THE IMMORTAL HEIGHTS

Also by Sherry Thomas

The Burning Sky

The Perilous Sea

THE
IMMORTAL
HEIGHTS

SHERRY THOMAS

BALZER + BRAY
An Imprint of HarperCollinsPublishers

Balzer + Bray is an imprint of HarperCollins Publishers.

The Immortal Heights
Copyright © 2015 by Sherry Thomas
All rights reserved. Printed in the United States of America.
No part of this book may be used or reproduced in any manner whatsoever
without written permission except in the case of brief quotations
embodied in critical articles and reviews. For information address
HarperCollins Children's Books, a division of HarperCollins Publishers,
195 Broadway, New York, NY 10007.
www.epicreads.com

Library of Congress Control Number: 2014959971
ISBN 978-0-06-220735-7

Typography by Sarah Creech, based on series typography by Erin Fitzsimmons
15 16 17 18 19   PC/RRDH   10 9 8 7 6 5 4 3 2 1
❖
First Edition

To everyone who has made it this far, this story is for you.
Live forever.

THE BOY FELL.

All about him, fire raged. Black smoke billowed against the night sky, obscuring the stars. In the distance wyverns dove and screeched, their silhouettes lit by their own flames, coppery light upon darkly iridescent scales.

"No!" someone screamed. "No!"

But the boy heard nothing. His heart had already stopped beating.

CHAPTER ✦ 1

SOMEWHERE IN THE MOST IMMENSE desert on earth, a thousand miles south of the Mediterranean Sea and just as far west of the Red Sea, rose a line of sheer sandstone cliffs. High in the night sky above this escarpment hung an enormous, flame-bright beacon, the war phoenix, the light of which cast an orange sheen for miles upon the surrounding dunes.

Beneath the war phoenix, the air appeared slightly distorted, due to the presence of a bell jar dome, which, when deployed in war, kept an opposing force penned firmly inside.

The bell jar dome had been put into place by Atlantis, the mightiest empire to ever bestride the mage world, headed by the Bane, the most powerful and feared mage alive. Trapped under the dome were a regiment of several hundred rebels who had neither handsome uniforms nor fire-breathing steeds, but only desert robes and flying carpets. Some rebels wore turbans and keffiyehs; others, roused from sleep and dressed in a hurry, were bareheaded.

Among this ragtag group of resistance fighters, looking not a bit out of place, were the Bane's quarries: His Serene Highness Prince Titus VII, Master of the Domain, and Miss Iolanthe Seabourne, the great elemental mage of their time.

From the day Iolanthe first summoned a bolt of lightning, she had been pursued by the agents of Atlantis. But it was not until recently that she'd learned the simple yet grotesque reason that the Bane wanted her: to power a feat of sacrificial magic that would prolong his life and maintain his chokehold on power.

Now surrounded, she was in a fight for her life. But at this very moment, she was not thinking about herself—not entirely, in any case. Her gaze was on the boy who shared her flying carpet, the one who held her hand tightly in his own.

Sometimes it amazed her that she had met him only a little over six months ago—it seemed as if they had spent their entire lives together, both running from and charging toward danger. She almost could not remember a time before she had been swept into this vortex of destiny, before she had made it her life's ambition to end the Bane's reign of tyranny.

His eyes met hers. He was afraid—she knew this because he did not hide his fear from her—but beyond the fear was an unbreakable will. All his life he had prepared for toil, peril, and the ultimate sacrifice.

She squeezed his hand. *We will outlive this.*

In her other hand she held Validus, the blade wand that had once belonged to Titus the Great, unifier of the Domain. She raised the wand high. Instantly, white arcs of electricity leaped across the star-studded sky. It had staggered her in the beginning and it staggered her still, that such sway should be granted to a mere mortal.

A shaft of thunderbolt plunged toward the desert, almost like the trunk of a brilliant tree growing from the top down. As it pierced through the war phoenix, the huge beacon shimmered and expanded.

Purpose surged in her veins. The sizzle of electricity was a rising tide in her blood. And a wildness beat in her heart—no more pretense, no more running, only drive against drive, power against power.

With an almost inaudible crackle, her lightning fizzled upon a shield that had been set outside the bell jar dome.

Cries of dismay rose all around her, drowning out her own gasp. She swore and reached for the elements again. Dozens of thunderbolts struck the shield, like so many brilliant needles thrown against a pincushion, or the fireworks of a new year's celebration gone mad.

The shield held.

A resounding silence echoed in her head.

"There is no surprising Atlantis twice," said Titus, with far greater calm than she felt.

Hours earlier—so much had happened since, it felt as if weeks, perhaps even months had passed—the two of them had been sniffed out of their hiding place and surrounded by wyvern riders. Iolanthe, with her memories still suppressed, had decided that there was no harm in trying to see whether the hidden writing on the strap of her satchel, especially the line *The day we met, lightning struck,* had been literal. She'd called forth a thunderbolt that had incapacitated the wyvern riders, enabling Titus and her to escape to temporary safety.

But this time Atlantis had come prepared. This time her command over lightning would not avail her.

As if to underscore Atlantis's advantage, the wyvern battalion roared en masse, a clamor that rattled her lungs against her rib cage. The wyverns had hovered in a tight formation, but now two prongs, like those of a pincer, thrust forward from the dark reptilian mass, companies of wyverns advancing to enclose the rebels in the middle.

The air displaced by their wings made the carpet beneath her bobble, like a raft on a sea growing choppier by the minute. The heat of their breath, even from a distance, prickled against her skin. And though she could not smell them through the mask she wore at the rebels' advice, her nostrils felt as if they burned with the stink of sulfur.

Mohandas Kashkari, Titus and Iolanthe's classmate from Eton College, came to a stop next to them. "We need to get into formation."

Belatedly, Iolanthe noticed that the rebels had maneuvered into groups of three.

"Two on offense, one on defense—that's me," Kashkari explained hurriedly as he helped Titus and Iolanthe onto individual carpets. "The carpets I'm giving you have been subordinated to mine—I'll steer for the group. Make sure to keep me in sight."

The carpets had been formed into an L shape, with a bottom ledge for standing on, a long vertical side for holding the rider upright, and the upper end rolled down to make a comfortable yet solid hand rest at waist height.

"Better fight standing up," said Kashkari.

Iolanthe kissed Titus on his cheek just before Kashkari set their carpets to the correct distance apart.

"May the might of the Angels propel you to unimaginable heights," said her beloved.

It was an old benediction, from a time when the powers of elemental mages decided the fate of realms. She sucked in a breath. The battle was fought around her; did its outcome also hinge *on* her?

"May Fortune shield you against all enemies," she replied, her voice trembling a little. "You too, Kashkari."

"May Fortune shield us all." Kashkari's answer was grim but firm. "And don't lose sight of me."

Her carpet leaped to the left. Her fingers dug into the hand rest— she hadn't expected the motion. Now she understood Kashkari's repeated instructions: she needed to keep him in view so that some part of her consciousness would attend to his subtle shifts of weight and prepare her for any abrupt changes in direction or velocity.

"Does the base have any strategy for dealing with a siege?" Titus asked Kashkari, his voice raised above the general din, as squads of rebels zigzagged about them, calling out to one another in a variety of languages.

"No," Kashkari answered, maneuvering them toward the center of the crowd. "Our strategy, in case of discovery, has always been to evacuate personnel and equipment as swiftly as possible—not to stay and fight."

But with the bell jar dome in place, that preferred option was gone. They all must stay and fight.

"Are you all right?" Titus asked her. "Sleepy?"

Less than three days ago, they had come to in the middle of the Sahara, knowing nothing of how they'd arrived there, knowing only that they must not fall into the grasp of Atlantis. But no sooner had they started their escape when they found out that Iolanthe had been penned in by a blood circle tailored specifically for her. Even with Titus weakening the power of the blood circle and the help of both a triple dose of panacea and a time-freeze spell, it almost killed Iolanthe to cross the blood circle. The panacea had since kept her under near-constant sedation, to preserve her life.

"I'm awake."

She had seldom been more awake, her nerves vibrating.

The rebels zoomed by, crisscrossing her vision. Beyond them, the wyverns, spread like a fisherman's net. And beyond *them* . . .

With all the chaos, she hadn't noticed that though a large number of wyvern riders had entered the bell jar dome, even more remained outside.

The arrival of allies was the surest way of breaking a siege—and she and Titus did have friends nearby: forces from the Domain were in the Sahara, alerted to the prince's presence by a war phoenix he'd deployed two nights ago. But could they breach *this* defense?

"Is anyone working on the translocators?" she asked, her chest tight.

Translocators provided instantaneous transport to distant destinations. The rebel base had two, but neither was functioning.

"Yes," answered Kashkari.

He did not sound entirely confident. Not to mention, they didn't know whether the rebels' translocators had suffered a simple breakdown or whether they had been compromised by Atlantis. Once a translocator had been compromised, there was no telling where a mage would end up.

Her uncertainty must have shown in her face. "Don't worry," said Kashkari. "We will protect you."

He had misunderstood her—she wished *she* could protect *them*. She knew the rebels had volunteered for a life of danger; but if it weren't for her, they would not be facing the deadliness of the wyvern battalion this very moment. "I can fight."

"And so can we. We may not have a specific plan of counterattack in case of siege, but we have trained for wyverns, which are not without weaknesses."

One might find an opportunity to attack a wyvern's tender underbelly—if one could last long enough before its fire and viciousness. She would have that opportunity: the Bane wanted her alive and in good shape; a dead elemental mage was useless in sacrificial magic. The prince too stood a chance: the satisfaction of getting rid of him was probably not worth an all-out war with the Domain, which, though well past its days of glory, still had enough might and mage power to be a thorn in Atlantis's side. Not to mention such a war would render Atlantis vulnerable to attacks on other fronts.

The wyverns spewed fire, a latticework hemisphere of flames crashing toward the rebels. A chorus of spell-casting rose. Most of the dragon fire was stopped by a wall of shields, but here and there the tassels and fringes of a carpet caught fire. Iolanthe had become accustomed to the more modern flying carpets, which resembled tablecloths and curtains more than they did actual rugs. But the carpets used in battle were of a more traditional appearance, a good deal thicker and sturdier than their counterparts meant for disguise and ease of carrying.

She commanded the fires on the carpets to extinguish themselves. Already the rebels on the front line were on the counterattack, diving lower so they could aim at the wyverns from underneath. Iolanthe expected at least a couple of wyverns to rear back in pain, their wings flapping wildly.

No reaction. It was as if the rebels had emitted rose petals and dandelion puffs, instead of spells that would have slaughtered elephants and rhinoceroses.

Shouts erupted in languages Iolanthe couldn't identify, let alone understand.

"The wyverns are armored," Kashkari interpreted. "Not metal, but plates of dragon hide on the belly."

Wyverns tolerated metal armor—dragon hide plates, not so much. Whether they clearly understood that they were being strapped into contraptions that had once been body parts of their own kind, nobody knew. But wyverns were intelligent enough that anything made of dragon hide repelled them.

Which meant that they had been given taming draughts ahead of time, so they wouldn't struggle against the donning of the plates. A taming draught given before a battle slowed a wyvern's normally lightning-quick reflexes. Atlantis must have decided that the protection of the plates outweighed the disadvantages of the taming draught.

"They are prepared for *you*," said Titus.

Of course. Metal plates against the most susceptible parts of the wyverns would have put them in danger when faced with a mage who command fire. Dragon hide, on the other hand, was immune to ordinary fire.

But it wasn't immune to dragon fire.

She pointed her wand and routed a stream of dragon fire back at the wyvern that had spewed it. The wyvern's rider wrenched it sharply to the side to avoid the jet of flames. Iolanthe gathered the flames of two nearby wyverns into two fireballs and hurtled them at the same wyvern, narrowly missing the ridge of one wing.

A noise like a thousand sharp claws scratching upon a thousand windowpanes grated against her eardrums. Instantly the night turned darker. She held her breath for several heartbeats before she realized that it wasn't some new and frightfully powerful act of sorcery on Atlantis's part. It was only that all the wyverns had stopped spewing fire.

So that she could not use their own fire against them.

You cannot surprise Atlantis twice.

The wyverns, without their fire, were scarcely less deadly. The sharpness of their talons and the toughness of their wings were matched only by their fierce intelligence. They came at the rebels, teeth and claws at the ready.

"I do not like this," Titus said darkly.

"You never like anything, darling." But she liked it no better than he did.

The wyverns advanced from all directions. The rebels retreated toward the center of their formation. The wyverns pushed in farther. The rebels pulled tighter.

All at once the wyverns on the front line charged. The rebels scattered like a school of fish bombarded by diving cormorants. Kashkari wrested Titus and Iolanthe left and up to get out of the way of a pair of hard-driving wyverns. Iolanthe, who'd forgotten again to keep Kashkari in her sight, grabbed on to her carpet, its motion a hard jerk in her neck.

More wyverns careened into the rebels, forcing each three-mage squad to fend for itself. Kashkari veered them to the right, to avoid being struck by a wyvern's wing. Iolanthe called for a ten-foot-wide sphere of fire and hurled it at the rider of the nearest wyvern—wyverns could not be harmed by ordinary fire; riders, not so invincible.

The wyvern knocked aside the fireball with its wing. Iolanthe summoned a fireball twice as big in diameter and sent it plummeting from above the wyvern rider.

A few feet from the head of the wyvern rider, her fire went out like a candle flame in a gale. She swore—there were other elemental mages nearby, interfering.

Or at least so she hoped—that it was other elemental *mages*, and not the Bane himself, as powerful an elemental mage as any who ever lived.

A trio of wyverns dove toward them. Kashkari swerved. Iolanthe hung on to her carpet, a string of spells leaving her lips as she zoomed by a wyvern—all of which, alas, were deflected by the wyvern's wings.

"Untether my carpet, Kashkari!" shouted Titus. "You get Fairfax back into the base."

Her beloved never feared anything without cause. But all Iolanthe could see were wyvern riders and rebels on carpets wheeling about. A fraction of a second later, however, it became clear that the three of them had been separated from the rest of the rebels and were surrounded by wyverns.

Without thinking, she willed a mass of sand to rise from the desert floor. The riders wore protective goggles, and the wyverns had hardy but transparent inner eyelids that made their vision impervious to flying specks. Still, sand impeded and sand obscured. If nothing else, a tornado of sand would make her feel less visible, less exposed.

But the desert floor seemed to have melted into a sea of glass. Not a single grain of sand leaped into the air at her command. The wyverns pressed in closer. She called for currents of air to push them back. The moment she did so, however, she felt the pressure of countercurrents—Atlantis's elemental mages were neutralizing her on every front.

She was not alone in her failure. Titus and Kashkari were trying all kinds of spells to no avail. She didn't know about Kashkari, but the prince was a veteran of dragon battles—at least in the Crucible, a book of folklore and fairy tales that he and Iolanthe used as proving grounds to train themselves for dangerous situations. But usually, in those stories, the dragons were few in number. And if they should be numerous, as in *The Dragon Princess*, at least the protagonist had a sturdy defensive position, like a dilapidated but still mighty fort, instead of flying carpets that provided no cover at all.

"Can I vault her into the base, or is that a no-vaulting zone?" Titus shouted the question at Kashkari.

"It's a no-vaulting zone!"

Titus swore.

Earlier this very night, he had made the two of them jump to the ground from a height of half a mile, with nothing to break their fall but her powers over air, because he hadn't wanted to risk vaulting her: vaulting so soon after a life-threatening injury could kill her outright.

Were they truly running out of options?

An incendiary idea flared to life. She had always called for lightning from above. But in nature, lightning didn't necessarily originate from the sky. Sometimes balls of electricity wafted from nowhere. Sometimes lightning traveled from the ground to the clouds.

Could she?

She aimed her wand downward, feeling as foolish as she had when she first attempted to summon a thunderbolt from above. "Lightning."

Nothing happened.

One particularly large wyvern surged forward and extended a claw—it would grab her off the carpet. The carpet dropped straight down and the claw missed her head by inches.

Two more wyverns followed the example of the first, attacking her from different altitudes, so that even if she were to drop or rise, she would not be able to evade both.

She tried again for lightning. Nothing.

Somehow Kashkari tugged them sideways, with the wyvern's talons slicing just past the prince's shoulder.

"Do you want me to vault you to the ground?" Titus yelled.

He and Kashkari shielded her from either side. Beyond the wyverns, the rebels were trying to break through this siege-inside-a-siege, the light of the war phoenix illuminating the anxiety and panic on their faces.

The wyverns advanced ever closer. The force of their wingbeats buffeted her from every side. She could see the glint of each individual scale on the nearest wyvern—and the eagerness of its rider, shoulders forward, fingers all but tapping against the reins.

She had given the wrong answer to the prince's benediction earlier. She exhaled and recited the correct response: "For I shall bear testimony to the might of the Angels. For I am power, I am mastery, and I am the hammer of immortality."

Titus snatched the two remaining hunting ropes out of their emergency satchel. "As the world endures." He completed the prayer as the first hunting rope left his hand. "As hope abides ever in the face of the Void."

The hunting rope caught the outstretched claw of a wyvern and twisted it back.

"Heads down!" Kashkari bellowed as he wrenched them out of the grasp of another wyvern.

Their last hunting rope shot out and missed the incoming wyvern altogether—the beast pulled in its legs and swatted the hunting rope out of the way with its wing. *You cannot surprise Atlantis twice.*

But the hunting rope wasn't aiming for the wyvern at all, but its rider, slapping itself around the latter's wrists and forcing the rider to jerk on the reins.

"Behind you, Fairfax!" called Kashkari.

She glanced back, expecting to see a pair of talons swooping down. They were, but Kashkari had put himself between the wyvern and her, facing the beast. He flipped backward, kicking his carpet toward the wyvern as he did so, and with a twist in midair landed behind Iolanthe, grabbing her by the middle so he wouldn't fall off the narrow ledge on which she stood.

"Come on," Titus shouted. "Bring down that hammer of immortality, will you?"

Ever since she'd been a little girl, friends and neighbors had asked her how it felt to wield direct power over the elements, without the intercession of words and incantations. She'd found it difficult to explain until she'd visited Delamer's Museum of Nonmage Artifacts on a school trip and had held a compass in her hand, lining up the quivering little needle with the magnetic north. *That* was what it felt like when she was in control of the elements, the alignment of her person with an invisible longitude of power.

Her previous attempts had wobbled wide of that perfect calibration. But this time she felt it, the difference between approximation and exactitude. She double-tapped Validus. Light radiated from the seven diamond crowns along the length of the blade wand.

She pointed it down and looked at Titus. "For you."

A flick of her wrist and a white-hot burst of electricity reared up from the floor of the desert.

CHAPTER 2

FOR YOU.

Time slowed. The syllables stretched out in Titus's ears as the lightning built spark by spark from the dark sands below, a spawn of brilliance hatching into a creature with claws, claws that lashed on to the nearest wyverns. The wyverns seized and fell, their wings lax and open, tumbling through the air end over end like paper dragons that had been carelessly flicked from a high balcony.

Silence, punctuated by the thuds of half a dozen wyverns crashing into the ground.

And another eternity of silence—which was probably only a fraction of a second—before the roar erupted, the screeching of wyverns mixed with the astonished cries of the rebels.

"What *was* that?" asked Kashkari, his left hand raised near his ear in an involuntary gesture of stupefaction.

This jolted Titus out of his own amazement. He put into effect a spell that gave his voice the amplitude to carry for miles. "Behold. Here is one who wields the divine spark, beloved by the Angels."

There were few followers of the Angelic Host in the Sahara. He was speaking not so much to the rebels as to the Atlanteans, who took their faith seriously.

"Remember," countered a high, clear voice that Titus recognized as belonging to the woman brigadier who had been on their heels since the moment he and Fairfax arrived in the desert, "usurpers often claim to be beloved by the Angels."

"And your Lord High Commander does not claim to be favored from above?" he retorted.

Atlantis's response was a clarion call. The wyvern riders regrouped. But instead of resuming their assault, they and their steeds left the bell jar dome entirely.

"Fortune favors the brave!" yelled a rebel.

Those closest to her shouted, "And the brave make their own fortune!"

"Fortune favors the brave!" she yelled again.

This time, almost everyone cried, "And the brave make their own fortune!"

It was noisy and jubilant. The rebels were beginning to laugh, from awe, excitement, and the draining of tension. They ribbed their friends for how afraid they had looked and boasted of their own fearlessness, only to be mocked in turn for trembling hands and misdirected spells.

Yet in the middle of this celebratory camaraderie, Titus's blood was turning cold. Atlantis did not give up so easily—or it would not rule the mage world.

"Let me guess, you like this even less," said Fairfax.

He turned to the girl in whose strength and character he had entrusted his fate. "I am an open book before you."

"If you are an open book," she answered, a hint of mischief in her voice, "then you resemble nothing so much as your mother's diary—hundreds of blank pages, followed by a few life-changing lines."

He could not help smiling a little. "By the way, you never cease to amaze me."

She steered her carpet closer and took his hand. "I admit to being rather amazed myself. But the part of me that is your protégée—you know, the eternal pessimist—wonders whether I haven't made even more trouble for everyone."

"It's all right," said Kashkari. "We are all here for trouble."

The rebels quieted as a drumroll came, followed by the pleasant female voice the base used for public announcements. "Armored chariots sighted."

Armored chariots, which were impervious to the power of a lightning strike.

Titus deployed a far-seeing spell: five squadrons, at the very limits of his enhanced vision. Three minutes then, possibly five, before they were on top of the bell jar dome.

Amara, the commander of the rebel base, zoomed over and

handed a new carpet to Kashkari, who was still standing behind Fairfax and holding on to her.

"Something strange is going on," said Amara. "I distinctly recall, while we were still inside the base, a warning about incoming lindworms. Where are they?"

It took Titus a moment—the warning had come before all his suppressed memories had emerged en masse, which produced a curious effect of distance on the immediate preceding events. But now that he cast his mind back, he did remember hearing the same pleasant female voice announcing the sighting of armored chariots, wyverns, and lindworms, when he and Fairfax still believed they could outrun Atlantis.

"Come to think of it," said Kashkari, "when the wyverns first entered the bell jar dome, there were lindworms to their rear—and circled by an odd sort of armored chariots, much smaller than any I'd ever seen."

Lindworms had terrible vision. In the wild they formed symbiotic relationships with mock harpies, which guided them to forage. Perhaps the much smaller armored chariots served the role of the symbionts, herding the armored chariots to Atlantis's purposes.

"Do you think the lindworms and those small armored chariots could have been dispatched to intercept our allies?" asked Fairfax.

"That wouldn't be a good use of the lindworms," said Amara. "I expect they had been brought because Atlantis meant to make a direct assault on the base itself—in close quarters, lindworms are terrifying. But for pursuits and such, they are so slow they are hardly useful."

"The armored chariots that are coming toward us now, are they the same ones you saw earlier?" Fairfax asked Kashkari.

"No. They are the usual kind."

Titus exchanged a look with Fairfax. Atlantis never did anything without a good reason. What, then, was the reason the lindworms and their accompanying small chariots were no longer on the battlefield?

"Should we—"

Fairfax stopped. He heard it too: hundreds of objects streaking through the air.

Her face lit up. "Bewitched spears!"

Five or six hours ago, wyvern riders had come quite close to Titus and Fairfax—and had been chased away by an ambush of antique bewitched spears. Titus had puzzled over the identity of the mages who used such weapons, until he recovered his memory and realized that they were forces from the Domain, and the spears those kept in the Titus the Great Memorial Museum for reenactment of historical battles.

From south of the bell jar dome the bewitched spears arrived, hissing like a storm of arrows, slender and lethal. Titus closed his fingers more tightly about Fairfax's and held his breath.

A huge net sprang up and caught the bewitched weapons, as if they had been a school of fish, swimming directly into a trap.

Amara grunted in frustration—it was a reminder that what seemed too good to be true usually was.

"Would the spears have lifted the siege, even if they reached the bell jar dome?" asked Fairfax with a frown. "I thought inanimate objects had no effects on such sorcery."

"Not under normal circumstances," said Titus, "but there are ways around it."

If there was some clever blood magic involved. And if the drop of blood at the tip of the spear was from a mage bound by blood to someone under the bell jar dome.

"One way or the other this siege will break," said Amara. "Mohandas has seen the future, and his visions have never led us astray."

When they first learned that they had been trapped under a bell jar dome, Amara had intimated that the rebels would take whatever measures necessary to keep Fairfax out of Atlantis's hands—including killing her themselves, if it came to that. And Kashkari, in what amounted to an outburst for him, had told Amara in no uncertain terms that a prophetic dream had let him know that Fairfax would not only survive this night, but venture as far as Atlantis itself, in a quest to finish the Bane in his lair.

Except Kashkari had been lying outright, as he had later admitted to Titus and Fairfax outside Amara's earshot.

Kashkari, as good a liar as Titus had ever met—and Titus was a world-class one himself—nodded gravely. "Thank you, Durga Devi."

Durga Devi was Amara's nom de guerre. Titus also addressed her thus, but for him it was less a term of respect than of distance: the woman had been willing to murder Fairfax to keep her out of the Bane's reach; he would never not regard her with several measures of suspicion.

Outside the bell jar dome, another net sprang up to catch a forest of—Titus had thought them all bewitched spears, but now it appeared that there were lengths of hunting ropes mixed in.

Why? To make the bewitched spears appear more numerous? Or was there some other purpose?

Amara's expression changed. She reached into a pocket, pulled out a notebook, and opened it.

"Is it my brother?" Kashkari asked immediately.

"You know those who go on raids are not allowed to take two-way notebooks." She turned to Titus. "It's your allies, Your Highness, requesting that Miss Seabourne be ready to deliver two dozen thunderbolts to the approaching company of armored chariots."

"Why are my allies contacting *you*?"

"But armored chariots are lightning-proof," said Fairfax at the same time.

"They said to tell you *'certus amicus temporibus incertis,'*" said Amara. To Fairfax's query she only shrugged—there was no answer for that.

Certus amicus in temporibus incertis—a certain friend in uncertain times—was one of the code phrases that Titus and Dalbert, his valet and personal spymaster, had agreed upon. A piece of communication bearing such a phrase signaled that it had originated from someone Dalbert deemed trustworthy.

Titus's preference was to trust as few people as possible. And to never undertake any action without having thoroughly investigated potential consequences. But at the moment he could not afford either luxury.

"You might as well," he told Fairfax.

They called for even more powerful far-seeing spells. The armored chariots, still several miles away, cut swiftly through the night, almost invisible except for the muted sheen on their underbellies, a reflection of the glow of the war phoenix.

"When?" asked Fairfax.

"Now," said Amara. "The entire lot, if you will."

Fairfax pointed her wand toward the armored chariots. The sky writhed with blue-white streaks; thunderbolts crashed as if the gods were drunk.

Twenty-four bolts of lightning in two seconds, followed by a long moment during which no one spoke—or breathed. Then all the armored chariots fell, as if they were so many boulders at last yielding to the might of gravity.

A deafening silence: fear and wonder were alike in their capacity to produce speechlessness. Even Amara, who must know that there was trickery involved, gazed with awe upon Fairfax.

The latter was the only one to appear more confused than dazzled.

"But that shouldn't have been possible. They are lightning-proof."

Titus signaled her to hold her questions. He raised his voice to speechmaking volume again. "Can anyone doubt any longer the power of the divine spark? Stand no more in the path of the one beloved by the Angels, and you need not fear their wrath."

Then, at normal volume, for her ears alone, "I could not let pass such a perfect moment for propaganda."

"Of course not. But do you know what is going on?"

"I might."

The arrival of yet another cluster of bewitched spears and hunting ropes, whooshing and hissing, roused the Atlanteans from their stupor. Another net sprang up as wyvern riders chased the few loose objects that had not been caught.

"I will tell you what is going on later. Now I need you to create as much distraction as possible. Keep everyone's eyes on high if you can. I will do the same." He pointed his wand skyward. *"Meum insigne esto praesidium meum!"*

The war phoenix had hitherto been a static beacon. Now, slowly, majestically, it flapped its enormous wings and descended toward a formation of wyvern riders outside the bell jar dome. The wyverns spewed fire at the war phoenix; but flame, like lightning, simply passed through it.

"Trust the Master of the Domain to always have something up his sleeve," said Kashkari, shaking his head.

Before the war phoenix's inexorable approach, the wyverns

scattered. One wyvern rider, who was too slow moving out of the way, screamed as the tip of the war phoenix's left wing brushed his shoulder. The war phoenix did not cause actual damage, but enemies who came into contact with it were said to experience a brief yet intense bout of pain.

"Here's my distraction," said Fairfax.

A ball of lightning, blue and eerie, hurtled toward a company of wyverns, sending them scattering.

"Send one like that into the war phoenix," said Titus.

She did. The war phoenix glowed with double the intensity and emitted a call that was wild and harsh, yet oddly stirring.

"Excellent. Keep it up."

The war phoenix continued its stately progress, while half a dozen spheres of sizzling electricity careened all about, keeping the forces of Atlantis scattered and in disarray. As one more cluster of bewitched spears and hunting ropes arrived, Titus directed the war phoenix eastward.

"I think it is safe to say our allies have quite a bit of experience with Atlantis," he explained. "They knew Atlantis would not be taken by surprise a second time and would be ready for the bewitched spears."

"So they send the bewitched spears in batches to see what kind of defense they would be dealing with?" said Kashkari.

"Exactly. I would not be surprised to learn that the clusters had come exactly ninety degrees apart on the compass, to best pin the net to the ground with all the hunting ropes."

Kashkari tapped a finger against his chin. "Should we expect to see spears and ropes coming in smaller clusters—twos and threes—to test that the net is well and truly pinned down?"

As if on cue, a pair of bewitched spears arrived. The Atlanteans shouted when they realized that their net could no longer spring up to catch the spears, but was squirming on the sand, held down by the hunting ropes.

They barely caught the spears, thanks to two particularly agile wyverns. The wyverns, spears in their claws, were being directed to head away from the bell jar dome. But the momentum of the spears was still strong, and the wyverns flapped their wings as if they were flying against a cyclone. "Tell your scouts with the keenest sight to look on the ground," Titus said to Amara. "That is how I would send in the one bewitched spear that counts. And tell them to keep quiet when they have spotted it."

"Understood." She flew off.

"When we do spot the spear we are looking for, the one carrying the blood spell that would act as proxy for the human touch," he said to Kashkari, "I will set Fairfax to safeguard its progress. Can you arrange for some additional distraction on the part of the rebels?"

Kashkari nodded. "Leave it to me."

Titus took Fairfax's hand. "And you, you smite anything that comes between the spear and the bell jar dome."

"Your wish is my command, sire," she said smartly.

He pulled her in for a quick kiss. "Good. Say that to everything I want."

She laughed. Even in the midst of chaos, the sound still made his heart lift.

Amara returned. "One of our scouts spotted something approaching from the northeast."

Titus immediately sent the war phoenix to the southwest of the bell jar dome, so that as little light as possible would fall on that "something."

He and Fairfax rode into a cluster of rebels and came out the other end with their heads covered in keffiyehs. Behind them, Kashkari had set up a spectacle: a dozen carpets floated end to end in midair, and several rebels made tumbling passes across the length of this makeshift stage.

"I'm tempted to neglect my task and watch that instead," said Fairfax. "And my life is on the line here."

She and Titus took the place of the pair of scouts originally stationed at the northwestern point of the bell jar dome, and each applied an angle-view spell, so that despite their tilted-up faces, they were watching the desert floor.

Cresting a dune about a half mile away, a bewitched spear slithered toward the bell jar dome. It was not dawdling, precisely, but then neither was it moving at anything close to full speed. Titus was fine with that relatively sedate pace until a scout called out, "More armored chariots on the way!"

But they had trouble from closer quarters too: several squads of wyvern riders swung by, their flight low, their gaze on the ground.

Titus swore. He raised his voice. "My esteemed friends from Atlantis, especially those of you who have met your Lord High Commander in person, have you ever wondered why he does not seem to age? Why, in fact, he sometimes seems to grow ten years younger overnight? Even by the most conservative of estimates, he should be a man well into his seventies. How does he not look a day over forty?"

The wyvern riders, forgetting their task, turned sharply toward the bell jar dome.

"It is because he is using a young man's body, one that bears a striking resemblance to his original body, before he threw himself down the hideous depths of sacrificial magic. That original body cannot ever be seen in public, as it is missing major limbs, perhaps the eyes and ears too; such is the cost of sacrificial magic.

"In all the long years of his reign, he has made it a point not to publicly disseminate his image. The official reason is that he never wishes to encourage a cult of personality. But conveniently enough, if the wider mage world does not know what he looks like, then it would not wonder why men who resembled him kept disappearing.

"Think about it next time you are asked to risk your life for him. Think about it now. Why does he want my friend the young elemental mage? It is because powerful elemental mages make the most potent sacrifices and will best invigorate his life force. Is this what you want to do? Fight to the utmost of your ability so that he can commit acts despised by the Angels?"

Unfortunately, not every one of the wyvern riders was riveted by his speech. One screamed at the top of his voice to alert his colleagues that a bewitched spear was on the ground and only a quarter mile away from the bell jar dome.

Instead of attacking those who had spotted the bewitched spear and were now diving toward it, Fairfax set up a much more elegant defense. Drawing on her command of lightning, she constructed a moving tunnel of electricity through which the spear passed unmolested.

A furlong. One-sixteenth of a mile. A hundred fifty feet. The spear came ever closer.

Titus's heart lodged in his throat.

The tip of the spear struck the bell jar dome; the entire dome shuddered.

The nearest pair of scouts yelled in jubilation and shot forward, only to be stopped by a barrier that was very much still in place.

CHAPTER · 3

"SHOULDN'T THE DOME HAVE DISINTEGRATED?" shouted Fairfax.

It should have, if Titus was right about blood magic having been applied to the spear.

Of course.

"Blood. I must put a drop of blood to the dome!" He fished for his pocketknife as he nudged his carpet forward.

She reached the dome the same time as he did and set her hand on it too. He felt a thrumming sensation in his palm, and then nothing but air.

Immediately he threw up a shield for her. She did the same for him—and not a moment too soon, as the wyvern riders aimed a barrage of spells at them.

"You should have been putting up shields for yourself," he admonished her as they flew higher. "How many times have I told you not to bother with me?"

"What? And assume the shields you've set up for me aren't strong enough? Besides"—she leaned over and rapped him on the head with her knuckles—"have you forgotten that there is no Chosen One? You are no less important than me in this—or anything else."

"I have not forgotten that." He took her wrist and kissed the back of her hand. "I speak not for the mission, but for myself."

She sighed. "And what am I going to do without you?"

For a fraction of a second, his prophesied death hung between them, a shroud that marked the end of everything. The next moment, she swung around and let loose a wall of fire.

Ordinary fire could not harm dragons. The wyvern riders, however, still dodged instinctively. It was a good tactical move on her part, but a less sound one strategically: now the Atlanteans once again knew her exact location.

But if anything, the wyvern riders drew back farther, the memories of the lightning-wielder's prowess still too fresh.

"Let no one escape!" came the clarion-like voice of the woman brigadier. "Reinforcement is almost here!"

The latest squadrons of armored chariots were now visible to the naked eye.

Kashkari came to a silent halt beside them. "The armored chariots are too high—the height they usually take to dispense death rain."

"Can our allies bring them down?" asked Fairfax. "I'll be happy to provide lightning strikes again."

Kashkari shook his head. "Amara already asked. They said one battery of armored chariots was the most they could sink in a short amount of time. We'd better retreat into the base."

"We should be all right with our face masks, shouldn't we?" asked Fairfax as they made for the great escarpment to the east. The rebel camp had been carved out inside the escarpment, and the only access—that Titus knew of, at least—was a vertical fissure that ran down the front of the range.

"Face masks would suffice against first-generation death rain. But lately we've been hearing reports that far nastier versions have been developed."

Fairfax glanced over her shoulder. "Look at the wyvern riders. Why are they not chasing us?"

As the rebels streamed toward the cliffs, the wyvern riders, who had reorganized into a semblance of order and formation, seemed content to merely observe.

"Why, indeed?" muttered Kashkari, frowning.

"Is it possible for us not to go so deep into the base?" Titus asked Kashkari. "Obviously we cannot flee in the open right now, but if we get in and are then surrounded, it might be difficult to get out again."

Kashkari nodded. He once again subordinated their carpets to his. Inside the fissure, they did not go on twisting and turning through the narrow opening as they had their first time, but instead took a side tunnel that Titus would have passed without seeing—the entire way was pitch dark—and flew up to what Kashkari called an observational post, entering through a trapdoor on the bottom.

As soon as they had alit from their carpets, Titus grabbed Fairfax for a hard embrace. She was still safe. They were all still safe. Every such moment must be savored, his fervent gratitude offered to the Angels. "You all right? Holding up?"

She stepped back and examined him. "I'm fine. You, on the other hand, are all ribs. Have you been eating anything at all?"

"Enough," he said.

Most of the time he probably ate a little less than he ought to—food being one of those things that he resented for taking time away from everything else that he needed to do. It was tougher to judge when his entire diet consisted of food cubes that tasted like solidified air. How much of *that* was sufficient?

She sighed, shaking her head. Then she turned to Kashkari. "How about you, old chap?"

It dawned on Titus that Kashkari had been watching them, a wistful expression on his face. There was probably very little that Kashkari would not give to be in their position, to love openly and without complication.

Titus could not imagine the kind of quandary Kashkari found himself in, being in love with a woman all his life, and meeting her much, much too late, when she was already his brother's fiancée.

"I'm all right," said Kashkari, turning away. "Let me show you how to open the view ports."

They pressed close to the long, rectangular view ports as the armored chariots, dark and silent, streaked past overhead. The wyvern riders raised their hands in salute. Titus squinted, but could not see whether anything had been dispensed.

"That's it?" asked Fairfax, after a minute or so of silence.

"That was all they needed to do," said Titus. "From what I remember, death rain is highly concentrated. It is harmless while in liquid form, but once it reaches the ground and evaporates . . ."

"Why didn't the wyvern riders evacuate?"

"Wyverns themselves are not susceptible to death rain. And Atlanteans are usually given antidotes before they go into battle."

Fairfax turned to Kashkari. "Is this observational post airtight?"

"The entire base is, once all the entrances have been sealed."

"How do we know when it will be safe enough to venture out again?"

"My colleagues in other observational posts will be taking air samples every half hour to test for toxicity."

"So we might be here awhile."

"We might."

"Then why don't the two of you take some rest? You are probably short on sleep, to have traveled so fast so far. And you"—her hand settled for just a moment on Titus's elbow—"I know you've hardly slept at all since we landed in the desert."

Titus did not want to sleep—he would go to his eternal rest all too soon, and he did not want to waste any minute he had remaining in a state of unconsciousness. He would much rather spend his hours and days with his arms around her, wide awake, accumulating memories for the Beyond.

Would that it were an option.

"I've been sleeping for days and woke up not very long before you came upon us, Kashkari. So let me take the first watch. In fact, let me also summon some water. You both look parched—finish what's left in your waterskins and I'll refill them."

While a sphere of water spun and grew in the middle of the observation post, she cleaned and rebandaged Titus's back, which had been wounded when they had passed through the Crucible the last time. It was getting better—but she was generous with the topical analgesic and he equally unsparing with the pain-relieving pilules.

She tsked as she worked, murmuring mild criticism on how little he took care of himself. Her touch was efficient, almost impersonal, as she took care of the wound. But when she was done, she rested her hand against his upper arm.

And he really, really wished they were alone. Kashkari was safeguarding them against known and unknown dangers, but he would give the man his castle in the Labyrinthine Mountains if he would go elsewhere in the base for fifteen minutes.

If he would stay away for half an hour, Titus would throw open the Crown Vault and Kashkari could have any of the treasures therein.

As if he heard Titus's thoughts, Kashkari, who had already stretched out on his carpet, got up again to look out of a view port, his back to Titus and Fairfax. Almost immediately her fingers climbed up his arm to his shoulders. There her hand splayed open, as if she wanted to touch as much of him as possible.

His breaths came in quicker.

With her other hand she traced his spine upward, vertebra by vertebra. His fingers sank into the deep pile of the carpet, trying to hold on to something. And then she shifted—a muffled sound upon the carpet—and kissed him at the base of his neck.

If she had struck him with one of her bolts of lightning, the sensation could not have been more electric. He barely managed to swallow a gasp. And surely she must have felt the tremor beneath his skin.

Do it again. Please do it again.

"I don't know what's going on," said Kashkari. "But you two had better come take a look."

Were Titus capable of commanding lightning, he would smite every single Atlantean in a hundred-mile radius that very moment. And the Bane he would gladly throttle with his own hands, for his stupid underlings never knew when to leave Titus alone.

She had to pull him to one side so he did not walk smack into the sphere of water. He half glowered at her, for the laughter in her eyes, for not physically suffering from desire the way he did.

She flung one arm about his shoulders and kissed him on his

cheek. He sighed, his frustration crowded out by sweetness and the simple pleasure of her company.

It was with much reluctance that he took his gaze off her to look out a view port. Immediately the levity in his heart dissipated. The wyverns were flying drunkenly, nearly crashing into one another. The riders, who a minute ago had been upright and alert in their high-backed saddles, were now slumped over.

Fairfax glanced at Kashkari. "Did your mages do this?"

Kashkari shook his head. "Our mages would have been too busy sealing the entrances and taking up defensive positions."

Fairfax turned to Titus. "Our allies?"

Titus could only shrug. He had no idea what was going on.

Kashkari took out his two-way notebook and scratched a few words with his pen. He looked up after a wait of several seconds. "Amara says no—she already asked them."

"Fortune shield me," cried Fairfax. "Do you see what I see?"

Titus pressed his face to the view port again and sucked in a breath. The wyverns were plucking off the riders and dropping them to the desert below.

Bits of dragon lore, read long ago and practically forgotten, surfaced in his mind. "The riders are dead. Wyverns cannot abide cadavers—that is why they are helping one another get rid of the riders."

The trapdoor burst open. They all jumped. But it was only Amara, her eyes wide, her hand clutched hard around her wand. "Would somebody please tell me what's going on?"

The question was for all three of them, but her eyes were on the lightning-wielder, she of the miraculous powers.

"I think I can venture a guess," said the lightning-wielder, her voice low and tired, the laughter in her eyes gone.

The moment she spoke, Titus understood the conclusion she had arrived at—and it chilled him from head to toe. Kashkari put a hand against the wall, as if he too were feeling unsteady.

"The Bane did this," came Fairfax's inexorable explanation.

Amara recoiled. "Why? Why would he kill his own loyal troops?"

"Because they heard His Highness accuse him of sacrificial magic. I don't know what kind of reputation the prince has among the Atlanteans, but he is still the Master of the Domain, and he made that accusation to the Bane's face, so to speak."

Amara's other hand clenched too. "But an experienced wyvern rider is very valuable—to train one takes years."

"Have you heard that the Bane can resurrect?" Fairfax asked.

"There have long been rumors."

"The Atlantean woman in my residence house had never heard of it—and she had lived outside Atlantis for a number of years. Granted, she probably always had to take care not to mix with the wrong people and lose her assignment, but doesn't that tell you something about the kind of information control the Bane wields over his own people?

"And it isn't necessary that they believe the prince completely. A sensational claim like that was bound to be repeated, however surreptitiously, to family, friends, colleagues in other regiments, and perhaps to strangers when one's had a bit too much to drink. Now multiply that dissemination by the hundreds.

"And notice that it is only the wyvern riders who have been eliminated—they heard what the prince said. The pilots inside the small armored chariots herding the lindworms would have been wearing special helmets that only let them hear instruction from their battle commanders—they were recalled and spared."

Amara rubbed a hand across her face. "If what you deduce is true . . . I've been a part of the resistance since I was a child, and this is the first time I've ever been afraid."

"My guardian once told me, 'Sometimes fear is the only appropriate response,'" said Fairfax kindly.

Amara shook her head and seemed about to say something when she stopped and felt her pocket. "Excuse me."

Out came her two-way notebook. "It's a message from a patrol—she was caught about ten miles from the base when the bell jar dome came down. When the second batch of armored chariots went by just now, she decided to follow them as far as she could. And she writes that they have just crashed into the desert."

The observation post was entirely silent as she wrote a response. Titus could hear her breathe as she stared at the page, waiting for the answer.

She exhaled carefully as she looked up. "Your allies say they had nothing to do with it."

The Bane again.

Amara turned to Fairfax. "Why them too?"

"Because if they were to learn that their compatriots died in the wake of their flight, they would have suspicions too." Fairfax gripped Titus by the arm. "And you know what? The Bane will want to pin the deaths on something else. Someone else. So he will send others to come and witness the carnage."

They had all better get out while getting out was still possible.

"The air is being analyzed right now. If it's safe to travel through with our breathing masks on, I will call for a general evacuation," said Amara. "Your Highness, Miss Seabourne, will you come with us or will you prefer to seek your own path?"

Fairfax glanced at Titus. "We will seek our own path."

As they had always done.

"Besides, you will be safer without us around, Durga Devi," added Fairfax.

"I will go with them," said Kashkari.

"Have you dreamed of it?" asked Amara solemnly.

Kashkari had once told Fairfax that his people did not consider visions as the future written in stone. Amara, on the other hand, seemed to take his prophetic dreams with extreme seriousness.

"No," answered Kashkari. "But I don't need dreams to tell me which way my destiny lies. Tell Vasudev I'm sorry we missed each other."

"I will. And I'll look after him for you—and trust that we'll meet again someday."

"Look after yourself too."

Kashkari's voice was oddly cracked. With some shock Titus realized that Kashkari was barely holding himself together—there was every chance he would not see either his brother or the woman he loved again. Ever.

Amara took his face in her hands and kissed him tenderly on his forehead. "Be safe and come back to us, my brother."

CHAPTER ✦ 4

SILENT AND SWIFT THEY FLEW, headed toward an eastern horizon that was beginning to be limned by a band of soft golden light, fading up to a still inky, star-studded sky.

It took Iolanthe some time to realize that she was shaking.

They had been in a rush, selecting fresh carpets and other tools and supplies that they might need. And then there had been the anxiety, glancing behind—and all around—every few seconds to make sure that they hadn't been spotted.

All throughout, however, the image of wyverns plucking dead riders off one another flashed again and again in her mind. She had been calm enough as she described the Bane's twisted reasons, but now, with immediate dangers fading, the anger that had been kept to a low simmer threatened to boil over.

Her experience with Atlantis, though harrowing, had been on an extremely personal level: Master Haywood's imprisonment, Titus's Inquisition, Wintervale's death, Atlantis's relentless search for her in the Sahara—not to mention the horrifying knowledge that her capture would lead to her being used in sacrificial magic to prolong the Bane's life. All this and more sometimes made it feel as if her family, her friends, and the Bane were the only ones involved in this struggle.

Even though she knew otherwise.

The sight of all the dead Atlanteans, however, at last brought the point home. Hundreds of soldiers who had served the Bane loyally and valiantly, dead because he could not allow even a smidgen of truth to tarnish his reputation at home. Because if they knew the truth about him, they—or at least some of them—would risk their own lives to end the travesty that was his rule.

Titus nudged his carpet closer. "You all right?"

"It has always been about him, hasn't it, this empire he has built?" she said, still seething. "He wanted control over the mage world not for the greater glory of Atlantis or the honor of the Atlanteans, but only so that he could immediately get his hands on the next great elemental mage."

"Oh, I do not doubt he also enjoys power tremendously," said Titus. "But I agree that in the end it has been driven by fear, by his unwillingness to leave this world because of what might await him in the next."

She glanced at him. He too was driven by a fear of dying. And he too had at times sacrificed personal integrity in order to further his goal. At the beginning of their partnership, a relationship then fraught with distrust, she had demanded angrily what the difference was between Atlantis and him, as they were both happy to hold her against her will.

But beneath the Master of the Domain's sometimes caustic manner and streak of ruthlessness was a boy of active conscience and fundamental decency. A boy who, if anything, judged himself too harshly for his imperfections.

As she studied him, her despair began to fade. They were not impotent bystanders. They would take on this tyrant and, should Fortune smile upon them, topple him from power.

Besides, it was almost impossible not to be filled with hope when she looked at her beloved.

They were still alive, still free, and still together.

He leaned against the upright side of the carpet, his shoulders slumped forward—he must be unbearably weary, having been on the run since their arrival in the desert, hauling her mostly unconscious person alongside without even knowing who she was.

But she knew that if she suggested he needed rest, he would brush it aside. Fortunately for him, she was not above playing the damsel in distress. "I hate to admit it, but I'm getting a bit tired. Can we stop for a minute?"

"Of course," he said immediately. "Let me find a good place."

❖ ❖

A suitable place, however, was not immediately to be had. There was nearly enough light to see, and the patch of desert they were traversing was flat and featureless.

As they searched, Iolanthe asked Kashkari, "Why did our allies contact Durga Devi during the battle? Do they all know one another?"

"You took the question right off my tongue," said Titus.

"She does know, after a fashion, some parties with a good deal of power from the Domain," answered Kashkari. "Remember when I was late coming back to school at the beginning of the Half?"

Terms at Eton College were referred to as Halves. For reasons that made sense only to nonmages, there were three Halves every year: Easter Half, which began in January and ended before Easter; Summer Half, wedged between Easter Holiday and summer holiday; and Michaelmas Half, covering roughly all of autumn.

The prince had brought Iolanthe to Eton at the beginning of Summer Half. They had become separated during the summer holiday, but had managed to reunite at school at the start of Michaelmas Half. That was when they had been informed that Kashkari's steamer had run into rough seas en route and had been delayed. Titus and Iolanthe had accepted the news at face value, neither suspecting that Kashkari might not be the nonmage Indian boy he very much seemed to be.

"I remember," she said. He didn't come back until that fateful house party on the coast of the North Sea. "You told Titus later that you were late because you and your brother were busy informing as many mages as possible that Madame Pierredure was long dead and any news of her emerging from retirement to lead a new resistance movement was Atlantis using her to round up those with rebellion on their minds."

"And while we were doing that," said Kashkari, "Amara was thinking on a more strategic level. We were no match for Atlantis either in the size of our force or the sophistication of our matériel. The plan had been to exchange training and know-how with other rebel bases, but with Atlantis's traps having reeled in so many rebels, she decided to investigate an offer of assistance she'd had from a mysterious source that claimed to be able to tap into the assets of a major mage realm.

"It was a huge risk, but Amara has never been afraid of risks. A meeting was arranged with a liaison in Casablanca. She then asked the liaison to prove that he truly had access to all the equipment and ammunition that he claimed. She was taken on a trip that lasted nearly twelve hours, and she was certain a large portion of it involved a sea voyage on a ship launched from a dry dock—even blindfolded and with her ears plugged, she could still smell the ocean and feel the rolling of the waves. When she was allowed to see again, she found herself in a huge cavern stockpiled with an eye-popping assortment of war machines.

"Amara is a cynic, so she asked how could she be certain that she wasn't looking at Atlantis's own stockpile. At which point she was blindfolded again. But this time, she was only led around on foot for about thirty minutes. When the blindfold was taken off, she stood on the side of a heavily wooded slope. And through the trees she glimpsed the Right Hand of Titus in the distance."

The Right Hand of Titus was a set of five mage-made peninsulas jutting out into the Atlantic from the coast of Delamer, the Domain's capital city. The Citadel, the Master of the Domain's official residence, sat upon the ring finger of the Right Hand of Titus.

"She was shown the facilities under the Serpentine Hills?" asked Titus, a speculative look in his eyes.

"Yes—she took a long, hard look at her surroundings to make sure she hadn't been tricked. Then she asked how could she be sure that she was actually dealing with someone with the power to deploy the war machines, and not just a lowly guard who had the password to the storage facilities.

"That was when she was informed of a diplomatic reception at the Citadel. She was told to walk in behind a cluster of late-arriving guests—and that she would have a five-minute window before she was discovered. Actually her instruction was to turn around and leave as soon as she got inside, to avoid discovery. But the matter of the new great elemental mage had been weighing heavily on her mind—it was an unknown that could change everything—and she resolved to speak to the prince directly about it."

That was how Titus had first met Amara, at that reception. She had asked him for his elemental mage and had escaped quite elegantly when the palace guards realized there was an intruder among the guests.

Kashkari sighed. "She is braver than any of us, but at times she can be quite impulsive. She regretted her action immediately, but it was too late. She had angered her contact, who saw her willfulness as a breach of faith. That potential alliance went no further.

"She returned to the base hours before I left for Eton. We discussed everything she'd seen—and her ultimate failure. That was when I decided to take the matter into my own hands. At that time we all thought that perhaps it was the Master of the Domain himself who was behind the overture."

Titus was not—he had always been adamantly against anyone knowing anything about his work. Nor were war machines his modus operandi.

"In any case," Kashkari went on, "it seems that Amara has been forgiven. It must have been the same mages who contacted her just now in her two-way notebook—that was how they had always got in touch with her, even though she had never matched her notebook with theirs."

"Do you think it might be Dalbert?" Iolanthe asked Titus.

"Not Dalbert himself—he is careful not to be mixed up in something like this. But it might have been mages he considered trustworthy."

"Good to know," said Kashkari.

"True, we are not entirely alone," replied Titus.

But his face was troubled, even as he uttered his apparently hopeful words.

They settled in a deep curve of a dune that undulated for miles.

Once Iolanthe discovered that the battle supplies they'd grabbed from the rebel base contained sachets of tea, she cleared a small space for them inside the dune, where she could summon a fire without being seen.

Over Titus's objection, of course. "You will overtax yourself," he said, shaking his head.

"Please, Your Highness, show some respect for the great elemental mage of your time."

They didn't have any cooking vessels, so she heated the sphere of water she'd summoned as it spun lazily a few inches above the fire. When she judged the water hot enough, she dropped in a pinch of tea leaves to steep.

The battle rations also came with pastries that had savory fillings of peas, potatoes, and spices.

"This is wonderful," she said wholeheartedly. "We've had nothing but food cubes since we woke up in the desert. What I wouldn't give now for one of those breakfast spreads at Mrs. Dawlish's."

Kashkari chewed meditatively. "When I was at Mrs. Dawlish's, I was always waiting for some dramatically eventful future to happen. But now that it's all happening, I wish I'd better appreciated the boring old days, when the most exciting thing I ever did was occasionally vaulting to London, or to the West Sussex coast for a walk by the sea."

Titus had already finished one pastry and was on to the next—this might be the fastest she'd ever seen him eat. "I miss rowing," he said. "Cricket was incomprehensible, so I chose rowing. At first I thought it was only a little less stupid as a sport. And then it turned out that when I rowed I paid attention only to the rhythm of my breaths and the rhythm of my pulls—I did not think at all."

Which must have been a lovely respite from the tyranny of his destiny.

In Summer Half, sometimes the cricketers walked down to the river and heckled the rowers. In her mind's eye she saw the four-man scull coming down the Thames, the rowers with their backs to the spectators, the blades of their oars slicing into the water in perfect unison and exact alignment.

She had been as enthusiastic a heckler as any cricketer, disparaging the rowers' form, speed, and general manliness. Titus usually ignored the cricketers, as befitting his lofty persona, but once—just once—he lifted his hand from the oar and flashed the cricketers an obscene gesture.

The cricketers had agreed that it was the best heckling session in their collective memory.

"I miss Cooper," she said. "I miss all of them. I miss the pictures of Bechuanaland from my room—they made me feel nostalgic, even though I'd never been anywhere near the Kalahari."

Into their warm enclosure a silence fell. Titus stared into the fire. Kashkari looked down at the sand at his feet. The sphere of hot water had turned a clear russet; she directed the tea into everyone's waterskins.

Then she exhaled and acknowledged the keenly felt absence. "And I really miss Wintervale. He would have loved to be here with us—he would have had the time of his life."

Kashkari lifted his head. "You were the last one to see him, weren't you?"

And by "him," Kashkari meant the real Wintervale, before he had been turned into a vessel of the Bane.

"I was, the day of the first cricket practice for the twenty-two. He'd been called back by his mother and just remembered that the wardrobe portal in his room no longer worked. And he was fretting over how long it would take to get home via nonmage transports." She blew at the steam rising from her waterskin. "Such an ordinary parting. I never thought anything of it."

"I last saw him at dinner that day," said Titus. The midday meal at Mrs. Dawlish's was referred to as dinner, the evening meal supper. "He was talking to Sutherland about the trip to Norfolk."

Where he had come to them—but by then he was no longer in control of his own body.

"It had been much longer for me," said Kashkari. "I last saw him before I left England at the end of Summer Half. We shook hands at the top of the staircase in Mrs. Dawlish's, and he told me that the next Half would be the best yet."

Titus sighed and raised his waterskin. "To Wintervale, an excellent friend and a good man. He will always, always be fondly remembered."

Iolanthe and Kashkari joined him in the toast. "To Wintervale."

The boys blinked and looked up. Iolanthe didn't bother holding back her tears; she only wiped the corners of her eyes.

In silence they ate the rest of the pastries. And then Kashkari asked, "So, where are we going?"

The fire wavered, throwing out a few sparks.

There were no drafts in this enclosure of sand. Nor was the fire fueled by anything that could shift and give movement to the flames. The flicker had been caused by the elemental mage who wielded the fire, a small lapse of concentration, perhaps.

Titus glanced at her. There were dark circles underneath her eyes and a new hollowness to her cheeks. She had always steadfastly protested that she was fine and that she had had all the rest she needed these last few days, sleeping plentifully under the influence of the panacea—choosing to gloss over the fact that she had very nearly died from crossing the blood circle and that the sleep had not been some lazy indulgence, but her body fighting for her very survival.

She turned to Kashkari. "We are going to Atlantis."

That was exactly what they were going to do, from the very beginning. Still, her words gave Titus chills.

Kashkari's hand tightened around the neck of his water canteen. "I thought so."

"You don't need to come with us unless you wish to," she said. "Your friends here will be glad of your help too."

Kashkari glanced westward, even though he could see nothing beyond the firelight and Titus's shadow on the wall of sand. "I wish to go with you," he answered quietly. "It might be delusional on my part to hope my actions will matter, but better that than sitting back in the belief that they won't. Not trying is the surest way of never making any difference."

"We are most grateful to have you," Titus responded, much to his own surprise.

His mother had once had a vision of two boys, seen from the back, approaching the Commander's Palace. Earlier he had assumed the boys to be himself and Wintervale, as one of the boys had some trouble walking—and Wintervale had never walked properly after his display of tremendous elemental power off the coast of Norfolk.

Titus had further assumed that the vision cemented the choice he had made to terminate his partnership with Fairfax, because she had proven not to be the One.

Now he knew better than to make any more assumptions. Now he knew the potential pitfalls of duplicating his mother's visions down to the last detail. He would no longer reject help simply because it did not seem to fit in with a future seen through a small lens at a very limited angle.

For all he knew, the two boys could be Kashkari and Fairfax, approaching the Commander's Palace after Titus was no more. And he prayed that she would have the help of someone as calm and competent as Kashkari, rather than be all alone in the end.

"Yes, most grateful," echoed Fairfax, offering Kashkari her hand to shake.

They all shook hands, sealing a pact that was a lifetime—and more—in the making.

"So," said Kashkari, still looking slightly stunned at what he had got himself into, "how exactly will we go to Atlantis?"

"Keep in mind that every option going forward will be terrible. My most workable solution right now is a destination disruptor for a translocator at Delamer East," answered Titus.

"I'm not sure I've heard of such a thing," said Kashkari. "A destination disruptor, that is. I know Delamer East is a big interrealm hub in the Domain."

"A destination disruptor does more or less what you think it does. It plays havoc with a translocator's route. The translocator my disruptor is tailored for handles a fair bit of transatlantic cargo. I was told that if I managed to get the disruptor to work properly, we might materialize within fifty miles of Atlantis."

Once upon a time, mage realms could only be found by those

who had seen them with their own eyes. In other words, no outsider, mage or nonmage, could locate a realm without the help of a guide who had already been there. But as commerce and travel between mage realms increased, the ancient system became increasingly unwieldy.

So a new system was put into place. Under the new system, one only had to know the exact location of a realm and its proper name to be able to make one's way there. The era of hidden realms was at an end; the age of the worldwide mage community had dawned.

Then, with the development and explosive growth of instantaneous travel, mages forgot altogether that a global accord ever existed to facilitate the tracking down of distant places—who needed to know how to locate a faraway realm when one could simply step into a translocator and be whisked there in seconds?

No one had bothered to update the protocol—not even Atlantis—and this meant that Titus, Fairfax, and Kashkari could grope their way to the shores of the Bane's stronghold, if they had the guts to do so.

Kashkari blew out a breath. "So we drop into the ocean somewhere around Atlantis—we hope—and then simply . . . approach?"

The coast of Atlantis was heavily guarded—Titus had heard rumors of floating fortresses that would make run-of-the-mill armored chariots look like gnats. To "simply approach" would give them odds of success roughly the same as those of a nonmage walking into a barrage of gunfire and emerging unscratched on the other side.

He shrugged. "It is the best plan I have been able to put into place."

Kashkari looked at Fairfax, something that was almost outright fear on his face.

She met his gaze squarely. "If I've learned anything since I brought down my first bolt of lightning, it's that you never need a mythical amount of courage—just enough to get through the day. And I'm fairly certain that today we will not end up off the coast of Atlantis."

She turned toward Titus. "If we are to implement this plan of yours, we need to go back to the Domain. I don't suppose you can send for your valet to come and get you."

In the upper reaches of the castle that was Titus's home, there was a translocator that had been built to resemble a nonmage private rail coach. It was how he always traveled from the castle to their school and vice versa.

"No."

"Then how? The sea route?"

The summer before, when they had been separated and Fairfax stuck in the Domain, she had left via the old-fashioned method of sailing on a sloop until she came to the nearest nonmage island, where she could catch a steamer and continue her journey.

"We could if we must, but the sea route takes a long time."

Kashkari picked up a handful of sand. "Do I remember you saying once that you must account for your movements every twenty-four hours?"

"I do, under normal circumstances. But when the war phoenix has been deployed, the rules change: I have seven days before I need to make my location known again. I summoned the war phoenix our first night in the desert, three days ago. So four more days before I must report in."

"Atlantis will know where you are then?"

"Alectus, the regent, will know where I am. And regrettably, as he is Atlantis's puppet, when he learns my whereabouts, it will be no time before Atlantis does too."

"And what if you don't report in?"

"The regent assumes the crown. I am not terribly fond of the crown, but there are many advantages to being the Master of the Domain, where our task is concerned. Not to mention Alectus would hand over the reins of government to Atlantis—and it would take many years and many lives to wrestle those back. So for both of those reasons, I do not wish to give up the throne unless I must."

"Does that mean we have to succeed in killing the Bane before your four days are up?" asked Kashkari.

Titus hesitated longer than he wanted to before he said, "More like seven days—four days until I make my location known plus the seventy-two hours' grace period before Alectus becomes the Master of the Domain."

The fire wavered again, a more agitated movement this time.

Kashkari might not understand it yet, but Fairfax knew what going to Atlantis portended: Titus's death.

"There is no absolute requirement that it must be done in seven days," she said. "And if the crown should go to Alectus because you can't reveal your whereabouts for a while, well, that can't be helped."

There was a silence.

"In any case, I must find out more about what is going on. If I can get back to my laboratory, I will be able to access reports from my spymaster and have a better understanding of the situation."

It worried him that his allies had revealed their capacity to take down armored chariots from the ground. At the time, of course, it seemed they had no choice but to do so. But now the decision appeared to have been premature.

In the heat of the battle, the Atlanteans might believe Iolanthe Seabourne to have summoned the kind of lightning strikes armored chariots could not withstand. But in retrospect, they would ask themselves whether the lightning strikes had not been a distraction for a different kind of weapon.

You cannot surprise Atlantis twice.

If the rebels lost this element of surprise, they would be deprived of a major advantage. Now more than ever, Titus needed Dalbert as his eyes and ears. Perhaps his lips and tongue, even, to direct those still loyal to the crown when he could not.

"Where is your laboratory?" asked Kashkari.

"It is a folded space. There are two access points—one close to Eton, one in Cape Wrath."

Kashkari let the sand in his hand slide down, a drizzle of a seemingly random pattern on the ground. "In Cairo there is a one-way portal my brother rigged up that goes directly to Mrs. Dawlish's. But it might not work if there is still a no-vaulting zone in place at Eton."

Titus shook his head. "Obviously Atlantis does not expect us to go back, but I would not be surprised if they still have people watching the place."

"And I'd have set a loophole for it in the no-vaulting zone," said Fairfax. "If you really want to find someone, you don't eliminate the possibility that they just might fall into your hands."

"Then how?"

"We do not all need to go to Britain." Titus took out the map from the emergency satchel and laid it on the sand. Their location appeared as a dot in the eastern Sahara. "If we proceed from here at about seventy degrees on the compass, we will reach Luxor some time before noon. You and Fairfax can probably find a place to stay for the day and I will vault to my laboratory."

"Scotland is at least three thousand miles away," Kashkari pointed out, sounding incredulous.

"I can vault that much in twenty-four hours without killing myself."

On the day he had discovered that the Chosen One in his

mother's visions had referred to Wintervale, rather than Iolanthe, he had vaulted four times from Norfolk to Cape Wrath and back, and then once more for good measure from Eton, which added up to approximately forty-five hundred miles.

"Doesn't mean you should," said Fairfax.

Her voice was low and controlled, but the flames before her shot up several inches.

"I'll go out and make sure it's safe to leave," said Kashkari, with his exquisite sensitivity. "You two can discuss our route a bit more."

"Don't go," she said as soon as Kashkari had vaulted out. "Don't go any place where I can't keep an eye on you."

"You know I would do anything not to leave your side, but I must know what is going on. And even if you were in perfect health, you still cannot vault that much distance in a short time."

"You don't need to be in that big of a rush. So what if we take our time getting to the laboratory?"

She rarely objected to his decisions so vehemently—most of the time she trusted him to look after himself. "What is the matter?"

She turned her face away, but not before he saw the grimace that she could not quite suppress. He caught her by the chin and tilted her face until she was looking at him again. "Tell me what is the matter, please."

"If we only have seven days left, then I don't want you out of my sight for a second."

"We do not know that we only have seven days left. Besides, did you not tell me that you are convinced I will outlive everything that is coming our way?"

"I did and I am. But . . ."

He knew what she could not quite bring herself to say. But what if she was wrong and his mother exactly right? And his mother had always been perfectly accurate in what she foresaw—the only mistakes she had made had been in the interpretation of her visions.

But how many ways were there to interpret death?

Fairfax closed her eyes for a moment. When she opened them again, she was once again in charge of herself. "I'm sorry. You are right. You do need to go and we need all the intelligence you can lay your hands on, if we are to have any chance of success."

"Do not apologize. I am flattered: no one else wants to spend time with me."

"That's not true: Cooper does. Desperately."

He could not help laughing. Then he kissed her. "I will be very careful, because I want to see you again, with a desperation Cooper can barely conceive of."

CHAPTER · 5

TITUS AND FAIRFAX GOT INTO another small disagreement over where to meet again. He wanted her to hide in Luxor and stay out of sight; she wanted to fly to the southern coast of Turkey, to shorten his return journey as much as possible.

"How about Cairo?" suggested Kashkari. "I've done the Luxor-Cairo route a few times. It isn't that difficult to remain unseen, even in broad daylight, provided we stay some miles from the Nile."

Titus grimaced. The longer she flew, the greater the chances of her being spotted by agents of Atlantis. But just as she reined back her desire to have him by her side all the time, he must also keep in check his need to never let her be seen again by anyone except him.

There was his overwhelming desire to keep his girl safe; but there was also his unwavering respect for the lightning-wielder.

"All right," he said.

"All right," she also said, "but on the condition that you sleep between here and Luxor—vaulting is more difficult and potentially more harmful if you are severely under-rested. You rest too, Kashkari. I'll fly us."

They did not argue with her. Kashkari had already put away the battle carpets they had flown thus far on and brought out the travel carpets, which were better suited to longer distances. He subordinated his and Titus's carpets to hers, and she took them a few feet off the ground and started accelerating.

Steering at such minimal altitudes took more skill and required greater concentration. But by staying low, the undulation of the dunes made it difficult for them to be spotted from a distance—and with the sun soon to rise, it was a far safer way to get to where they needed to go.

"Wake us up if you need anything," Titus told her.

"I will. Sweet dreams, you two."

Barely a minute later—or so it felt—a hand was gently shaking him on the shoulder. "Titus. Titus," she called him, first softly, then with greater urgency. "Titus!"

He turned and sat up so abruptly their heads almost knocked. "What—"

What is going on? he was about to demand, when he realized that they were no longer airborne. He was still on his carpet, but the carpet was on the hard floor of a dim, stuffy cave. And Kashkari, not far from him, slumbered soundly.

"We are in Luxor—in the Theban Necropolis," said Fairfax, as if she had heard his questions. "You and Kashkari were both dead asleep when we arrived. I didn't want to wake you up to ask where we should stay, so I just came here."

Still groggy, Titus rubbed his eyes and made a face. "The mummy hotel?"

No self-respecting mage community had tolerated burial as a funerary practice after the Necromancer Wars. And the very idea of bodies preserved to last forever, perfect for serving as foot soldiers the next time a twisted archmage decided to reanimate corpses for his or her own nefarious purposes—he grimaced again.

She laughed softly. "There are piles of pottery deeper in the cave. Maybe they contain embalmed organs."

He stretched—the hard ground had made his back stiff. "How did you come across this place?"

"I knew about it from talking to Birmingham—he had definite plans to excavate here someday. Wait, you were there that day."

It took him a moment to remember Birmingham—their former house captain at Mrs. Dawlish's—and the lovely, lovely days of the latter part of the Summer Half, with the Inquisitor dead and the Bane pondering his options, not yet ready to sally forth again. Life during those miraculously safe weeks seemed to consist entirely of sports, sunshine, and merrymaking. She was never not in the corridor, talking to clusters of boys, either about to set out and do something fun or newly returned from such an excursion.

And on that particular day, a Sunday, after morning service, when he had gone to his laboratory for something or another, she, Cooper, Wintervale, and Kashkari had come back from a walk in the country with, of all things, a pewter freezing-pot. By the time Titus set foot in Mrs. Dawlish's again, the house was in an uproar, with boys being sent out to obtain all manners of items, a tub from the laundry room, ice from the nearest ice well, and the cook's recipe book from the kitchen.

The Master of the Domain was dispatched to find a gallon of fresh cream at an hour long after the morning's milk had been delivered. He had somehow accomplished this Herculean task, and that afternoon the boys had flown kites and played tennis while taking turns stirring the cream until it began to congeal.

A gallon of ice cream was a drop in the ocean where dozens of boys were concerned. By the time she had doled out a serving to everyone, there was barely a spoonful left for the two of them. It had certainly not been the best ice cream he had ever tasted, only the most wonderful.

And that was when Birmingham had declared that he would be sure to take a freezing-pot with him, when he undertook his future digs in Upper Egypt. Birmingham had gone on to describe what must be this exact place. She had listened attentively, curious as usual about what nonmages did with their lives, but Titus had only looked at her, while terms such as "Temple of Hatshepsut" and "Valley of the Queens" washed in and out of his hearing.

He reached out and touched her hair, feeling its softness between his fingers.

"Thinking of the ice cream?" she murmured.

"Of course," he said.

Every bright, beautiful memory was always associated with her. Until she came along, he had never understood the concept of boyhood, of those years in a man's life that should be full of fun and laughter. Now he only wished he had met her sooner—that they had spent more time together.

He wrapped his hand around the back of her head and pulled her closer. She gazed at him, her thumb grazing across his chapped lips.

Kashkari cried out.

They drew apart, their heads turning in unison toward their friend. He seemed to be still asleep. A bad dream, most likely. They waited a few seconds, glancing at each other, holding back laughter of both frustration and mirth.

She reached out toward him again.

Kashkari bolted upright, breathing hard.

Titus and Fairfax scrambled to their feet. "You all right?" she asked.

Kashkari looked up at them, blinked, and gasped.

They both immediately glanced behind. But no enemy was approaching from the outside. All the same, Titus gestured for Fairfax to go to Kashkari while he himself took up a defensive position near the mouth of the cave.

"Is something wrong?" she asked, kneeling down beside their friend.

Kashkari rubbed his face. "No, I'm fine. Probably got startled by a dream, that's all. Where are we? And what time is it? How long have I been sleeping?"

"We are in the hills west of Luxor, across the Nile. And it's . . ." She hesitated. "It's sometime past noon."

"What?" Titus exclaimed. "How long did you let me sleep? I should have left hours ago."

"You needed your rest. A few hours won't make any difference one way or the other."

"They very well might," he shot back.

"Let me—let me go outside for a moment," said Kashkari.

Titus had already begun to apply cleaning spells to himself as Kashkari slowly got up. As the latter made for the mouth of the cave, he went deeper inside, to a different chamber, and changed into a fresh set of clothes that had been part of the rebels' battle supplies.

When he reemerged, Fairfax was waiting. She lifted his tunic from behind and ministered to his back. Then she opened a small jar, also part of the rebels' kit, and dabbed some balm on his lips. "You never look after yourself," she said.

Her touch was gentle and warm. Her words fell somewhere between an accusation and a lament.

"I will learn."

She shook her head. "That'll be the day."

He took her hand as they walked out. The cave was near the top of a completely barren hill, its rocky bones baking in the hot sun of the afternoon. The land dropped off in the distance, the brown, bare ground abruptly turning into startlingly green fields as it neared the Nile, the lifeblood of Egypt. And on the other side of the river sprawled Luxor, with its ancient ruins and modern brick buildings, both very nearly the same color as the desert beyond.

About fifty feet away, Kashkari sat on a small outcrop, his head in his hands.

A thought came to Titus. "You think he has dreamed of my death?" he asked under his breath.

Her hand tightened around his. "He had better not."

His mother's vision of his early demise was easier to deny on its own. Corroborated by Kashkari, it would be that much harder to pretend that there was any escape from a fate that had already been written.

Kashkari rose and headed in their direction.

"Will you drop in on my guardian in Paris, if you can?" Fairfax asked Titus.

"That is already on my itinerary," he told her. "And will you take some rest? You have been awake too long."

She nodded.

When they met up with Kashkari, Titus asked outright, "You have any prophetic dreams I should know about before I head out?"

Something flickered across Kashkari's face, but his answer was mild and even. "I'll let you know when I do. In the meanwhile, may Fortune walk with you."

They shook hands. Titus embraced Fairfax. Then he took a deep breath and vaulted.

Iolanthe stared at the empty spot where he had been.

Every good-bye could be their last.

"He loves you," said Kashkari quietly, "in a way that is beyond me."

She turned to him. "Thank you . . . and is it gauche to admit that I haven't the slightest idea what you mean?"

Kashkari smiled a little. He seemed back to his old self. "What I mean is that you are everything to him. When he sees you, he sees the one with whom he has been to hell and back—the one who would accompany him to hell again, no questions asked."

Whereas he and Amara did not have that history of shared struggle. That as much as he loved her, it was as a bystander, looking in from the outside.

"Titus and I have been fortunate in each other," she said.

And how she missed him.

It wasn't his absence that she minded—the Master of the Domain was always off somewhere, doing something; that had been the way ever since they first met. It was this fear she could not shake, now that they were close—and edging ever closer—to the moment of truth.

Could she save him—or would it prove all hubris and wishful thinking? And if she couldn't . . .

"Why don't you take some rest?" said Kashkari. "You look tired."

She would have preferred for them to start for Cairo right away, but she had promised Titus that she would rest, and she *was* beginning to feel drained. "Don't let me sleep too long."

"We'll be in Cairo before the end of the day," Kashkari assured her.

No, she thought, he was not back to his old self. She knew the old Kashkari, she knew his resolve, his courage, and his secret heartache. None of it had gone away, but there was something different about him.

He was . . . saddened. He hid it well, but he was weighed down, in a way he hadn't been before he'd awakened in the cave, gasping for breath.

What exactly had he dreamed of?

Her own slumber was blissfully free of dreams, but when she woke up her head was crammed full of memories that had been suppressed for years and years.

Memories of herself as a baby, inhaling the subtle narcissus perfume of the warm body that cradled her own, falling asleep in a cloud of contentment.

Memories of herself as a toddler, running her fingers over the rich silk velvet of the overrobe of this unbelievably beautiful woman who was her mother. Her *mother*.

Memories of herself as a little girl, wishing this one day every two years that she could spend with her marvelous mother would never, ever end, that the clock would stop one minute short of midnight and not move again.

Memories of herself as a slightly older girl, her eyes wide at learning that her father was none other than the hero of the January Uprising. And two years later, she and her mother weeping together over Baron Wintervale's sudden passing.

That would be the last good year before Master Haywood's troubles began. Before she started to plead with her mother to help the man who cared for her, whom she loved like a father. Before she received the answer that had chilled her to the bone: *He is only the help, my darling; you don't need to worry about him.* Before she had no choice but to understand that this man who had devoted his life to her mother meant nothing to the latter. He was but a cog in the machinery she'd built to keep herself and her daughter safe.[1]

She could never again love her mother with the purity and wonder of those more innocent days. Their relationship grew testy. Lady Callista was not happy with a daughter who was no longer adoring and biddable; Iolanthe grew ever more frustrated and distrusting.

Their last meeting had been downright antagonistic. Master Haywood had just lost his position at a third-tier lower academy for taking bribes from students for better marks, forcing him to accept a position as a schoolmaster in one of the most remote villages of the Domain.

Iolanthe had been furious with him, but the moment memories of her secret life had come back, all her fury transferred to Lady Callista. When Lady Callista had come for her a few minutes after midnight, Iolanthe screamed and railed. She was going to go to Master Haywood that instant and tell him everything. She didn't care that his possession of the knowledge might threaten Lady Callista's position or her own safety. There were gray areas in life, but this was not one of them. What had been done to Master Haywood was heinous, and she would not allow another moment of it to pass unrectified.

Lady Callista had listened quietly, seeming to pay attention, but then, with Iolanthe in midsentence, she'd raised her wand.

That was the end of that meeting. The memories of Lady Callista, old and new, had returned to their vault deep in her mind, and Iolanthe had awakened the next morning, aching and upset, and had thought it was only because of her despair over Master Haywood and her increasing distress over her own future.

"Are you all right?" came Kashkari's soft voice.

She realized that she'd been staring at the ceiling of the cave. Something about the situation with Lady Callista bothered her—something besides her mother's callous treatment of Master Haywood. But she couldn't quite pinpoint what it was.

She sat up. "I'm fine. How long did I sleep?"

"About three hours."

The cave, which opened to the west, was now filled with a golden light. She noticed the two-way notebook in Kashkari's lap. "Have you heard from Amara and your brother, by the way?"

"Yes, from both—they are safe and regrouping," he answered— but did not meet her gaze.

Was it because he did not want to reveal his inner thoughts as he spoke of the one he loved and the one *she* loved? Or was it something else?

"What about Mrs. Hancock? Anything from her?" Mrs. Hancock, special envoy of Atlantis's Department of Overseas Administration stationed in Mrs. Dawlish's house, had turned out to be a staunch enemy of the Bane and their secret ally.

"Nothing from her. I hope she's all right."

"I wonder if West has been discovered missing yet," she said slowly.

West, a senior boy who bore an uncanny resemblance to the Bane, had been abducted from his resident house, setting off the chain of events that led to Titus and Iolanthe's abrupt departure from school.

"That we don't have to worry about, for now. Mrs. Hancock set up a number of otherwise spells. People at school believe him to be on extended leave. His family thinks he can't get away from school for various reasons."

Kashkari still didn't look her in the eye. What was the matter with him?

He closed his notebook. "Do you know anything about the Commander's Palace?"

She supposed it was natural enough for him to be thinking about the Bane's stronghold, since it was their eventual destination. "Yes, a few things Titus told me."

She related what she knew—the fortress's location in the uplands of Atlantis, the rings of defense that surrounded it, the wyverns and armored-chariot-carried colossal cockatrices that crisscrossed the air above, ever vigilant on behalf of the Bane's safety.

"And how did Titus learn everything?"

She brought up the rupture view that resulted from Titus's interrupted Inquisition and the spy Prince Gaius, Titus's grandfather, had sent into Atlantis many years ago.

"That's remarkable," mused Kashkari. "Atlantis receives no diplomatic delegations on its own soil and issues no visitor visas. And I hear that floating fortresses guard the entire coastline, watching for any approaching intruders. How did this spy get in?"

"I don't know. I assume he snuck in somehow."

As they would.

Kashkari nodded, seemingly deep in thought. Then he rose to his feet. "Shall we get going then?"

CHAPTER · 6

TITUS POSSESSED A ONE-TIME VAULTING range of three hundred miles, a rare gift. But such a gift was not terribly useful unless the world was a network of nodes he had visited in person, each node less than three hundred miles apart from the next nearest connection point—vaulting was only accurate when the destination could be visualized from personal memory.

After he arrived at Eton, at age thirteen, he set out to create just such a network for himself. It started with a Sunday afternoon stroll to a railway station in nearby Windsor, and a ticket purchased for London. When he reached London, he walked about Paddington Station and some of the surrounding streets, then got on the underground and took himself to Euston Station and King's Cross, two other railway termini.

Once he knew all of London's major railway stations by heart, he would vault to one after lights-out and board a night train somewhere, taking care that he did not accidentally go beyond his vaulting range. Soon he could materialize directly in rail stations in Bristol, Manchester, and Exeter—and take the train farther afield. It was not long before he vaulted handily to any major population center in Britain, plus a number of remote, scenic places.

With Britain under his belt, he set his sights on France, beginning with a night crossing from Dover. Once he reached Paris, the biggest railway hub in France and achievable in a single vault from Mrs. Dawlish's, the rest of France lay open to him.

Over the years he expanded this network to many corners of Europe that were readily accessible by rail, and some that were not. He had, however, never penetrated east of the Balkans. But this was where Alectus did him a favor.

Usually he was left alone on his school holidays to be looked after by Dalbert—Titus could be very unpleasant company. But each summer Alectus, Lady Callista, and Aramia went on a holiday abroad, and for that Alectus always insisted that he come along too—for the appearance of family unity, if nothing else.

Two summers ago they sailed the eastern Mediterranean on the crown yacht. Alectus delighted in calling at nonmage ports, pretending that they were the ruling family from the nonexistent principality of Saxe-Limburg. They visited the great pyramids at Giza—not the ones the nonmages flocked to see, but a series of six upside-down structures buried nearby that comprised an ancient translocator said to be able to, in its day, send a mage anywhere on earth. They even took a smaller craft from the yacht and set sail from Cairo, one hundred miles up the Nile.

Thanks to that trip, Titus was able to vault, in two segments, from Luxor to the vicinity of Giza, then northwest to Alexandria. Two more vaults and he was in Tobruk, which lay directly south of the isle of Crete.

From Crete he hopped to Zakynthos, an island in the Ionian Sea, west of mainland Greece. One more hop and he was in the easternmost spot of continental Italy.

The back of his head was beginning to throb painfully; he had no choice but to stop for a while. The sun shone warmly on his face; gulls wheeled and dipped; a breeze made fish-scale patterns on the surface of the bright-blue sea. He sat on the rocky shore and drank the last of the tea Fairfax had made in the morning.

As it often happened, when he allowed his mind to wander a little, he thought of her future. She had never told him herself, but he knew, from the material Dalbert had collected on her a while ago, that she would like to attend the Conservatory of Magical Arts and Sciences.

The Conservatory had a lovely campus on the shoulder of the Serpentine Hills, overlooking the Right Hand of Titus and the ceaseless Atlantic beyond. He could see her walking along the flagstone paths between buildings, talking with her friends, perhaps making plans to gorge on ices later at Mrs. Hinderstone's sweets shop, which she had often visited as a little girl.

The summer before, he had sent Dalbert to Mrs. Hinderstone's, to obtain a selection of the tastes and textures she had adored during her years in Delamer. Dalbert, always one to go above and beyond the call of duty, had brought back not only baskets of foodstuffs and beverages, but also postcards that captured the shop from every angle: the small, round tables on the sidewalk under a white-and-blue-striped awning; Mrs. Hinderstone herself standing beside huge display cases full of bonbons and chocolates; the lunch menu on the wall, done in iridescent wand-writing, with a notice at the bottom that proudly declared, *We are happy to pack picnic baskets for two or two hundred—and our famous ices are guaranteed not to melt for at least eight hours.*

Titus rarely injected himself into these reveries. But now he saw himself walking into Mrs. Hinderstone's and asking for one of those picnic baskets. He could see Mrs. Hinderstone's round, smiling face as she took down the particulars of his order. He could feel the weight and coolness of the coins he handed over. And he could sense the curious gazes of the other patrons, at the presence of the Master of the Domain.

But where would he take Fairfax for their picnic? In the Labyrinthine Mountains, overlooking a slope of brilliant red poppies, on the deck of a sailboat anchored in a sheltered bay south of Delamer, or on the great lawn of the Conservatory of Magical Arts and Sciences itself, in the shade of a late-blooming starflower tree, as bells tolled the passage of leisurely hours?

His mind, so adept at processing danger and making split-second decisions, was incapacitated before this cornucopia of pleasurable options. He did not want to choose. He wanted only to wallow in the endless possibilities of such a future.

He did not need to die, whispered a small voice inside. It was too soon, too unnecessary. His mother's grand vision had proved, if not outright false, then highly misdirected. There was no Chosen One, no certain path. There was no obligation to do more—not on his part, at least, he who had already sacrificed his entire childhood.

While other boys played, he had toiled. When he was not taking lessons from his ancestors in the teaching cantos, he was fighting every creature with teeth and claws in the fairy tales. Instead of sunshine and fresh air, the scents of his youth were old books and the scorch of dragon fire.

He had lived so little. When was the last time he took a walk in the Labyrinthine Mountains for pleasure? No, when he had time to spare, he had instead run on those unforgiving slopes, to make sure he would be fast and nimble when the time came.

Had he ever taken a day just for himself?

He dragged his mind back, gasping with effort. There was a reason he only thought of her in that mythical future: when he included himself, this monstrous greed for life burst forth, willing to destroy everything in its path for one more day, one more hour, one more breath.

But it was too late to turn aside now, too late to embrace cowardice.

He swallowed a dose of vaulting aid, closed his eyes, and pictured Naples.

Naples. Rome. Florence. When he materialized in Florence, he experienced a sharp pain behind his eyes. Instead of sitting down somewhere and waiting for the discomfort to pass, however, he used his recovery time to acquire some nonmage clothes that were better suited to Europe than the Sahara Desert: essentially buying everything off a dress dummy on display. But then again, he was handy with tailoring spells, having had hundreds of hours of practice so he could make sure the clothes he had prepared would fit the elemental mage who would assume the identity of Archer Fairfax.

Fairfax.

When he thought of the future this time, there was only her on the picnic blanket on the great lawn of the Conservatory, a book on her knees, a half-eaten sandwich to the side. But she did not remain alone. A friend would come by and sit down, then another. Soon a sizable cluster had gathered around the picnic blanket, and she was surrounded by laughter and joie de vivre.

He closed his eyes again.

Genoa. Turin. Geneva. Dijon. Auxerre.

By the time he reached the bell tower of Auxerre's largest

cathedral, hunched over, his ears ringing, he knew he had taken one vault too far. This part of France was too densely populated for flying on a carpet, so he bought a coat—in sunny Italy he had underestimated the amount of clothes he needed—got on a train, and let himself be transported by nonmage technology, clickety-clacking the remaining distance to Paris under a gray, rainy sky.

Two hours later he exited Gare de l'Est in Paris and hired a hansom cab to take him to the sixteenth arrondissement. Streetlights flickered to life along the broad boulevards of the city. He stayed in the hansom until traffic degenerated into a logjam that did not budge in any direction, then got out and walked the rest of the way, shivering despite the coat.

The concierge at the apartment building where Fairfax's guardian lived smiled as she saw him. *"Bonsoir, monsieur."*

He had used the apartment earlier as an on-site laboratory, and had given her the impression that he was a friend of the family. He nodded. *"Bonsoir, madame.* Is Monsieur Franklin at home?"

"Yes, *monsieur.* Such a lovely gentleman. He will be glad to see you, *monsieur.*"

Horatio Haywood was indeed overjoyed as he opened the door. But his smile wavered when he realized that Titus had come alone.

"She is fine," Titus said quickly. "May I come in?"

"Yes, of course. Do please forgive me, Your Highness."

He was shown to the *salle de séjour,* with its enormous paintings of nonmages frolicking in the countryside. Haywood ran to the kitchen and came back with a tea service and plates of puff pastry with savory fillings.

The man would probably have gone to the kitchen again to fetch more things, but Titus bade him take a seat and recounted what had happened since they were all last in a room together: the real story behind Wintervale's spectacular display of elemental power, their hasty departure from Eton, and their few but eventful days in the Sahara Desert.

"When I left earlier today she was safe and well, or at least as well as could be under the circumstances. And I trust that our friend is looking after her to the utmost of his considerable ability—although at any given moment she could be looking after him, for all we know. She is very good at keeping her friends alive and in one piece."

"Fortune shield me," murmured Haywood. "I was worried—I thought she would have come to see me again, but I never anticipated that so much could have happened."

They were quiet for some time. "So you remember everything now?" asked Titus.

The older man nodded slowly. "Yes, sire."

He would have been able to guess at Lady Callista's betrayal, judging by what they had learned the day they found him at Claridge's Hotel in London. But to be engulfed by a tide of memories, to remember the fervor of love that had driven him to lie, cheat, and steal for her only to be abandoned so completely—Titus could not imagine his anguish.

His regrets.

"I would like to ask you a question, if I may."

"Certainly, sire."

"I can piece together most of the story, even if the details are somewhat sketchy. But one part puzzles me. What is Commander Rainstone's role in all this?"

Commander Rainstone was the crown's chief security adviser. She had also, at one point, served under the late Princess Ariadne, Titus's mother.

"You said she introduced you to Lady Callista," Titus went on. "I understand Commander Rainstone comes from a humble background. How did she and Lady Callista become friends?"

"Oh," said Haywood, taken aback. "You didn't know, sire? Commander Rainstone and Lady Callista are half sisters."

Iolanthe and Kashkari did not risk flying into Cairo, which had its share of mage Exiles. And where there was a substantial gathering of mage Exiles, there were informants and agents of Atlantis.

Nor did Kashkari want them to walk in each carrying a carpet. They had covered the distance from Luxor to Cairo on travel carpets, but they still had their battle carpets, which were much more substantial in thickness and could not be folded into tiny squares and shoved into pockets. He feared that even rolled up, those carpets might still signal their mage origins.

Instead he bought a donkey on the outskirts of the city and laid their battle carpets across the donkey's back. He offered the donkey to Iolanthe, but she declined firmly: she'd much rather walk than wrestle with an unfamiliar beast.

So Kashkari rode and Iolanthe walked behind him, her face largely hidden beneath her keffiyeh. The buildings they passed were like none she had ever seen, with each story projecting farther out than the one immediately below. Two top-floor residents on opposite sides of a narrow street could almost embrace across what little distance remained between them.

Their destination was a clean and hospitable guest house. The proprietor embraced Kashkari and greeted him by name. Sweets and cups of coffee appeared as soon as they'd entered their room, followed by bowls of a delicious green soup and heaping plates of dolmas, which were grape leaves wrapped around a savory rice filling.

"You've been here before?" she asked Kashkari as they ate.

He nodded, reaching for a dolma. "My brother has been in the Sahara for a while. I would come to visit him every holiday, and it was always a hassle to get me back to school at the end of it. Somebody somewhere might have a mobile dry dock, but there wasn't always a vessel available—and we couldn't exactly ask to borrow the emergency boat. So sometimes they could launch me to the Mediterranean and take me to the coast of France. Other times I had to fly back most of the way.

"One day Vasudev had enough of the uncertainty—he also didn't like me flying so far by myself. He decided to rig me a one-way portal here in Cairo, since most rebel bases had a translocator that could reach Cairo or Tripoli. So we came here and stayed a few days. And then we went to school together, so he could finish the portal's other end."

"He visited Eton?"

"Met Mrs. Dawlish and Mrs. Hancock—and Wintervale too. Wintervale and I squired him around the school—walked the playing fields, rowed a bit on the river."

"He didn't meet the prince?"

"No, he left before Titus arrived that Half. And it's a shame you didn't have the chance to meet him, while we were still in the desert."

Did the timbre of his voice change? And was it sadness that once again darkened his eyes? The flame of a lantern flickered upon his face and threw his shadow on the wall, against a fretwork panel of arabesque patterns.

She set aside her plate. "What manner of man is he, your brother?"

Kashkari blew out a breath. "He's a bit shy—our sister, his twin, has always been the vivacious, assertive one. When Amara spoke at the engagement gala, she said that during his first six months at the base he never said anything to her that wasn't related to equipment production and maintenance."

"Is that what he is responsible for?"

"He's a marvel, a true wizard, when you need any devices built, improved upon, or invented from scratch. But don't let that fool you into thinking he's only fit for a workshop. He's also a deadly distance spell-caster—taught me everything I know."

And Kashkari had been quite the sniper.

"Do you think he and Durga Devi are a good match?"

"They are not an obvious match, but yes, I do think they are good for each other. He needs someone full of life to tear him away from his workbench once in a while. And he is a steadying influence on her, as she can be rash at times."

Before she could reply, he reached into his pocket. "Will you excuse me?"

He moved away from the divan on which they'd been eating to read his two-way notebook. His expression changed.

Iolanthe rose. "Is everything all right?"

He looked at her, his face now blank. "Vasudev writes that they are married. As of five minutes ago."

Iolanthe was stunned, and she wasn't even in love with one of the parties. "I take it today wasn't when the wedding was scheduled."

"No, they'd never set a date."

But she and Titus had brought Atlantis to the rebels' doorstep. What was the point of waiting longer, when there might not be a tomorrow, let alone a next week?

"I'd better tender my congratulations," he said.

Impulsively she stepped forward and hugged him. "I'm sorry it wasn't meant to be. I'm sorry for all the pain this has brought you. And I'm sorry it will hurt worse before it gets better."

He stood quiet and motionless in her embrace. She let him go, feeling a little self-conscious that perhaps she had overstepped the bounds of their friendship, which made it all the more surprising to see the sheen of tears in his eyes.

"Thank you," he said. "You have always been a very kind friend."

Something about his response disconcerted her. She laid a hand on his shoulder. "You get on with your reply. I'll put up some anti-intrusion spells."

Anti-intrusion spells were immaterial in their situation: even those that could hold off a determined housebreaker were of no use against the might of Atlantis. But she wanted to give Kashkari some space to grieve, without her standing next to him.

She went into the adjoining room and pulled out her wand from her boot. No lamps had been lit in this room, but as soon as her fingers closed over the wand, she remembered that she still had Validus. Titus had given it to her before the battle in the desert, hoping that the blade wand would be a magnificent amplifier of her powers.

And it had been.

She hesitated over whether to call a bit of flame, decided against it, and murmured a few spells with Validus pointed at the window. The diamond-inlaid crowns along the length of the blade wand were barely visible in the feeble light that drifted in from the other room. The facets of the gems seemed to . . .

She opened her eyes wider. Were the crowns growing brighter and then fainter in turn? The second-lowest one was now perceptibly brighter than the rest, now the third lowest one, going up in an orderly procession, then coming down again.

"Kashkari."

"Yes?" he answered immediately, his voice reflecting the tightness of her own.

"Extinguish the lantern and come here."

The outer room fell into darkness. Kashkari arrived silently. "What's the matter?"

"I need you to take a look at Validus."

He took the wand from her. She waited, a nameless dread trickling down her spine.

"Is it always like this?" he asked, after a minute.

"I don't know. The wand belongs to Titus. He gave it to me last night because he thought I might put it to better use."

"Could it be a signal from him?"

"If it is, he has never told me about such a use for this wand."

"Have you checked your tracer?"

Titus had a pendant that broke apart into a pair of tracers. At the moment he held one, and Iolanthe the other.

"I have and I can't tell the difference." Titus was so far away that the tracer had been ice-cold for hours.

Kashkari was silent for some time. "What does your gut say?"

She was slow to answer, not wanting to speak aloud the words gnawing at her nerves. "That it can't be good."

Kashkari did not disagree, but moved closer to the window. She joined him there. The window opened onto a dim, quiet courtyard, illuminated only by light from the surrounding guest rooms.

He opened the window a crack and murmured something in a language she didn't understand—Sanskrit, probably. She could just make out something dark taking shape in his palms. And then it flapped its wings and took off—a bird made of the very shadows of the night, it seemed.

"Our canary, so to speak," explained Kashkari.

She had been a canary once, one of the most harrowing experiences of her life. "What dangers would it alert us to?"

"Anything that might imperil a flying entity, or so I hope." He released several more such birds.

In front of him, a few specks of light came to be. Iolanthe was confused for a moment until she realized they weren't stray bits of fire that she didn't remember summoning, but tiny representations of the birds.

"Nice piece of wizardry," she whispered.

"My brother is working on a far more ambitious version—should he succeed, we'd be able to see what the birds are seeing, a three-dimensional rendering of their surroundings."

One of the birds disappeared in a microscopic shower of sparks. "Did it fly into something?"

"No, they avoid mundane obstacles like houses and pedestrians— even cats."

He bent forward, so as to be level with the smidgens of lights that stood for the remaining shadow canaries.

A second bird exploded, followed by a third. She turned cold: the danger was not at Titus's end, but theirs.

"They are destroyed when they fly higher," said Kashkari, his voice clenched.

"By what?"

"I don't know. But it's fairly certain that we also can't fly high, at least not nearby."

"Why is there such a thing overhead? Do you—do you think Atlantis knows we are here?"

"It might, if the wand has been broadcasting its location."

His words hung between them. Her throat burned with the very idea of such a betrayal. How could *Titus's* wand, of all things, turn on them?

She was shocked to hear herself speak in an even, collected tone. "If that's the case, then we had better be on the move."

How long had they been in Cairo? In the guest house? Was it long enough for Atlantis to pinpoint their location?

"Leave the wand behind," said Kashkari.

"But it once belonged to Titus the Great." A priceless heirloom, not just for the House of Elberon, but for the entire Domain.

"It will be the end of you if you keep holding on to it."

She bit the inside of her cheek. Then she held the wand aloft with a levitation spell and sent a sphere of lightning crashing toward it. For a fraction of a moment, everything inside the room stood out in sharp relief: the wand, Kashkari's startled gaze, the line where the wall met the ceiling.

When she grabbed hold of the wand again, it was hot to the touch and smoking a little, but as far as she could tell, the diamond-inlaid crowns were no longer changing in luminosity, however subtly.

"Let's go," she said.

They left on a single carpet—Kashkari's skills were a better match for the close confines of an urban district. Iolanthe held on to him from behind and kept her gaze upward, but she couldn't see anything overhead, other than a narrow alley of dark sky, between the nearly kissing top stories of the houses to either side.

The air smelled of spent coal, bread, and a faint undernote of donkey droppings. The night was becoming cooler, a breeze from the sea pushing out the residual heat from the day. Kashkari steered carefully, inching them forward.

A movement caught in the corner of her eye. But when she looked to the side, she didn't see anything. What was it? A reflection on a still-open window, which meant the object was . . .

"Go! Fast as you can," she hissed.

The thing behind them was a miniature armored chariot, a pod scarcely bigger than the desk in her room at Mrs. Dawlish's and almost the exact same shadowy color as the night. A pair of claws, attached to long cables, shot out from the pod's snout, aimed directly at her.

The carpet accelerated with a leap and took a sharp right turn tilted almost perpendicular to the street—only to careen headlong into the embrace of another pair of big claws.

Kashkari grunted and steered the carpet even lower, flattening it out completely. They passed under the incoming pod with scarcely an inch to spare above their heads.

Iolanthe sent a bolt of lightning toward the sky—their location had already been discovered, might as well find out what exactly loomed overhead. A gossamer net shimmered briefly, a thin, beautifully latticed web that stretched as far as she could see.

Fortune shield her. Had they covered all of Cairo?

Ahead three more vehicles blocked the way. Two pursued them from behind, and the way up was sealed.

She threw a barrage of opening spells at the nearest house. Kashkari banked a stomach-lurching turn. They shot past the front door into a dark, narrow passageway and saw the stairs just in time to pull up the carpet. At the top of the stair landing, Kashkari made her squeal by turning the carpet completely sideways. They fitted through a slender window—and barely avoided becoming caught in a tangle of laundry lines outside.

A half-wet sleeve—or was it a trouser leg?—slapped her on the shoulder as they dipped into an alley no wider than her arm span.

"What if they have sealed off the entire city?" Fear soaked her question. What if all they managed, by evading the armored pods, was to run into that lacy, bird-killing web somewhere down the road?

More laundry. Was that a donkey they avoided? Another pod barreled toward them. Kashkari jerked the carpet into a door Iolanthe opened for him. Strange odors assailed her nostrils—had they plowed into a gathering of hashish smokers? The faces that turned toward them, from low divans all around the walls, wore expressions of vague surprise rather than outright astonishment.

Then they were out another door into a walled garden. Kashkari kept the carpet as low as possible as they went over the walls—she could feel the jagged bits of glass embedded at the top of the wall scraping the bottom of the carpet. Thank goodness they were on a battle carpet and it was thick.

"Do you dare go back to Eton?" came Kashkari's question, between a sudden dip and another tight turn.

A pod dropped down from nowhere. Its claws hurtled toward Iolanthe with terrifying speed. She yelled as she sent the water of a nearby well toward the claws—as ice, freezing them so that they could not close around her person.

"Just get us out of here!"

More twisting, ribbon-narrow alleys, more humble houses flown right through. The streets became wider, straighter, illuminated by gas lamps; the houses to either side sprouted balconies and elegant latticework windows and wouldn't have looked out of place along a major boulevard in Paris.

Kashkari seem to know the neighborhood well: she could hear the bustle and crowd on the next street, but the one down which they charged was entirely empty of pedestrians, its residents either eating dinner genteelly inside or having gone to the busy thoroughfare for their evening entertainment.

"See that building? That's the opera house. Don't think the season has quite started yet, so it should be empty. Open all the windows and doors as you did before. Do you have anything that can look somewhat like us, to act as dummy doubles?"

She thought wildly. "I've a tent. It can take various shapes."

"Have it ready."

She fished the tent out of her satchel—the tent that had served as Titus's and her shelter during their days in the desert. They shot into a side door and came to a sudden halt that almost threw her off. Kashkari jumped down from the carpet and motioned her to do the same.

She shook the tent open and shaped it roughly to look like two slender, conjoined cylinders. They strapped the tent onto the carpet. Kashkari bewitched it to fly down a long corridor and toward the open door at the other end. "Come with me."

He led her down to the level beneath the stage, a warren of corridors. They turned and turned, seeming to go around in circles, before Kashkari pushed open a door into a dark and cramped storage room and called for mage light.

He swore. "I don't see it."

"Are we in the right place?"

"Yes. When I went to England at the beginning of Michaelmas

Half, it was here. It's always been here."

"What is it, exactly?"

"A double-door wardrobe. Huge. Curlicues and whatnots every-where. You can't miss it."

They came across shelves and racks and trunks, but no ward-robes, armoires, or freestanding cupboards, huge or otherwise.

She gripped him by the arm. "Do you hear that?"

They were no longer alone in the basement. They'd taken too long—the Atlanteans had discovered their ruse.

She tamped down her panic. "Wait! Did you say the theatrical season hasn't *quite* started yet? When *does* it start?"

He stared at her a second. "This way!"

They raced up to the auditorium level. The theatrical season was about to start, which meant there must have been rehearsals. Nei-ther of them had ever taken part in Eton's dramatic productions, but Sutherland had and sometimes talked about his experience. The later rehearsals were always conducted with the stage dressing in place, so that the actors would know where the props were and how to negotiate their way across the proscenium.

But there was nothing onstage except a bed, draped in rather gar-ish silks and velvets. They stared at each other, stricken.

Then, with a soft cry, Kashkari rushed toward the stage. He yanked off the red and gold counterpanes and heaved aside sev-eral layers of padding. Now it became clear that underneath the bedcovers had not been a bed frame, but an enormous armoire lying on its face.

Iolanthe lifted it with a levitation spell and set it back down on its feet. They scrambled inside and closed the doors.

"Out of the frying pan, at least," she said.

Kashkari exhaled. "Here's to going into the fire."

CHAPTER • 7

"SAY THAT AGAIN," TITUS DEMANDED.

"Lady Callista and Commander Rainstone are half sisters."

One was the regent's mistress, the power behind the throne, and the other the woman in charge of defending the realm from external threats. And yet Titus, the Master of the Domain, had known nothing of it.

"Who else knows?"

"I don't know, sire. I can tell you that I was never told, but overheard an argument between the two of them. Commander Rainstone was lambasting Lady Callista for having no grasp of the concept of loyalty. For not understanding why Commander Rainstone was so distraught that she had been dismissed from Her Highness's service. 'To you everyone's value is only in what they can do for you,' she said to Lady Callista. And then she added, 'I wish I'd never discovered that we were sisters.'"

Commander Rainstone had been let go by Princess Ariadne, Titus's late mother, after the latter caught Commander Rainstone snooping in her personal diary, in which she recorded all her prophetic visions. Neither Titus nor his mother had been able to make sense of this transgression on Commander Rainstone's part. But now Titus was beginning to see how Commander Rainstone could have been pushed into it, by a sister who desperately wanted to know if there were prophecies inside that diary concerning her daughter.

"I never mentioned to either of them what I'd overheard," Haywood went on. "But I'm fairly certain they stopped spending time together after that—the matter with Her Highness was probably the weight that snapped an already fraying bond."

Titus thought back. Had he ever seen Lady Callista and Commander Rainstone in the same place? Yes, he had, at the garden party at the Citadel that Amara had crashed. But the two women had been separated by the crowd, and Commander Rainstone was well known for her disinclination to attend social functions at the Citadel.

"But whether they'd reconciled in the years after I gave up my memory, I can't say. I never had any dealing with Lady Callista after that. And even with Commander Rainstone, we gradually grew apart, given my own troubles."

A silence fell. Titus studied the man who had suffered so much for his devotion to Lady Callista. He could fault Haywood for not having treasured Iolanthe as well as he should have in those latter years of his "troubles"—and a younger version of himself might very well have done so.

But how could he, when he had hurt her just as much? Perhaps more.

"She thinks the world of you, your ward," he told the older man.

Haywood smiled, the smile of a man trying to hold back greater emotions. "I don't quite deserve it, but I am beyond grateful that it is so."

"And I believe she much prefers having grown up with you than with Lady Cal—"

He carried his half of the pendant in his trouser pocket, wrapped in a handkerchief. Even through the fabric, the sensation of cold had been unmistakable. But all at once the temperature of the pendant changed enough for him to notice. He pulled it out of his pocket, unwrapping the handkerchief impatiently.

The metal half oval inside was barely cooler than the ambient temperature.

Her location had changed thousands of miles. What happened? Had Atlantis snared her at last? Was she en route to the Commander's Palace?

"Sire?" asked Haywood tentatively.

Titus leaped up. There was a map on the wall of the apartment, a nonmage map. Nonmage maps were by their very nature inaccurate, but he should still get an approximate idea of her location.

He pressed the pendant against the map and recited a long

cascade of spells. A dot appeared off the shore of Corsica. "What the hell."

"If I may, sire," said Haywood. "I haven't been very busy of late, so I've tried to convert this map into a mage map. Though I'm afraid my accuracy leaves much to be desired. *Revela omnia.*"

The lines on the map wriggled and writhed as continental mage realms squeezed themselves into place and land masses that had never been seen by nonmage eyes appeared in the oceans.

Now the dot fell in the middle of the English Channel.

What the hell.

Then he remembered what Kashkari had said: *In Cairo there is a one-way portal my brother rigged up that goes directly to Mrs. Dawlish's.*

The odor of quicklime assaulted Iolanthe's nostrils the moment she and Kashkari materialized in the dark, crowded broom cupboard. She attempted to vault, with Kashkari's hand on her elbow. They went nowhere—the no-vaulting zone was still in place.

Already footsteps pounded in their direction, swift and ominous. Iolanthe and Kashkari burst out of the broom cupboard, she calling for illumination, he shaking open a spare carpet.

The room was crammed with soaking tubs, cloth presses, and drying racks. She didn't bother to try the door or the flat window set high on the wall. The laundry room was a later addition to the house, stuck onto one end. She raised her hand, and a flash of lightning shot up and blew a hole in the ceiling.

They climbed onto the carpet and sped up into a drizzling and cold night. Mist closed in, the vapors vaguely orange in the light of the streetlamps.

Windows opened in nearby houses. A voice that sounded very much like Cooper's rang out. "What's going on? Did we get struck by lightning?"

Iolanthe closed her hand. All the flame illumination within a two-hundred-foot radius went out. The night turned pitch dark.

"Head west," she told Kashkari.

The carpet sliced through the night, out of the town in seconds—Eton was much longer than it was wide, and the residence houses were already near its western boundary. Iolanthe let the fire return to the lamps and sconces—it would not do to mess with gas-burning devices.

"How far west?" Kashkari asked.

The question stumped Iolanthe. She had vaulted many times to the abandoned brewery that housed the southern entrance into Titus's laboratory, but had never traveled there by conventional means. She, in fact, had no idea exactly how far it was or whether she could even recognize the place from outside in broad daylight.

Then she felt it, the half pendant on her person abruptly heating up. "Titus is here!"

She pressed the pendant into Kashkari's hand. "Keep going in the right direction and it will continue to get hotter."

The night turned bright as day—a squadron of armored chariots had arrived, shining their harsh, merciless light upon the country-side. From their metallic bellies dropped the desk-sized pods that had chased Kashkari and Iolanthe all over Cairo.

In Cairo they'd had the advantage of the urban landscape. Here it was open and flat, with no places to hide—and not even darkness to help them disappear.

Already, despite the tailwind she'd applied to the carpet, the pods were closing in. She willed the soil beneath a clump of trees to loosen, hoisted the trees with levitating charms, and sent them toward the pods.

The pods dodged her missiles.

She summoned the water of the Thames and erected a wall of ice. One chariot ran smack into the wall, but the others pulled up in time.

Instead of throwing up another ice wall, she ripped apart the existing one and threw boulder-sized shards at her pursuers. Two of the chariots were hit broadside and knocked off their trajectory. But the rest extended their mechanical arms and either caught the ice chunks or swatted them aside.

And there were so many of them, an entire swarm. Where was the brewery? If they didn't find it now, they might never be able to.

Even more pods fell from the sky, a particularly pernicious hail-storm. Their long mechanical arms reached for Iolanthe from all directions, and Kashkari was already flying them as low as possible without scraping the ground.

"Do something!" cried Kashkari.

But what else could she do? She looked about wildly and saw nothing but claws and metal underbellies.

"Vault!" Titus's voice rang out, clear as a church bell. "You are out of the no-vaulting zone now!"

Kashkari's hand already grasped her arm. She closed her eyes and thought of the inside of the brewery. The next instant she and Kashkari were crashing to the floor of the brewery, thrown against a pile of old barrels by the residual velocity of their carpet.

Before they'd come to a complete stop, they were already hauled to their feet. Titus—and Master Haywood!

"Come on. Hurry!"

The door to the laboratory was open, light spilling out of the familiar interior, with its long worktable and walls upon walls of shelves and cabinets. They raced inside. Titus entered last, slammed the door shut, and shouted, *"Extinguatur ostium!"*

Iolanthe clung to Titus, her entire person shaking, her breaths in fits and wheezes. He all but crushed her in his arms.

"Fortune shield me," he said, his voice hoarse. "For a moment I thought they had you."

Now she was hugging Master Haywood. He kissed her face and caressed her hair. "I thought there had to be some archival magic I could wield. But I drew a complete blank. I was scared witless."

"We're all right," she answered, gasping. "Don't worry. We're all right."

She also embraced Kashkari, who, like her, was still panting heavily. "That was some very fine flying, old bloke. You saved us."

"I thought we were done for. I thought that was how—"

He stopped speaking abruptly. An unease that was becoming all too familiar coiled around her heart, but he only raised his hand to his temple and gingerly felt around the cut that must have resulted from his having slammed into a cider cask head-on.

Titus had already dampened a cloth with some potion. He ordered Kashkari to sit down. "And are *you* all right?" he asked Iolanthe as he cleaned Kashkari's wound. "Any headache, nausea, or weakness?"

"I'm fine. Are you sure all connections between the brewery and the laboratory have been severed?"

"Yes." When he had affixed a bandage to Kashkari's temple, he extracted several vials from various drawers and handed them to Iolanthe. "Take these to be on the safe side. You were not supposed to vault within seven days of any trauma severe enough to require panacea."

She'd forgotten about that altogether. After she had poured the remedies down her throat, Master Haywood once more enfolded her in his arms, his heart thudding a staccato beat against her chest. "Fortune shield me. I think I'm still scared witless."

"I'm safe now. We are all safe now."

Inside the folded space the laboratory occupied, they could not be traced or found.

Eventually she let go of Master Haywood and presented Kashkari to him. All the men shook hands.

"What *happened*?" asked Titus. "How did Atlantis find you?"

Iolanthe dug up a charred Validus, handed it to Titus, and recounted the anomaly involving the diamond-inlaid crowns along the length of the blade wand.

Titus's expression turned grim. "Unless I am very much mistaken, Atlantis now has access to Validus's daughter wand."

"What's that?" everyone else said in unison.

"Most blade wands come in pairs, a mother wand and daughter wand. The daughter wand is not particularly remarkable—it does not amplify a mage's power any more than an ordinary wand—but it does inherit the mother wand's properties should the latter be destroyed.

"When Hesperia the Magnificent held Validus, she made modifications to its daughter wand, so that it could be used to track down the mother wand. Because of this, Validus's daughter wand is kept at a secret location, not to be used unless the one who wields Validus is deemed dead or captured."

"But you are neither," said Iolanthe.

"Try telling that to the regent." He frowned. "Come to think of it, I am not sure that Alectus knows this at all. Someone like Commander Rainstone is more likely to be in possession of such knowledge."

"Can you ask Dalbert to find out?" It was why he had left them in the first place, to retrieve what intelligence Dalbert might have gathered.

"You do that," Titus said. "I will go get some water for tea."

"Surely I may fetch water for you, sire," said Master Haywood.

"It is dark out. You would not be able to find the pump."

Even Iolanthe didn't know where the pump was—whenever she came to the laboratory, the kettle was always full. And then, at the confused look on Master Haywood's face, she explained, "The prince isn't going back to where we came from. The laboratory is also connected with a lighthouse at the northern tip of Scotland."

She tapped out a message on the typing ball Titus used to communicate with Dalbert. Then she inserted a sheet of paper underneath, to receive any messages the latter might have sent during their time in the desert. The keys clacked.

As she was rolling the paper back out, Titus returned. "There is a tremendous fog outside. I walked by the pump twice before I found it."

He put the water to heat, read the messages with her, and relayed what they learned to Kashkari and Master Haywood. "There was a meeting of the regent and his closest advisers the night Fairfax and I found ourselves in the desert—the night I summoned the war phoenix. There have been frequent meetings since, between the regent and his advisers and between the regent and the current Inquisitor. Apparently Lady Callista is still being held in the Inquisitory."

Master Haywood placed his hands together on the desk. Iolanthe recognized it as a sign of nerves on his part—after all this time, he still cared about Lady Callista. "If they threaten her safety, the regent is sure to give them what they want."

Was there a trace of pity in Titus's eyes as he glanced toward Master Haywood? "That is a romantic view. I am afraid the regent would have given them what they wanted even if Lady Callista were perfectly safe—by nature Alectus longs to bask in the reflection of power. He does not have it in him to deny any request Atlantis makes."

Kashkari frowned. "Is that everything your spymaster has to tell?"

"There is a little more. Nothing has yet been said to the public. And my subjects have no particular suspicions at the moment, since I do not typically make appearances in the capital. They still believe me to be in my mountain fastness, studying like a good little princeling."

Titus looked at Kashkari. "But you are right. I had expected a great deal more. Now I wonder if my spymaster is himself in custody."

"Then what are we to do now?" asked Kashkari.

The kettle sang. Titus made tea and handed out biscuits from a tin. "We arrange for everyone to have a place to sleep. The lighthouse has a pair of rooms for visiting commissioners and travelers stranded by bad weather. It looks like one of the rooms is already taken. Since Miss Seabourne should still refrain from vaulting, as much as possible, I recommend that we let her have the remaining room. The gentlemen can stay at the inn in Durness, twelve miles away."

The gentlemen murmured their assent.

They drank their tea. Kashkari and Titus discussed the armored pods, while Iolanthe asked Master Haywood about his life in Paris.

"I've grown to be quite fond of the bakery around the corner. Their mille-feuille reminds me of those we used to buy at Mrs. Hinderstone's shop. You remember Mrs. Hinderstone's shop?"

"Of course," she said. "It was one of my favorite places in Delamer."

"There is a sign in there that you adored, left behind from when the place was a bookshop."

"'Books on the Dark Arts may be found in the cellar, free of charge. And should you locate the cellar, kindly feed the phantom behemoth inside. Regards, E. Constantinos.'"

"Yes, that one. You always laughed at it. You always understood that it was a joke."

He smiled with the memory of the little girl she had been. Her chest tightened. "Did you like to go there because that's where you first met Lady Callista?"

"No, I went because I loved the way your face lit up whenever you crossed that threshold. There were other places that sold similar fare, but Mrs. Hinderstone's was the one for you. And you always liked to sit at the same table by the window, and watch everyone go by on University Avenue."

"Someday we'll go back there," she said impulsively. "Someday when all this is behind us, we'll ask His Highness for a special dispensation to give you your old professorship back. Then you can teach there again and maybe I will even take some of your classes, if I can manage to get myself admitted."

"Let's have a special dispensation for that too," said Master Haywood, getting into the spirit of things.

She laughed. "And we'll have our old house back too. And it'll be as if . . . as if . . ."

She realized how silly she must sound. How could they pretend as if nothing had changed when they both knew now that the arrangement that she had found so wonderful had been the source of so much pain and confusion to him?

Her guardian set his hand on her shoulder. "Yes, let's do, if at all possible. Those were some of the happiest days of my life. I would be thrilled to go back to the Conservatory, go back to the old house, except this time with you all grown up and attending my classes."

She took his hand in hers, overcome by both joy and sorrow. "Thank you. I would love that."

They didn't say anything else for a while. It dawned on her that the laboratory had fallen silent, that both Titus and Kashkari gazed upon them, the former with wistfulness, whereas the latter . . .

Kashkari looked upon her with grief.

He quickly turned to Titus. "It's been a long twenty-four hours and I'm worn out. Is it possible to go to the inn soon?"

"Of course. I will vault you there. Master Haywood, you are welcome to stay here for as long as you would like. I can come back for you later."

Master Haywood rose. "No, sire. You've already vaulted too much this day. I will go too."

He hugged Iolanthe again. "I'm so glad you are safe."

She kissed him on both cheeks. "Likewise. Until tomorrow."

With Master Haywood and Kashkari waiting outside, Titus kissed Iolanthe on her forehead. "I will bring back some supper for you," he promised.

"I already ate," she reminded him.

"I know," he murmured.

And kissed her again before he left.

The inn was simple, almost crude, but it was warm inside and the food decent—Titus could attest to the quality of the cooking, as he had bought the occasional soup and sandwich from the place.

It was getting late. The proprietor informed his new guests that they had better hurry if they wanted anything to eat. Haywood bowed to Titus and decamped to the taproom.

"Will you put some food in a basket for me? I am not hungry now, but I might feel peckish later," Titus said to the proprietor.

"That can be done," said the man in his thick Scottish accent.

"Will you want it in your room, sir, or will you wait for it?"

"I will wait for it."

"Anything for you, young man?" the proprietor asked Kashkari.

"No, thank you. I'm fine." Kashkari turned to Titus. "May I have a word with you?"

Something about the solemnity of Kashkari's tone made Titus's stomach drop. "Yes, of course."

They stepped outside the inn, which was enshrouded in fog. Kashkari set a sound circle. Titus stuck his hands into his pockets and willed himself not to shiver—what was barely enough clothes for Paris felt like sheets of paper in the near arctic cold of the very northwestern tip of Scotland.

Kashkari had changed into a set of Titus's spare nonmage garments from the laboratory. He ought to be freezing too, but he seemed not to feel the teeth of the air. "Before you left Luxor today, you asked me whether I had any prophetic dreams you should know about."

"And you said you would let me know if you did."

In the feeble light cast by a lantern hung over the door, Kashkari's features drifted in and out of the fog. "I had a dream this morning."

The vapors penetrated through all the layers of Titus's clothes to enclose him in their bitter embrace. "I thought so."

"It was not a happy dream, and I woke up hoping it would fade from memory—occasionally I have nightmares, just like everyone else. An ordinary dream disappears in time, but a prophetic dream only grows in clarity and detail." Kashkari scraped the bottom of his boot against the short turf underfoot. "This one did not fade."

So cold—and growing colder by the second. "You dreamed of someone's death, did you not?" Titus heard himself ask.

Kashkari was taken aback. "How did you guess?"

Instead of the fog, Titus saw the campus of the Conservatory of Magical Arts and Sciences. The students on University Avenue. The bell towers. The open expanse of the great lawn. He saw Fairfax sitting on a blanket under the starflower tree. The tree was in bloom, full of petals of the faintest pink. Whenever a breeze blew, tiny flowers would glide down onto her blanket, her shoulders, her hair.

He would never sit there with her. They would never share a picnic basket from Mrs. Hinderstone's. And he would never know what she would look like in ten, twenty, thirty years' time.

"That death has long been prophesied," he said. "And the person in question has known it for years."

Kashkari looked both incredulous—and relieved. "Are you sure?"

"I am."

"But—but I listened to Fairfax speak to her guardian just now, and it didn't sound as if she had the slightest idea."

For the longest time, Kashkari's words drifted between them, not making any sense at all. Then all at once Titus had his hands on Kashkari's lapels, almost lifting the latter off the ground. "What did you say? What do you mean, Fairfax did not have the slightest idea? What does she have to do with prophetic dreams about death and dying?"

Kashkari stared at him. "I thought you said she knew."

Titus stumbled back a step. Then another. "You saw Fairfax? *Fairfax?*"

Kashkari's voice cracked. "I'm afraid so. I'm sorry."

"Where? Where was she?" Titus was shouting, but only so he could hear himself over the uproar in his head.

"She was lying across a marble floor with inlays of the Atlantean whirlpool design."

"How do you know she was dead? She could just be unconscious."

"You were in my dream too. You were shaking your head, with tears in your eyes."

Titus could not breathe. In his mind he saw the Conservatory again. The students, the bell towers, the great lawn, the lovely starflower tree in bloom. But now the blanket under the tree was empty.

Kashkari was still speaking—or at least his lips were moving. But Titus heard nothing.

All he wanted was for her to come through unscathed—to have a wonderful life, surrounded by love and laughter. All he wanted was a single hope to light his way, when all ambition and courage had failed.

He held up a hand. Kashkari's lips stopped moving. He gazed at Titus, his eyes dark with sorrow.

But he was only losing a friend. Titus was losing everything.

The heavy door of the inn opened. The proprietor leaned out, a basket in his hand. "I be off to bed now. Anything else you need, gentlemen?"

Titus took the basket and shook his head. The proprietor disappeared back into the warm interior of his establishment, to his peaceful, orderly existence.

"Is there anything I can do?" asked Kashkari, his voice barely audible.

Besides cowering, what could anyone do when the boot heel of fate descended?

Titus vaulted away without another word.

He rematerialized on Cape Wrath and stood in the fog, shivering.

The tang of the sea burned his lungs with every breath. The unseen Atlantic crashed against the headlands, wave upon unceasing wave. Overhead the beacons of the lighthouse cut ghostly trails through the thick vapor, a stern warning to maritime vessels to keep away from the treacherous cliffs.

His entire life he had been headed to just such treacherous cliffs. But somehow he had managed to delude himself that *she* would avoid that fatal crash, would spread wings in time to save herself and soar above.

He had endowed her with all the immortality he wished he could possess. But she was only flesh and blood. She could all too easily stumble and fall, her eyes blank, her limbs lifeless.

And she would.

He wanted desperately to hold her in his arms, to feel the beat of her heart and the warmth of her skin. But he could not make his feet move, even though he was chilled to the bone, scarcely able to feel the fingers clutched around the handle of the basket.

Out here he was still in a daze, still numb with shock and disbelief. The moment he saw her he would fall to pieces.

A door opened in the rectangular base of the lighthouse, where the guestrooms were located. Light spilled out, limning a figure in the doorway, peering. It was her, checking for his return, becoming worried that he was taking too long.

He could not face her. He could not face the rage and the grief that were beginning to pulsate in his veins. He could not face a future in which he lived only for duty, not after he had at last known what it was like to hope with every breath and every thought.

He lifted his wand and pointed it at his head. It was the most cowardly of choices. But he would allow himself this: a few hours free of the knowledge of her impending death.

A few hours of him, her, and a future that included sunny days underneath a starflower tree in bloom, with friends about to drop by any moment.

CHAPTER · 8

IOLANTHE WAS DEBATING WHETHER TO clear the fog so she could see farther out when Titus emerged from the swirling vapors.

She ran to him. "What took you so long? Fortune shield me, your hands are frozen. Where have you been?"

His lips too were icy as they pressed against her cheek. "Sorry. I was just standing outside."

She pulled him in and shut the door tight—his teeth were chattering. "Why? What did Kashkari tell you?"

He leaned back against the door, his eyes half-closed. "He told me what he saw this morning in his prophetic dream."

Her heart stopped. "What did he say?"

Titus exhaled slowly, carefully. "I have suppressed that memory for now. It will come back by tomorrow, but at the moment I have no idea what he said."

The only other memory he had ever suppressed concerned the

details of the prophecy about his death. She felt light-headed, as if she stood on the edge of a chasm, and its bottomless depths were drawing her forward.

Her fingers tightened around his—so cold, his hand. She ignored the fearful clamor in her head and tugged him down the corridor toward the bath. "There is a hip bath inside. I already filled it with hot water. Get in and get warm."

"You probably filled it for yourself. I do not want to take away your soak."

She indicated the pajamas she wore—ever since they'd started preparing to leave school at the drop of a hat, the laboratory had become much better equipped with such supplies as food, linens, and spare clothes. "I had my wash—you go thaw yourself out."

The inside of the bath steamed, an echo of the conditions outside, except it was warm and smelled of the handful of dried silver moss she had found in the laboratory and tossed into the water.

"I am sorry," he said, as they stood on either side of the doorway. "I am sorry I bring terrible news without being brave enough to tell you what it is."

The ravage of the desert was still on him. His eyes were hollow, his cheeks equally so. Her heart broke. "Let's not think about it."

"How? How do you not think of an impending disaster?"

How indeed. She set her hand on his lapel, the wool still damp from the fog. "Do you remember the reason I brought down my first bolt of lightning, in Little Grind-on-Woe?"

"You said you were trying to correct a batch of light elixir that had been ruined."

"I'd volunteered to make the light elixir for a wedding—not out of the goodness of my heart, mind you. The villagers were complaining about Master Haywood, because he wasn't a very good schoolmaster to their children. And I was hoping that by doing everything I could for Rosie Oakbluff's wedding, her mother, who had the power of dismissal over Master Haywood, would let him remain in place until after the qualifying exams for upper academies.

"Except I hadn't been properly schooled since we got to Little Grind. With luck I might pass the qualifying exams, but the chance for me to do well enough to be awarded a grant was almost nil. Our finances were quite depleted at that point; without a sizable grant, an upper academy education would have been beyond our means."

And no university would look at a candidate who hadn't been through the rigorous preparatory program of a good upper academy.

"But every day, after I finished teaching Master Haywood's students, after I corrected their homework, scored their tests, and prepared for the next day's practical, I sat down at my desk and stared at an old calendar full of pictures of the Conservatory. And then I studied during whatever hours remained of the day.

"I plied Mrs. Oakbluff with favors and even went so far as to call down a thunderbolt to revive the silver light elixir for her daughter's wedding, all for something that was essentially hopeless from the very beginning." She smiled. "Sound familiar?"

He gazed at her, his eyes solemn and beautiful. "Somewhat."

"It's the same here. The prophecies will most likely come to pass, but I won't concede anything until then. I won't despair now because a shadow might fall tomorrow." She touched his hair, also damp from the fog. "Or perhaps I've already despaired—and decided that while despair is fine as an occasional indulgence, it can't be served three times a day."

He took her hand and pressed her fingertips to his lips. "Is it as simple as that?"

"What? A big helping of stubbornness plus a gentle sprinkling of lunacy? Of course. If you need more of either, I'm sure we can find some in the laboratory." She kissed him on his cheek. "Now get in that tub before the water freezes."

She carried the basket of foodstuffs back to the laboratory. It contained a flask of soup, sandwiches, and a pudding. Solid English fare—and except the flask of soup, all stone cold. She reheated everything as best as she could, watching her flames carefully to make sure they didn't scorch the pudding or lick the sandwiches.

The next second she was sobbing, prostrate over the worktable, grief inundating her like a storm-driven surge, each wave more pitiless than the one before.

How deranged she had been, to believe that she could make the difference. That she would single-handedly save him from certain doom. And every time they cheated death, every time they emerged unscathed from an impossible situation, her belief had grown stronger. Why should she have been given control of the divine spark, if it weren't to defy all such ill-written fate?

What had Princess Ariadne foreseen? What terrible detail had Kashkari's dream added to that inevitable future? Did they see her kneeling by his lifeless body, screaming with rage and futility? Did they mention that she would destroy everything in her path afterward, leaving nothing but fire and ruin?

A hand settled on her shoulder. "I have stubbornness and lunacy side by side on this shelf here. Which one was it that you could not find?"

At the sound of his voice, her sobbing only became more uncontrollable. "Do you have a jar of delusion too? I depleted all of mine."

He lifted her from the worktable. "No, I am all out of extra delusion. But I do have a bit of sense left, if you want it."

"What's that?"

He wiped her tearstained face with a soft handkerchief. "You should not despair now because a shadow might fall tomorrow."

More tears trickled down her face. "Fortune shield me. Where have I heard that old chestnut before?"

"A barmy mage told me before I went into my bath. Perhaps you have met her: beautiful girl, but scary—will electrocute you if you are not careful."

Despite herself, she felt her lips curve in the beginning of a smile. "And what do you do to make sure she doesn't electrocute you?"

"I distract her with bushels of rose petals. She loves that sort of sentimental rubbish."

She snorted. Rose petals had been something of a running joke between them from the beginning of Michaelmas Half, except she had been the one ridiculing *him* for using them as a shorthand for romance.

"You want to see some of the other distractions I had prepared, so she would not smite me?"

"Let me guess: the moon and the stars?"

"Close enough." He walked to a locked cabinet, opened it, and extracted a sphere the size of the snow globe Cooper kept in his room at Mrs. Dawlish's. Dimming the light in the room, he said, *"Astra castra."*

The sphere burst open. Countless tiny stars emerged and floated in the air, like an overabundance of pixie dust. Gradually, the tiny stars organized themselves into the familiar shape and brilliance of the Milky Way.

She held her breath: the miniature galaxy was mesmerizingly beautiful.

But all too soon, the stars vanished.

He gave her fireworks next, diminutive yet intricate blazes. After that, a small, glowing seed that turned into a sprout, a sapling, and then a large, wonderful tree, the rustle of its tender green leaves like music, the swaying of its boughs releasing a gentle rain of tiny silver petals.

"I always imagine you sitting under such a tree on a warm day, on the great lawn of the Conservatory, with a carton of pinemelon ice from Mrs. Hinderstone's by your side."

She shook her head. "There are no trees on the great lawn."

"Now you tell me. Well then, I had better order one planted, so it will be there for you when you are a student at the Conservatory."

"Will it look like this tree?" She tilted her face up for one last glimpse of the green canopy, which was already disappearing.

"Yes, of course."

She glanced back at him. Until this moment, she hadn't noticed the pajamas he wore. She had seen him half-dressed a few times, but she had never seen him casually dressed. No matter how early she arrived in his room for their morning training sessions in the Crucible, he was always already in his school uniform.

He returned the light in the laboratory to its normal brightness, and she saw that the pajamas were soft-looking dark-blue flannel, with the top button of the shirt undone. Her heart thudded: she couldn't look away from the skin that one open button exposed.

And she didn't want to. "Kiss me."

He took a pretty glass jar from the cabinet. The jar was filled with sweets. He opened the jar and held it out toward her. "Try one."

She put a green-striped bonbon in her mouth. And when he kissed her, the bonbon melted with a burst of freshness: mint, basil, and a hint of silver moss. But it was he who made her pulse race: his hands in her hair, the sinew of his arms beneath her fingertips, the scent of Pears soap that still clung to his hair and skin.

"What do you think?" he asked softly, his eyes dark.

Her fingers toyed with the second button on his pajama shirt. "Did you make all these yourself?"

"I stole everything from Lady Callista last summer. Want another one?"

She placed an iridescent, almost glass-like lozenge on her tongue. It was marble-cool and tasted like it too. She snapped that second button on his pajama shirt open and pressed the pad of her finger against his skin.

He sucked in a breath—and kissed her so thoroughly that her head spun and the sound of distant wind chimes echoed in her ears.

"Open your eyes," he murmured.

She did so reluctantly and saw that they were standing under a rainbow. And the soft tintinnabulation of wind chimes still vibrated the air, growing fainter as the rainbow faded.

They were pressed together from shoulders to knees. He touched his lips to her ear, sending a current of electricity through her. "Still think rose petals are a terrible idea?"

She encircled his wrist with her fingers—his pulse was as erratic as her own. "You, Your Highness, are made of clichés."

"Hmm. I take it you do *not* want me to make it rain hearts and bunnies?"

"Of course I want to see something that ludicrous!"

He dug deeper into the cabinet and extracted yet another sphere.

"*Delectatio amoris similis primo diei verno.*"

Love's delight is as the first day of spring.

The sphere split open. No hearts or bunnies emerged, but hundreds of sparkling butterflies did, flitting around in the laboratory, landing on beakers and drawer pulls before evanescing, leaving behind a pastel shimmer in the air and a barely perceptible fragrance, like that of meadow flowers drenched in bright sunshine.

She half laughed, caught between the absurdly sentimental nature of the tableau and its innate and unabashed sincerity. She laughed again, only to find her eyes stinging once more with tears.

She cupped his face in her hands. "You didn't make it rain hearts and bunnies."

"Next time," he murmured. "May I stay here tonight—with you?"

Her heart rolled over. "I thought you'd never ask."

"By the way, Your Highness, you lied," she said, much later, her head on his shoulder.

He laced their fingers together. "Hmm, shocking. What did I lie about this time?"

"About there being occupants in one of the rooms of the lighthouse. There's no one here except us."

"A most desirable outcome." He lifted her hand and kissed the back of it. "You are sure that there are no trees on the great lawn of the Conservatory?"

"None when I lived there."

"I will need to pretend some had been planted in the years since you left."

She turned toward him and trailed her fingers along his arm. "Have you ever visited the Conservatory?"

"No, I have only seen it in pictures. On the whole I spent very little time in Delamer. Most of my childhood was in the mountains."

"What was it like, living in the mountains?"

"It was home. For the longest time I did not realize that not everyone lived in a castle—and that not every castle sat on a mountain range that moved. Did you ever get a glimpse of the upper terrace of the castle?"

The first time she had visited the castle, she had been in the form of a canary. Usually mages retained no memory of the time they spent in beast form, under a transmogrification spell. But she did on that particular occasion, because then they had been linked by a blood oath.

"Yes, I saw it while you were walking down a corridor with open arches that led onto the terrace. It had a beautiful garden."

"It is several hundred feet above the courtyard level of the castle. My mother and I used to stand at the balustrade and pretend that the garden was in the sky, drifting along, because we could see the mountains move. She loved that garden, and I often found her sitting under a vine-covered pergola. That vine gave small clusters of golden flowers, and we used to make circlets of them to wear as crowns."

In the teaching cantos of the Crucible, each ruling prince or princess since Titus III had a classroom of his or her own. The inside of Titus VII's was a garden, with vines knotted into intricate arabesque patterns on the walls, and spreading into a lovely canopy overhead.

"Your classroom in the Crucible, you made it look like your mother's favorite spot on the terrace."

"I did. We had some wonderful hours there." He combed his fingers through her hair. "Did you have a garden of your own?"

"The Conservatory provided housing for faculty members. They were small town houses built in a row. In the front there's barely enough room for a patch of grass and two rosebushes. In the back the view is nice, but the land drops off too steeply for gardening.

"But behind the faculty library, there is a garden open only to professors and their families. And in this garden, there is a fountain. When Master Haywood needed to do some work at the library, I would read in a corner of the garden. And sometimes I would play with the water of the fountain and make it look to those inside the library as if it had started to rain."

"I always knew you were rotten."

"Oh, to the core."

They were silent for a minute. The he turned her toward him and kissed her gently. "I wish this night would last forever."

"'A moment of grace echoes in Eternity,'" she quoted the Angelic Canon.

He cupped her face. "You have been all my moments of grace."

Her heart clenched. "Why are you speaking as if this is already our last hour together?"

"Because our last hour together I might be in no condition to tell you that you are the best thing that has ever happened to me."

She didn't want reality to intrude, but reality was always just outside the window, banging. "All right then. Here's what I have been saving for the bitter end: I have no regrets, none whatsoever."

He gazed at her. "Really?"

"Well, except the raining hearts and bunnies part. I'd have liked to see that."

He thought for a moment, then got up, a sheet wrapped around himself, and left the room. When he came back, he had two more snow-globe-sized spheres. And when he had set *them* off, it rained hearts and bunnies.

She laughed until she could scarcely breathe. Until tears once again threatened to fall. She pulled him back into her arms and held him tight. "Now I truly have no regrets. Not a single one."

◆ ◆

Memory returned as it always did, an assault to the mind.

Titus did not scream. He did not smash the furniture. He did not crumple to the floor, sobbing.

He lay perfectly still, listened to the soft breaths of her peaceful slumber, and wept in complete silence.

I love you. I will love you until the end of the world.

CHAPTER ✦ 9

TITUS KNOCKED ON THE DOOR with a seam of light at its bottom edge.

Soft, quick footsteps moved across the floorboards. The door opened. Kashkari did not appear at all surprised to see Titus, though his jaw tightened—it was not every day that the Master of the Domain arrived before his friend with red-rimmed eyes. He stood aside to let Titus pass, then closed the door and set a sound circle.

The room's furnishings were rudimentary. Kashkari offered Titus the only chair and sat down on the edge of the bed.

"Were you able to get some rest?" asked Titus.

His voice sounded strange to his own ears, as if his vocal cords had been badly scratched.

Kashkari shook his head. He looked worn—an insomniac's body craved the rest to which his mind could not succumb. "I tried to sleep, but I couldn't. So I've been writing letters."

There was a finished letter on the table, already in its envelope. "To be sent by Her Majesty's post?"

"The British post is very reliable."

The reach and efficacy of a realm's postal service was usually the rough equivalent of the reach and efficacy of its power.

Kashkari rose and added some more coal to the grate. "And you? I don't suppose you spoke to Fairfax—or she would be here to see me herself."

Instead she was sound asleep, still blissfully ignorant. "No," Titus admitted. "I could not tell her. I am as much of a coward as you are."

Kashkari gave a soft, bitter laugh. "I hate this ability. Hate it."

Titus closed his hand around the collar of his coat—he was cold again despite the warmth of the small room. "My mother was a seer and she hated it too."

Kashkari had picked up the poker to jab into the grate. At Titus's words he stilled—then slowly turned around. "When we spoke earlier, you mentioned a death that has long been prophesied. By your mother?"

"Yes."

Kashkari's eyes were wide with dismay. "Fortune shield me. Whose death? *Yours?*"

Titus nodded wearily, beyond caring.

Kashkari gripped the edge of the mantel. "I'm so sorry. I'm so very, very sorry."

Titus sighed. "My mother could not tell me face-to-face either—left it to her diary to decide when it should be revealed."

"Was that why you told me that the person I dreamed about already knew of the prophesied death?"

"Both Fairfax and I suspected that you had dreamed about me, confirming my mother's vision. Never in a million years would I have guessed that—" Titus still could not bring himself to speak those words aloud. "Upon my death, Alectus assumes the reins of power and that will be an unfavorable development, but it only worsens the current situation by degrees. Whereas . . . the rippling effect of what will happen to Fairfax was what you were trying to warn me about, was it not, when I walked out on you a few hours ago?"

Were she to fall into the Bane's hands, the consequences would be unthinkable.

Kashkari lifted the poker again and redistributed the coal in the fireplace. "It's the dominant view among western mage realms that one must never tamper with what has already been seen. But as I told Fairfax a while ago, we of the eastern heritage do not have such a draconian stance on the flow of time. For us, what I dreamed yesterday morning would be considered a shot across the bow, a warning from above."

"Against what?"

"Against that very eventuality. Fairfax should not step onto Atlantis."

Titus set his elbow on the desk and dropped his forehead into his hand. "You think we stand a chance without her?"

That prophecy of his mother's, that of two young men approaching the Commander's Palace—had she meant Titus and *Kashkari*? Fortune shield him, he had come across that vision right after Kashkari had revealed himself as not only a mage, but a mage bent on the downfall of the Bane. And when he had opened her diary that day, he had wanted specifically to know whether she had seen anything about Kashkari.

"We don't have Fairfax's powers, obviously. But we also don't carry the same liability. If we fail, we are just two more dead mages."

In Titus's mother's vision, those two young men, whoever they were, had reached the outermost ring of the Commander's Palace. They were still as far from the Bane's crypt as a snail in Iceland was from the summit of Mount Everest—but they were closer than anyone had been in at least a generation.

"Perhaps your mother's vision was a warning too," said Kashkari.

"What? I should not go to Atlantis either?"

Was it wrong how much he wished Kashkari were correct?

"Maybe not now. Maybe at a different time."

"You forget that I cannot simply lie low—not without ceding the throne to the regent."

"But you yourself said that the harm of such a course of action is incremental."

Titus sighed. "Compared to the catastrophe of Fairfax falling into the Bane's hands, I suppose the harm of everything else is incremental."

"Then think about it."

Titus pressed two fingers against the space between his brows, his head throbbing. "My mother saw two young mages getting as far as the outermost ring of the Commander's Palace. Are we giving that up too?"

It was Kashkari's turn to rest his forehead against the edge of the mantel. "Damned if we do and damned if we don't."

Titus rose to his feet, drained. *"Debattuimur omni modo."*

"You can say that again."

He took a vial from his pocket. "I brought some sleep remedies. Two pilules are calibrated to give me four hours of uninterrupted sleep. The effect might vary for you."

"Will they affect my dreams?"

"They should not."

"Then I will gladly accept them. Thank you."

Twenty minutes later Titus was back in the lighthouse, after covering the distance on his flying carpet. Fairfax was still sleeping. He swallowed a dose of sleep remedy, lay down, and wrapped his arm around her.

She sighed softly in her sleep.

He laid his head in the crook of her shoulder. While Kashkari talked, it had been easy to accept that prophetic dreams might be no more than warnings. But in the silent darkness, a lifetime of ardent belief in the supremacy of prophecies reasserted itself.

True seers were never wrong in what they saw. Sometimes, as his mother had, they misinterpreted the significance of their visions. But he had yet to come across an instance where his mother erred in her recording of events. Nor did he have any reason to suppose that Kashkari was any more prone to such mistakes.

To have an unambiguous outcome already specified, and then to try to prevent just that outcome . . . His mind overflowed with all kinds of spectacular ways for everything to go wrong—and for Fairfax to end up dead anyway.

He was grateful when the sleep remedy finally manifested its powers and pulled him under.

A summer day. A clear blue sky dotted by clouds as white and fluffy as spring lambs. Crowds as far as the eyes could see, men in gleaming top hats, women in straw boaters with fluttering pastel ribbons. On the riverbank, boys were ready to launch their boats, boys wearing black-and-white-striped jackets and hats trimmed like a flower seller's baskets.

The Fourth of June.

"Fortune shield me," Titus groaned. "Not this circus again."

"Oh, come," Fairfax countered cheerfully, poking him in the arm. "Deep down you love it passionately. And you can't wait to come back each year."

"That is not true. Deep down I tolerate it passionately and give thanks that it comes around only once a year."

"In either case, you always enjoy yourself. So spare me the— Wait, here comes Cooper. In which case, carry on with your melodramatic moaning, but put some majesty into it. You know he lives to hear you judge everything as unworthy."

Indeed, there was Cooper, with the same round eyes and eager face, except he had acquired a considerable paunch. His trousers, which had not been tailored to accommodate for this extra girth, now hung an inch too short.

Titus opened his eyes abruptly and stared, disoriented, at the bare, unfamiliar ceiling. The entire room was bare, almost drab: white-painted walls, a desk, a washstand, and a bed with a nightstand.

It was only as his eyes settled on the other occupant of the bed that all the events of the previous night came rushing back.

"Good morning," said Fairfax, smiling a little. It was only a quarter after five, but she was already dressed. She sat against a pair of pillows, a book open on her knees. "How are you feeling, Your Highness, after the most utterly wonderful night of your life?"

For the first time in his life, he wished he had Kashkari's gift. So that his dream would come true, a dream in which their lives did not end on Atlantis, but extended far enough into the future for Cooper, who was currently as lean as Titus, to have nurtured a sizable belly with good food and comfortable living.

He sat up, his heart as heavy as the foundation of the lighthouse. "There is something I must tell you."

She flipped a page of the book on her knees—belatedly he

recognized it as his mother's diary, blank as usual. "I thought so. Let's hear it."

He raked his fingers through his hair. "Will you give me a moment?"

He was not accustomed to facing the day, let alone this kind of a day, in only a set of flannel pajamas. He kissed her on the cheek, left the room, and returned fully dressed, necktie, shirt studs, and cuff links perfectly in place.

"That bad, eh?" she said, after one look at him.

The bed had been made during his absence. She now sat on top of the counterpane, his mother's empty diary still open before her. He tried to gather himself. But how did he find the right words for something like this, even if he had a hundred years and piles of dictionaries as big as the pyramids?

She waited—and kept turning the blank diary, page after page.

"About Kashkari's dream . . . remember that he does not take it as the future written in stone."

She gazed at him—and turned another page.

But this time, there was writing on the page, his mother's familiar, neat hand. "The diary!"

She looked down, surprised.

"Let us read that first." *Please.*

She nodded. He sat down next to her, put his arm around her shoulders, and kissed her on her temple.

31 August, YD 1013

A most fantastical day.

*I slipped out of a command performance of Titus III, evaded my
ladies-in-waiting, and hurried to the Emporium of Fine Learning and
Curiosities, Constantinos's shop. As I walked into the shop, the vision
repeated itself an unprecedented seventh time.*

*This time, I saw clearly the distinctive ring on the hand wielding the
stylus.*

*When the vision had faded, I lifted my own hand in shock. On my right
index finger is an identical ring that had been wrought for Hesperia the
Magnificent. There is not another like it in all the mage realms.*

The woman is me.

I laughed. Well, then.

"We have read this before, haven't we?" she asked.

He too recognized the diary entry, a pivotal one that they had
read together the night of his Inquisition six months ago. He did not
know why, but the hair on the back of his neck stood up.

*Once I had a vision of myself telling my father that a particular
Atlantean girl was going to be the most powerful person in the Domain.
Then, when I saw the girl in truth, I told him what I had seen myself
tell him—since one cannot deliberately change what has been seen to*

♦ 140

happen. He was terribly displeased to be faced with the possibility that
he, a direct descendant of Titus the Great, would one day no longer be
the absolute master of this realm.

But this time I would offend no one.

I found the book, dragged it to the table, lifted the stylus from its
holder, and vandalized the book as I had done in the vision.

In the margins of the book, his mother had written, *There is no*
elixir, however tainted, that cannot be revived by a thunderbolt. Nearly seventeen years later, those very lines would spur Fairfax to bring down
her first bolt of lightning.

The one that changed everything.

Only when I was finished did I remember the desk calendar. In the
vision it is always 25 August. But today is 31 August. I looked at the
calendar on the desk. 25 August! The device had stopped working a week
ago.

I am not often cheered by how right I am: the ability to see glimpses of
the future is frustrating and hair-raising. But at that moment, I was ever
so thrilled.

On impulse, I opened the book again, turned to the section for
clarifying draughts, and tore out the last three pages. The recipes given
on those pages are riddled with errors. I was not going to let some other
poor pupil suffer from them.

The end of the page. And the end of the record of this particular vision, too, the previous time. But this time, when they turned the page, the writing continued.

"Abominable book, isn't it?" said someone.

I jumped. It was a young man of about my own age, very handsome, with kind, smiling eyes.

"I am—I am going to buy this book," I mumbled, thoroughly mortified. Why had I not seen this coming?

"That will be a much greater crime," he said. "I cannot possibly permit you."

I could not help but smile. "Did they teach you from this book?"

"We had to bow before it too, as if it were the Epiphanies."

My eyes must have bulged. He laughed. "I was kidding. It didn't become quite that absurd, but the book is atrociously overrated and only good for a stepping stool."

"But still, I damaged it. And I should pay for it."

"Buy a few good books then, to compensate the bookseller."

Struck by divine inspiration, I asked, "Do you have any recommendations for good books?"

He did. We spent a happy half hour browsing through the aisles. All too soon my pocket watch began to throb, reminding me that it was time I returned to the theater. He helped me carry my books to the counter. Only then did I realize that of course I did not carry any coins on me.

Such things were beneath the heir to the throne.

"Don't worry," he said. "I will buy the books for you, if you will buy a cup of tea and a slice of apple cake for me tomorrow at the Wand and the Willow."

Tomorrow I have to sit all day with Father and his advisers. We decided on the day after tomorrow at three o'clock in the afternoon—and changed the locale from a busy public establishment to a scenic but rather empty stretch of the coast south of Delamer.

I cannot believe what I have agreed to, and I cannot wait for the hours to pass.

2 September, YD 1013

I was almost half an hour late to the rendezvous. But he waited for me. He even brought apple cake from the Wand and the Willow.

I had a lovely, lovely time.

4 September, YD 1013

He asked me whether Father would approve of my meeting with someone like him.

Father, of course, would be apoplectic. But I am already in love.

"It is all right," I told him. "We will find a way."

9 December, YD 1013

We are so happy I am afraid to write of it.

10 December, YD 1013

I should have listened to my own advice. Why did I ever mention our happiness?

17 December, YD 1013

It has been a week. I could neither bring myself to record the vision nor say anything to him about it. I love him so fiercely. I dread the future almost as much.

29 January, YD 1014

The vision has come true. I am numb with shock and misery. I had not expected it to happen so soon.

22 February, YD 1014

I am with child. Overwhelmed with joy, frozen with fear, I do not know what to do.

Titus shook. Whatever it was that he had expected the diary to reveal, it was not this.

"Your father," said Fairfax softly.

"My father," he echoed, his chest tight.

A loud pounding came at the front door of the lighthouse. They both leaped up. It was still dark outside, so it could not be the lighthouse keeper trying to get in, to shut down his machine and record the oil level in the fuel tank.

"It's Kashkari. Open the door."

"Let me check," he told her.

He vaulted to a higher level of the lighthouse and looked out the window. It was indeed Kashkari, and he was not alone. With him were Horatio Haywood and—

Titus had to squint to make sure he was not seeing things. But standing next to Kashkari, wrapped in a thick coat, was none other than the woman of Kashkari's dreams.

Amara.

CHAPTER · 10

"DURGA DEVI, THIS IS UNEXPECTED," Titus said coolly.

Almost coldly.

He could feel Fairfax's exasperated glance. So Amara had once entertained the possibility of killing Fairfax rather than letting her be captured by the Bane—was he always going to carry a grudge?

Yes, he was. He would not forgive Amara for having had the thought, and he would always suspect her of wanting to get rid of the one he loved.

"It is unexpected for me too, Your Highness," answered Amara.

"Do please come in, everyone," said Fairfax.

And glared at Titus to move out of the way, which he did reluctantly.

They would be too crowded in the laboratory, so she ushered the visitors into the parlor of the lighthouse. Titus remained behind to execute a strong keep-away spell for the door; he did not want to be inconvenienced by the lighthouse keeper arriving for his morning duties.

When he walked into the parlor, Fairfax had already summoned a roaring fire in the grate, put the kettle to boil, and set out a plate of biscuits. Upon his entrance, Haywood rose and bowed. Titus gestured for him to be seated, reddening slightly as he did so. Were it not for Amara's unexpected arrival, he would have gone back to the inn at some point, to keep up the appearance that he had slept there. But now Haywood must have realized that Titus had instead spent the night here.

And nobody asked whether they ought to worry about those fictional other travelers staying at the lighthouse.

Fairfax sat down next to her guardian and took his hand in hers. "Allow us to congratulate you on your marriage, Durga Devi."

Titus's surprise must have shown. Fairfax turned to him and added, "I'm sorry we forgot to tell you, Your Highness, what with everything else going on."

"Felicitations," he said curtly.

"Thank you," said Amara. "We thought there would be plenty of time for weddings and celebrations after we put away the Bane. But then we realized there is no point waiting."

Fairfax passed around the plate of biscuits. "I assume it probably wasn't your choice to spend your honeymoon here with us. And how did you get here so fast?"

"Mohandas probably told you that one of our satellite bases

has a dry dock that can launch a boat into the Mediterranean. I was taken to the coast of Andalusia and flew the rest of the way."

Flying carpets, for all their marvelous uses, could not travel for long distances over water. From Spain to Britain, the only major body of water she had to cross would have been the English Channel, which was narrow enough between Calais and Dover for a well-made carpet to make it across before it started to lose altitude.

"And as for why I am not enjoying my husband's company . . ." Amara took a deep breath. "My parents left the Kalahari Realm many years ago, before I could remember. Last night armored chariots paid a visit to the settlement where they once lived."

Titus clenched his hand—no good ever came of armored chariots paying anyone a visit.

"The population of the settlement is about twenty thousand. I am told that at least half of the inhabitants are confirmed dead. Twenty-five percent of the rest are not expected to last more than a few days. And of those who will survive, many will suffer: blindness, lesions on internal organs, the accumulation of fluid in the lungs so that they exist in a constant state of near drowning."

The only sound in the room was that of the fire in the grate, leaping and crackling. And then the water, beginning to agitate inside the kettle.

"You believe the attack was a direct retaliation against you, personally, for the assistance you gave us?" asked Titus.

Amara shook her head. "If only that was it. The settlement's elders received a message afterward that said, 'This will be Delamer in seven days, unless...'"

"Unless what?" asked Fairfax, her voice no more than a whisper.

"That was all it said, 'unless...'"

Unless she was handed over to the Bane.

The kettle hissed. The room seemed to grow darker, a shadow as enormous as the world itself creeping upon them.

"Do you believe the threat credible?" Titus heard himself speak to Amara, his tone entirely flat.

"Atlantis has never made idle ultimatums. And the fact that they specified a week lends credence to the threat—even Atlantis needs a few days to stockpile the quantity of death rain necessary to cover all of Delamer."

"What . . . what should we do?" came Haywood's hesitant question.

Titus could not think. He was responsible for the welfare of his subjects—he could not possibly allow them to die by the hundreds of thousands. On the other hand, he would never voluntarily give up Fairfax, never allow her to be taken by the Bane.

Fortune shield him. Was *that* what Kashkari had seen in his prophetic dream?

As if the thought had occurred to him at the exact moment, Kashkari said, "Could that be what my dream was all about?"

They looked at each other, aghast.

Fairfax rose and removed the kettle from the fire. The room was once again dead quiet, so much so that he could hear every wave breaking against the cliffs.

And then she asked the question he had been dreading. "What exactly did you dream of, Kashkari?"

Kashkari could not seem to meet Iolanthe's eyes; instead he turned toward Titus. Her spine tingled with alarm.

His face ashen, Titus stood in place, a stone statue of a boy.

"Answer me," she demanded.

Another endless moment passed. Titus gripped the top of a chair and at last looked back at her. "He dreamed of your death."

"No!" someone shouted. "No!"

But it wasn't her. It was Master Haywood, on his feet, pale and shaking.

She glanced down at the kettle in her hand. There seemed no point in doing anything except pouring out the boiling water. So she did, into the teapot—and only then remembered that she hadn't put any tea leaves inside.

She set the kettle back on its hook, which had been swung out of the grate, put down the towel she had used to shield her hand from the heat of the kettle's handle, and reached for the tin of tea leaves.

"Did you not hear what His Highness said?" came Master Haywood's anxious, high-pitched question.

"I heard him."

But she comprehended nothing—yet.

She counted out five spoonfuls of tea leaves, one for each person, replaced the lid on the tin, and then put the teapot's lid back on. "I always forget to warm the pot first," she said. "His Highness makes a much better cup of tea."

"Iola," said Master Haywood.

She went to him, eased him back down onto the long, padded chaise, and took a seat next to him. "It isn't the end of the world—not yet."

And wouldn't be until her shock wore off. "What exactly did you see, Kashkari? I want to hear everything."

Kashkari closed his eyes for a moment. "I was riding a wyvern and peering intently ahead. It was dark except for a glimmer of starlight, just enough to give the idea that I was flying above an angular and desolate landscape. And then I saw a pool of light ahead, growing brighter and nearer with every stroke of the wyvern's wings.

"At that point my dream, as dreams sometimes do, cut away to a different locale. I was in the air again, on a huge terrace or platform that floated forward, and I was looking down on a floodlit valley surrounded by a jagged rim. There were rings of defenses and dozens of wyverns in the sky."

"The Commander's Palace," Iolanthe murmured.

She remembered now that Kashkari had asked her about the Commander's Palace. He had been trying to understand every detail of his dream, to give it its proper context.

"Yes, I believe so," said Kashkari. "At this point my dream jumped forward in time again and I was running across a rubble-strewn floor. But even with the damage I could see the pattern underfoot, a huge mosaic of the Atlantean maelstrom.

"And—and there was your body, next to a column. His Highness was already there, kneeling by your side, your wrist in his hand. At my approach, he looked up and shook his head."

Iolanthe listened carefully—or at least it felt as if she were listening carefully. She could see what Kashkari described, in more detail than she wanted. But still none of it felt real. "You saw my face?"

Kashkari nodded.

"You are sure?"

He nodded again.

"And I looked the same as I do now?"

"Exactly the same. Except . . ."

Her heart pounded. "Except what?"

"Except your sleeve was torn. And on your left upper arm you wore a gold filigreed armband set with rubies."

"But I don't wear any jewelry. And I don't have any." She turned to Titus. "Do you have such a piece in your possession?"

She knew Master Haywood didn't.

Titus shook his head.

"Then it couldn't possibly be me. I wouldn't accept jewelry given to me by anyone except my guardian or the prince."

As soon as the words left her lips, she realized how naive—even asinine—she sounded. This was exactly how every single dunce tried to reason his way out of his fate, by holding on to some detail that could be vigorously denied. *I would never go there. I would never eat that. Why would I meet my end on a mountaintop when I do not even care to climb stairs?*

The future had its way of twisting and turning, so that events that seemed both improbable and perfectly avoidable ended up inescapable, when enough time and circumstances had unspooled.

Master Haywood took her hand in his. Their clasped hands shook, and she couldn't tell who was trembling harder. Titus, across the room, seemed to need all his concentration to remain upright. Amara, next to Kashkari, had her head bowed, as if in prayer.

Only Kashkari leaned forward in his seat. Now that the news had been broken to Iolanthe at last and his dream described at length, he had reverted back to his composed, determined self. "Remember what I told you, Fairfax, that it isn't necessary to view a future that has been seen in a vision as set in stone, especially not this one."

Yet everything he had ever seen had come to pass. Sometimes the true significance of his prophetic dreams had been misunderstood, but *what* he had dreamed had unfolded exactly as foreseen.

"How should we view this vision then?" asked Master Haywood, his voice tense yet not without hope.

"As I told the prince earlier, we should see this as a warning: instead of heading to Atlantis right away, we should—"

"You were going to *Atlantis*?" exclaimed Master Haywood.

It took Iolanthe a long moment to remember that he didn't yet know about this part of her plan. "I'm sorry. There hasn't been time to tell you."

The lines on his forehead had never appeared so deeply furrowed, or his eyes so sunken. "But that's *mad*."

"Yes, I know," she said softly.

"We live in unhinged times." The comment came from Amara, who had been silent for a while. "Such times often call for extraordinary measures."

A brave statement, but one delivered in a completely flat tone, devoid of any derring-do.

"So they do, and our decision was to strike at the heart of the Bane's dominion, in the crypt where he keeps his original body." Kashkari reached out and poured tea for everyone—tea that Iolanthe had forgotten was steeping in the pot. "Last night I'd suggested to the prince that we should wait for a more opportune time to strike. But the news my sister-in-law brought this morning changes things again."

Titus pulled a chair up next to Iolanthe, sat down, and pressed a cup of tea into her hands. His eyes reflected nothing but ruin—exactly as she remembered, when she'd pulled him in from the fog the night before. She ought to have guessed then and there that Kashkari's dream concerned her, not him: he had long ago made peace with his own death; it was only hers that could have devastated him to such a degree.

She set aside the saucer and wrapped her hands directly about the cup, needing its scalding heat against her skin. He did the same, his hands clutching his teacup so tightly that it was a wonder he didn't pulverize it.

"We must go after the Bane," continued Kashkari. "Only now we have an implacable time constraint—and we must do it without Fairfax, if we've learned anything from my vision. Nobody who goes to Atlantis expects to come back alive. But if Fairfax were to fall, everything we've ever done would be in vain."

Iolanthe's head throbbed. "Then what do I do?"

And who would save Titus?

"You hide. Preferable somewhere none of us can even guess, in case we are captured by Atlanteans."

She shook her head—this went against the grain of everything she had been taught about prophecies. "We are asking for trouble. You interfere with a prophecy and the end result will always be worse than if you'd let it happen."

"But what can possibly be worse than your being taken to the Bane's crypt and sacrificed? And it was the Bane's crypt I saw; that much there could be no question."

Beside her Master Haywood gasped softly, but said nothing. She glanced at him, then at Titus, who sat with his neck bent, his breaths shaky.

She shook her head again. She couldn't think very well, but even so, something about Kashkari's vision made no sense. "Why wouldn't either you or His Highness have made sure that Atlantis didn't take me alive?"

"I've taken a blood oath that doesn't allow me to harm either you or His Highness. I don't know whether His Highness is capable of lethal acts against you. Besides, we could have become separated as we made our way across Atlantis."

She took a sip of tea. It was bitter—she never did make very good tea. Titus tasted his and grimaced. He rose, left the room, and came back half a minute later with a small plate of sugar cubes. She dropped two cubes into her cup; he took the rest.

"But perhaps we are looking at this the wrong way. Perhaps my death, far from the worst thing that could happen, was instead the necessary step that allowed the two of you to go as far as you did. You were in the Bane's crypt. And you were still alive and well. There was nothing to prevent *you* from finishing the Bane."

No one said anything. She drank from her tea again and was astonished at the difference in the taste. Whatever had gone into making the sugar cubes gave the tea not only sweetness, but subtle yet delicious hints of citrus and stone fruits.

"I can't believe that everyone here takes the matter of a vision so cavalierly," she went on. "I'm all for making a vision prove itself, and even I do not argue the validity of this one. Whereas . . . whereas you all seem to treat it as no different from a mere rumor."

Again, silence.

"My beliefs in the matter differ from Mohandas's," said Amara. "I do understand his point of view, that the future has not yet happened—that every decision we make now has an impact on what will take place down the road.

"Growing up, however, I was very much influenced by my paternal grandmother, who emigrated to the Kalahari from a Nordic realm and was a firm believer that only events that *are* chiseled in stone are transmitted in visions. The entirety of the future may yet be unwritten, but no one can deny that certain forces and developments are so powerful, trying to stop them would be like a fly getting in the way of an armored chariot.

"But even I, who hold staunchly to the view that no one should try to alter a future that has been revealed, can't find anything particularly wrong in what Mohandas suggests. After we met again this morning he confessed that he'd lied about having seen you reach Atlantis on your own power and of your own will. Given that, are there actual known visions of you marching onto Atlantis?"

"No," Iolanthe had to admit.

"Then no one is trying to refute a future that has already been seen."

Iolanthe set down her empty cup. Something didn't add up— something one of the mages in the room said or indicated. But she couldn't seem to think. In fact, she was listing hard to her left.

She clutched at Titus and missed. But his arm banded about

her and kept her from toppling over.

"What's the matter?" came Kashkari's voice, sounding very distant.

"Iola? Are you all right, Iola?"

Her vision shrank. The last thing she saw was Titus's eyes, from which all light and hope had fled.

"She is fine," said Titus, setting her down. "Master Haywood, would you mind getting a blanket from one of the bedrooms?"

Haywood ran out and was back within seconds. Titus tucked the blanket carefully around her. "She will come to on her own in two or three hours, if not sooner."

He did not need to explain his action any further. He knew Fairfax. She was stubborn and loyal—and she bowed to no prophecies. She would never stand for her friends to brave the perils of Atlantis without her.

So they must leave her behind.

"You will forgive us for not discussing our plans in your hearing, sir," he said to Haywood.

Haywood nodded—he understood that the moment his ward awakened, she would demand to know where her friends had gone.

"Make sure you build a fire and keep her warm."

With her falling unconscious, the fire she summoned had dissipated. The grate, the bricks of which still radiated heat, was empty.

Titus looked down at his most stalwart friend for a moment

longer, before he made himself head for the laboratory, Kashkari and Amara in tow.

Amara inhaled deeply as she took a seat before the worktable. "What is this lovely fragrance in the air?"

It was from the butterfly tableau of the night before, the scent of a meadow in bloom. He remembered how Fairfax had looked, with both laughter and tears in her eyes.

His heart felt as if it had been branded, a scalding pain through which he could barely breathe. This task was always going to take everything from him in the end—but he always woke up each morning hoping he had at least another day.

After this day, there would be no more reprieve.

"I have more bad news," he said, ignoring Amara's question.

When he had come into the laboratory to fetch the "sugar cubes," he had spied a new message from Dalbert. The first paragraph explained that Dalbert had had some trouble accessing his end of the transmission device, but had since managed to move it to a different spot—and that was the only good news the message contained.

Half of the rest dealt with the massacre in the Kalahari Realm and the threat that had been left for Titus, which was as Amara had reported. The other half conveyed developments that were almost as dire.

"There was a raid last night on the armory underneath the Serpentine Hills—the one Durga Devi was taken to see. All the war engines were destroyed, including a large number of annihilators—the machines that can bring down armored chariots."

Leaving the Domain defenseless when the forces of Atlantis arrived in six and half days.

This was what Titus had feared: that by tipping their hand in the desert, his allies courted disaster.

Now it became ever more imperative that they succeed in bringing down the Bane.

Without Fairfax.

In the long, dark shadow of her prophesied death.

"I'm sorry to hear that," said Amara.

Titus turned to the typing ball and tapped out a message to Dalbert. An answer came almost immediately.

"What more news does he have?" Kashkari's voice was tense. The way things were going, any news would almost inevitably be bad news.

"I did not ask for further news. I asked whether he had ever prepared a means for me to return to the Domain, without the aid of our usual translocator."

"And?"

Titus exhaled. "He had."

Haywood rose as Titus reentered the parlor. "Sire."

"We are leaving." The words lacerated him, as if he spoke with pieces of broken glass on his tongue. "And so we have come to say our farewells."

Haywood bowed. "May Fortune ever smile upon you, sire."

"Fortune already did, when your ward became my friend."

And now everything that had been given would be taken away.

As Haywood wished the kindness of Fortune upon Kashkari and Amara, Titus knelt down by Fairfax and took her hand in his. She looked peaceful, unencumbered by care, like Sleeping Beauty in her hundred-year slumber. Yet the image that flashed across his mind was one of himself prostrate before her lifeless body.

Even now he had no hope. He was certain that no matter what he did, disaster was barreling toward her. But he had to do something, had to at least make an attempt, however idiotic, to keep her safe.

To keep her alive.

Let this be their final farewell. Let him not see her again, ever. He could handle leaving her behind, if he must. He could not bear walking into a future in which she had been murdered by the Bane—the end of everything worthwhile, the beginning of all his nightmares.

"Live forever," he said softly.

And then, to Haywood, "Long may Fortune walk beside the two of you. And when she awakens, tell her that I do not regret my decision this day, only—only that we will never share a picnic basket from Mrs. Hinderstone's."

CHAPTER ✦ 11

THE LABORATORY HAD ONE MORE exit than it had entrances, and that exit led to a dilapidated barn in southeast England. From there, Titus vaulted his companions to London.

They made their way to the Victoria and Albert Museum. Among the exhibits of Renaissance France, there stood a large and elaborate wardrobe with marquetry doors and ormolu trims.

"This is the one," said Titus.

It was early in the day and late in the year; the museum was not crowded. They had no trouble clearing out that particular gallery with a few keep-away spells. The wardrobe was big enough that the three of them—and Amara's bulky coat—had no trouble fitting inside.

Titus murmured the password and the countersign Dalbert had given him. Almost instantly they found themselves in a more cramped space, bumping up against stacks of crates and buckets. When Titus opened the door a crack, the tang of the sea greeted him, as well as the sound of waves.

He waited a minute to make sure there was no ambush, before he opened the door more fully. They were in a large, natural cavern. The mouth of the cavern was hidden behind an outcrop, but there was light slanting in from outside, glinting on the tips of the wavelets.

A twenty-foot-long sloop, swaying slightly, was suspended from the ceiling of the cavern.

"So we sail?" asked Amara.

"We sail," answered Titus.

He called for mage light. With the help of the blue illumination, he was able to find where Dalbert had wound the chain that kept the boat up high. Together, the three of them lowered the boat down into the water.

Titus took out the map from his satchel and placed it against the damp cavern wall. A red dot appeared on the silky map, just outside the Domain's maritime borders.

As he had thought. Dalbert, unlike Lady Callista with her connection to Atlanteans, could not create a loophole through the barriers Atlantis had erected around the Domain against unauthorized entries and exits by instantaneous means. So he had opted to get them as close as possible.

In the small structure that served as the portal, which looked more like a nonmage bathing machine than anything else—except without wheels—they found oars, poles, and fishing implements, as well as food cubes, water, and changes of clothing.

The equipment was moved easily enough to the boat with levitation spells. They themselves managed to board without falling into the water. Since it had long been Titus's plan to approach Atlantis via its coast, he had trained himself to sail in a number of the stories in the Crucible that involved sea voyages.

But it was one thing to steer a vessel in open ocean, quite another to get it out of the narrow and cramped cavern, with waves rushing in and creating unpredictable currents that threw the sloop this way and that. They rowed. They pushed with oars and poles. At one point, Titus and Kashkari jumped into the frigid water to get the boat unstuck.

The cost of leaving their elemental mage behind.

But the far greater cost was the emptiness within Titus. It was as if he were somewhere outside himself, watching the struggle with the boat. His muscles worked, diligently and tirelessly, but he did not care anymore.

He remained in his icy wet clothes for a good long while afterward, until he was sure the boat was far enough from the cliffs of the uninhabited island that he did not have to worry about it being blown back and dashed to pieces on those unforgiving rocks during the time he changed.

If only—

He cut off the direction of his thoughts. What he had done, he had done for himself, because he could not live in a world without her. If this was the universe punishing him for his hubris and stupidity, then so be it.

Iolanthe's head felt as if someone had stuffed an entire English boiled pudding inside: a wobbling mass. Her eyelids were as heavy as bricks, resisting all attempts at lifting them. Strange: she wasn't as fanatic an early riser as the prince, but usually when she awakened, she felt refreshed and ready to face the day, and not drugged, as if she were stuck in a woolly abyss, unable to pry herself out.

Drugged.

Titus—the futility in his eyes. The tea with its wonderfully evocative flavors. The sugar cubes. Titus, putting all the remaining sugar cubes into his own tea, and then never taking another sip.

She groaned and sat up, her muscles as limp as the macaroni served at Mrs. Dawlish's house.

"Iola! Are you all right?"

Master Haywood's face slowly swam into focus before her, his expression as guilty as it was anxious.

She didn't even bother to ask *whether* everyone else had gone. "How are they getting to the Domain?"

"They didn't discuss it within my hearing."

She pinched the ridge of her nose. "And you were glad for it, weren't you, when the prince told you that he would hold his discussions elsewhere, so that you couldn't possibly relay any information to me?"

"Iola—"

She held up a hand. She didn't want to argue with him. What she did want was to put her hands around Titus's throat and throttle him to within an inch of his life. How dare he make a decision of such magnitude for her? And how dare he make it in such a cowardly manner? She might yet acquiesce to the group's consensus, if they absolutely felt they could not have her along—but not until after she had made a proper case for herself.

She got to her feet and staggered to the laboratory. The place was as neat as ever, not a single item out of place. She was familiar enough with its contents to see what they had taken: vaulting aids, sailing aids, all kinds of other remedies for trauma and injuries. But her ability to inventory the missing items did not give her any idea of how they had gone back to the Domain—or from where.

Only as she turned away from the shelves and cabinets did she notice the few things that had been left on the worktable. Kashkari and Amara's two-way notebooks lay side by side, with a note from Kashkari underneath.

Dear Fairfax,

These notebooks contain intelligence that affects the safety of many. Since the pages cannot be adequately secured, we have decided to leave

them behind, rather than risk their falling into the wrong hands. If you
would be so kind, please send them both to my parents and ask that my
sister-in-law's be given into my brother's keeping.

I am sorry we cannot say a proper good-bye. It has been a pleasure
and a privilege to know you. Long may Fortune guard your path.

Fondly,
M.K.

On the other side of the worktable sat Titus's most prized possession. And he too had left her a note.

Beloved,

I debated fiercely whether I should take my mother's diary with me.
In the end I chose not to, because I do not wish for it to become lost
or destroyed, and because the time for prophecies has come and gone.
Please keep it well, for in it is written your story too. Our story.
And please forgive me my trespass. I love you with every breath and I
always will.

Titus

It was a measure of her love for him that she did not burn his
note then and there. But she did scream, calling him names that

would have melted a hole in the paper were she to set them down in writing.

When she was hoarse from shouting, Master Haywood, who had followed her into the laboratory, said tentatively, "My, living in a boys' school has certainly changed your language."

"I hate to shatter your innocence, sir," she answered curtly, "but I didn't utter any words I didn't already know since I was twelve."

She laid her elbows on the worktable and buried her face in her hands, as exhausted as she was furious. Was this it? After everything they had been through, he expected her to sit quietly and wait for *The Delamer Observer* to tell her when half the city's population had been destroyed by death rain? And when his state funeral was held, assuming that Atlantis would even bother to return his body—did he expect her to learn that from the papers too?

"Iola, my dear—"

"Please leave me alone." She hated to be rude to Master Haywood. But he was glad that she hadn't gone, and she couldn't face that gladness now.

"I'll be happy to give you all the space you wish. But do please remember that we must decamp at some point, if only to the inn. You can't stay here forever."

She could, just to spite Titus. "I understand. Would you mind leaving me for a few minutes? You can take the paper if you want."

The laboratory had a copy of *The Delamer Observer*, the contents of which refreshed every few hours—and sometimes even more frequently.

"That's all right. I already read every article inside while you were sleeping. Some earlier visitor had left a copy of the *Times* in the parlor—I'll have a look at that instead."

Silence. Emptiness. The sound of her own trembling breaths. The hollow sensation of no longer being needed. Ever.

The rain of hearts and bunnies. The Sahara Desert, his long, lonely walk each night, watching over her. The lightning erupting from the ground up, white-hot and deadly. *For you.*

Anger, seething. The violence inside her, a dark cauldron. His hand as she pulled him into the lighthouse, so cold, so very, very cold. *You and you alone. Live forever. I love you with every breath and I always will.*

She clutched her head. She could not bear the upheaval. Peace, calm, tranquility—she needed something. If not, then at least a blessed numbness, a cessation of this vehement churn of emotions and memories.

The blankness she longed for came all of a sudden. But it was not peace, calm, or tranquility: her mind had seized onto something, forsaking all other thoughts in order to pull a phantom of an idea out of the chaos.

She sat up.

But what can possibly be worse than your being taken to the Bane's crypt and sacrificed? Kashkari had demanded. And Master Haywood had gasped. She, naturally enough, had interpreted it to be a sound of dismay and distress.

What if she had been wrong?

"Iola!" Master Haywood set aside the *Times* and rose from his seat. "Are you feeling better?"

She had seldom felt worse.

At her silence, he fidgeted a little. Then he tapped the paper. "You will not believe what I just read: a funeral announcement for your friend, young Wintervale."

That indeed wasn't something she would have expected to find in a nonmage paper. Still she said nothing.

"Iola, are you all right?"

She wasn't, but her mind was now working furiously. "Do you remember Professor Eventide?"

"Hippolyta Eventide? Of course."

Professor Eventide had been an unforgettable personality, a big, loquacious woman with a head of bright-red hair, a wardrobe full of sequins and polka dots, and a mind as powerful as a blade wand. Her research specialty was the Dark Arts, which mage societies as a whole shunned. The in-depth understanding of the Dark Arts, however, was considered to be an unfortunate necessity, if only so that there were those who could recognize and help defend against such practices.

Most major centers of learning had a resident expert or two

on the Dark Arts. It was Iolanthe's understanding that they were usually awkward loners who eschewed the company of their fellow academics, even as the latter gave them the cold shoulder. Professor Eventide, by dint of her warmth and conviviality, was an exception. She was welcome everywhere and never lacked for invitations to social gatherings.

When Master Haywood had worked at the Conservatory, Professor Eventide had taken a maternal interest in him and was determined to find him a wife. That project never came to fruition, but the two had become great friends and would sometimes throw dinner parties jointly. On those occasions Iolanthe had loved to sit at the top of the staircase, out of sight, and listen to the grown-ups as they discussed everything under the sun.

It was from those discussions that she'd gleaned enough knowledge to figure out what had happened to poor Wintervale. And it was another one of those snippets of knowledge that now led her to reevaluate what Master Haywood had understood from Kashkari's words.

"When I was seven, there was a dinner to celebrate your promotion." The last promotion he would ever receive from the Conservatory—or anywhere else. "During the meal, someone asked Professor Eventide about the primary sources she used for her research. She declined to discuss it in detail, saying it was forbidden. But after the guests left, the two of you sat and talked for some time. And at one point you asked her about those primary sources, whether it was true that records of actual practitioners of the Dark Arts had been allowed to survive."

Master Haywood became very still, almost as if he had stopped breathing.

"She said yes," Iolanthe went on. "She warned you to keep everything confidential, and then she went on to describe some of what she had read in those primary sources. I kept listening and kept regretting what I'd heard. Afterward I did my best to forget, because what she said gave me nightmares.

"But some things you never really forget. I remember now what she told you about sacrificial magic, how mages mistakenly equated blood magic with sacrificial magic because a rite of sacrificial magic began with the drawing of a small quantity of blood from the victim, to ascertain how powerful the sacrifice would be. I also remember she went to say how grotesque sacrificial magic was. And how messy, since all the best parts of the body—eyes, brain, organs, and marrow—had to be extracted while the victim's heart still beat."

Her breaths grew agitated from the horrifying memories— and from the accusation she was about to make. "My friends are knowledgeable, but few mages alive know anything concrete about sacrificial magic. By the time we learned that sacrificial magic was the reason for the Bane's quest for a great elemental mage, none of us had time to do any reading on it—we were too busy preparing to leave Eton at the drop of a hat.

"Today, in their ignorance, my friends assumed that what

Kashkari's prophetic dream revealed was that I would die from sacrificial magic, giving the Bane another century of unparalleled power. That was the reason they left me behind, even though they had come to count on my abilities.

"But you, all along you knew that they were wrong. That I would not be used for sacrificial magic, at least not successfully. And you kept it to yourself. You let them go. You let—" Her voice caught. "You let the one I love walk into certain doom without me."

He said nothing.

"Am I right?" she demanded. "Is that what you did?"

Still he said nothing.

"Answer me!"

His throat moved. "Yes, you are right. I let them think your death would be caused by sacrificial magic, even though your friend's description of the dream suggested otherwise."

She slumped into a chair, her legs no longer able to support her.

"But don't you see, Iola, that even if it will not be by sacrificial magic, by going to Atlantis you will still die?"

Wearily she raised her head. "I know that. I have known it since the day the prince first asked me to help him in this endeavor. That was why I ran from him. That was why he had to trick me into a blood oath so that I'd stay. But somewhere along the way I changed my mind. I understood what is at stake. And I realized that sometimes the loss of a life, even if that life is my own, isn't too great a price to pay."

He shook his head, his eyes stricken. "I can't let that happen. You are still a child. You are too young to make such irrevocable decisions."

"I may be still underage, but I haven't been a child for a very long time. You know that. And I have some idea how devastating it might be for you, to let me choose my own path. But it's the same for me, don't you see? There is a prophecy of the prince's death. He would meet his end on Atlantis. Do you think it never occurred to me that perhaps he ought to stop pursuing this course of action that would lead him to Atlantis? But I don't say anything to dissuade him, and I don't stand in his way. He has already chosen, and I must respect his choice."

A tear rolled down Master Haywood's face. "But what about the Conservatory? If you set foot on Atlantis, you will never return. And you will never study at the Conservatory."

"Did you really think that by tomorrow or next week I would change my mind, and be content to throw myself into my studies so that I might yet do well on next year's qualifying exams? And even if I did, have you forgotten who I am? Have you forgotten that as long as the Bane endures, I will never be safe?"

Master Haywood covered his face with his hands. Iolanthe got to her feet. What else was there to say?

She returned to the laboratory, sat down on her usual stool, pressed her fingers to her temples, and tried to think. There was always the sea route, of course. Titus had an account with the Bank of England to which she had access, and there was enough money in the account for her to hire a vessel—or buy one outright—to cover a thousand miles of open ocean. But the speediest steamer would still take at least thirty hours to traverse that distance. And even she, with her powers, could not create an ocean current that moved much faster.

The pages of Kashkari's two-way notebook moved—as if someone had set a thumb against their edges and riffled them.

She stared at it. She had used two-way notebooks when she was a child—most schoolchildren had, buying them from hawkers, as no parents or parental figures would make such purchases, given that their predominant use was for chatting with friends during class, while still looking as if one were taking notes and paying attention.

Over the years two-way notebooks had been adapted so that they could receive messages from much longer distances, rather than from only a few feet away. But because part of the underlying construction was so flimsy, no one had ever been able to make them truly secure. Titus had always refused to carry one, for fear it would give away too much if his person was ever searched.

The pages of the notebook flipped again.

Even if Iolanthe wanted to, she wouldn't be able to read the message, unless she knew Kashkari's password. The security was lax, but still enough to stop a casual peeper.

The contents of the front page of *The Delamer Observer*, which lay next to the notebook, changed. Not that much could be gleaned from the front pages of any newspaper these days—valuable information was much more likely to be found concealed among the tiny and numerous advertisements on the back inside pages.

She blinked and pulled the newspaper toward her. At the bottom of the front page, a small headline read, *Cargo Loads Diverted to Delamer North as Hubs at Delamer East Undergo Maintenance.*

The article was short.

Several of the Domain's longest-serving freight translocators were demolished this morning. Translocators 1 to 4 had long functioned as the capital's, indeed, the realm's most reliable vessels for transatlantic cargo shipment. That slack has now been taken up by translocators at both Delamer North and Riverton West. Delamer East's translocators are expected to be rebuilt to current standards and return to service by the beginning of next year.

Translocator 4 at Delamer East was the one for which Titus had a destination disruptor!

Was the message in Kashkari's notebook from them? Had Titus too discovered this unhappy turn of events and was trying to contact her? But why *her*? What could she do from a lighthouse at the very north of mainland Britain?

Of course, the diary. Faced with such a challenge, Titus would immediately want to consult his mother's record, to see whether any of her visions might provide a clue as to how he ought to proceed.

She picked up the notebook and tried to think from Kashkari's perspective. Two-way notebooks did not work with countersigns, and they did not tolerate long, complex passwords. So it had to be something relatively simple. And Kashkari, who spent the majority of his time at school, would want something that his classmates could not guess, something that belonged to his secret life as a young rebel.

"Amara," she said.

That was not it.

"Durga Devi."

No.

"Vasudev."

Still not right. Of course, Vasudev Kashkari had come to Eton and met quite a few people in Mrs. Dawlish's house. So his name would not do. Was it their sister's name, then? Or his parents' names? She didn't know what any of them were called.

Wait. What was it that Kashkari had said was his nom de guerre? "Vrischika!"

She grunted aloud as she proved wide of the mark again. She was on the wrong track here. Kashkari did spend part of his year with the rebels, so he would want something the rebels couldn't easily guess either, in case someone nosy stumbled upon his notebook.

She walked several times around the worktable. Kashkari had gone to Eton to keep Wintervale safe, but all the variations of Wintervale's name fell flat. She consulted Princess Ariadne's diary, but no new visions were revealed. She did find, tucked into a pocket on the back cover, a letter from Lady Wintervale to Titus, written years ago, when the latter first began his career at Eton. But it was no use to the problem at hand.

You will best help him by seeking aid from the faithful and bold, came the long-ago advice from the Oracle of Still Waters. Could it be? *Fidus et audax,* which had been the password for the wardrobe in Wintervale's room, was in fact—Titus had told her later—the Wintervale family motto.

Could Kashkari have taken that as his password, because of what he believed to be his prophesied connection with Wintervale?

"*Fidus et audax,*" she said.

The notebook opened. And on the page it opened to was written, *I remember now where I saw a book exactly like the prince's volume of fairy tales: on the shelves of Royalis's grand library, when I last worked there.*

Iolanthe nearly dropped the notebook. She didn't need the tiny Atlantean whirlpool symbol at the corner of the page to know who had sent the message.

Mrs. Hancock.

Where are you? she wrote back.

No answer came.

If she were Mrs. Hancock, she would be careful too, especially if she received a reply that wasn't in Kashkari's handwriting. Iolanthe almost identified herself to Mrs. Hancock, but that would be too risky, if the notebook were to fall into the wrong hands.

Or was already in the wrong hands.

Her head pounded. What was really going on? What would Titus, Kashkari, and Amara do once they found out that they could not proceed as they'd hoped? And what was her role in all of this? Did she merely pass on the information to Dalbert and hope for the best or . . .

She got up and walked back into the parlor. Master Haywood sat in an armchair, his hands in his lap, staring straight ahead.

Her heart pinched, but she only said, "If you can show me where it is, I would like to see Wintervale's funeral notice."

Titus had taken their emergency satchel. But fortunately for her, his preparedness was world-class, and in the laboratory there were duplicates of almost everything—including, thankfully, another plain spare wand, since she planned to leave Validus behind. She found a satchel similar to the one they'd used and stocked it with remedies, tools, and everything else she could fit inside.

Master Haywood, his face grim, did the same, filling the bag he'd brought with him from his apartment in Paris.

"You don't have to come," she told him.

"I want to."

"You don't want to. You would rather stay behind."

"So would you, Iola. We are none of us that brave."

"At least I made my decision long ago, after careful consideration. You are just being rash."

He stopped and turned to her. "My dear girl, you may criticize me on anything else—and goodness knows I have failed on many fronts. But for nearly seventeen years now my life has had no purpose other than to keep you safe. When I destroyed your light elixir, it was an attempt to keep you safe. When I said nothing and let the prince and his friends go, likewise. And now I am coming with you, because nothing matters more to me than your safety. Maybe I am being rash, but my decision too was made very, very long ago."

She swallowed. "I'm sorry. Please forgive me."

His voice softened. "Only if you also forgive me for overstepping my bounds."

She set aside her bag, wrapped her arms around him, and laid her head on his shoulder. "I want so much for you to have years and years ahead. Good years—too many were stolen from you."

"I want the same—but not because I had anything stolen from me. I was the one who threw away those years we could have been happy together. I want to do everything right by you, should we be given another chance."

She touched his face. "You have always done everything right by me."

He hugged her fiercely, then kissed her on her forehead. They finished packing and checked each other's bags to make sure no important items had been left behind.

When there was nothing more to be done, Iolanthe closed the

door of the laboratory. She wished she had time for one last stroll on the headland. It was an austerely beautiful place, Cape Wrath, and she'd seen very little of it, despite the number of times she'd visited the laboratory.

Someday. Someday when all the prophecies in the world went up in flames.

She took a deep breath. "Ready?"

"No," said Master Haywood.

"I know what you mean. No one can be ready for what we are about to face."

"No, that is not what I meant at all."

She glanced at him. Had he changed his mind? "Then what do you mean?"

From the abandoned barn in Kent, Iolanthe vaulted Master Haywood and herself to Gravesend, then to central London, then West Drayton, six miles east of Eton. She didn't know exactly how far Atlantis's no-vaulting zone extended, but they arrived in West Drayton without mishap, and from there took a train to Windsor and Eton Central railway station, immediately on the doorstep of Windsor Castle.

The castle was inside the no-vaulting zone, which was still very much in effect. High walls and guarded entrances, however, were no matches for two mages with breaking in on their minds. In fact, the only problem Iolanthe had was in determining the precise location of the room she used to vault into, for meeting with Lady Wintervale.

But she knew it faced north and was on an upper floor. And she gave a detailed enough description for a footman, under an otherwise spell that made him believe that she was one of the English queen's ladies-in-waiting, to know exactly which sitting room she was talking about.

Later that day, her voice rang out clearly from inside the room. *"Toujours fier."*

What Lady Wintervale had told her to say, to summon the noblewoman from her lair deep in the castle.

Except this time those words summoned only the agents of Atlantis, lying in wait.

CHAPTER ⋅ 12

TITUS SAILED THE SLOOP SOUTHWARD. The sea was steel gray and choppy, the spray cold as knives. Kashkari and Amara were huddled near each other toward the aft, but they seldom spoke. Amara, despite the sailing aid Titus had given her, looked as if she were desperately trying not to lose her breakfast.

If he thought about it, it was strange that Amara had tagged along—he vaguely recalled whispered exchanges between Kashkari and her, while they were still in the laboratory. But Titus did not devote much time to the oddity of her choice: everyone who was not Fairfax was free to try his or her luck on Atlantis.

They were all going to die anyway.

It was nearly dark before they sighted land—a rock heap that belonged to the Nereids Isles, one of the Domain's outlying archipelagos. Titus more or less ran the boat aground. They were lucky it did not tip over and injure someone.

Just as he had done with the countries of Europe, Titus had methodically taken himself to many parts of his own realm. He gave Kashkari and Amara each a hefty dose of vaulting aid and vaulted them to a bigger island ninety miles away.

Another hop and they were on a third island, this time before an old temple that had fallen into ruins. In the inner sanctum of the temple, Titus pointed his wand at the floor. "*Aperito shemsham.*"

The huge stones receded, leading to a passage down.

"Hesperia," he said, by way of explanation.

Hesperia the Magnificent had spent a significant portion of her childhood under imprisonment. After she wrested power from the Usurper, she was determined never to lose her freedom again. Everything she ever built had multiple means of escape that led everywhere in the Domain.

The secret chamber beneath the inner sanctum had a portal that led to a similar secret chamber underneath a similarly dilapidated shrine, this time in the Labyrinthine Mountains.

Finding places in the Labyrinthine Mountains was always tricky. Titus asked Kashkari and Amara to remain in the vicinity of the shrine, while he himself vaulted about to see how the mountains had shifted. That is, he blind vaulted—vaulting with his eyes wide open, staring at where he wanted to go, instead of using actual memories of a place that he had visited before. In the Labyrinthine Mountains, where everything moved, vaulting did not work as well as it did elsewhere.

It would have been easier for him to use a carpet and scan the landscape from a higher vantage point, but he did not dare make himself so visible. After his fourth vault, he finally materialized near the safe house: he recognized the sound of the Sonata Stream.

Up close, the Sonata Stream was but another mountain brook, the kind that was everywhere to be found in these parts—clear, cold water, rocky banks, red and gold fallen leaves carried swiftly on the currents.

It sounded ordinary too, the burbling of water, the rustle of tree branches overhead, the chirp of an occasional bird or insect. But if one happened to be at just the right distance, all the commonplace sounds somehow combined to form music. Not figurative music, but literal, as if the stream had learned to pluck lyres and strike tiny triangles to mark the rhythm of its progress.

Whenever he and his mother went on a long walk, she always made sure to pass by the Sonata Stream. This had been their mountain, their playground, their safe refuge from her despot of a father and the attention of Atlantis, circling ever closer. And she had wanted him to feel its magic in his bones, to always hold in his heart a deep well of reverence and wonder.

He allowed himself a minute to listen. This would be the last time he stood upon the loamy soil of his childhood, the last time he breathed in the scent of home.

Then he vaulted back to ferry Kashkari and Amara to the grassy slope beneath a sheer rock face. Behind the rock face was a surprisingly large living space, room after rough-hewn room, the furniture simple and sturdy, the granite walls faintly reddish in the light of the sconces.

It was where Fairfax would have stayed during the previous summer, if things had not gone ill for them. They had made such plans. Every moment he could have stolen away from the castle they would have spent together, training and strategizing, but also just holding hands and leaning on each other, storing up a reserve of happiness and hope to see them through the darker days to come.

Instead they had spent no time together at all. And as much as Titus wished to draw on the good times they *had* shared to keep despair at bay, he felt like the safe house, full of should-have-beens and little else.

"There is a bath in the back, with hot water," he told his companions. "Go ahead and make use of it."

He walked into the kitchen. There were no fresh foods in storage, but a large variety of preserved and dehydrated nutrients. He set a pot of water to boil over a flameless stove and added an assortment of ingredients to make a vegetable potage. As the soup bubbled, he opened several packages of waybread, soaked the brick-like pieces in water, then put them in a warm oven, as per the heating instructions.

When he was done, he leaned against the rough stone counter, more exhausted than he cared to admit. Only the first day of the journey, and already he felt as if he had been traveling for years.

More than anything he wanted to swallow a dose of sleep aid and pass a few hours in blissful oblivion. But first he had to make sure his companions were properly fed. Maybe he ought to put out some dried fruits on the dining table, or—

"Titus," came Kashkari's voice.

He turned around. "Yes?"

Kashkari stood in the doorway of the kitchen, a copy of *The Delamer Observer* in his hand. The expression on his face made Titus's heart sink even before he said, "I'm afraid I have bad news."

Titus could scarcely credit what he was reading. *Demolished. Return to service by the beginning of next year.*

"Can your disruptor be used on a different translocator?" asked Kashkari.

Titus shook his head. He had not been involved with the making of the disruptor, which he had inherited from Prince Gaius, his grandfather, who had long sought ways to get into Atlantis. But the instruction had been very clear: it would work only on that particular translocator.

Which was the reason translocators 1 to 4 of Delamer East, though becoming obsolete, had never been replaced: it was a security weakness in that particular generation of translocators that the disruptor sought to exploit.

Could this have been a coincidence, the demolition of the translocators when he most needed them to function as usual? And who, besides himself, Fairfax, and Kashkari, even knew of the existence of the disruptor?

"So what do we do?" asked Kashkari.

Titus threw aside the paper. "We seize an armored chariot and make it do our bidding?"

"You know as well as I do the moment Atlantis realizes the vessel is outside of its control, we'd drop like a rock."

If they had Fairfax, dropping out of the air would not be a problem. But they did not.

"Will you look after the food?" he asked Kashkari. "I need to track down my spymaster and find out what is going on."

Titus stood atop the rock face, the edge of his tunic whipping in the gale. The last few scattered rays of light from the sunset were disappearing; the full mantle of night lay upon the mountains.

Why had Dalbert not come to the safe house yet? Before Titus left the laboratory, he had let Dalbert know to expect him in the mountains. He did have a few other way stations, but Dalbert should have understood that he meant to make for the safe house. And Titus would have expected Dalbert, always meticulously organized and prepared, to have arrived well ahead.

He tried to recall the exact words Dalbert had used in his earlier communiqué, but could only remember the gist of it, something about the spymaster not being able to send messages for several days.

What exactly had happened in the castle while Titus had been in the desert? Was Dalbert also on the run—or in hiding, as it may be?

"Your Highness," came the sound of a familiar voice.

Dalbert stood at the base of the smooth cliff, his round face upturned. He was not a liveried servant, but at the castle he always wore a white capelet, embroidered on the back with the image of a two-headed phoenix, the emblem on Titus's mother's personal standard. This time the capelet was missing and he was in the simple tunic of a woodsman, a worn leather bag slung over his shoulder.

"Dalbert!" Titus was more than glad—he was thrilled. He vaulted down and gripped his valet and spymaster by the shoulders. "Are you all right?"

Dalbert bowed from the waist. "I'm quite well, sire. I had hoped to arrive sooner and have everything in the safe house ready for Your Highness, a meal and a bath in particular."

Titus waved his hand. "I can see to those myself. Come inside and tell me what is going on instead."

Amara and Kashkari were setting the table when they walked in. Titus made the introductions, and together they brought all the supper items from the kitchen and sat down.

"Thank you, Master Dalbert," said Kashkari, "for having the foresight to provide us a translocator."

"Indeed," said Titus. "When did you put that in place?"

"After we were informed that Your Highness was expected to attend a nonmage school in England, I was among the mages sent to

Mrs. Dawlish's to make sure the dwelling was sound. I took advantage of that time to examine some locales in London. With every subsequent trip, I did some work on the wardrobe at the Victoria and Albert Museum. It was ready to use by your third Half at Eton."

"Well done, of course. But how did you anticipate that I might require something of the sort?" Titus had never spoken of his mission to Dalbert: his policy had always been secrecy. And yet here he was, finding out that Dalbert had long been implementing emergency measures on his behalf.

Dalbert smiled slightly, a smile with a trace of melancholy. "When I was fourteen, I became a page to Her Highness. After she came of age, she dismissed the personal secretary Prince Gaius had assigned her and entrusted the post to me instead. At the same time she confided in me that she saw visions of the future, and much to her regret, she was eerily accurate in those visions.

"A few years later, she caught Commander Rainstone snooping in her diary, in which she kept a record of her visions. After that, she put a blank charm on the diary, so that even if someone knew the password to the diary, they would still see only bare pages—the touch of her hand was needed to show the contents.

"But when she understood that she would die young, she faced a quandary. Many of her visions concerned you, sire. It was important that you had access to them, but it was also crucial that you not be overwhelmed by everything at once. She didn't have enough time to configure the spells necessary for the diary to only give up what you needed to see at any point in time. That task was handed to me instead, with the understanding that in the course of fulfilling it, I might come across certain of her visions. I had permission to read those: she charged me to look after her son and I must have the necessary knowledge."

Titus's brows shot up. "You never told me that—that she gave me into your charge."

Dalbert bowed his head. "It was a conscious choice on my part, sire. Her Highness had been too trusting by nature. Knowing the mission she had set out for you, I felt that you must hold your cards close to your chest—trust no one, if possible."

Titus gazed, flabbergasted, at this man he had known all his life. Not so much at what Dalbert said, but because all at once he saw Dalbert's influence on him, something he had been unaware of until this moment.

Trust no one. He had always believed that he had become as suspicious as he was simply because of his circumstances. But no, there had also been Dalbert's unobtrusive sway at work.

Together they had reinforced his isolation. In isolation there was safety. In isolation no one could betray his trust. He wondered now what Dalbert thought of the companions he had gathered along the way.

And the one he had left behind.

As if he had heard Titus, Dalbert said, "One must be careful to remain alive and free. But the point of staying alive and free long enough is to tackle the great task—and that cannot be accomplished alone. For that I am beyond grateful that Your Highness has found a fellowship of common purpose.

"I've known for many years that Your Highness has been charged to find the great elemental mage of our time. Like everyone else, I couldn't be entirely sure whether Your Highness had indeed found her. But like Atlantis, after the events of the Fourth of June, I also suspected that Lady Callista might be involved in some way.

"When I heard Atlantis had at last pried information from Lady Callista that she had long hidden about the elemental mage, I wanted to warn you in person, but couldn't as I didn't have authorization to take your personal translocator out of the Domain. When news came that you had disappeared and your belongings had been confiscated, I managed to get that go-ahead by arguing that someone from the Domain should also be on the scene."

"I've been wondering, Master Dalbert," said Kashkari, "when you arrived at Mrs. Dawlish's that day, how were you able to tell that I was a mage? Did you recognize my curtain as a flying carpet?"

"No, I'm sure I didn't, Master Kashkari. What caught my eye was the small altar in your room. You had the usual accoutrements of oil lamps, ghee, and spices. But instead of vermilion, the small heap of red powder on the plate was ground fire moss."

"Oh, I took it from home. I thought our altars were exactly the same as our nonmage neighbors'."

"They look quite similar, but ground fire moss is of a slightly different texture—and a more pungent scent, if one places a pinch close to the nose. So I chose to give the message concerning Lady Callista's confession to you. I didn't know whether you would be able to pass it along to His Highness, but it was a better chance than entrusting it to anyone else in that house.

"As I was leaving, I was detained by agents of Atlantis. Fortunately, I had the authorization, so I could honestly report that I'd simply been following orders. But still, half a dozen agents of Atlantis accompanied me on the way back.

"When I realized that they meant to interrogate me under truth serum, I made a getaway. I had anticipated trouble of the sort and had already removed my end of the message conveyor from the castle. Unfortunately, matters accelerated faster than I'd foreseen, and I hadn't yet had the opportunity to retrieve certain crucial items from the monastery—both the castle and the monastery have been under heavy guard by those in Atlantis's pay since the beginning of the summer.

"That's what I've been doing for the past few days. Getting into the monastery wasn't hard, but getting out proved quite a hassle. It was only last night that I succeeded in leaving undetected."

He took an item out of the bag he carried and placed it on the dining table. Titus almost rose out of his chair. "Hesperia's wand."

Which had also been his mother's.

Dalbert nodded and then brought out something else: The

monastery's copy of the Crucible. "Atlantis already confiscated the Citadel's copy and Your Highness's personal copy. I didn't want the last copy still in our possession to be found and taken."

Titus smoothed his fingers across the aged leather cover. "Thank you, Dalbert. My gratitude is immense. But you must know that it can no longer be used as a portal, not while the other copies are held by Atlantis."

"I beg to differ, sire. I heard from Miss Seabourne today while Your Highness was still in transit."

"Is she well?" The question left Titus like a shot.

They were only a thousand miles apart—they had been separated by far greater distances in the time they had known each other, or even during the past forty-eight hours. But this time it was not merely physical space that divided them, but the line between life and death.

He was already dead. But she could still live.

"She made no mention of her health," answered Dalbert, "but I feel confident in deducing that she is safe, at least."

Safe, at least. He supposed that was all he could ask for, though he wanted so much more. "And what did she say?"

"She reported that Master Kashkari received a message in the two-way notebook he had left behind. She begged Master Kashkari's pardon, but under the circumstances she felt she had no choice but to guess the password and read the message."

"I would have urged her to do the same," said Kashkari.

"The message was from Mrs. Hancock."

A collective intake of breath reverberated in the stone chamber.

"According to Miss Seabourne," Dalbert continued, "about a week ago, on the night of the disappearance of a student named West, the Oracle of Still Waters said to Mrs. Hancock something along the lines of 'Yes, you have seen it before.'"

"I remember that," said Titus. "Mrs. Hancock thought the Oracle meant the Crucible, which she had seen many times in my room, before I took it away."

"As it turned out, the Oracle did mean the Crucible, but a different copy, which Mrs. Hancock now remembers that she had seen in the library at Royalis."

Royalis was the lavish palatial complex in Lucidias, the capital of Atlantis.

This time Titus did leave his seat. "Fortune shield me. My grandfather told us the fourth copy of the Crucible had been lost. But it never had been."

Instead, Prince Gaius must have sent the copy as a gift to the Bane. That must be how he had sent in the exceptional spy who had managed to get a good look at the rings of defense outside the Commander's Palace.

And that copy of the Crucible had remained on the shelf of the library at Royalis all these years, gathering dust.

Dalbert also came to his feet. "I see the news pleases you, sire."

It did. And it terrified him too.

But he only nodded. Then he turned to Kashkari and Amara. "It would appear that we have found another way into Atlantis."

After they had gone over the logistics, Amara wished to spend some time in prayer and asked Kashkari to join her. This left Titus and Dalbert alone.

"Miss Seabourne asked that I keep an eye on your back, sire," said Dalbert. "May I take a look at it?"

Titus had nearly forgotten about his injury. Despite his strenuous day, his back had not hurt. Dalbert too pronounced himself satisfied—apparently the remedies had worked as they ought to and he did not need to be bandaged anymore.

They sat down again around the dining table. "Any more questions I can answer for you, sire?"

Dalbert knew him very well—something else Titus had failed to appreciate. He exhaled. He might as well, as the opportunity would not come again. "I encountered mentions of my father in my mother's diary for the first time this morning. You served my mother during the time of their courtship. What can you tell me about him?"

Dalbert seemed to be considering his choice of words. "He was . . . a simple man, simple in the best sense of the word—frank, kind, and lively without being silly or irresponsible. Had I a daughter or a sister, I would have been pleased if she'd brought home such a young man."

"But?"

"But my daughter or sister would not someday become the Mistress of the Domain. She would not be expected to face complicated and difficult situations—or deal with a hostile enemy that required the most careful and delicate of handling. Your father would not have been an asset to a woman in such an environment—but a liability. A princely house is no place for a man who does not understand treachery or deceit."

"Are you certain he does not understand such things? He is Sihar, is he not? Is it possible for a Sihar man to come of age without understanding something of the complexity and cruelty of the world?"

The Sihar, for their practice of blood magic, had long been shunned by the rest of the mage community. And though it was no longer acceptable to openly discriminate against the Sihar, the old bigotry had endured in subtler and sometimes more insidious new guises.

"You would think that the prejudice that surrounds them would breed bitterness in every Sihar heart. And yet I have found that is not always the case. Sometimes the response of those who receive a disproportionate share of the world's ugliness is a startling beauty of character, a warmth and joie de vivre that one cannot help but be attracted to and moved by. Yet I was convinced that he would wither if she were to make him her consort—it requires a certain sternness, a certain ruthlessness, if I may say so, to successfully wear the crown. Her Highness, as such, did not possess enough sangfroid. If she were to ally herself in marriage with a man even more temperamentally unsuited to rule . . .

"In any case, I recommended that she go about it the old-fashioned way: marry one of her barons to strengthen her position and keep her lover away from the gaze of the public. But Her Highness was an idealist. She didn't want to follow my advice, even though she acknowledged that it was sound.

"We disagreed strongly over the matter—it was probably the most strained our relationship had ever been. Then one day she came, distraught, and asked that I never seek to harm her beloved. I was hurt that she thought I would overstep my bounds to such an execrable extent, and I told her so.

"For the first time in all the years I'd known her, she wept. She told me that something terrible would befall him and begged me to promise her that it would not be at my hand or my instigation—as I was the only one in whom she had confided his identity, who had the means and motive to remove him from her life.

"To put her at ease, I volunteered to take a blood oath. She declined to bind me with one, saying that my word was good enough. She next agonized over what to do about her father. He was not opposed to a youthful indiscretion or two on her part, but she had kept her affair in extraordinary secrecy because she feared what he might do if he were to find out that her lover was Sihar. In the end she decided not to say anything to Prince Gaius and to marry only after she ascended to the throne, when no one could gainsay her—or arrange for her beloved to meet with an unfortunate accident.

"The second week of January 1014, your father went on his annual volunteering trip abroad. The Sihar community of the Domain is far wealthier than those in many other realms, and the young people of the community often traveled overseas to help their less fortunate kin—this was in the years before the January Uprising, when mages still had the freedom of instantaneous interrealm travel. Though Her Highness missed him desperately, she was glad he was away from the Domain, away from her father's caprices.

"He was expected to return in a fortnight, before the start of spring term, but he never did. When he was confirmed missing, I spoke to everyone who knew him. His friends who had gone abroad with him agreed that he started his return journey before they did, with every intention of resuming his everyday life in Delamer. But somewhere along the way he disappeared.

"I reported my findings to Her Highness. She rose, pale and shaken, and told me that she had already seen a snippet of my report in a vision—except she'd thought she would have more time.

"She asked me to keep searching. When every avenue of inquiry came to a dead end, she confronted her father at last. They had an awful row. He was adamant that he'd had nothing to do with it—that had he known, he would have indeed done something, but there would have been no secrecy, at least not between father and daughter. He would have let her see exactly how he'd deal with this unsuitable young man.

"She did not believe him. She told him that the child of 'this unsuitable young man' would sit on the throne. Well, you are the Master of the Domain, sire."

Titus gripped his hands together. "Do you believe Prince Gaius?"

"I don't know that I do. He certainly took pleasure in telling the ugly truth, but he was not above a convenient lie or two. After all, if he had been behind it, what was the point in confessing at that late stage?"

Titus nodded slowly. "Do I . . . do I look like him at all, my father?"

"You have something of his aspect, sire; but in the main, you bear a far greater resemblance to Her Highness."

"Did my mother keep any images of him?" Would he at last have a glimpse of his father? Would he recognize something of himself in the smile that his mother had loved so much?

"If she did, I did not find any among her belongings after her passing."

Disappointment cut sharp and deep—it was not to be, then. Titus should be accustomed to yet one more of his heart's desires not being granted, but the feeling of emptiness inside Titus only intensified.

He pushed aside the sensation of loss. "You said he was expected to return before the start of spring term. Was he a student?"

"Yes, sire. At the Royal Hesperia Institute." The Royal Hesperia Institute, situated at the other end of University Avenue from the Conservatory, had been built by the Sihar so that their children too could receive an advanced education. "He was a student of botany."

Realization dawned. "The vine that my mother loved to sit under? Did he give it to her?"

"Yes, sire."

How often had he seen his mother, caressing the stem or a leaf from the vine? And when was her room without a garland of the small golden flowers, draped over a mirror or a bedpost?

Titus swallowed the lump in his throat. "Am I named after him?"

"Yes, sire, you are. His name was Titus Constantinos. His father—"

"Was Eugenides Constantinos, who ran the Emporium of Fine Learning and Curiosities on University Avenue." Now it all made sense. "What happened to him?"

What happened to my grandfather?

"Titus was his only child, and I'm afraid the loss was too much. He sold his shop and moved back to Upper Marin March. He died a few years later."

And Mrs. Hinderstone had bought the place and opened her sweets shop, where Fairfax loved to go for pinemelon ice, not knowing that she was sitting in the very same spot where her fate was first written. And where his parents had met and fallen in love.

"Thank you, Dalbert," he said. "Let me not keep you with any more questions."

Much still needed to be done before they left the mountains.

Dalbert rose to his feet. "If I may, sire, I would like to accompany you."

It was tempting, terribly tempting, to say yes. "I would give my wand arm to have you. But war and destruction are coming to these shores, and you will be desperately needed here. You know who can be trusted. Help them to protect my people."

Dalbert inclined his head. "I understand, sire."

Titus rose and touched his forehead to Dalbert's. "Thank you, Master Dalbert. Thank you for everything all these years."

Dalbert, with a sheen of tears in his eyes, bowed and left.

Titus wiped the heels of his hands across his eyes as he watched the departure of the man who was the closest thing he had to a father figure.

There was nowhere to go now but Atlantis.

CHAPTER · 13

PALACE AVENUE, THE BIGGEST THOROUGHFARE in Delamer, passed before all five mage-made peninsulas that constituted the Right Hand of Titus. It was not the liveliest place at night, as most of the grand edifices on either side housed the various agencies and departments that ran the business of the realm—the House of Elberon had always understood that the trick to surviving a few incompetent rulers was a strong bureaucracy capable of seeing to the day-to-day operations of the Domain even if an idiot sat on the throne.

But usually one could expect to see some flow of traffic and pedestrians, attending a concert in the public parks or going down to the beach for a moonlight stroll. Tonight the avenue was utterly empty and the reasons, scores of them, hovered motionlessly overhead, each metallic bird shining a harsh light upon the capital city, which together mashed into an overbright ceiling that shut out the stars.

Armored chariots.

There were none directly above the Citadel, but the nearest one was at most a mile away. And for five miles around the Citadel, it was a no-vaulting zone.

Titus whispered a prayer and leaped onto his carpet. He shot out of the shadows of a grove of blue linden, crossed Palace Avenue, and sped up Citadel Boulevard. There were guards along Citadel Boulevard, but as he passed overhead, instead of challenging him, they saluted: the underside of the flying carpet glowed with the image of a phoenix and a wyvern guarding a shield that bore seven crowns, his personal standard.

The gate of the Citadel opened. He hurtled past, not slowing down until the walls of the palace itself blocked his way. Wrenching the carpet to a sudden stop, he jumped off onto the grand balcony.

What he was about to do offered neither strategic nor tactical advantage. In fact, it was a colossally inconvenient feat to attempt, for which he would have to sacrifice the last copy of the Crucible still in the House of Elberon's possession. But some things could not be helped. He was the sovereign of these lands, and on the eve of war, he must address his people.

He strode to a podium near the balustrade, placed both hands on its smooth, cool marble top, and recited the password and the countersign.

There came the sound of a small bell being struck, a soft reverberation that did not seem as if it would carry far. Yet it would be heard inside every home, classroom, and place of employment in the Domain, as would his voice.

Already, lights from the armored chariots were swinging toward the Citadel.

He inhaled deeply. "To the mages of this great city and this great realm, I speak to you as a crisis approaches. For months you have heard the rumors, of unrest far and near. But now Atlantis has declared hostilities upon us, upon all who will no longer tolerate its oppression. Protect yourselves, safeguard the ones you cherish, and shield those who cannot shield themselves. Better yet, fight for them.

"I cannot defend every one of you, but I will defend this realm to my last breath." Which would be drawn elsewhere, for he would never see his own country again. "Remember always: Fortune favors the brave."

The armored chariots careened toward him. And was it his imagination, or did he hear a faint but rising chorus of "and the brave make their own fortune"?

There was no time to listen more closely. He placed the Crucible on the podium. "I am the heir of the House of Elberon, and I am in mortal danger."

As the last syllable left his lips, a hand closed around his arm.

Titus flung the hand away, his wand drawn and pointed, his heart pounding. But the person who landed in the tall grass with a cry was not an Atlantean soldier. Her eyes round, her hands held out in a gesture of supplication, she cried, "Please don't hurt me, Titus!"

Aramia, Lady Callista's daughter.

Behind her, Sleeping Beauty's castle loomed in the distance, its turrets illuminated by light from torches and cressets far below. The dragons that guarded its entrance roared, a bit too loudly for the minor disturbance of their arrival on the meadow.

Instantly he was on alert, scanning the sky above.

"I wanted to tell you to get out," said Aramia, getting to her feet. "Uncle Alectus has already informed Atlantis of your presence at the Cit—"

Titus yanked her behind himself. *"Praesidium maximum!"*

The strongest shield he could summon was barely enough to defend them against a shower of swords and maces. He swore. Bewitched weapons of this quantity—provided someone had not been editing the stories—could only belong to the Enchantress of Skytower, who should be busy besieging Risgar's Redoubt.

Yet the massive silhouette outlined against the hills west of the meadows was none other than that of Skytower itself, a bulbous-looking stronghold set atop a huge rock formation roughly in the shape of a cone.

What the hell? Risgar's Redoubt was a good hundred miles away. And Skytower, for all its other impregnable virtues, did not travel terribly fast. To keep Kashkari and Amara safe, he had stowed them inside the Crucible before he approached the Citadel, no more than fifteen minutes ago. How had Skytower managed to cover so much distance in so little time?

And where were those two?

". . . me come with you."

He turned sharply toward Aramia. "What?"

She swallowed. "My mother will now always be known as the one who betrayed you and your elemental mage. I need to redeem her, to undo some of the damage she has unwittingly caused."

But he had already stopped listening. Kashkari and Amara zoomed toward him, pulling up into a vertical climb to check their breakneck speeds. Their carpets circled back and hovered ten feet overhead.

"Get off the ground!" shouted Amara. "Now!"

Belatedly Titus remembered that once the Enchantress's weapons dropped down, they only became more dangerous. He shook open his carpet, pushed Aramia onto it, and jumped on himself, gaining just enough altitude to avoid being hacked to pieces by a line of rampaging swords.

"That's the woman who crashed the party," said Aramia.

Titus ignored her and spoke to Kashkari. "When did Skytower get here?"

"An eternity ago," said Kashkari. "Or five minutes. You weren't kidding when you said it was dangerous inside the Crucible."

He had warned them in no uncertain terms to expect the worst when they got inside. But *he* had not expected this much trouble. As far as he could tell, the Crucible became more dangerous the longer it was kept open as a portal. When he had reentered the Crucible from the library of the Citadel to find the wyvern he had used for his steed lying in pieces on the meadow, the Crucible had been in use nearly an hour, if not more. But this time the Crucible had been open all of fifteen minutes.

"Praesidium maximum!" he cried, as another swarm of bewitched blades hurtled toward them, razor-edged and sibilant. He turned to Aramia. "Say 'And they lived happily ever after.'"

"No. I'm coming with you."

"You are not. Get out."

"You have to make me."

Under normal circumstances, he only had to take her by the arm, say the exit password, incapacitate her while they were outside, and then come back in again. But he could not possibly leave the Crucible right now, not when it must be surrounded by Atlantean soldiers on the grand balcony.

Nor could he push Aramia off the carpet and leave her to fend for herself until she came to her senses, not with the forest of hacking broadswords underneath them. And he did not have time to reason with her—Atlantean soldiers would follow them into the Crucible any moment now. But if she left the meadow, she would no longer be able to leave the Crucible at will, no matter how many times she shouted, "And they lived happily after!"

Not while the Crucible was being used as a portal.

"This is your chance to live."

She shook her head, her face set.

He swore and spoke to Kashkari and Amara instead. "North-northeast. Fast as you can."

He would just have to get rid of Aramia later.

"Who is she?" asked Kashkari as they sped in the direction Titus had specified.

"Lady Callista's daughter. She grabbed on to me when I got in."

"How can we trust her?" demanded Amara.

"If I go back out, the Atlanteans will interrogate me under truth serum," Aramia pleaded. "And they'll put me in the Inquisitory and keep me there, because they'll know that I wanted to come and help you."

"The Inquisitory is the better option for you," Titus said impatiently. "Where we are going, everyone will die."

"And it's that much worse than spending the remainder of my life in a windowless cell in the Inquisitory, never to see the sky again?"

His answer was unequivocal. "Yes."

Aramia fell quiet.

They flew at blistering speeds. Already they had passed over the market town from "Lilia, the Clever Thief." Dread Lake, in the distance, was visible by its waters, which glowed an eerie red. And beyond that . . .

"Where is she?" asked Aramia, shouting to be heard above the rush of air. "Where is the one who is my mother's real child?"

"She will not be coming with us."

Aramia's voice rose. "Why not? Isn't that why you have protected her all this while?"

He said nothing, but glanced behind. Dozens of wyverns were in pursuit, far enough away that they would not catch up in time.

He turned to Kashkari and Amara. "Remember, when we are escorted into the great hall, make absolutely sure you do not look at the lady."

"You already warned us against that before we entered the Crucible," said Amara.

Titus's grip tightened on the edge of the carpet. "Have I warned you that she looks exactly like Fairfax?"

Several portals had been set up in the Crucible. To go from the monastery's copy of the Crucible to the copy now in the grand library at Royalis, they must pass through a portal deep inside Black Bastion, the stronghold of Helgira the lightning-wielder and one of the most dangerous places in the Crucible. "My mother once saw Fairfax in a vision, standing atop Black Bastion. Afterward she changed the illustration for Helgira in all the copies of the Crucible to which she had access."

Kashkari and Amara exchanged a look.

"So I can see what she actually looks like, Iolanthe Seabourne?" murmured Aramia. "Is she as beautiful as Mother?"

"Other than the Inquisitor, every woman I know is more beautiful than Lady Callista."

His words did not sit well with Aramia. "Mother has never harmed you."

"Maybe not, but no one who is that selfish is ever truly beautiful. Kashkari, Durga Devi, start decelerating."

Black Bastion loomed ahead, massive and forbidding. The last time he had approached it had been when Fairfax saved him from a phantom-behemoth-riding Bane. He had trembled with gratitude as he had landed on the upper terrace and slid off his steed. And once he had realized that the young woman who stood waiting for him was not Helgira, but his faithful friend . . .

This time it would only be Helgira, ruthless and unforgiving.

Soldiers surrounded them the moment they landed on the rampart of Black Bastion. "We've been attacked!" Titus cried. "The Mad Wizard of Hollowcombe promised the peasants land and riches in exchange for our lives."

It was more or less the same ruse he had used the previous time he had passed through—except with the necessary changes to accommodate his three companions. The ruse worked more or less as well as it had earlier in getting the suspicious captain to summon his soldiers and escort them down the rampart into the fortress.

The great hall was merry and crowded. There was music and dancing. Helgira, clad all in white, her long black hair cascading, sat at the center of a long table upon a great dais, drinking from a chalice of gold.

He ought to know better. He did know better, and yet he stopped dead. Four spears pressed into his back—and already he could feel a dull throb where Helgira had sliced his arm open. Still he could not move a single step.

Behind him the captain chuckled, "Gets 'em bumpkins every time, she does."

The déjà vu was so strong he was dizzy.

Helgira raised her hand. The musicians halted. The dancers retreated to either side of the hall, clearing a path in the middle.

Titus was shoved forward. Slowly Helgira stood up. Already he felt her rage at his insolence. Watching her rise to her full height inspired the same dread and awe as seeing Fairfax's bolt of lightning, the one that surged up from the desert floor to take down half a dozen wyverns at once.

The captain smacked him on the side of his head and yelled at him for disrespect. He sank to his knees, but he did not lower his gaze as he repeated his tale. Let her knife slice through him again. What was a little blood and agony when he was already headed for his end?

She walked off the dais and slowly approached him. Had he finished telling his story? He had not the slightest idea. He only knew that he dared not say another word before the fury that emanated from her.

Had he enraged her this much last time? Did it matter?

"Forgive me, my lady," he croaked, not even certain what he was saying.

She slapped him so hard he was sure his neck snapped. Then she slapped him again, backhand, on his other cheek.

As he reeled, she growled, "You may rise and follow me, the four of you."

The sound of her voice stunned him. He remembered Helgira's voice, high and sharp. But the syllables that issued from the woman before him were low, almost gravelly.

She was not Helgira. She was *Fairfax*.

CHAPTER · 14

THE LETTER FROM LADY WINTERVALE to the Master of the Domain, dating from the beginning of his very first Half at Eton, read,

Your Noble, Serene Highness,

It is with both pleasure and sadness that I welcome you to England. I should not be here and neither should you. But since we are, we must make the best of it.

We Exiles have had to abandon a great many traditions, which probably explains the fervor with which I made a place at Eton for my son, Leander. You may not remember him, but he does remember you from his childhood days in the Domain, and he is very much looking forward to being your companion at school—a role my uncle served for your grandfather, and Lady Callista for your mother.

I always loved your mother dearly—many, many people loved her dearly. It was impossible not to be drawn to her kindness and the depth of her sincerity. Her death devastated me. And it devastates me to this day that no matter what I or anyone else does, she cannot be brought back.

But I see in Your Highness a spark of the greatness that she never had the chance to realize. I pray Leander can help you achieve that greatness—he aches for a purpose in life and longs to prove himself in the wider world. For now, I hope you will be good friends and faithful companions at Mrs. Dawlish's house.

The house is one step above a hovel, but changes that shake the world have come from unlikelier places.

Your humble servant,
Pleione Wintervale

P.S. Before he passed away, Baron Wintervale had commissioned a hot air balloon for Leander's tenth birthday, forgetting that his son is terrified of being that high above the ground. If Your Highness should be so inclined, the apparatus can be found in the main carriage house of Windsor Castle—before he passed away, Baron Wintervale and I often entertained at the English queen's home; his funeral, too, was held there.

Perhaps Your Highness will find the hot air balloon amusing. Consider it a gift, from someone who has never stopped mourning the loss of your mother.

As agents of Atlantis swarmed over Windsor Castle, Iolanthe said to Master Haywood, "I think I've got it. On my count, one, two, three."

She struck a match. It flared to life. At the same time, Master Haywood worked a force pump that was attached to two cans of paraffin oil, driving the fuel into an overhead cistern. Flames shot up into the opening of the hot air balloon's envelope. The balloon ascended farther.

"All right. Let's practice it a few more times."

They did. Then they practiced some more with Master Haywood striking the match. When he no longer looked as if these nonmage fire sticks were entirely foreign to him, they let the balloon go on rising as they strapped down the contents of the gondola.

They were high above Salisbury Plain, more than a hundred miles west of Windsor Castle. It had been Master Haywood who had pointed out that Iolanthe was being far too optimistic in thinking of going to Lady Wintervale for help getting back into the Domain.

"What's the first thing Atlantis would have done?" he'd asked her. "I've been in a similar situation, and I don't think the protocol has changed in the past six months. They would have interrogated her under truth serum, and she would have told them about every last interaction she'd had with you, including where you last met.

"And if they still keep Eton under a no-vaulting zone, do you think they wouldn't have kept a similar watch on that room in Windsor Castle, especially after they lost your trail in the desert?"

His doubts made all too much sense. But from what other quarter could she ask for help? Iolanthe had turned to Princess Ariadne's diary, which gave her nothing. In desperation, she reread the letter from Lady Wintervale to Titus, which she had only glanced at before.

The detail that leaped out at her was the location of Baron Wintervale's funeral, which affirmed Master Haywood's suspicions. Even if Lady Wintervale had been released from Atlantean custody in time to plan for her son's last rites, she would not have held his memorial in some little-known church in London, as stated in the notice in the *Times*, not when she had set her husband's pyre in the middle of the English queen's castle.

It was only as Iolanthe was once again restlessly pacing in the laboratory that it struck her: she ought to at least go and see whether the hot air balloon was still at Windsor Castle. When mages stowed their belongings among nonmages, such belongings remained undisturbed until either the original owner came for them or another mage searched specifically for those items. She had never heard Titus mention having gone on a hot air balloon ride, so there was a chance that the hot air balloon Baron Wintervale had commissioned for his son had remained undisturbed in the carriage house at Windsor.

And so it had. She and Master Haywood wove a series of otherwise spells, which compelled the castle's staff to transport the balloon and everything it came with to the railway station and into a luggage car. Meanwhile Iolanthe found a footman who knew the location of the parlor where she used to meet Lady Wintervale. About two hours after Iolanthe and Master Haywood's train departed Windsor and Eton Central Station, the footman delivered a small stone bust to the room.

The prince had had such a bust in his room at Mrs. Dawlish's, which would answer for him at lights-out when he was away elsewhere. Iolanthe dug up a similar bust in the laboratory and put it to good use: as they began their ascent in the hot air balloon, she wanted Atlantis's attention focused squarely on Eton, seeking her frantically in the vicinity, instead of widening the scope of the search.

With all the cargo in the gondola secured, Iolanthe donned a pair of goggles that had come with the hot air balloon and handed another pair to Master Haywood. "Ready?"

"Ready."

She gathered a fierce current of air and propelled the balloon toward the Atlantic.

Iolanthe sat in a corner of the gondola, her eyes half-closed, a pocket watch from the laboratory in hand. The watch, much like the one Titus carried on his person, worked as a timepiece. But more importantly, it also gave readings on their direction, altitude, and velocity. At one point she pushed the balloon to nearly 190 miles an hour, but that had proved too taxing even for the mage-reinforced lines that held the gondola—and for her too. After that she settled into a speed somewhere around 150 miles an hour.

Master Haywood, wrapped in an enormous fur coat, his eyes almost invisible behind the goggles, watched the skies, moving every few seconds from one side of the gondola to another, and from time to time murmuring a new far-seeing spell.

They were some three hundred miles southwest of Land's End when he shouted, without turning around, "I see something!"

Iolanthe exhaled and gradually—but not too slowly—let up on the air currents she had been herding. The balloon, subject to atmospheric conditions, began to drift northward.

"You are absolutely certain the Irreproducible Charm is intact?"

"Yes."

The Irreproducible Charm that had been set on her when she was an infant made it impossible for her image to be captured or transmitted outside the Crucible. As long as the charm remained intact, only those who had met her in person could recognize her.

"My God, what are those?" he shouted. "Come look, Miss Franklin!"

The act had begun, even though the enemy was still some distance away—in case anyone incoming could read lips.

Iolanthe rose to her feet, grabbed a rifle, and joined him at the side of the gondola. "Good gracious, are those Haast's eagles?"

"Can't be. Haast's eagles have been extinct for centuries—and they never inhabited any islands this far north."

They stared, agape, at the fast-approaching wyverns, the sound of whose wingbeats echoed in her ears, their brimstone odor already drifting into her nostrils. She shook without having to try.

"Christ almighty, what the hell?" Master Haywood's voice trembled too. "Are those . . . are they . . . *dragons?*"

With a thump, he fell to the floor of the gondola—it had been decided earlier that he should pretend to faint at the sight of any wyverns or Atlantean aerial vehicles. The rebels Titus had met in the desert oasis had done that, and Titus had never once questioned their authenticity as caravanists. Not to mention it would also spare Master Haywood, who had been in the Inquisitory for weeks and did not have an Irreproducible Charm protecting his image, from as much of the Atlanteans' attention as possible.

She aimed her rifle—another trick borrowed from the rebels of the Sahara—at the rider in the lead, whose steed now hovered only ten feet from the gondola.

"Come no closer or I'll shoot!" she cried, her voice cracking. "Who are you? *What* are you?"

"Who we are is none of your concern. Identify yourself and your companion and state where you are headed in this vessel."

"I am Adelia Franklin and this is John McDonald, my father's old batman. We are balloonists traveling from the Azores to England, to claim a— Keep your beasts away from the envelope of my balloon! We cannot have any scratches or burns."

"For what purpose do you undertake such a journey?"

"For money, what else?" she bellowed. "There is a prize of a thousand pounds for the first team to complete a thousand-mile journey without touching down before the end of the year. And we are not that far from England now. So if you would just get out of our—"

The lead wyvern rider waved a hand. Two of his subordinates urged their mounts forward, until they hovered just below the gondola. Getting up from their saddles, they grabbed the cables that wrapped all around the gondola and started climbing.

Iolanthe aimed her rifle at them. "You have no permission to come inside!"

"Put away that primitive weapon of yours, if you do not wish your balloon burned to a cinder," the leader of the wyvern riders said coldly.

The two Atlanteans inside the now-crowded gondola examined the burner, the ballasts, the additional containers of fuel, which had all been part and parcel of Baron Wintervale's commission. They also looked at the trunk of clothes, the tins of biscuits and potted meat, and the cooking and eating implements—Iolanthe had raided the kitchen, the pantry, and the laundry department at Windsor Castle, as well as borrowing a few rifles that belonged to the queen.

One of the Atlanteans nudged Master Haywood with a boot.

"What happened? Who are these ruffians disarranging our things? Where are my glasses? Let me put them on. Dear God in heaven, there is a—"

Master Haywood wilted again, his face conveniently pressed into the side of the gondola.

"Oh, for Christ's sake," shouted Iolanthe. "Look what you have done to the poor man. I can't operate this apparatus all by myself from here to England—it needs attention round the clock. Careful that you don't do anything rash with the fuel—it's highly combustible. And don't even think about throwing out one of the ballasts—it will make my balloon jump up right into the talons of your dragons overhead!"

How closely were the Atlanteans going to search everything? She wasn't worried about her watch. But their emergency bags, which she'd secured to the top of the balloon's inside envelope, would give them away immediately.

She summoned just enough air to jostle the gondola. The Atlanteans stumbled. She grabbed on to the side of the gondola too.

"Careful! Over the open ocean it's full of rogue air currents."

"What is this?" asked an Atlantean, pointing at the typing ball, which she had decided was worth the effort to drag along.

"Don't you know anything? It's a typewriter. Up so high fountain pens leak, so we use a typewriter for our daily logs."

But she had not thought to create a logbook ahead of time. What if they were to ask to see it?

She had better go on the offensive. "Anyway, who are you people? Those dragons of yours, mind if I snap a photograph of them? This is going to take the scientific world by storm—it'll make the Loch Ness Monster about as interesting as a lizard in a tub. My God, I could sell the negative to the *Times*! Where is my camera?"

She had also swiped one of those from the castle. The Atlantean nearest her yanked the apparatus from her hand.

"Hey, hey! You can't just toss my camera overboard."

The Atlanteans returned to their mounts and left without another word, while she screamed after them, "Where are you going? Come back here. You must compensate me for the destruction of my camera. That cost me twenty-five American dollars to buy when I was in New York City last!"

The flapping of dragon wings grew more distant. She kept on shouting for some time. Presently Master Haywood got up and came to stand next to her, staring at the retreating backs of the wyvern riders— to do anything else would be out of character for nonmages who'd been brought up on the idea that dragons were strictly fictional.

After the wyvern riders disappeared from view, there were no celebratory hugs. Instead they searched every inch of the interior of the gondola for any tracers the Atlantean might have left behind. Then they took advantage of a huge cloud bank and sailed into its midst for Iolanthe to check the outside of the gondola and even the outer envelope of the balloon itself.

They found eight tracers, six inside the gondola and two on the envelope. To keep them was to let Atlantis oversee their progress. To destroy them or throw them into the ocean below would be a clear signal that these seemingly convincing nonmages actually knew what tracers did.

Iolanthe agonized for ten minutes before she sprang into action. She cut the stiff silk from the skirts of one of the gowns she had swiped—yards and yards of fabric those gowns had—and secured it to a frame made from segments of wicker that she snipped from a picnic basket that held some of the foodstuff. Then she attached all the tracers to the kite and set it aloft with a gentle current.

It would float above the Atlantic, drifting with the wind, and signal a false location.

Once again, she applied strong currents to the balloon.

She had worried that by arriving while there was still daylight, they would be all too visible. But the weather cooperated. A band of rain covered the sky over Ondine Island, eighty miles east of the Domain's mainland, and they were able to land unseen, on the shoulder of a mountain that thrust up above the clouds.

Iolanthe picked out a message on the typing ball. Then she deflated the envelopes of the balloon and retrieved their emergency bags.

"So we wait?" asked Master Haywood.

"And have some tea."

The English queen's tea was quite good, as were her shortbread biscuits. Beneath their feet, the cloud cover extended for miles in every direction, made a warm gold by the light of the westerly sun.

"Remember when we went camping that time in the Siren Isles?" she asked.

They'd spent the night on a great conical peak not unlike this one. At dawn Master Haywood had awakened her to watch the sun rise over an ocean of fog that stretched from horizon to horizon. It had been one of the most indelible memories of her childhood, the beauty of that sunrise—and her complete happiness, to stand at the top of the world with the father figure she adored.

"Yes, I remember. You were five and you'd had your front tooth knocked out a month earlier, playing airframe-jousting with much older children. And you refused to have a cosmetic tooth put in— said the gap made you look scarier when you snarled."

She smiled a little. Elemental mages were almost always violent and overly energetic as tots, and she had been no exception. One of the older boys she jousted against had suffered a concussion—and had studiously avoided her for months afterward, gap-toothed snarl not required.

"I wonder if there would be time for us to stop by the campus of the Conservatory," said her guardian.

She sighed. "I doubt it."

She had very much wished to walk about Eton one last time. To say a proper good-bye to the boys who must still be wondering what had happened to their four friends.

So much of her life had been hasty departures and friends left behind when circumstances suddenly changed. And in the case of the Conservatory, it would be too painful to see the bare branches and fallen leaves, knowing she would never again be there to welcome the arrival of another spring.

She glanced at her guardian. "When we get to the mainland, there is a safe house in the Labyrinthine Mountains. It's chiseled into the rocks, has a supply of fresh water, and plenty of berry bushes and leafy plants scattered just outside—not to mention a pantry stocked with enough staples to last for years. Will you . . . will you consider staying there?"

Master Haywood's eyes had lit up as she'd described the safe house. But when he understood that she would not be making use of it, he shook his head.

"I have trained for this," she reasoned with him. "You haven't."

He placed another biscuit in her hand. "That is not entirely true. After Lady Callista asked for my help and before my memories were locked away, I made a rather thorough study of the deadlier archival magic spells."

Her eyes bulged. His research specialty had been archival magic, which dealt with the preservation of practices that had fallen out of popular usage. And while a good deal of sorcery became obsolete in time due to the development of better, easier, and faster spells, the more dangerous hexes and curses were often abandoned because they had been powered by self-sacrifice, which was no longer considered acceptable in this day and age.

"Besides, my dear, you are assuming that I'm driven by altruism. Nothing could be further from the truth. I'm driven entirely by selfishness—I'm coming with you because I won't be able to bear a life without you. So unless you can guarantee your safe return, there is nothing you can dangle before me to change my mind."

She bit the inside of her lip and shook her head. But before she could say anything, a man appeared, wand in hand. He was about Master Haywood's age, a little rotund, yet light on his feet as he moved.

Iolanthe had seen him before and he Iolanthe, though not while she was in human form.

"Master Dalbert," she said. "A pleasure to meet you at last."

CHAPTER · 15

TITUS FELT AS IF HE were plummeting, the bottom of the abyss rising all too fast.

"No." His denial was hoarse, almost inaudible. *"No."*

She should have been left behind. *Safely* behind.

He should have realized, when he saw Skytower at the meadow before Sleeping Beauty's castle, that the Crucible had not been open for mere minutes, but at least several hours. And Dalbert knew—and had said nothing.

"No?" Fairfax narrowed her eyes, eyes as ruthless as Helgira's. "Then perhaps I should have you escorted to my dungeon. It is a most hospitable place for mages who say no."

She would do it. She would have him locked up in the bowels of Black Bastion while she ventured forth to her doom.

He shook. "Please reconsider, my lady. Please."

Please stay here. Please come no farther. Please do not make me watch you die.

Around him, his companions were rising, since she had ordered them to their feet. Titus remained on his knees.

"Get up or be dragged to the dungeon," she said softly, coldly.

He gazed up at her pitiless features, his cheeks still stinging with the imprints of her hand. "Please, I beg you."

Her expression seemed to soften. His heart leaped—the last time they had been in Black Bastion together, she had looked at him exactly like this, with both fury and tenderness. And it had been the beginning of the happiest time of his life.

"Blindfolds," she said.

Soldiers blindfolded Titus and everyone he had brought. The strip of black cloth over his eyes tightened into a band he could not remove.

"No!" he shouted in panic, as someone pulled him to his feet and shoved him forward. "You cannot send me to the dungeon."

"Then shut up and walk," came her curt reply from somewhere behind him.

The sounds of footfalls were all around him. He could not tell where Kashkari or Amara were, though occasionally Aramia whimpered a few feet to his right. They were escorted down corridor after corridor, and up steep flights of stairs—heading toward Helgira's bedchamber, the prayer alcove of which served as the actual portal.

What could he do? The guards' weapons were at his back again, and when he walked too slowly he felt the chill of the sharp points of their spears, spears that could travel more than a mile to hunt him down.

They came to a sudden stop.

"I have changed my mind about the young woman in the green overrobe," said Fairfax. "About thirty-five miles south-southwest of here stands an empty castle surrounded by bramble and guarded by dragons. Take her to the meadow west of the castle and leave her there."

"Please, please don't!" cried Aramia. "My mother—and yours— if the Bane doesn't fall, she will never leave the Inquisitory."

So she had figured out that they were dealing not with Helgira, but Fairfax.

"And that should concern me?" Fairfax countered flatly.

"Everything she has ever done was to keep you safe."

"Everything she has ever done and will ever do is to keep *herself* safe. The sooner you realize that, the sooner you will stop making excuses for her."

Aramia made a sobbing sound. "I know you don't think of her as your mother, but she is my mother and she has never been unkind to me. Please let me do what I can to help her—and you. I am far more useful than I look."

"If I may," said Kashkari. "The meadow before Sleeping Beauty's castle is something of a war zone right now. Skytower is in the vicinity, and my lady's soldiers might have trouble getting through."

Titus could almost see Fairfax's lips twist. "We are going to die, Miss Tiberius, every single one of us. If you wish to die for Lady Callista, that is your choice. But the moment you become a hindrance, you will be left behind to fend for yourself."

A door opened and closed, her footsteps disappearing inside. The door opened again. Titus was once more made to move. He kept trying spells that would undo the blindfold. But some older forms of magic had no exact modern counterparts.

A few seconds later their blindfolds were removed. He recognized the interior of Helgira's bedchamber. Haywood stood near the door, listening. Fairfax, across the room, was no longer in the wig or the white dress, but a simple blue tunic and trousers, her short hair still mussed from the wig's removal.

"Don't try anything," said Fairfax, her voice uninflected. "We are already in the copy of the Crucible on Atlantis. And I have sealed the connection."

His blood ran cold. He had thought she had only marched them into Helgira's bedchamber. But no, she had already guided them past the prayer alcove inside the bedchamber, which served as the actual portal.

Why? Why will you not let me save you?

"So it really is you," said Kashkari, shaking his head a little.

She nodded. "You should know, though, the lady of the fortress in this copy of the Crucible looks nothing like me, but fortunately,

I was able to convince her that I was a messenger from her beloved Rumis and that he is in trouble. So Helgira is temporarily absent. We'd best leave before she comes back."

"But—" said Kashkari.

"Miss Tiberius, would you mind keeping my guardian company for a minute?"

Aramia looked at Fairfax, then glanced at Titus. He signaled her to go to Haywood as Fairfax had ordered. She did so, dragging her feet as she went.

When she was no longer a part of their cluster, Fairfax set a sound circle around the four of them. "The Bane will not succeed in sacrificing me."

"What do you mean?" asked Amara, her voice tense.

"A mage who dies from sacrificial magic looks nothing like the neat, highly recognizable corpse Kashkari saw."

Relief spiked through Titus, until he realized that not dying from sacrificial magic did not imply that she would live. By coming with them, she would still die.

"My guardian understood this and didn't tell you." She shrugged. "But anyway, I'm here now."

"So you've been in the Crucible all this while, waiting for us," said Kashkari.

"And clearing the way for you. The prince still carries a scar from the last time he came through."

"But why wait until now to reveal yourself?" asked Amara. "Why didn't you meet us at the safe house?"

Fairfax looked at Titus. "Because His Highness here would have done everything in his power to leave me behind again—that I will not die from sacrificial magic makes no difference to him. Am I not correct, Your Highness?"

He said nothing. Of course she was right. He would give up his own life, but never hers. Never willingly or knowingly.

He was as selfish about her as his grandfather had been about the throne.

"Well, I for one am glad you are here," said Amara. "But what should we do about that girl? I don't trust her and neither does anyone else."

"Unfortunately, Black Bastion is no place to abandon a battle-hardened warrior, let alone someone who has led a sheltered life—and when the Crucible is being used as a portal, entries and exits are only possible on the meadow before Sleeping Beauty's castle. I say we take her there and leave her."

"The meadow is not always a safe place." Titus spoke for the first time since they had arrived in this copy of the Crucible. "And the longer the Crucible remains in use as a portal, the more dangerous and unpredictable it becomes. How long were you in the other copy of the Crucible?"

"We were at Black Bastion for about two and half hours before you arrived." She sounded reluctant, as if she still did not want to speak to him.

"So the Crucible had been open about three hours altogether before I reached the meadow, with Miss Tiberius hanging on to me. It was a scene of lethal chaos."

"We'll make sure she has the password to exit."

"But after she gets out, she will be on *Atlantis*," Kashkari pointed out. "It will be no time at all before she is arrested and interrogated. And then the Bane will know *we* are inside Atlantean borders."

"Master Haywood is working to suppress her memory of the past twenty-four hours. She will be unconscious after that, which will give us time to travel to the meadow. And we will stay with her until she starts to come to and leave a note in her hand before we go. That way, even if she exits the Crucible directly into the waiting embrace of the Bane, she won't be able to tell him anything."

"How can your guardian achieve that?" asked Kashkari. "You are speaking of precision memory magic, and that is contact requisite. How would he have accumulated all those hours of contact with her?"

"She was born Iolanthe Seabourne, the child of two poor students. Her birth was quite a bit premature and necessitated a long stay in the hospital. The physicians recommended as much physical contact as possible, to help her develop. Her parents had to remain in school—their scholarships were their only sources of income—and couldn't stay with her as much as they wanted to. So they recruited their friends to go in their stead and hold her. My guardian went many times, often for four or five hours at a stretch—that was how he accumulated enough hours of contact."

Fairfax's lips flattened. It came to Titus that this must have been a story she had loved hearing: her guardian, devoted to her from day one. But it had been a different infant in his arms, someone else altogether.

Amara exhaled. "I still don't like it. But I suppose when there is no good solution, we must accept the least terrible one."

Fairfax, who had been watching her guardian, frowned. Titus looked in the direction of her gaze. The sound circle only blocked the sounds inside from traveling out; they could hear Aramia talking animatedly about Lady Callista, glad to have at last found a receptive audience.

Haywood waited until Aramia had come to a stop, then excused himself.

"Would you mind keeping Miss Tiberius company for a minute, Kashkari?" asked Fairfax.

Kashkari was nonplussed, but he left readily enough. They redrew the sound circle to include Haywood.

"My spell didn't work, and I can't understand why," said Haywood. "I could have sworn I'd held her for at least seventy-two hours."

"You have," said Fairfax. "I saw the visitors' log of the Royal Hesperia Hospital with my own eyes."

"But the spell refused to take."

Fairfax pressed the heels of her palms against her temples.

"There's something not quite right about all this. But never mind that. Can you do this instead, Master Haywood: wait until we are on the meadow, ready to exit, then use a blunt force memory spell on her?"

Haywood grimaced but nodded.

Fairfax erased the sound circle and opened the shutter outside the window. "Get on your carpets, everyone. We are leaving."

Titus climbed onto Iolanthe's carpet. It hurt to look at him: he seemed a mere husk of his former self.

He took her hand. She shook his grip loose as she accelerated, leaving Black Bastion behind.

"We are all going to die soon," he said, his voice barely audible. "Do you really wish to waste time being angry at me?"

"Yes," she hissed. "I remain an unrepentant optimist. If I see that I am about to die, or you, I will forgive you. But not until then, you bastard."

She hadn't called him "bastard" since the earliest days of their acquaintance.

"I will not apologize, you know. We all thought you would end up being used for sacrificial magic, and that must be avoided at all costs."

"And have I asked you to apologize for that? No. But you had better grovel hard for your high-handed methods. You *drugged* me. Were you out of your mind?"

"Yes."

She was taken aback by his admission. "That was no excuse. You've lived through many trying situations. You should have been able to think more clearly."

He said nothing for a long time. Then he sighed. "I am sorry for my methods. I panicked. And when I panicked, all I could think about was myself, how I could not go on knowing that the hour of your death had already been declared. Forgive me."

What could she say to something like that? How could she maintain her anger in the face of his despair?

He pulled the hood of her tunic more closely about her head—the temperature was nowhere near as frigid as that of the north of Scotland, but the night air was still chilly. "Please. We have so little time."

And they hurtled at such a breakneck speed toward that eventual rendezvous with destiny.

"When we are in the Crucible," he said, "we are in a folded space, much like the inside of the laboratory—and our location cannot be pinpointed. But the moment we exit, we will be on Atlantis itself."

Which wouldn't be long now—already the turrets of Sleeping Beauty's castle were visible in the distance.

"In case conditions are adverse once we leave the Crucible and I do not have the that one last opportunity, Fairfax . . . I love you."

Once upon a time they'd had a falling-out because he had not wanted them to act on their feelings for each other—he had thought love would interfere with their task, would make them weak and indecisive.

Now she wondered whether he hadn't been right after all. Until this moment she had been driven by rage, which was a despot of an emotion: when rage ruled, it ruled alone; the mind was void of everything except anger.

But now that he had defused her wrath, now that he had brought up love, fear came rushing back: fear of loss, fear of dying, fear of failing in the end, after every sacrifice had been made.

She did not say anything. But this time, when he took her hand again, she did not push him away.

CHAPTER · 16

THE MEADOW BEFORE SLEEPING BEAUTY'S castle seemed peaceful enough—they had not been in this copy of the Crucible long enough yet for all hell to break loose. Still Kashkari and Amara, who had borne the brunt of the chaos in the other copy, held their wands tightly and circled again and again before they deemed it safe to land.

"No sign of Skytower, at least," said Kashkari.

Fairfax and her guardian stood with their hands clasped, their heads bent toward each other, speaking in voices too soft for Titus to hear. They were probably discussing how best to get rid of Aramia without causing the latter grave bodily damage, but the sight of their closeness, their obvious affection for and reliance upon each other, made his heart constrict.

"So where is this copy of the Crucible?" asked Aramia.

No one answered.

"We will be on Atlantis, won't we, once we exit?" Her voice quavered.

Still no answer.

"Fortune shield me." She bit her lower lip. "And are you planning to leave me behind here?"

"It would be for the best," said Fairfax.

"Maybe, if you were headed elsewhere. But here it would be a mistake. What do you know of Atlantis?"

Fairfax glanced Titus's way. They had studied, as much as they could, everything about Atlantis that might be relevant to their tasks—he more than she, as he had been at it for far longer. The problem was, the information they had was often out of date.

Atlantis, when it had been poor and on the verge of destroying itself, had been of little interest to the more prosperous and powerful mage realms. And when its fortune had turned, it had likewise shunned close diplomatic ties with the wider world. No doubt the Bane's desire to keep his secret at any cost also played a role—if the rest of the world did not know anything about Atlantis, they would have a much more difficult time coming after him.

Titus had read most of the books and articles about Atlantis that could be dug up and studied the rudimentary maps that the more adventurous mages of yesteryear had made. From time to time, Dalbert, in his unobtrusive way, would present Titus with a report. But even Dalbert could only do so much.

"Aha," said Aramia triumphantly. "As I thought, you know the depth of your ignorance. But my mother always collected intelligence everywhere she went, and everyone *loved* to confide in her."

Haywood winced. Fairfax narrowed her eyes at Aramia, who gulped. In the Sahara Desert, Titus had called Fairfax "the scariest girl in the world." Aramia obviously agreed with him.

But she carried on, if visibly less smug. "It's nighttime outside. Do you know Atlantis has had a curfew in place for decades?"

"Of course," retorted Amara. "That's common knowledge."

"So it may be. But do you also know that the towns and cities of Atlantis are brightly lit at night?"

She looked around. This time, no one told her that she was repeating old chestnuts.

"Well, they are," Aramia continued. "Except for the biggest boulevards, which are continually patrolled, most streets do not have trees, but short, neatly trimmed shrubs that offer very few hiding places. Even the architecture is unfriendly to any illicit activity— there are no narrow alleys between houses where one might hide from the night patrol. And houses with their backs to each other do not share a common garden, as they sometimes do in the Domain. Even with raising land from the ocean, terrain suitable for construction is always at a premium on Atlantis, so their houses and apartment buildings simply back into one another with no spaces in between, and the communal gardens are on the roofs, which, again, have flowers and shrubs but no trees, making it very easy for patrols to see everything."

Every word she uttered was unwelcome news. Not that Titus had counted on arriving at night to be an advantage—he too knew about the long-standing curfew and understood movements at night to be potentially troublesome. But Aramia's information revealed just how profoundly uninformed he was about Atlantis as a society—it would be almost impossible for them to be in the open without betraying themselves.

If Fairfax felt as he did, she did not reveal it. "It isn't enough for you to point out what we don't know. What solutions can you offer to help us counter such disadvantages?"

"Obviously I've never stepped onto Atlantis either. But I do know that Atlanteans themselves have found various ways around the curfew. There are mages who have legitimate excuses to be abroad at night: private security guards, late shift workers, or technicians who are summoned for emergency repairs—and I believe it is a fairly common practice to either barter favors with them or bribe them outright for their night passes."

"And you think we can do that without being immediately reported? Wouldn't most people have already arranged for these night passes before they left their houses in the evening?"

"There are always those who fail to plan ahead. They'll have to pay more, of course." Aramia looked around at them. "Is this copy of the Crucible in Lucidias?"

She received no answer, but that was apparently enough answer for her. "My mother knows about the tunnels underneath the city. Roads leading in and out of Lucidias have checkpoints. If we can get into the tunnels, then we can avoid the authorities altogether."

"How do we get into the tunnels?" Fairfax asked.

"That I cannot divulge until we leave the Crucible. I've seen first-hand how dangerous it can become when it is used as a portal." Aramia smiled. "Anyway, shall we make our exit? It won't be safe to stay here for much longer."

The moment Titus left the Crucible—and stepped onto Atlantis—his long-suppressed memory dropped back into his head, piercingly, regrettably vivid. Normal memories faded and distorted over time, but those that had been suppressed always reemerged with perfect clarity and accuracy.

He had been thirteen, in his first Summer Half at Eton, rowing on the Thames River with a scowl. He hated rowing, he hated this school, and he hated England: frankly, there was not a single aspect about his life he did not detest resoundingly.

At the end of two miles going upstream, they turned around to head for the boathouse. The crew sat with their backs to their destination, so Titus happened to be facing west. For an entire week, it had been drizzly. But now the clouds parted, and the sunlight that fell upon him had such a rich, saturated golden hue that it took his breath away.

And then one of the other three rowers in the boat, a boy named St. John who also lived in Mrs. Dawlish's house, his mood probably likewise buoyed by the sudden flood of light, said, "Tell me this, who is the greatest chicken-killer in Shakespeare?"

Titus rolled his eyes. He regarded the nonmage boys with whom he was forced to share the school as absolute bumpkins—absolute and incomprehensible bumpkins.

"Who?" asked another boy.

"Macbeth!" St. John cried. "Because he did murder most foul. Get it? Murder most *fowl*?"

The other two rowers groaned. Titus very nearly smiled: he had actually understood the joke and found it rather ticklish.

And when they had pulled the boat ashore and started walking back toward their resident houses, instead of feeling sore and grumpy, as he usually did, he felt strong and . . . almost happy.

The sensation startled him. His mind raced: perhaps being sent to school in a nonmage realm was not the punishment he had always believed it to be. Here he was just another boy, without the tedium of court etiquette or the weight of a country's expectations. And if he tried, he might come to enjoy such an adolescence, far from everything he hated about being the Master of the Domain.

And maybe, just maybe, he could even ignore for a few years the demands his mother had put on him. After he had thoroughly enjoyed himself, the Bane would still be there. What was the hurry? What was the harm in not spending every spare second preparing himself?

The vista of possibilities that opened before him was dizzying. He could have fun. He could have friends. And he even knew exactly how he would go about making friends—the hot air balloon that Lady Wintervale had told him about, still sitting in the carriage house at Windsor Castle, which would make for a grand eye-opener for the boys at Mrs. Dawlish's house.

His excitement kept building. He never knew he could have this many ideas about having fun. Back at Mrs. Dawlish's, after he had changed and washed, he sat down to imagine some more of this potentially sublime future.

By habit he knocked his finger against the cover of *Lexikon der Klassischen Altertumskunde* and turned the German reference book back to what it really was, his mother's diary. Again by habit, he began turning the blank pages. But his mind was not on the diary: he was already thinking about what he could do to make Wintervale feel included, when the latter would rather jump off a cliff than ride in a hot air balloon.

By chance he looked down and was astonished to see writing on the pages. The diary was the one true link he had to his mother, and its revelations were rare enough that his heart pounded. What did he need to know now?

25 April, YD 1021

The day before she died.

This is the worst yet, a blow so heavy that I am prostrate with grief.

It is a world on fire, everything burning. Somehow I discern figures flying through the storm of smoke. They are pursued urgently, by mages on wyverns towing spell accelerators.

Distance spell-casting can be deadly. Many incantations of the genre mete out mortal damage. And only the best equip themselves with spell accelerators.

I hold my breath. The very sky seems to be aflame. Spells fly. One of the fleeing mages falls. "No!" A scream pierces the night. "No!"

The falling mage does not strike ground. Instead some force breaks his fall twenty feet in the air. A flying carpet zooms down, and the rider pulls his body onto the carpet.

"Revivisce omnino!" *the rider cries hoarsely.* "Revivisce omnino!"

The fallen mage shows no reaction at all. He is dead then.

The spell is a powerful one, but not even the most powerful reviving spells can bring a mage back from the dead.

"Don't you dare die! Not now! Don't you dare, Titus!"

No, not my Titus.

Then I see his face, and it is my child, no older than his late adolescence and already felled.

As the world burns.

The vision has faded, but the damage is done. I have been destroyed.

Only yesterday I made Titus promise that he would do everything in his power to topple the Bane. He did, my solemn child who already had the weight of the world on his shoulders.

And this was his reward for that promise, a brutally short life and a violent death.

I have never hated myself more.

Next to me my son sleeps soundly. I kept him up deep into the night, wanting to spend as much time with him as possible before my execution. And he gamely stayed awake until exhaustion overtook him.

Could I? Could I, when he woke up in the morning, tell him to forget about Atlantis altogether and simply enjoy all the privileges that came with his station in life?

I almost shook him awake to do just that. But with my hand on his shoulder, I could proceed no further. One does not stand in the way of a future that has been revealed, not even if one were a vessel of the Angels.

After a long time of further hesitation, I opened my diary, which hardly leaves my side these days, and recorded this vision, placing it just behind the one in which I saw him moving about surreptitiously in the library of the Citadel, followed by a scene of Alectus and Callista crowded around the Inquisitor. I have not the slightest idea whether these visions form one unbroken thread of the future, but Titus, in the moment of his death, had on a hooded tunic that looked very much like the one he had worn in that vision.

When I am done, I will take my child's hand and rest it against my cheek and I will apologize to him silently, endlessly. It will not make up for what I will take from him, but there is not much else that I can do.

Forgive me, my son.

Forgive me.

Titus could scarcely understand his mother's words—the pages shook badly. And when he set the diary on his desk and clenched his still trembling hands at his sides, he found that he still could not see the letters—not through the moisture in his eyes that blurred and distorted every line.

The last words she had spoken to him, minutes before her execution, had been, *Not all will be lost.* And always he had comforted himself with the belief that she had found some measure of peace and equanimity.

Instead she had gone to her death shattered by what would happen to him.

Tears rolled down his face. He was already an adolescent. How much time did he have left? *How much?* Was it enough to accomplish this great task she had thrust upon him? In the Beyond, when they met again, he would like to reassure her that his years had not been brutally short after all, for no one who toppled the Bane could be said to have lived anything less than a remarkably full life.

But he had not even found the great elemental mage yet. And

there was no telling how much longer it would take him. He buried his face in his hands. He would have to be far more prepared than he was.

Far, far more prepared.

A burst of laughter came from somewhere outside his door. A gaggle of other junior boys were talking together in the corridor, planning for something fun. With a needle-stab in his heart, he remembered his brief hour of almost-happiness, of the possibility of a normal life.

There was no question of that now—no newly made friends or legendary outings on the hot air balloon. There would be only work. And then, after that, more work.

He pulled out his wand, pointed it at the corner of the last page of the vision, and marked it with a skull symbol. And then he pointed the wand at his own temple.

Titus swayed.

He had lied to himself. The suppression of the memory had never been about forgetting its particular details, but all about not remembering his mother's utter heartbreak—and that soap-bubble-in-the-sun moment when he could have taken his life down a very different path.

Someone squeezed his hand—Fairfax. "Are you all right?"

He nodded.

No one else seemed to notice him. They were all busily—and

warily—examining their new surroundings. He had hoped they would find themselves in the cavernous interior of a state library, housed in a palace so opulent that it bankrupted the royal treasury and caused the downfall of the last king of Atlantis.

What he had not expected was a cramped, disorderly study, full of books on every horizontal surface. The light spilling in from the gap between the curtains illuminated plates littered with cake crumbs and bits of bread crust, cups with dried rings of tea at the bottom, and a miscellany of slippers and socks under the big desk before the window.

Fairfax touched her palm to his face. "Are you *sure* you are all right?"

He shook his head. He was only so brave—and no braver.

"I'll keep you safe," she said.

His heart leaped a little. "Have you forgiven me?"

"You overestimate my magnanimity. I'm not done slapping you yet—and that's why you aren't going to die anytime soon."

The corners of his lips lifted slightly.

The pad of her thumb caressed his cheek. "Remember that."

Kashkari was the first to state the obvious. "I don't believe we are in the grand library of Royalis—at least not in the stacks."

"Is that where we are supposed to be?" Aramia asked, her voice squeaky. "If so, could we be in a librarian's office?"

Haywood, who was peering out from behind the curtains, answered, "Doesn't seem like it, unless the library at Royalis is surrounded by an ordinary residential street. We are several floors up, by the way."

Titus looked out the window himself. The street below was lit as if for an evening event, except it was echoingly empty. Lining the sidewalks were perfectly spherical bushes trimmed to less than two feet in diameter. The apartment buildings opposite, of fewer stories than the one in which he stood, were joined at the seams and smooth of facade. The communal garden on the roof was nice enough, even in the harsh light that flooded it; but it, too, offered no nooks or crannies where a toddler could conceal himself, let alone a full-grown mage.

Then he realized that the buildings across the street were not shorter, but were situated lower—they were on a slope. And he had a clear view all the way to the waterfront and the sea beyond. The maelstrom of Atlantis was fifty miles from the coast and too far to see, but Lucidias was a rather remarkable place in and of itself, a great metropolis built on the slenderest ribbon of workable land, a city that was largely new and seemingly perfectly regulated.

There were certain districts in Delamer that never slept—at most they quieted for an hour or so before dawn. The waterfront near Delamer Harbor was one such place. But its equivalent in Lucidias was as empty as a classroom during school holiday.

Little wonder, when it too was lit like an outdoor stage. Where was the source of the light? He looked up—and the hair on the back of his neck rose. Something hung high above the waterfront, something enormous. A floating fortress that was very nearly the size of the Citadel, light flooding out from its belly.

Across the room, Kashkari opened the door a crack and peered out. "Looks like an apartment of some kind."

Titus was about to reach for Fairfax and alert her to the floating fortress when she said, "Shhh."

Kashkari immediately closed the door. Titus listened, his head bent. A bed creaked somewhere in the apartment. Footsteps, then the sound of a commode being used. More shuffling steps, and a body of seemingly considerable weight fell into a mattress, making the bed groan just a little.

Titus exhaled.

"Here, look at this," Aramia whispered, even though they had a sound circle in place.

She had turned a coat hanging on the back of the door inside out. On the lining was sewn a label that said, *If found, please return to Professor Pelias Pelion, 25 Halcyons Boulevard, University District, Lucidias.*

"I think I can guess what happened," continued Aramia. "The book was in the grand library. But even books in a grand library can be loaned out, especially to those with academic credentials. Professor Pelion borrowed the Crucible, and that's why we are in his home."

This was a problem. In the library they could expect to wait undisturbed until morning before venturing out, to avoid running afoul of the curfew. But in a private home, with a restless sleeper . . .

"What about the option Miss Tiberius mentioned?" said Haywood. "That of bribing a night worker?"

Kashkari frowned. "Where do we find a night worker?"

"Shouldn't there be one in such a building?" asked Haywood. "If only to make sure no one slips out during the curfew hours?"

"I can go down and have a look," said Kashkari.

Fairfax held up her hand. Titus heard it too: someone had bumped into something, and that sound came from the opposite end of the apartment from the professor's bedroom.

It was easy enough for a careful mage to stop a door or a floor from creaking, but an accidental collision still made sounds.

Was it the professor's adolescent child sneaking back home after a wild night out? Or perhaps even his servant? Or was that too benign a direction of thought? Had the Bane somehow already discovered the exact place to capture those who had come for his downfall?

They took up positions on either side of the door. Outside the wind howled. The professor coughed in his bedroom, an explosive noise in the quiet of the night.

The door opened, slowly, soundlessly. A short, squat, masked figure tiptoed inside, closed the door—and crumpled sideways.

Kashkari sprang forward, caught the intruder, and laid the mage on the rug before the professor's desk. Titus sneaked a look into the corridor to make sure no one else was coming.

Then he closed the door again and nodded at Kashkari, who peeled back the mask from the intruder's face.

He, Kashkari, and Fairfax sucked in a collective breath.

Mrs. Hancock.

CHAPTER ⋅ 17

KASHKARI HAD USED A FAIRLY mild stunning spell. It was not long before they brought Mrs. Hancock around.

Fear flooded her eyes as she found herself surrounded, but she relaxed somewhat once she recognized the faces closest to her. "You are already here," she whispered.

"Sorry for striking you unconscious," said Kashkari, the volume of his voice just as low.

The professor, on his bed, coughed again.

"Go back into the book," said Mrs. Hancock. "Let me take you to my place. We'll be safer there."

Titus hesitated. If Mrs. Hancock was now acting on Atlantis's behalf, then they were doomed. But then he recalled that Mrs. Hancock was bound by a blood oath not to harm either him or Fairfax. "All right, but let me close the book and reopen it, so that it will be safer inside."

He had come out of the Crucible with a brooch he had picked up from the top of Helgira's ivory-inlaid chest. When the Crucible was used as a portal and something was brought out, then the book did not "close," and one could quickly return.

But the inside of the Crucible became increasingly dangerous if it was left "open" for too long. "I'll come with you," said Fairfax.

They returned to the Crucible with wands drawn. No shower of swords and maces rained down upon them, but strange creatures were emerging from the woods west of the meadow, skulking toward Sleeping Beauty's castle.

At the sight of a band of ogres, Titus quickly dropped the brooch to the ground and said, holding on to Fairfax's hand, "And they lived happily ever after."

Three minutes later, the entire company that had come to Atlantis was once again on the meadow, which looked peaceful enough for the moment.

"What could possibly draw so many characters from so many tales this way?" asked Fairfax.

Titus was already setting up a perimeter defense. "It might be Sleeping Beauty's story. I have a vague recollection of my mother telling me that some previous prince or princess had added the description of a stupendous treasure hidden inside the castle. But my mother did not like how crowded that made the area around the castle—the lure of lucre is apparently much stronger than the lure of Sleeping Beauty herself—so she stripped out that addition in her copy of the Crucible, which later became my copy.

"I did not see evidence of anyone streaming toward the castle in the Citadel's copy. But that one had a phantom behemoth guarding the castle, and I would say that is in itself more than enough to keep away those who are merely greedy and opportunistic."

Fairfax looked at him with narrowed eyes.

Suddenly he remembered that once upon a time he had refused to let her look at Sleeping Beauty in his copy of the Crucible. In the days before they trusted each other completely, he had modified Sleeping Beauty in his copy of the Crucible to look exactly like her—and had not wanted her to know or guess why he would not allow her to ascend to the garret of the castle where the princess slept her years away.

"When we get to Mrs. Hancock's house," he said, "I will take a look at the text of Sleeping Beauty's story and see if I can undo the change."

She plucked a blade of the knee-high grass that covered the meadow. "Maybe not."

"Why not?" asked her guardian.

"It might confer an advantage on the way back: those of us still left standing will know what to expect; Atlantis, not so much."

He supposed it was true that other than Fairfax and himself, no one else had been prophesied to die. That meant nothing, however, when it came to their chances of survival. But he did not want to say no to her—they had so little time left. "I will leave it as it is then."

"I hope some of you live to take advantage of that," she said to the company.

Haywood winced. Kashkari looked grim; Aramia, suitably afraid.

The only one who seemed to be made of blithe assurance was the commander of a rebel base. "Thank you, Miss Seabourne," said Amara. "I have every intention of doing just that."

Mrs. Hancock lived on a street of small two-story row houses. The houses were of identical frontage and height, their combined rooftop enclosed by low, decorative parapets.

The floating fortress could not be seen from Mrs. Hancock's window. Titus had described it as best as he could to his companions, while they were still in transit in the Crucible. But for something like that, seeing was believing.

He slid the shutters into place and pulled the curtains shut. "You may turn on those sconces now," he said to Mrs. Hancock.

A soft light with a hint of apricot came on, illuminating an interior not unlike Mrs. Hancock's parlor in Mrs. Dawlish's house. Mrs. Dawlish's house had been full of print chintz and embroidered flowers, but Mrs. Hancock's parlor had always been bare to the point of austerity. But whereas her English parlor had drawer pulls marked by the stylized whirlpool that symbolized Atlantis, here there were no such patriotic decorations.

"How are you?" asked Fairfax, embracing Mrs. Hancock warmly. "We wondered what became of you."

"I thought you'd run and hid yourself somewhere in England," said Kashkari.

London, Titus would have wagered, in one of the more crowded districts where the addition of a middle-aged woman who dressed in brown sacks would never have been noticed.

"Sit down, please," said Mrs. Hancock, distributing several plates of unfamiliar-looking snacks. "I considered it. In the first minutes after Mrs. Dawlish's house became overrun with Atlantean agents, every other moment I had to restrain myself from slipping away and disappearing among the English. And then I came to my senses. If my superiors suspected me, I would already have been arrested. I wasn't—so I decided I must use my position to its greatest advantage.

"I made every effort to look eager to help my compatriots. Poor Cooper was quite distraught that I was so civil, indeed obsequious, to the men who were carting things from your rooms. And it hurt more than I thought it would, to lose Cooper's good opinion. But I had to do what I had to do.

"What I didn't expect was that I was immediately recalled to Atlantis for questioning. Though I readily agreed, once again I very nearly fled. In the end I told myself it was providential: if I was to help topple the Bane, it would not be from some hidey-hole in the slums of London.

"So I came back. I'd bought this house shortly before I was assigned to Eton College. I return twice a year to appear normal—our superiors are suspicious of anyone who seems to be cutting ties with Atlantis. I pay to keep the house and the garden in good shape, host dinners for my neighbors, and tell them how much I look forward to moving back when I'm retired.

"And I submitted cheerfully to the interrogations—under truth serum, of course. But what my interrogators didn't know was that I'd taken an anti-truth serum before I left my house."

"What?" exclaimed Titus. "An anti-truth serum exists?"

She sighed and nodded. "It was one of the things that haunted Icarus Khalkedon."

Icarus Khalkedon, while he yet lived, had been the Bane's personal oracle, providing answers to the Bane's most pressing questions.

"I told you that the Bane often asked about those who presented future threats to his rule. One of the answers Icarus gave was the name Ligea Eos. Mrs. Eos was troubled by the Bane's practice of interviewing his senior staff under truth serum on a regular basis— her husband being one of those senior staff. The moment her husband began questioning the regime, she knew he was doomed, unless she could do something.

"And that something was the invention of an anti-truth serum, which prevented the truth serum from taking effect—and gave safety to those who didn't entirely agree with the Bane. Or would have given safety, if she'd been able to disseminate the antidote as she'd have liked. As it was, agents watched her carefully for months. When she finally succeeded in producing a batch of anti-truth serum, they confiscated her entire output and took her away. She was never seen again.

"But her creation was not immediately destroyed. Instead, it became a carefully guarded cache at the Commander's Palace. The Bane was considering giving doses to his military commanders on the eve of campaigns, so that they could not give away strategic secrets even if they were captured. I don't know that he ever did, but Icarus, during his seemingly innocent exploration of the palace, managed to pilfer a small quantity of it, in case I needed to lie under truth serum someday.

"My actual interrogation was relatively uneventful. The one who questioned me was someone I'd never met before—someone far higher up the chain of command than those I usually thought of as my superiors. She was quite annoyed that somehow I'd managed not to discover the plot against the Bane, despite having lived under the same roof for so long.

"I pointed out that by all appearances, the Master of the Domain was attending to classes and sports just like the other boys. Not to mention that he showed up on time for meals and Absences. And despite not being particularly warm or helpful, he gave no trouble as far as anyone could see.

"Thankfully, in this regard I could hide behind the Bane's own failure—he lived in that household for a number of weeks without realizing that the one he sought was just a few doors down. Of course I didn't say such a thing aloud, but that he didn't perceive it went a long way toward absolving me, a simple woman whose powers of observation by no means rivaled his.

"When they were satisfied I'd been guilty of nothing more than incompetence, they put me on temporary suspension and let me go. I went to the nearest cathedral to give thanks and then, for old times' sake, I went to the library at Royalis and sat down in a garden."

"Royalis, throughout the Bane's reign, has always been open to the public—it was one way in which he sought to distinguish himself from the old kings, who hoarded the wealth of the realm and left the people to starve. He was determined to show himself a kind overlord. Royalis was and is available for weddings and other celebratory receptions for only a nominal fee, and the mage on the street is welcome anytime—except during curfew hours—to enjoy the beauty of its many gardens.

"From what I understand, in the early years of the Bane's reign, Royalis was a practically never-ending wave of revelry in honor of nuptials, milestone birthdays, and so on. We were at last a realm prosperous at home and respected abroad, and the populace as a whole was in a festive mood that lasted a good long while.

"And then something changed. A chill crept in. The Bane was no longer just revered, but both revered and feared. Perhaps ordinary Atlanteans weren't exactly aware of this fear, but they knew they didn't want to hold their weddings on the grounds of Royalis, even if the venue was magnificent and practically free.

"By the time I was working at the library in Royalis, it had few visitors—sometimes out-of-town tourists still wanted to see the place, but not too many others. When the Bane stayed at Royalis, its administrators strong-armed local schools into sending their pupils for educational visits, and various branches of government would hold award ceremonies and annual dinners at which attendance was compulsory, so that the Bane would still be under the impression that Royalis, the symbol of his generosity to his people, remained a popular and well-loved destination.

"As a result, when Icarus and I used to meet, the garden we most preferred was almost always deserted. No one knew of our association, and while the Bane might think it odd that Icarus named me to Eton, he probably thought it no more odd than any other oracular statement the significance of which had yet to be borne out by time.

"So there I was, once again sitting on our bench in that beautifully kept but lifeless garden, and it came to me out of the blue what the oracle in the prince's book had meant when she said, *And yes, you have seen it before.*

"At the time I thought she'd meant the copy of the Crucible in the prince's room, and I said that of course I'd seen it before—it had been there for years. That was truly spectacularly dense of me. A few months before, the Acting Inquisitor had held up a copy of such a book and asked whether the prince had used it as a portal—I should have realized then that multiple copies of this book existed. But you must understand that the prince had never remotely been my priority—to me he was largely incidental, someone who was involved only because I needed an excuse to be waiting at Eton when the Bane walked in, after the great comet had come and gone.

"On that fateful day, after agents of Atlantis walked out of the prince's room with the Crucible, it finally dawned on me that the Acting Inquisitor had not been spouting nonsense, that the book truly was a portal. And it was while I sat on the bench in Icarus's and my favorite garden that I realized where exactly I had seen it, on that very bench, near the beginning of our friendship.

"And then I remembered that Icarus had said he'd borrowed the book from the library and had intended to return it later that afternoon. The present-day me jumped up from the bench and rushed into the library. Because the library is so vast, most patrons made their requests at the help desk. But since I was a former librarian, I knew where the catalogue room was and headed directly there.

"The cataloguing system we had was somewhat old-fashioned, but still enough to let me know that the book had been checked out for the entire academic term by Professor Pelion of the Grand Conservatory of Lucidias. I broke into the professor's office at the university last night but couldn't find the book. Tonight I went to his home and, well, found you."

A kettle sang somewhere in the house. Mrs. Hancock disappeared for a minute, came back with a large tea tray, and poured for everyone.

"Well, we're here, against all odds—or as preordained," said

Kashkari. "What do you advise, ma'am? What's the best way to get to the Commander's Palace?"

"You mean, the least terrible way? I have been thinking about it for years and I'm still not quite sure how."

Mrs. Hancock handed the first cup of tea to Titus, out of deference to his position. Titus handed the cup to Fairfax, who in turn gave it to her guardian.

"So how did the Bane commute between the uplands and the capital city?" asked Kashkari, bringing the discussion back on topic.

"A griffin-drawn cavalcade."

"No portals or other translocators?"

"Icarus never found any such thing at the Commander's Palace—any portal that could be the Bane's easy transport elsewhere could turn around and become someone else's easy way into the Commander's Palace. And the no-vaulting zone around the palace is said to extend a hundred miles in any direction."

"How is that possible?" Amara exclaimed. "The amount of work necessary to create a no-vaulting zone a mile across is already an immense undertaking. How big is the no-vaulting zone around the Citadel?"

"Five miles in radius," said Titus. "And it was a controversial undertaking, for how much time and treasury outlay it consumed."

"This no-vaulting zone wasn't achieved in one year, one generation, or even one century," said Mrs. Hancock. "Let's not forget how long the Bane has been around.

"Once Icarus's oracular abilities divulged the Bane's true age, I began piecing together his story. A great deal of the time, the founder of a new dynasty or regime presents a sanitized and glorified version of himself or herself, but the background of the mage who became known as our Lord High Commander seemed to need no cleaning up or embellishing.

"His family was highly respected—beloved even. They hailed from the west coast, on the far side of the massifs that harbor the Commander's Palace, a poorer, harsher part of what was already a poor, harsh realm. Unlike many landowning families who exploited their peons, members of the Zephyrus clan were celebrated for their humility and generosity.

"Young Delius Zephyrus wasn't exactly a child prodigy. Until he was fifteen, he was almost completely undistinguished, except for his youthful good looks. But then his beloved great-grandfather died, and it was commonly believed that his death propelled young Delius to make something of himself.

"From that point on, his ascent was remarkable. This was more than fifty years ago. Atlantis at the time was ruled by a collection of warlords, each controlling a parcel of the realm, each trying to expand his or her own territory at the expense of another warlord's. There was constant unrest. The harvests were terrible due to the displacement of the peasants, and the fisheries were close to being depleted again, because mages were struggling to feed themselves. Everyone feared we would tip over into another widespread famine, and that was when young Delius took up his wand and organized his own people, who were probably better fed and better treated than any other group of peasants in the country, and persuaded them to follow him into battle, as no tribe could ever enjoy good fortune alone: if they, better-off mages who were surrounded by misery, did nothing except wallow in their own superior luck, sooner or later misery would penetrate whatever barriers they thought they had erected against it.

"'I wish to help because I cannot bear not helping,' he'd said, in a speech before many eyewitnesses. 'If that is how you feel, join me. If that is not how you feel, you should still join me. Because our destinies are not divided from our fellow Atlanteans, and in helping them, you help no one so much as yourself. And you would go to the end of your days knowing that you have been brave and wise, that you did not cower in your own little safe haven as chaos marched in, but fought for order, for justice, for a cause that is bigger than yourself.'

"I know it well, this speech. The first time I read it, I wept. I was so moved by his courage and so enormously proud to be an Atlantean under his stewardship. At school we reenacted the scene every year, and for years it used to touch me anew.

A wistful light came into Mrs. Hancock's eyes. All at once Titus could see her as a young girl, bursting with pride and joy at her homeland's remarkable rebirth.

"And so this young man who had nothing but pluck and the favor of the Angels marched against the warlords with his ragtag band of supporters. And they won victory after victory, the oppressed everywhere swelling their ranks, because they saw hope for the very first time. And they were so hungry for a better life, for a society characterized by peace, prosperity, and fellowship, that they did not mind giving their lives to that noble goal.

"Soon he became unstoppable. When his forces took Lucidias, and he declared the realm rid of the warlords and the brutal old ways that kept the ordinary mage downtrodden, such jubilation there was, such euphoria."

Mrs. Hancock sighed. "The thing about this story is that it's overwhelmingly true, at least the facts on the surface. For years, I worked under the librarian in charge of the historical archive at the grand library. And in that capacity, I visited many private collectors to arrange for the purchase or donation of primary sources to the archive. And while I went about my official duties, especially if I happened to be on the west coast, I collected documents and anecdotes that might help me piece together the puzzle of who the Bane really was.

"The more I learned about the Zephyrus clan, the more my attention came to focus on its founder, a man by the name of Palaemon Zephyrus, who lived until age ninety-one."

Mages seldom lived to sixty-five, and almost never past seventy—it was something that for all the wonders of their powers, they could not change. Hesperia the Magnificent, who reached eighty, was not only the longest-living of all the heirs of the House of Elberon by a large margin, but also the third-longest-lived mage in the entire recorded history of the Domain. Titus's grandfather, who had died at sixty-two, was considered to have been in full old age.

For a mage to live to his nineties was unheard of, a life span almost 50 percent greater than the expectancy of even the most privileged and well cared for.

"Did he live to ninety-one by natural means?" asked Fairfax.

"That question was very much on my mind. I also wanted to know whether that was his true age—or whether he had lied when he claimed to be a young man when he arrived on the west coast. But my biggest question was: 'What evidence can I find that he actually died?'

"Since there was no strong central government at the time, documentation for life events was spotty. The Bane had actually donated his family's papers and letters to the historical archive at the grand library. Bit by bit—since I didn't want to appear to be too curious—I combed through those papers.

"A less suspicious researcher would have come away with the impression of a family that was completely above reproach—there were innumerable thank-you notes from mages they had helped over the years. And yet members of the family met with a slew of misfortunes, especially in the earlier years, as attested by the almost equally innumerable condolence notes.

"A flood of such letters came when Palaemon Zephyrus was in

his seventies, condolences on the loss of his son and daughter, his only two children. There were also a number of get-well-soon wishes for himself. I was able to locate a copy of a seigneury circular from that time. A seigneury circular was a paper published by a land-holder for his tenants to inform them of the goings-on in the area, and sometimes in other parts of the realm and maybe even abroad. It was a common practice of the era, since the ordinary mage didn't have any other access to news. It was also used to announce signifi-cant events on the estate itself.

"According to that particular edition of the Zephyrus seigneury circular, Palaemon Zephyrus and his children had the grave misfor-tune of running into a giant serpent."

Titus cocked a brow. "Do giant serpents truly still live on Atlantis?"

He had seen a replica of a giant serpent skeleton in the Hesperia the Magnificent Museum of Natural History. He did not doubt that they had slithered the earth at some point, but it was the general belief that giant serpents had long ago become extinct.

"Here on Atlantis we tend to give a little more credence to the reports of their existence. There are very few eyewitness accounts, because it is said that giant serpents are fiercely territorial and will kill without any other provocation. But sometimes hikers come across bone piles characteristic of those left behind by giant serpents—usually as territory markers—and they immediately turn back. The truly public-minded might file a report with the Department of

Interior Resources. Most don't, because such reports could lead to unwelcome questions. 'What were you doing in that area?' 'Why did you stray from the boundary of the nature reserve?' 'Where else did you go besides the place where you claim to have seen the bone pile?'

"In any case, we believe in the existence of giant serpents enough that when my sister disappeared, everyone sincerely thought it was what had happened to her. She had been on an approved nature reserve with her classmates, but the place was said to have been infested with giant serpents at one point, and that was where all our minds went.

"So Palaemon Zephyrus's account was not questioned. He was a man respected and beloved, not to mention he'd lost half an arm in the incident himself. The clan mourned and life went on. Almost exactly ten years later, there came another flood of condolence notes, this time over the death of Palaemon Zephyrus's youngest granddaughter.

"He had married late. His children were in their thirties when they perished. And this granddaughter, born after the death of her father, was only nine at the time of her death. That month's edition of the seigneury circular said she was swept away by a sudden flash flood. No body was ever recovered. It also said that Palaemon Zephyrus lost an eye in the search for his granddaughter."

Kashkari pinched the skin between his brows. "So you are saying, ma'am, that he sacrificed his own children and grandchild?"

"I have no direct evidence, but that is very much my conclusion."

Aramia looked as if she might faint—or retch. Instead she gripped the edge of her chair and stared at the clock on the wall.

"After that," Mrs. Hancock went on, "the next round of condolences were finally for Palaemon Zephyrus himself. The obituary published in the seigneury circular mentioned that he had been heartbroken after the death of his children and grandchild and had spent the last few years of his life in isolation in his mountain retreat—and passed away there, according to the circular."

"So the retreat in the uplands existed even before Palaemon Zephyrus was officially dead," mused Fairfax.

"It looks that way."

"Was he put on a pyre?" asked Haywood.

In realms that fell under the banners of the Angelic Host, a deceased mage was burned on the pyre with just enough covering for modesty. The face was never concealed.

"In those years, Atlantis as a whole was so impoverished that even the well-to-do didn't have proper pyres for their funerals. We never had a great deal of woods on Atlantis, most of the original forest had already been cut down, and importing timber for pyres was beyond the means of all but a few. The bodies of the deceased were preserved for the day when they could be properly cremated, their ashes offered to the Angels. Until then, they remained underground, tightly wrapped, so that the Angels could not see their shame at having been buried."

"Are these bodies wrapped even at the funeral?"

"Yes."

"So no one ever actually saw Palaemon Zephyrus's dead body?"

"Except one person, a nephew on his late wife's side, who wrapped his body for the funeral. And he died very soon afterward, in his sleep. The cause given was sudden massive heart failure."

Titus and Fairfax glanced at each other. The last time they had heard the term, it was in connection with Baron Wintervale, who had not suffered a heart attack after all, but had been felled by an execution curse.

"Killing off a witness who might know that Palaemon Zephyrus wasn't really dead," said Amara.

"Please tell me the atrocities against his own family end with his 'death,'" said Aramia, paler than pale.

"That was my hope. Alas, a few years later, a baby newly born to the family, a great-grandchild of his, was stolen. It was news even in Lucidias—I found letters from the era referring to the kidnapping. There were some exorbitant ransom demands, so it was believed bandits and other criminals must have been involved, perhaps with help from some of the servants. There was a huge search, ransom demands stopped coming after a few weeks, and the baby was never found, though his parents refused to give up for years and years."

Aramia shook visibly.

"Is there such a thing as sacrificial magic being more powerful, if it is your own flesh and blood that you sacrifice?" asked Kashkari.

"Was it a deliberate choice on his part to keep sacrificing younger and younger children?" Fairfax asked at almost the same time.

"Have any of you ever heard of a book called"—Mrs. Hancock hesitated, as if reluctant to even let the words pass her lips—"*A Chronicle of Blood and Bones?*"

Everyone shook their heads, except Haywood, who said, "That's the best-known manual on sacrificial magic, isn't it? I thought all the copies had been destroyed."

"I had to dig deep into the library's records. Apparently, days before the fall of the last king, a copy was confiscated in Lucidias and set aside for destruction. Then it was lost in the subsequent chaos."

"That would have been around the time the Bane was born."

"Correct. I don't have positive evidence on whether he ever came into that copy or how, but during my research, I did read about a young man of Lucidias, by the name of Pyrrhos Plouton, who was miraculously cured of a deadly disease that was within days of killing him. And I came across his story by searching for people who had disappeared without a trace. In his story, it was mentioned that his recovery was bittersweet, as his best friend was believed to have been one of the curious onlookers who got too close to the newly appeared maelstrom of Atlantis and were swept in."

Mrs. Hancock looked at Fairfax. "Remember what you said about the elemental mage who created the maelstrom having probably been the Bane's first instance of sacrifice? You were exactly right. And decades later he moved across the breadth of Atlantis—no mean feat in those days—to become Palaemon Zephyrus."[2]

"What happened after the baby was taken away?" asked Aramia, her voice low and tight.

"The curse on the family seemed to lift after that—no more unnatural misfortunes. And then came Delius, who changed from a rather mediocre boy to an immensely accomplished young man almost overnight. Oh, I do want to mention that Delius had a twin, who is said to have died in one of the battles. Buried. Once the Bane took power over all of Atlantis, he put many of his ancestors and relatives on one huge pyre and finally offered their ashes to the angels."

All evidence destroyed, in other words.

"To sacrifice your greatest enemy is evil enough. To practice sacrificial magic on those who love, trust, and respect you—that is despicable beyond words. Especially"—Fairfax briefly clamped her teeth over her lower lip, as if trying to control a bout of nausea—"especially since he knows exactly what sacrificial magic entails, the unspeakable agony the victims must endure, the extraction of brains and marrows and goodness knows what else while their hearts still beat."

Aramia covered her own mouth, as if she feared she would vomit otherwise.

"Sorry about that," said Fairfax. "It is what it is."

"I got completely distracted, didn't I?" said Mrs. Hancock to Kashkari. "All you asked was how best to get to the Commander's Palace, and here I wouldn't shut up about everything that happened decades ago."

"No, no, of course. It always helps to know what we are

dealing with," answered Kashkari. "And you did mention that the no-vaulting zone around the Commander's Palace is a hundred miles in radius. Do Atlanteans never have cause to go into the area?"

"Our population has always been concentrated in the coastal regions. The interior of the realm is largely empty of inhabitants, especially the region around the Commander's Palace. The terrain is ill-suited for just about everything—the land mass is too young and the volcanic rock hasn't had enough time to become rich volcanic ash. Some places you can scarcely walk. The land beneath your feet is like a forest of knives."

Obsidian flows sometimes produced such landscapes, the volcanic glass, upon cooling, fracturing to produce blade-sharp edges.

"Would you happen to have a map?" Titus asked.

"Maps are to be had everywhere. But none of them will have the location of the Commander's Palace marked. You can, however, have a guess as to its general area. It would be the sector in the northwest quadrant of the island that is entirely covered by wilderness preserves."

Mrs. Hancock moved to a desk and opened a drawer. "Here are two maps. One of Lucidias and one of the entire realm. I've marked them where I thought there might be inaccuracies or information you could use."

Titus took the maps and offered his thanks.

"Now you just have to get out of Lucidias."

"Via the tunnels?" asked Amara.

"The tunnels have their uses, but are hardly necessary for you: I still have freedom of movement. Tomorrow morning I will take the Crucible, with all of you inside, for an outing in the country. There are a couple of designated recreational nature areas not far from here. Once you are there, you can proceed with far fewer eyes on you. And I bought some simple tunics and cloaks for all of you, so that your clothes won't stand out."

Kashkari leaned forward in his chair. "Can you not vault out of Lucidias directly? That would make it safer for everyone."

Mrs. Hancock shook her head. "The entire city is a no-vaulting zone."

This was not welcome news.

"Will we stand out?" Amara gestured at Kashkari and herself.

"Somewhat, but we do have a small population of mages who moved to Atlantis from realms in the Indian Ocean. So your appearance alone won't get you dragged off to be interrogated." She rose. "If anyone is still hungry, I have some eggs in the kitchen and I can make omelets. Would that be all right?"

"That does sound good," said Haywood. "I will not mind a fresh omelet at all. Thank you."

"When you've eaten," Mrs. Hancock went on, "we'll see how we can bed down everyone as comfortably as possible. You'll need a good night's rest."

It might be their last.

Titus was accustomed to late nights and little sleep. But it had been a long day, both physically demanding and emotionally draining. And the thought of a few hours of uninterrupted sleep sounded more tempting than he wanted to admit, for someone who really ought not to waste any more time sleeping.

He moved closer to Fairfax, intending to ask how she was holding up.

"No!" Aramia screamed.

Every single person stopped mid-motion.

"Don't eat. Don't sleep. You must leave this house now! Go to the tunnels, get out of Lucidias this minute."

Titus stared at her. Suddenly he knew what she was about to say next.

"I'm carrying a tracer. I entrusted the other half to Uncle Alectus to give to the new Inquisitor. It would take them a while to find us, but we have been here a while."

Of course. If all she wanted was to free Lady Callista, it would be much easier to help the Bane than to defeat the Bane. Titus could have throttled himself. Aramia had the uncanny talent to portray herself as a victim, a girl too weak to matter, someone who would never intentionally serve as an accessory to murder.

Was *this* what would lead to Fairfax's death?

"No!" Fairfax shouted, clamping her hand on him and pushing his arm down.

Belatedly he realized that he had his wand pointed at Aramia, with every intention of completing an execution curse.

The room turned dark all at once. He blinked before he realized that Kashkari had extinguished the light, in order to look outside without attracting notice. As he drew back the shutters, a bright-blue light rushed in.

"Hurting her now would serve no purpose whatsoever," said Fairfax.

"I didn't know that's why the Bane wanted her," whimpered Aramia. "I didn't know that it was to use her in sacrificial magic."

"So it was quite all right for you when you did not know that specific fact?" Titus growled. "What did you think was going to happen? That the Bane would treat her to a nice afternoon tea and let her go?"

Fairfax's hand tightened on his arm. "Stop wasting time. We have to leave." She turned to Aramia. "Hand over your tracer."

Aramia dug under the folds of her overrobe and surrendered a small round disk.

"Get started on the password to the Crucible. I'll send the tracer as far away as possible."

"We won't have enough time to get into the Crucible," said Kashkari, from the window. "They are coming."

CHAPTER · 18

IOLANTHE RAN TO THE WINDOW. In the clear, cool light of the streetlamps, it was all too easy to see the swarm of armored pods, the kind that had chased her in Cairo and Eton, speeding toward them.

She swore and threw down the tracer.

"I've a half portal!" cried Mrs. Hancock. "Quick. This way."

A fully functional portal required a starting enclosure and an end enclosure. A half portal, on the other hand, could send a mage a certain distance, but there was no telling just how far one would be dislocated, or even in which direction.

They grabbed their emergency bags. Mrs. Hancock urged everyone into a closet in her bedroom, packed as tightly as if they were spectators at a parade.

"What about me?" cried Aramia. "If Atlantis interrogates me now, they'll learn that I'd helped you after all."

"Then you had better make sure they don't interrogate you," said Mrs. Hancock as she closed the door in Aramia's face, shutting her out.

The next moment, they found themselves standing in a garden of some kind, surrounded by low, burbling fountains and parterres made of dwarf shrubs. The city spread out to the south—a thin, dense strip. And in the distance, the sea, the foam of its choppy waves a strange shade of blue-green under the light of the floating fortress—Titus had told them it was big, but her imagination had been no match for the size of the colossus in the sky.

Mrs. Hancock looked about. The garden was as brightly lit as everywhere else in Lucidias. "We are in River Terrace Park," she said, a name that meant nothing to the non-Atlanteans, "about three miles from my house."

"Is it safe here?" asked Kashkari. "And are there any tunnels around?"

"There are no tunnels nearby," said Mrs. Hancock, waving at them to follow her as she walked toward the west. "Public spaces in Lucidias are carefully watched during the day and even more so during curfew hours, because they might have features that can offer places of concealment. We need to get out of the park."

"And then what?" demanded Titus.

Even if they could find someplace to hide until morning, the original plan of being carried out of the city in the Crucible by Mrs. Hancock was no longer feasible—Mrs. Hancock herself would now be considered a fugitive from the law.

Mrs. Hancock led them closer to a high retaining wall, above which was another terrace like the one they were traversing—the park had been carved out of a hillside. And if Iolanthe listened carefully, she could almost hear the roar of the river referenced in the name of the park.

"There are some colleges in this direction," said Mrs. Hancock. "Usually colleges are allowed to police their own campuses. The Interrealm Institute of Languages and Cultures is said to be lax about enforcing the curfew. I hope we can stay there until sunrise."

"There are actually places on Atlantis where mages are interested in the languages and cultures of other lands?"

Mrs. Hancock stopped. "Your Highness, with all due respect, *of course*. Just because you have met a few philistines who happen to be Atlanteans doesn't mean the rest of us are all ignorant and incurious. It means that we live in conditions hostile to our way of thinking and we are less inclined to join the bureaucracy that sends mages abroad because we tend to disagree with the official position of disdain and brutality."

A moment of silence. Iolanthe felt ashamed of herself: she hadn't said it aloud but she'd thought the same thing.

"My apologies, ma'am," said Titus. "I will remember your admonishment."

Mrs. Hancock resumed her hurried walk. "Apology accepted, Your Highness. And thank you for—"

A thump. Iolanthe glanced up as Titus took hold of her arm. A fraction of a second later, two uniformed guards fell at Mrs. Hancock's feet. She leaped back, her hand clasped over her mouth.

"I might have stunned the guards too late," said Amara, cool and unflappable. "They could have already spread the word."

Mrs. Hancock's jaw worked. "There's a flight of steps ahead. Let's move the guards there."

The flight of steps had been cut into the retaining wall to permit access from the lower terrace to the upper terrace. The steps were broad and shallow—again, designed to offer as little place to hide as possible. But at the edges of the steps they were less likely to be seen, unless from directly overhead.

They pushed the unconscious Atlanteans beneath the handrails. Titus peered out from the top of the steps; Kashkari and Amara did the same at the bottom. Mrs. Hancock had her hand over her heart, catching her breath. Master Haywood leaned against the stone wall that held back the hillside from the steps, his hand in a fist and the flat of the fist against his forehead.

Iolanthe took his hand. "It's all right. We might be luckier than we think. If those guards had already informed their superiors or sent for reinforcements, they'd be here by now."

But his shoulders only slumped farther. "If only I hadn't failed to suppress Miss Tiberius's memories. If only I had managed that . . ."

She gaped at him. At the back of her mind, bits and pieces of information that had refused to come together to make sense did just that in an avalanche of insight. Her grip on his hand tightened. "You never could have done it, because she wasn't the one you held for hours and hours. It was *me*. I'm not Lady Callista's daughter—I am the real Iolanthe Seabourne."

Master Haywood stared at her. "But that's impossible. I switched the two of you myself."

In her excitement she grabbed Titus by the back of his tunic and pulled him toward her. "Remember when we encountered the blood circle in the Sahara? We each sent a drop of blood toward the blood circle. Yours reacted with the blood circle, if weakly; mine didn't at all."

Now he too was slack-jawed. "Fortune shield me. My blood reacted with the blood circle because Lady Callista and I are distantly related. But yours . . . and hers . . ."

"Exactly! I should have put two and two together the moment I remembered everything. But we were so busy with the battle and everything that followed—there was no time to stop and think."

She was giddy: the supremely selfish Lady Callista and the supremely cowardly Baron Wintervale were *not* her parents.

"I still don't understand what happened," said Master Haywood dazedly.

"The explanation is obvious. By the time Aramia was born, I'd been in that hospital nursery for six weeks. The night nurses might not recognize Aramia, but they must have recognized me, figured that I'd been somehow put in the wrong bassinet, and switched us back."

"So there is nothing deceptive about my memories after all," Master Haywood said slowly. "I was a man raising my schoolmates' daughter, whom I loved above all else. That was all true, every bit of it."

She squeezed his hand. "Yes, that was us. That *is* us."

He squeezed her hand back. "I can't tell you how thrilled I am for Jason and Delphine Seabourne, that their daughter has turned out to be everything they could have possibly wanted in a child."

"Because you did everything right by me. Never forget that."

A watery light shone in his eyes. "I didn't. But I will never forget you said that—it makes everything worthwhile. *Everything.*"

Her vision too was growing misty. She leaned forward and kissed him on his cheek. "We'll—"

She whimpered at the hard pressure Titus's hand exerted on her shoulder. He was staring at Mrs. Hancock, who was—who was—

Mrs. Hancock glowed, as if she had turned into a giant lightning bug. She gaped at her hands with their faintly poison-green luminescence, her mouth wide open, her eyes terrified.

Master Haywood scrambled to his feet. "I don't think it was just truth serum Atlantis gave her. This looks like the work of a beacon elixir."

He gripped Iolanthe by the arm. "Get out your carpet! You must get as far away from—"

Mrs. Hancock erupted into a beacon of light that shot high into the sky, glaringly visible even against the bright background illumination of the Lucidian night. The same light swirled about her, encasing her as if in a tube. Her face was frozen in a scream of horror.

"Go! Go now, all of you!" cried Master Haywood. "She is already dead. Move!"

"But where?" shouted Amara.

Kashkari shook open his carpet. "Away from that!"

"That" was a floating fortress, charging toward them with the speed of an armored chariot.

They fled in the opposite direction from where they had been headed, the sanctuary of the security-lax college now a hopeless mirage. Iolanthe's carpet had been subordinated to Amara's, the latter being the fastest and most experienced flyer among them. But even with their carpets advancing at a dizzying speed, the floating fortress was already on top of them.

Worse, its edges were extending downward. It was going to physically confine them in a place where they could not vault, where once penned in, they had no way of getting out.

Her heart pounded like the pistons of a steam engine that was about to overheat. Was this it? Was this the beginning of the end?

She ripped off chunks of the hillside and aimed them at the floating fortress. Volcanic rock produced very satisfactory thunks against the underbelly of the juggernaut, but had no practical effects whatsoever.

The floating fortress was now exactly above them, its speed identical to theirs, its edges halfway to the ground. Amara banked hard and reversed their direction. But the floating fortress, the size of a city district, matched their movements without the least hesitation.

"Kashkari, head in a different direction!" Titus ordered. "I will do the same."

The floating fortress ignored their attempts at creating confusion and stuck with Amara, Iolanthe, and Master Haywood.

Iolanthe jerked at the sudden pressure she felt on the strap on her shoulder. But it was only Master Haywood digging in her emergency satchel. He shook open her spare carpet, embraced her with one arm, and kissed her on her cheek. "I love you." To Amara he shouted, "Get out from underneath the fortress!"

Then he was on the spare carpet, dashing up toward the floating fortress itself.

"What are you doing?" Iolanthe screamed.

Whatever he intended would only get him killed.

His receding figure began to glow, much as Mrs. Hancock's had done. "No!" Iolanthe screamed again. What had Atlantis given *him* during his time in the Inquisitory?

Impossibly, the flying fortress too began to glow. For a moment, her mind refused to comprehend what she was seeing: a last-mage-standing spell, enormously destructive because it was powered by a voluntarily given life.

Master Haywood's voluntarily given life.

The entire floating fortress glowed orange, with cracks of red showing through. It wobbled and slowed, even as its edges continued to descend. Iolanthe forced herself to concentrate. The tailwind she summoned flung them forward; Amara barely hung on to her control of the carpets. They spun as they slid out from underneath the fortress's enclosure.

The flying fortress broke apart and plummeted. A tide of debris crashed toward them. Iolanthe called for the strongest shields she knew and sent a strong countervailing current of air—still she had to raise her emergency satchel to her head to shield herself from the smattering of small fragments that pelted down.

Out of the cloud of smoke and dust appeared Kashkari and Titus. But there was no time to inquire after their well-being, not even to catch her breath. Beneath the din of the floating fortress's destruction there came slithering sounds in the grass. Hunting ropes, hundreds, perhaps thousands in quantity.

Hunting ropes that knew the scents of their quarries, if they had been first taken to Mrs. Hancock's house. And traveling by flying carpet would not deter the hunting ropes from following their scents.

But hunting ropes, thankfully, had one imperfection: they only worked on dry land.

"To the river. Now!" Iolanthe commanded.

The river was only a stone's throw ahead. The debris cloud was beginning to clear; Titus called for a large, powerful smoke screen. Under different conditions something like that would have been a dead giveaway of their location. But as it was, their location was already known, and all they needed was for Atlantis not to know their next move.

The river was far more swollen than Iolanthe had anticipated, the currents dark and swift. She inhaled deeply and made a motion with her hand, as if she were yanking apart a stuck window.

The water parted, revealing an irregular-looking riverbed, the kind where there was no good place for setting foot. And while the channel wasn't too steep, there was a noticeable incline.

"Get down and crouch low." Due to the slope, the river wasn't too deep, at most eight feet.

No one looked overjoyed at what she proposed. But they all obeyed immediately. She leaped in after them.

"Wait," said Titus, as Iolanthe readied an air bubble.

He took out a hunting rope from his own satchel, rubbed it across the back of her hand a couple of times, and then flung it onto the far bank of the river. She hoped his trick would keep the other hunting ropes busy for a while.

Taking another deep breath, she let the river resume its thunderous progress toward the sea. The air bubble she had anchored to the riverbed held, keeping them safely in place.

But staying in place was not their goal. Sooner or later those who sought them would circle back to this spot: they needed to move.

"Put away the carpets," she said. "Then we levitate one another an inch or two above the riverbed and make our way upstream."

It would have been far easier to go downstream, but that would only wash them out to sea.

The carpets were put away. Iolanthe and Titus, who each carried an emergency raft, took out the oars that came with the kits. Fully unfolded, the oars would measure six feet in length. But they only let the oars out to eighteen inches or so.

In the Sahara, Iolanthe and Titus had used levitating spells to get through a tunnel she excavated in the bedrock. Here the trick worked again: floating three inches above the riverbed, they each used an oar to push themselves forward.

Iolanthe reduced the size of the air bubble as much as possible without suffocating everyone inside—the more water going over them, the less likely they would be seen. Kashkari coordinated their moves. Titus kept an eye on their speed, altitude, and oxygen supply—reminding her regularly that it was time to bring in some fresh air—as she wrestled with the air bubble, pushing it along the bottom of the river at the rate of their progress.

Amara remained silent, except to ask once, "Is it difficult keeping the air bubble intact?"

"No," Iolanthe answered. "The hard part is keeping it underwater. This much air exerts a lot of buoyancy."

And it was a constant struggle to keep the air bubble down and not let it bounce them all up to the surface.

Their progress was slow, torturous—and often taking place completely in the dark. When Titus deemed the water deep enough, he would allow a bare flicker of light. Otherwise they proceeded without any illumination, groping their way forward.

It felt to Iolanthe as if she'd spent her entire life crawling in this cramped and unnatural way, her shoulders aching, the back of her head throbbing, when Titus said, "Our levitation spells are weakening. We might have to stop for a bit."

They happened to be traversing a relatively flat stretch of riverbed. Titus took out an emergency raft, which, when inflated, made for a decent mattress. "The water here is fifteen feet deep. You can make the air bubble a little bigger."

"How far have we come?" asked Iolanthe, collapsing onto the raft.

Not far enough, that much she already knew, as the same bluish light that illuminated Lucidias elsewhere filtered down from the funnel she had made to the surface for the exchange of air.

"About a mile and a half. But the river's course turned a couple of times. So as the crow flies, we are only about four-fifths of a mile from where we started."

"Still in Lucidias?"

"Yes." Titus handed her a small vial of remedy. "The good news is I have been studying the map of Lucidias Mrs. Hancock gave us, and I am certain that one, the river will take us out of Lucidias, and two, it will do so at a spot where there is no checkpoint. The bad news is, of course, since Atlantis did not think it necessary to install a checkpoint, we will find it punishing in some other way."

The contents of the vial, when she tipped it into her mouth, tasted quite familiar, with its burst of orange flavor. He had given her the exact same wellness remedy on the day they'd first met.

The day she had sat inside a dark trunk, read Master Haywood's letter, and learned just how much he had given up to keep her safe.

There would be no triumphant return to the Conservatory for him, no life of ease and plenty. And they would never share another sunrise on the Siren Isles, leaning into each other as the birth of another day suffused them with hope.

She knew she was crying, but she didn't realize she was shaking until Titus wrapped his arms around her and held her against him.

"He wanted to keep you safe, and now he has."

"For how long? I won't leave Atlantis alive—we all know it."

"We can never judge the full effect of any action in the immediate aftermath. But remember, it was not only you he kept alive and free, it was the rest of us too."

A soft lament floated to her ears. For a moment she thought she had imagined it, but it was Amara, singing quietly. "It's a paean to those who have led worthy lives," said Kashkari, a catch to his voice. "Your guardian and Mrs. Hancock neither lived nor died in vain."

For as long as Amara sang, Iolanthe let herself weep, her head on

Titus's shoulder. When the final note of the lament had drifted up to the ears of the Angels, she wiped her eyes on her sleeves. They had a long way to go yet, and she must focus on the tasks at hand.

But Amara sang again.

"A prayer for courage," murmured Kashkari, "the kind of courage for facing the end of the road."

It was quite possibly the most beautiful song Iolanthe had ever heard, as haunting as it was stirring.

"'For what is the Void but the beginning of Light?'" said Titus, quoting from the Adamantine aria. "'What is Light but the end of Fear?'"

Iolanthe heard her own voice joining him in the rest of the verse. "'And what am I, but Light given form? What am I, but the beginning of Eternity?'"

You are the beginning of Eternity now, she said silently to Master Haywood. *You have arrived at the end of Fear. And I will love you always, for as long as the world endures.*

CHAPTER · 19

THEIR PAINSTAKING PROGRESS CONTINUED THROUGH the night. By midmorning they came to a huge waterfall, and Fairfax declared that it was time for everyone to get out of the river.

Titus was accustomed to mountains—he had grown up in the heart of a great mountain range. But the mountains north of Lucidias—the Coastal Range—were like none he had ever seen. There were no *slopes*. Everything reared up at a near-vertical angle. Even the banks of the river were precipitous and strewn with enormous and sharply edged boulders. They had to fly out of the riverbed, after Fairfax once again parted the currents.

Titus made a number of blind vaults until he was high enough to see the dense, crowded city that consumed every square inch of feasible land between the sea and the mountains. Above Lucidias hung several floating fortresses, slowly rotating. Between them wove squadrons of armored chariots. As for the intensity of the search on the ground, he could only imagine.

Or it could all be a spectacle put on to fool them into thinking that Atlantis still believed them trapped in Lucidias.

Unfortunately, the mountain rose higher behind him and he could not see what was happening elsewhere in Atlantis. And to think these mountains were but gentle hills compared to what awaited them farther inland.

He returned to find Kashkari and Amara, despite their skill, thwarted by the flying carpet's other great intrinsic weakness: it could only travel so high above ground. They could see a ledge some two hundred feet up. But it was on a sheer cliff without a foothold anywhere, and they simply could not ascend that high on the strength of the carpets alone.

In the end, an exhausted Fairfax summoned a strong and precise air current to lift them past the required height, which allowed them to more or less glide into place—and collapse en masse.

Titus volunteered for the first watch. But the ledge was not big enough for more than two persons to lie down.

"I'll join you for the watch," said Kashkari.

Titus tucked a heat sheet around Fairfax. The ledge was not exactly smooth and even; he could not imagine that she was comfortable, even with the thicker battle carpet beneath her. But she was already asleep, her fingers slack in his hand.

Behind him the great waterfall thundered down, generating so much spray that even a quarter mile away stray droplets occasionally struck them. He wiped one such tiny bead of water from her cheek and wished for the ten thousandth time that he could protect her from what was to come.

Eventually he took a seat beside Kashkari and handed the latter a food cube. "The ladies forgot to eat."

"If I could, I too would sleep now and eat later, rather than the other way around." Kashkari bit wearily into the food cube. "What did you see?"

Titus described the scene over Lucidias and mentioned his suspicion that it could be all for show.

"While they strengthen the defenses around the Commander's Palace? That makes sense."

"I hope the Bane does not decide to move his real body somewhere else."

Kashkari flicked a few crumbs from his fingers. "That would be unlikely. The Commander's Palace has provided him with shelter and secrecy for close to a century, if not more. That's where he feels safest. Not to mention, to move the body, he would have to accept the risk of the transit: he'd be more exposed and more vulnerable than he has been in a long, long time. And what awaits him at the other end can't be as well fortified as the Commander's Palace.

"Moreover, the idea of Fairfax coming to him must be terribly exciting. She has proved elusive elsewhere, and the hunt has cost him time and again. But now she's in his territory. The way he sees it, she's making a huge mistake and would sooner or later run up against the impenetrability of his defense and be caught. He only has to sit tight and another century of life will fall into his lap—if, that is, he still has a lap left."

Titus dropped his head to his knees. "That is exactly what will happen, is it not?"

Kashkari was silent for a long time. "But you and I, at least, will still be alive after Fairfax is no more. And that is what we must plan for now."

Iolanthe must have been asleep for no more than ten minutes when someone shook her on the shoulder. "Wake up, Miss Seabourne. Let the boys have some rest."

Amara.

Iolanthe pried apart her eyelids and shuddered at the precipitous drop bare inches from where she lay.

"Let her sleep more," said Titus to Amara, an edge to his voice. "It was not necessary to wake her up."

"You need your rest," Amara answered calmly. "If you're too tired, you'll become a liability to the rest of us."

Iolanthe carefully got to her feet so she could switch places with Titus. "She's right. Sleep."

As they passed each other, he held her against him for a moment. Nothing of their surroundings seemed quite real, not the roaring waterfall, not the sheer cliffs, not their precarious perch above the scabrous surface far below—and she was so drained she couldn't even remember how they'd got there.

"So you were not born on the night of the meteor storm, after all," he murmured.

She vaguely recalled something about not being Lady Callista's daughter, just plain old Iolanthe Seabourne, who was born six weeks before the meteor storm.

"The arrival of my greatness needed no such gaudy announcement," she half mumbled.

He snorted softly and pressed a food cube into her hand. "We missed celebrating your birthday in September. You have been seventeen for a while."

"No wonder I've been feeling old and tired lately. Age, it creeps up on you."

"Then lie down and sleep some more."

"Durga Devi is right. If you are under-rested, you'll be of no use to us. Now vault me someplace where I can see Lucidias."

He sighed, kissed her on her lips, and vaulted them both to a nearby peak. She examined the concentration of floating fortresses and armored chariots. "Did it look like this when you last saw it?"

"More or less."

"You think they believe us to be still somewhere in the city."

His arm around her shoulder tightened. "That might be wishful thinking." He expected that more trouble than ever awaited them where they were headed—and that was why she would not survive.

When they returned to the ledge, Kashkari was already asleep, laid out flat. She tucked Titus in and watched as he dropped off into a fitful slumber.

"So you have forgiven him?" asked Amara.

Iolanthe sat down next to her. "Provisionally—in case I die very soon."[3]

"And if not?"

"Then I'll have the luxury of time in which to hold a grudge, no?"

Amara chuckled softly. Iolanthe stared: the woman was amazingly beautiful, perfect from every angle. It occurred to her that though they had become comrades in a life-and-death struggle, she knew very little about Amara besides her stupendous loveliness and that she was the object of Kashkari's impossible longing.

She summoned some water and offered it to Amara. "Did you say that your grandmother came from one of the Nordic realms?"

Amara unscrewed the cap of her canteen and let Iolanthe direct a stream of water inside. "You've heard of the good looks of the gentlemen mages of the Kalahari Realm, I trust?"

"Oh, yes." There had been students from the Kalahari Realm at the Conservatory, and some of them had been spectacularly handsome—all that mingling of the bloodlines produced a most unusual beauty.

"My grandfather liked to joke that as a grass-green immigrant, my grandmother stepped out of her transport, laid eyes on the first nearby Kalahari man, and immediately proposed."

"Did your grandmother ever admit to it?"

Amara held up a hand, indicating that her canteen was full. "She insisted until the day she died that he was the third man she encountered after her arrival, not the first."

Iolanthe chortled and absentmindedly spun the remainder of the sphere of water she'd summoned.

"They were my father's parents. My mother was born and raised on the Ponives—the same archipelago Vasudev and Mohandas's grandparents hail from, incidentally, though not the same island. My father visited the Ponives on some sort of official business, and he met my mother while he was there. The way my mother told it, she nearly fainted with wonder when she first saw him—but only after they were married did she realize that among other Kalahari, his looks were considered mediocre at best."

Iolanthe chortled again. Until this moment, she hadn't been sure whether she liked Amara. Or perhaps it would be more accurate to say that until this moment she had never seen Amara as an actual person. "You said your parents left the Kalahari Realm when you were very small."

"True. I never got to experience this overabundance of male pulchritude myself."

"Why did they leave?"

Amara shrugged. "Atlantis, what else? The Kalahari Realm has the first Inquisitory Atlantis ever built overseas."

Iolanthe was embarrassed: she hadn't known that—and she

probably should have. "Why did the Kalahari Realm interest the Bane so much?"

"I never understood it myself until I learned about Icarus Khalkedon from Mohandas—he wrote a great deal when he was flying to us in the desert. The Bane wanted control over our realm because he wanted our oracles. We are—or were—famous for our oracles. That's why so many mages from all over the world had come there in the first place, to consult the oracles."

"You mean there are others like Icarus Khalkedon?"

"No, I'd never heard of another human oracle like him, but there was the Prayer Tree, the Field of Ashes, the Truth Well, and a number of others throughout history. I imagine the Bane probably inquired at every one of them when and where he could find you."

"Not me, just the next potent elemental mage—that was probably long enough ago that even Kashkari's uncle's powers hadn't yet manifested themselves."

Amara nodded. "You are right. It was forty years ago that the Inquisitory was built. He must have learned something from all our oracles, because he took over the Ponives just in time for Akhilesh Parimu to come into his powers."

The story of Kashkari's uncle never failed to give Iolanthe chills: killed by his own family, so that he did not fall into the Bane's hands.

"After the establishment of the Inquisitory, did Atlantis become the only entity that could ask questions of the oracles?"

"No, ordinary mages were still allowed to consult them, but far less often. And of course all questions had to be approved by the acolytes, who were now either Atlanteans or those allied with Atlantis—to prevent just what Mrs. Hancock was able to do: using the power of an oracle to ask how the Bane could be brought down."

In the Beyond, was Mrs. Hancock already reunited with her sister and Icarus Khalkedon? And Master Haywood—who welcomed him on the other side? His parents? His sister who had died early? When Iolanthe arrived, would he be happy to see her—or sad that she had outlived him by mere days?

She brought her mind back to the present—the ways and means of the Beyond she would know soon enough.

"The only oracle I've ever consulted is in the Crucible—there is no queue of supplicants waiting for answers. But a real oracular site must be swamped with mages desperate for answers. How do the acolytes choose which supplicants they will favor?"

"It runs the gamut. Some decide on the relative merit of the supplicants' questions; some, obviously, on who can pay the most; and some charge a nominal fee and let the oracle itself decide."

"So the supplicants just toss their questions to the oracle and see if they get an answer?"

"That's how the Prayer Tree worked. One gave a few coins in alms for the needy, then wrote a question on a leaf that had fallen from the tree and dropped it anywhere among the roots—and those roots cover a large, large area. If the tree decided to answer a question, a white leaf would grow on the branches, and an acolyte would climb up to record the answer and copy it to their register.

"By the time my parents asked their question about me, they could probably have paid with the leftovers of their lunch. Oracles don't last forever. The Prayer Tree had largely withered, and hadn't answered any questions in years. But my parents thought they might as well try it, since they didn't have the means to afford a more robust oracle."

"You were ill?"

"Very. The physicians weren't sure whether I would live past my first birthday, and my parents were frantic. But the Prayer Tree roused itself to give one last assurance."

"So what did the Prayer Tree tell you?"

Amara took a sip of water from her canteen. "I will need a vow of silence from you."

Without quite noticing it, Iolanthe had created a complicated waterscape in the air, slender streams threading in and out of a shallow pool of water, the entire thing bright and sparkling under the early afternoon sun. And now, in her surprise at Amara's request, the waterscape dropped ten feet straight down. "Why?"

"You'll see."

"All right," said Iolanthe. She didn't see how that would matter one way or the other, for a question answered at least two decades ago about a baby girl's life expectancy. "I solemnly promise to never mention it to anyone."

"The Prayer Tree said, 'Amara, daughter of Baruti and Pramada, will live long enough to be embraced by the Master of the Domain.'"

"*What?*" The waterscape disintegrated altogether and fell with a loud splash to the boulders far below.

"Quite an answer, eh?"

Iolanthe sucked in a breath. "So that's why you crashed the party at the Citadel."

"Wouldn't you, if you were told that you would be embraced by a prince? I'd outgrown the curiosity I had about him when I was younger. And of course Vasudev and I were already engaged, and I couldn't imagine ever letting another man embrace me, unless it was a quick hug from someone like Mohandas. But still, I was curious."

"And then you met him and realized he was a man who embraced no one."

That was an exaggeration, but not by much. Iolanthe was certain that after his mother, and maybe Lady Callista when he was a tot who didn't know any better, she was the only person he had ever touched at length.

"Which bodes well for my life expectancy, does it not?" Amara laughed, a high, abrupt sound.

Iolanthe gazed at her for some time, perhaps at last seeing behind the perfect surface. There was an adamant resolve to Amara, but at the same time, a bleakness that nearly rivaled the desolation of these mountains.

"Why have you come with us?"

Kashkari would not have denied Amara anything. And Titus most likely had been too distraught from having to leave Iolanthe behind to object to a replacement. But why had Amara decided that she wanted to be part of their hopeless venture?

And *when*?

She certainly had expressed no such interests when they had all been in the desert together. And it wasn't as if she had led an idle, useless life: the woman commanded an entire rebel base; she had already dedicated her life to fighting the Bane. Could the massacre in the Kalahari Realm really have changed things so much for her that she was willing to abandon not only her new husband, but all her longtime colleagues, for something that was at *best* a suicide mission?

"I have come to help you, of course," said Amara, her voice quiet and sincere.

A chill ran down Iolanthe's spine, not because she didn't believe Amara, but because she did.

They sat quietly for some time. The sun disappeared behind the higher peaks to the west. A shadow fell upon the ravine.

"I mentioned that there is an oracle inside the Crucible," said Iolanthe. "She specializes in helping those who seek her advice to help others. Would you like me to take you to see her?"

Amara pulled her cloak more tightly about her. "No, thank you. I already know exactly how I will contribute."

"How?"

"You'll see."

Silence fell again. They each nibbled on a food cube. Iolanthe stared at the great cascade, her mind as agitated as the pool at its base—and that was before she remembered what Dalbert had told her. On Ondine Island, after they'd met, she'd pressed him for more information on the massacre of civilians in the Kalahari Realm and the subsequent threat aimed at Titus and herself.

It happened about two hours after midnight, Dalbert had said, to start his account.

That particular detail had not leaped out at her then. But now it did. The massacre had taken place in the small hours of the morning, whereas Amara must have left the Sahara Desert the night before to begin her long flight to Scotland.

Whatever had caused her to leave everything behind to join them had not been the mass killing of her kinsfolk.

Then what had it been?

The question was on the tip of her tongue when Kashkari bolted up, thrashing. Instinctively she called for a current of air to press him toward the wall of the cliff, pinning him in place, so that he wouldn't lose his balance and plummet from the ledge.

Kashkari held up his hand to shield his face from the fierce wind. "I'm all right. I won't fall off."

Iolanthe stopped. The air turned still, the only sound in the ravine that of water leaping toward the sea.

"Another prophetic dream?" asked Amara.

Kashkari glanced at Iolanthe. Her chest tightened. "About me again?"

He didn't answer, and that should have been answer enough. Still she heard herself say, "Tell me."

Kashkari folded the sheet-like flying carpet that he had used to cover himself. "It's you, on your pyre. And the pyre is already burning. Above the flames I can see the outlines of a great cathedral—it has wings extending from its roofs."

Her ears rang. But at the same time, a ray of hope pierced her heart. "That's the Angelic Cathedral in Delamer—I don't know of any other cathedral with a silhouette like that. Only state funerals are held there—we must not have failed too badly, for me to receive a state funeral. Did you see who lit my pyre?"

Let it be Titus. Let it be him.

Kashkari shook his head. "I wasn't shown that."

Disappointment swelled in her chest, making it difficult for her to breathe. "In that case, no need to mention anything to—"

No need to mention anything to the prince. But the prince's eyes were already open. And judging by his grim expression, he had heard everything.

"Well," said Amara, breaking the fraught silence, "since you are awake, Your Highness, you might as well do some more blind vaulting and help us find a way out of these mountains."

CHAPTER · 20

BEFORE THEY LEFT, AMARA ONCE again asked for time for prayers. While she and Kashkari prayed, Titus took Fairfax to a crater lake he had come across. The day was getting late, and the water of the lake was a cool, dark blue. Reflections of clouds that had been tinted a rich mango hue by the westerly sun floated upon its surface. Along the edges of the lake, wild plants and shrubs grew, some still flowering, festooning the inside of the caldera with garlands of cream and yellow.

"What a beautiful place," she murmured.

He draped his arm around her shoulders. She looked more exhausted than he had ever seen her, her eyes somber and wistful.

"What are you thinking about?" He could not get the image of her burning pyre out of his head, her still, lifeless body surrounded by flames.

"I was wondering whether Mrs. Hancock ever stood here. Also, whether she had ever seen anything of Britain."

"Probably not." Year in and year out, Mrs. Hancock had waited for the Bane to walk into Mrs. Dawlish's, rarely straying from the resident house, and likely never outside the boundaries of the school.

"I'm glad that this time I left Britain in a hot air balloon—saw more of the country than I ever had before. It's a beautiful island, especially the coasts—reminded me of the northern wilds of the Domain."

Was she already looking backward toward all the people and all the places she had known and loved?

As if she heard his thought, she turned to him. "Don't worry. I'll keep going."

"Then I will too."

She took his face in her hands and kissed him very gently. "I've had an epiphany concerning happiness," she murmured. "Happiness is never thinking that each kiss might be your last—to be so assured that there will be countless more that you don't bother to remember any single one."

"For what it is worth, this *is* happiness for me," he told her. "This is what I have always wanted—that we should be together at the end."

She gazed at him a long moment, and kissed him again. "You know what I regret?"

"What?"

"My former disdain for rose petals. In the greater scheme of things, they really aren't so evil after all."

He chortled at her unexpected admission. "If that is all you regret, then yours has been a life well lived."

"I hope so." She sighed. "All right, enough philosophical indulgences. Now let's have your confession, Your Highness. Why did you refuse to let me see Sleeping Beauty when we first fought dragons at her castle?"

On the far side of the mountains, the land lay tumbled and broken, as if someone had shrunk the Coastal Range to a fraction of its size and then strewn copies about willy-nilly: the rocky ground was full of cuts, gashes, and stone slabs leaning at drunken angles.

They started after sunset, and still they flew with one eye on the sky. But no pursuers appeared over the top of the Coastal Range, which to Titus served to underscore Kashkari's point: the Bane was more than happy to wait for them to come to him.

Their progress was swift, but not *that* swift. Amara steered the carpet she and Kashkari shared and set the pace for the group. Titus had the sensation that she did not want to hurtle toward the Commander's Palace at a blistering speed.

Who did?

No one spoke. Titus and Fairfax shared a carpet, but they only held hands: everything that needed saying had already been said.

They were past declarations of love, loyalty, or even hope. It now remained only to be seen what they could accomplish before their prophesied deaths.

Titus kept them in a northwesterly direction, stopping from time to time to spread maps on the ground and gauge their progress. A waxing crescent was low in the sky, when they came to a huge, vertical escarpment that the carpets could not ascend.

Titus attempted a blind vault—and went nowhere. "We must be inside the no-vaulting zone now."

A hundred miles—or less—from the Commander's Palace. They could be there within an hour, if they were to fly without interruption. Titus felt a weakness in his fingertips: he was frightened, after all.

He had always been.

Fairfax tried to boost them up, but around six hundred feet or so above ground, the force of air she generated was only enough to keep them hovering, not to gain any more altitude. And the top of the cliffs was still two hundred feet farther up.

"Should we climb or should we go around?" asked Amara, her voice tight.

"The fault line seems to stretch as far as I can see," said Kashkari, surveying the expanse of the cliffs with the help of a far-seeing spell. "You've more experience with escarpments, Durga Devi. What do you recommend?"

Amara clamped her teeth over her lower lip. "I say let's fly a mile or two toward the southwest—the cliffs in that direction seem lower."

Unfortunately, the impression of lesser height turned out to be an illusion of perspective. Amara signaled them to stop. "We passed a protrusion. Might be the best we can do under the circumstances."

The protrusion was barely enough of a foothold for one. Amara pulled out a length of hunting rope from her bag. They all contributed what ropes and cords they carried. The hunting rope, pulling the entire length of the ropes knotted together, shot up the face of the cliff and disappeared over the top.

The end of the rope was attached to Amara, who used the hunting rope's pull to run up the cliff, as graceful as an acrobat. Titus and Fairfax, both still on their carpet, exchanged a look of head-shaking admiration.

"I will probably bruise my face going up," said Titus.

"No, not that. That's my favorite part of you."

"Really? You told me something else altogether in the lighthouse."

It was the first time either of them had brought up their night together. She slanted him a look. But then the hunting rope returned and Kashkari made ready for his ascent, so they had to situate themselves underneath him and pay attention, in case he fell.

Kashkari reached the top without mishap. As they waited for the rope to come back again, Fairfax leaned over and whispered, "When I said that, it was just to make you happy before you died."

He whispered back, "I am touched. You said it very, very loudly.

You must have been really concerned about my happiness."

This time her eyes narrowed. Briefly he wondered if there would not be a bolt of lightning in his near future. But she only caught the rope and ascended the cliff, acquitting herself nicely.

Titus did not smash his face during his run up the precipice, but once he was on flat ground again, he struggled to release the rope from his person. The line kept yanking him forward at the pace of a sprint. He lost his balance and was dragged forward on his stomach. Amara hissed to recall the hunting rope. Fairfax and Kashkari threw themselves on him so he would not slam into one of the huge boulders that littered the top of the escarpment. He frantically tried every untying spell in his repertoire.

The knot slipped all of a sudden, leaving him a few feet short of a boulder, with Fairfax and Kashkari each hanging on to one of his boots. Slowly they sat up, panting hard. The knees of his trousers were bloodstained: the trousers had not torn—mage fabrics were stern materials—but his skin was much more fragile.

Fairfax was already seeing to his scraped knees when Amara at last managed to recall the hunting rope. She came and stood next to them, her breath as irregular as theirs.

"Sorry about that."

"What did you have the hunting rope chase?" asked Fairfax.

She had already cleaned his scratches and was sprinkling a regenerative elixir onto them. He would have told her to save the elixir for more significant wounds—but it was not as if they had a great deal of time left to accumulate more serious injuries.

"I said to find a snake," answered Amara. "Maybe one was close by. Hunting ropes accelerate when they are near a quarry."

"I hope we don't accidentally disturb a giant serpent," said Kashkari.

No one commented. Titus might not believe in the existence of giant serpents, but he did not want to remark on it one way or the other. He did not want to say anything at all. Even though no one spoke above a whisper, on top of the escarpment their voices carried, a disturbance that he could almost see in the clear, cool air.

Fairfax had finished with her ministrations. She put away her remedies and gestured for everyone to hand over their canteens and waterskins for her to fill. No one objected to prolonging their stop, even though their containers must still be nearly full—the conditions were not the kind that required frequent hydration. Titus thought longingly of the ledge above the ravine. What he would not give to be that far from the Bane again.

He got up, took a few gingerly steps, and called for a far-seeing spell. The moon had set. The land they had flown over, a dark, forbidding expanse that unfurled at the foot of the cliffs, was scarcely visible. Here and there a jagged outcrop of obsidian glinted in the starlight. And if he squinted really hard, he could make out gullies and fissures, as if someone had hacked away at the land with an enormous broadsword.

Little wonder the interior of Atlantis remained almost as empty as the day mages first settled the newborn island, barely cooled from the paroxysm of its creation. Had they been on foot, they would still be stuck in the Coastal Range, trying to find a way out of a pathless land.

But as daunting as he found the terrain behind him, it was the landscape yet ahead that filled him with dread. Ten miles or so northwest another escarpment reared, even higher than the one they had just scaled. Much of its surface was as smooth as fondant on a cake, but nearer its base, the cliffs seemed to be riddled with darker patches. Were they caves of some sort? Lairs for giant serpents? The desire to turn back, to hide forever among the hard-gouged ravines of the Coastal Range, grew ever more potent.

Fairfax put a hand on his elbow and gave him his waterskin. They stood together for some time. Then, wordlessly, they made ready to go on.

They were airborne barely seconds before she leaned over the side of the carpet. "Wait! What's that? Did you see?"

Titus swung the carpet around for a better look.

"Are those . . . bones?" she whispered.

They were bones indeed, spread over a relatively even area, perhaps three hundred feet or so from the edge of the cliffs, hidden from their view earlier by several large boulders. The bones were scattered, but some seemed to be still stuck together, not as part of an animal or human skeleton, but as if they had been set with mortar.

"Do you think they'd been in a stack earlier, those bones, and that the hunting rope knocked it over?" Fairfax asked Amara.

Amara swallowed. "It's possible."

A stack of bones. What had Mrs. Hancock told them? *Sometimes hikers come across bone piles characteristic of those left behind by giant serpents—usually as territory markers.*

Kashkari raised a few of the bones with a levitating spell. "How old are they?"

Or rather, how fresh?

"Fairly weathered," judged Amara. "I would say they've been in the elements several years, at least."

"Let's be careful," said Kashkari. "Giant serpents shouldn't be an obstacle if we stay airborne."

But he, like Titus, was looking at the great precipice that loomed in their way, and the openings that seemed a perfect size for giant serpents.

Fairfax tapped Titus on the shoulder. "I hear something."

Visions of giant serpents swarmed his head. But the sound was only that of beating wings—wyvern riders on patrol. They landed in a hurry and hid themselves in the cracks between overlapping boulders, wands at the ready. The wyvern riders, however, passed high overhead, swooping down toward the lowlands.

It was the first time they had seen wyvern riders since their arrival on Atlantis proper. Yet another sign that they were most assuredly getting closer to the Commander's Palace.

Titus glanced at Fairfax. If she was thinking of her lifeless body in the Bane's crypt, she gave no sign of it. Amara, beside her, showed more strain, her fingers digging into the boulder.

But after the wyvern riders had disappeared from sight, it was Amara who said, "Let's go. The end is near."

Titus kept one eye on the ground for bone stacks. He saw no more of them, but that did not comfort him: if the piles marked the boundaries of a giant serpent's territory, did it mean that they were now deep inside what the beast considered its private dominion?

His other eye he kept on the sky. They flew higher off the ground than he liked—the fear of an unexpected attack from below manifesting itself. This greater altitude made them more visible from every angle.

At the sight of a team of wyvern riders far to the northeast they landed and concealed themselves. Fairfax set a sound circle. "Do I remember you saying, Kashkari, that in the first part of your prophetic dream concerning me, you were riding a wyvern?"

"That's correct," answered Kashkari, if a little reluctantly.

"Have you thought about how you might obtain a wyvern?"

Stop, Titus wanted to say. *Do not help him make any part of his dream come true.*

But she was right. If they all had to sacrifice everything to get Kashkari inside the Commander's Palace, then that was what they must do.

"I have," said Kashkari, "but I don't see how—not yet, in any case. They are flying in much bigger groups than I was expecting. And I'm sure that the moment we attack one group, the riders will alert everyone else."

For the next ten minutes, they discussed various possibilities. But no one could come up with a plausible scenario where the benefits of commandeering a wyvern outweighed the overwhelming disadvantages.

After they climbed back on the carpets again, they had not gone two miles when Amara said, "I hear them again. Behind us."

There were no perfect hiding places immediately nearby. They took cover in a crease of the ground and hoped that the darkness of the night would safeguard them from unfriendly eyes. A squadron of wyverns shot up from the lowlands. They circled. And circled—right above where Titus guessed the knocked-over pile of bones must be.

"They know we are here," said Kashkari.

They debated whether to get on the carpets again or to proceed on foot. The question was settled when Amara swore. "They are dropping down hunting ropes."

As they took to the air again, Titus and Fairfax gripped each other's hand tight. On the next carpet, Amara and Kashkari did the same.

The end is near.

The next escarpment came all too soon. They tried to find a way up that did not require them to leave the protection of the carpets.

Above the openings leading into possible giant serpent lairs, however, the cliffs were as even and vertical as a wall, with barely a toehold for a goat, let alone a full-grown mage. And they dared not use a hunting rope again, for fear it would disturb something far worse than a stack of bones.

"We have to move forward somehow," said Amara, her face set. "No point going back, and we can't st—"

Kashkari gripped her wrist and pointed down. From the shadows at the base of the cliffs, almost directly below them, something was emerging. Its head was the size of an omnibus, and its body even thicker around.

In the distance, from beyond the top of the cliffs, came the sound of dragon wings.

Was that what giant serpents ate between long bouts of inactivity? Wyverns—and wyvern riders?

The flapping of dragon wings grew louder. The giant serpent below came to a stop. Titus stared, unable to help himself: the bulbous head, the stillness, the dimly metallic glint of its scales.

He braced himself for the emergence of an enormous forked tongue. It never came. He frowned. The castle in the Labyrinthine Mountain housed a small collection of local reptiles. And every time he saw the snakes, they were always flicking their tongues in the air.

He looked around, hoping not to find any more giant serpents. But what were those things silently slithering up the face of the cliff? Juvenile giant serpents, lured by the scent of a nice, fresh meal? His heart stopped. No, they were long, mechanical claws, far bigger and longer than those extending from the armored pods chasing Fairfax and Kashkari in Eton, but of essentially the exact same structure.

And they came out of the giant serpent.

Which was no serpent, but a mechanical contraption of Atlantis's. Of course the real giant serpents were already extinct. Of course the Bane would have a counterfeit one. Of course he would want Atlanteans to believe that giant serpents still existed: it became so much easier to not only keep civilians away from his stronghold, but to explain an occasional disappearance, like that of Mrs. Hancock's sister all those years ago.

"Fairfax!"

Titus barely managed to squeeze the word past his throat. But she had seen and understood. Two great boulders flew up from the plain below and smashed the claws right at their "wrists," breaking them off altogether.

The claws scraped along the cliff as they fell, and met the hard rock of the plain below with an enormous clamor.

"We have to hide," said Fairfax, her voice shaking.

Amara was already steering her carpet lower. "Follow me."

She led them into one of the openings on the face of the escarpment. It was easily the worst hiding place possible, except their only other option was to remain in the open—an unacceptable choice.

Amara listened at the mouth of the cave. "More than just

wyverns are coming. I can hear bigger beasts."

Titus could not hear anything over the frenetic beating of his own heart. He had not wished to meet any giant serpents. But he had trained in the Crucible for battling such straightforward monsters his entire life. The ferocity of a beast was always, always preferable to the cunning and treachery of anything devised by the Bane.

"Is there a back wall to this cave?" Kashkari asked.

"I don't think so," said Fairfax, who had the best night vision. "Not for some distance, at least."

A good thing, for the unmistakable sound of hundreds of slithering hunting ropes rose to Titus's ears.

"Can we outrun hunting ropes?" asked Amara.

She meant by going deeper into the cave, into the labyrinth of connected tunnels that the real giant serpents of yesteryear had left behind in the base of the escarpment.

"Maybe not," said Fairfax. "But I can burn them if they come too close."

Provided they themselves did not run smack into a dead end. There were so many perils of heading desperately down a path they knew nothing about—

Kashkari swore. "Something is coming from the inside."

Fairfax, always quick to react, brought down enough rocks to collapse the passage.

They barely had enough time to turn away, to avoid the flying debris brought on by the roof of the passage giving away. They were cornered, with no escape, not even a dark, dangerous, and utterly unfamiliar warren.

The first wave of hunting ropes wriggled up the cliffs. Instead of fire, Fairfax called for a torrent of air to blow them away. But whatever they did now was only stalling for time. Outside the Atlanteans called to one another, advising care as they positioned "cliffwalkers" in place. Titus crept as close to the opening as he dared and saw that cliffwalkers were entities that resembled armored chariots, but had feet that drilled into rock to keep them anchored to the vertical surface—had they been carried up by the bigger beasts Amara had heard?

"Get back here!" Fairfax growled.

Titus made a hurried retreat. Fairfax collapsed the front entrance to the cave. Now they were well and truly trapped. To one side the cliffwalkers were noisily clearing away the rubble blocking the entrance. At the other end of the cave, the unseen entity, either the same counterfeit giant serpent they had seen earlier or a different one, judging by the metallic clangs it made, rammed repeatedly against the rocks in its path.

They had at most a minute or two before their defenses were breached.

A garland of flame came into being, the firelight illuminating Fairfax's stark but determined eyes. "Looks like this is the end of the road for me. I know Titus cannot bring himself to kill me—and probably not Kashkari either. Will you do me a favor, Durga Devi, and make sure that I am not captured?"

No! No! screamed a voice inside Titus's head. But he only stood with his hand clenched uselessly around his wand.

"Yes, I will do you a favor," said Amara, her voice hoarse, yet with a note of triumph. "Just not the one you ask."

She set her hand on Fairfax. A moment later, *two* Fairfaxes stood in the center of the cave. The one who was Amara in truth cast aside her thick coat, pushed up her sleeve, and revealed an intricately wrought ruby-studded band.

And on your upper arm you wore a gold filigreed armband set with rubies, Kashkari had said at the lighthouse, as he described Fairfax in his prophetic dream.

But I don't wear any jewelry, Fairfax had protested. *And I don't have any.*

And Amara had been there, sitting quietly among them. Had she felt the metallic pressure of the armband against her skin? The unbearable weight of a future that had been set in stone?

Titus stumbled a step back, shock pounding like a hammer at the back of his head.

The real Fairfax gasped. "You are . . . you are a mutable."

Kashkari only made small, choked sounds, as if he had been mortally wounded. The one he had seen lying dead in his dreams had not been Fairfax, but Amara in Fairfax's form.

"The three of you hide in the Crucible," ordered Amara, a beacon of calm and authority in the rubble heap the cave had become, when everything they had believed about their future had been turned upside down. "I know it might be unstable in there, but you can handle it for a short time. I'll make sure the book is disguised as a rock."

"I will come with you," Titus heard himself say.

"What?" exclaimed Fairfax.

He turned to her, deathly afraid yet strangely elated that he was the one headed to his doom, and not the one he loved. "They know I am here. They will keep searching if they do not find me. But if they capture me, I can convince them that everyone else died in Lucidias. If they believe me, they will be more likely to be lax. A better chance for the two of you to reach the Commander's Palace undetected. Besides, Durga Devi might look like you now, but she does not sound like you—and the Bane knows what you sound like. I will speak for both of us and delay that moment of discovery for as long as possible."

"But—"

"Do not waste time arguing. We have been given an opportunity. Use it." He exchanged their wands—he did not want the wand that had belonged to both Hesperia and his mother to fall into the Bane's possession. Then he kissed her on her lips and shook the nearly catatonic Kashkari. "You too, Kashkari. *Go*."

Amara kissed her brother-in-law on his cheek. "Don't think about what you should have done differently. The troth band has been on my arm since summer. It's all meant to be."[4]

Still Kashkari remained frozen in place, shaking. Fairfax had to grab his hand and put it on the Crucible. They disappeared inside. Titus changed the book's appearance, then hid it as best he could.

"Would you mind if I stunned you?" he said to Amara, his voice quaking with both fear and gratitude. "That way I can pretend that I have botched an execution curse—it would make sense to the Bane that I would rather kill you than let him have you."

And so that her voice, which remained her own, would not give her away.

Amara nodded. He knew that it was Amara. He knew that the real Fairfax was safe for now, inside the Crucible. But it was Fairfax's eyes looking at him, eyes wide with fear yet resolute at the same time.

He hugged her tight. "If I do not have the opportunity to say it again later, whatever happens, we are forever in your debt."

She smiled strangely. "So I have lived long enough to be embraced by the Master of the Domain. May Fortune guard your every step, Your Highness."

He did not know exactly what she meant, but there was no time to ask. He pointed his wand at her. She crumpled to the ground just as the cliffwalkers broke the cave wide open.

CHAPTER · 21

ON THE MEADOW BEFORE Sleeping Beauty's castle, chaos reigned: creatures of all descriptions in melees, dragons spewing fire, swords and maces running amok as Skytower rose from beyond the hills.

An ogre lumbered toward them, only to have its head disconnect from its body as soon as Kashkari lifted his wand. A cyclops belonging to the Keeper of Toro Tower met a similar fate.

Iolanthe had never seen Kashkari in such a rage.

She left the killing to him and busied herself opening the tent she had brought from the laboratory. She covered the tent with a layer of sod to shield it from sharp implements and the view of marauding creatures. When the shelter was ready, she dragged Kashkari inside, hissing at the sight of his blood-soaked trousers.

Hurriedly she cleaned and bandaged his wound. "You are not allowed to be so careless, Mohandas Kashkari. Do you understand, damn it?"

He threw aside his wand and crumpled, his face wet with tears.

She knelt down next to him. "I'm so sorry. I am so, so sorry."

"I sent her to her death. I told her everything about that dream, even describing the troth band in detail. That must be how she recognized herself. That was why she married my brother and set out to find us all in the same day, not because of the massacre in the Kalahari Realm, but because of my dream."

Iolanthe remembered now what Amara had said that morning at the lighthouse, about her staunch belief that events that had been foreseen were not so much inevitable as unstoppable.

The prayer for courage that she had sung—it had been a prayer for herself, that she should be brave enough, when the time came.

And her calm, sincere answer only hours ago atop the stone ledge, when Iolanthe had asked her why she had come to Atlantis. *I've come to help you.*

I've come to help you.

And she had. She had saved Iolanthe and, in that process, saved them all. But at what cost to herself? At what cost to those who loved her?

Iolanthe wrapped her arms around Kashkari and wept too, for him, for Amara, for the husband who had been left behind.

Kashkari dropped his head to her shoulder. "I first dreamed of her when I was eleven," he said, as if to himself. "In my dream it was night, there were torches everywhere, and she was dancing. She had on this emerald-green skirt, and over that, a silver shawl with such heavy beading that it sounded like raindrops falling every time she spun around. She wove through the crowd, smiling and laughing, hugging all the women and kissing all the babies—I'd never seen anyone look so happy.

"That would turn out to be the evening of her engagement party. The dancing lasted well into the night—and my brother never once took his eyes off her." His voice caught. "Now he'll never see her again."

As a child, a mutable could mimic the appearance of another, and then resume her own without any trouble. But as an adult, if a mutable changed her appearance, it stayed altered. In life and in death, Amara would henceforth always look exactly like Iolanthe.

None of them would see her extraordinarily beautiful face again. Ever.

Iolanthe closed her eyes and imagined herself at Amara and Vasudev's engagement party: the firelight, the music, the stomping feet of the dancers, the hint of perfume and spice in the air. And Amara, full of love and a zest for life, blissfully ignorant of the deadly prophecy that awaited her.

Despair swamped her—destiny was the cruelest master. Every chosen one was damned. Even those who were simply swept along by the tide were towed under more often than not.

When she opened her eyes again, the bland interior of the tent greeted her, lit by the mage light she had summoned, everything cool, blue, and utilitarian. There was no joy, no music, and no celebration in her ears, only the din of the pandemonium outside.

She raised her wand, wanting to do something and not knowing what. Only then did she notice that she wasn't holding a plain spare wand. Vaguely she recalled Titus taking that from her and giving her his wand instead.

She had never seen this wand, made from a unicorn's horn. On it was etched the symbols of the four elements, along with the words *Dum spiro, spero.*

While I breathe, I hope.

She had come upon those words the day she first called down a bolt of lightning. And now here they were again, near the very end.

Was it divine inspiration or cosmic joke?

It didn't matter now. With or without hope, they still had work to do.

"Come on," she said, giving Kashkari's shoulder a shake. "You don't believe in the inevitability of visions. Let's go. If we can reach the Commander's Palace soon enough, maybe it'll end differently."

Her words were fervent, yet empty for all their urgency. Perhaps at the moment of his prophetic dream, the future had not yet hardened. But now . . .

Kashkari allowed her to wipe away his tears. "You are right. Let's do what we can."

He sounded as hollow as she had, but his eyes burned, despair with an edge of desperate hope.

She took his hands in hers and said—wishing with all her heart the exit password was anything but—"And they lived happily ever after."

Dozens of hunting ropes rushed into the cave and bound Titus and Amara tight. Mages holding actual battle shields crowded the cave and stripped Titus of the plain wand that had been in Fairfax's hand a minute ago. Next, they not only blindfolded him, but gagged him as well—presumably the Bane did not want him telling anyone else about the Lord High Commander's penchant for sacrificial magic. He was then put under a temporary containment dome, to be sure he would make no trouble for the Atlantean soldiers.

He was afraid they might plug his ears too, but they did not seem to care that he could still hear perfectly well.

"She is unconscious, but her life signs are strong," reported someone. "We are readying the astral projector, sir."

An astral projector would cast her image—and speech also, had she been capable of it—to a remote location. It was a piece of Atlantean wizardry that no one else had managed to duplicate.

The audience at the other location was apparently satisfied, for the next commands that boomed were for the astral projector to be dismantled and packed away, and for the "elemental mage" to be transported with great care.

The gag in his mouth was yanked out. "Where's the book?"

"In her bag, under a disguisement spell."

Amara carried a book of prayers with her. Titus could only hope that the Atlanteans would buy his answers.

"Turn it back."

"The spell is hers. I do not know the countersign to it."

"Where are the others who came with you?"

"They died in Lucidias."

The gag was shoved back into his mouth. Something like a metallic barrel closed around his torso.

"All right. Let's go quickly," ordered the same soldier who had interrogated Titus.

Titus was lifted bodily. The barrel was most likely attached to a cliffwalker. Briefly he felt the chill of the open air before he was set down again, the pressure around his chest easing as he was released from the metallic hold. A door slid shut. A few seconds later the cliffwalker was airborne.

He scooted around in his cell—almost certainly a containment cell—but Amara was not there. A debate raged in his head. Should he try to consciously remind himself that this woman who looked exactly like Fairfax was someone else, or would it be safer for everyone if he stopped the reminders and let his instincts take over instead?

Kashkari's prophetic dream had not included the real Fairfax. What would have happened to her by the time he, Amara, and Kashkari were together again? Would she be simply a few steps behind Kashkari or . . .

Knowing that Amara was the one in Kashkari's dream did not eliminate harm to Fairfax. In fact, it took away the one guarantee that she would not be used in sacrificial magic. Now there was no telling what would happen to her. Everything was possible, including the worst failure of all.

All too soon, the door of the containment cell opened and he was yanked to his feet.

A wyvern roared uncomfortably close by. But no flame scalded his skin and no talons hooked into his person—only his nostrils were assaulted by a sulfurous stink.

For a moment his imagination ran wild. Atlantis was the most geologically active of all mage realms, was it not? Who was to say that there was not a volcano nearby? The Bane might mistake it as dead, but it was only dormant, waiting for one with the power to reawaken it. And would that not be a worthy spectacle for the Angels to see the Commander's Palace engulfed in lava, swallowed by the earth itself?

But no, the smell of brimstone had been stronger in the desert, when he had faced the wyvern battalion. If any volcano slumbered nearby, it slept soundly indeed.

He was marched up a long flight of stairs, and then the faint odor of rotten eggs was completely gone. The air became bracing—the brisk, salty scent of the sea. He wondered whether he was imagining things. But as he advanced, his footsteps and those of a phalanx of guards echoing against high ceilings and distant walls, the scent only became more noticeable.

The Bane had grown up on the coast. When he left Lucidias, he had settled on a different coast. But the Commander's Palace was far from the sea. And the one who could not leave, the one who must remain hidden, buried in the bowels of this fortress, missed the scent he loved, the scent from the days when he had been whole and free.

It was terrifying to be reminded that the Bane was still human—it made him only more monstrous. What had Mrs. Hancock said? That he had used his first act of sacrificial magic to cure himself of a fatal disease. So he must remember his fear and anguish before that impending death. And yet he could not care less that he doled out such fear and anguish on an industrial scale.

His humanity extended only to himself.

The timbre of the footsteps changed. Titus's boots had been clacking against hard, smooth stone. But now he was walking across a different material, one that felt and sounded almost like . . . wood.

They came to a stop. Titus's gag and blindfold were removed. He was in another containment cell, a transparent one that allowed him to see that the floor of the chamber in which he found himself was indeed a fine, golden-hued wood, the rain ebony of the Ponives. And on the walls, instead of paintings, murals, or tapestry, hung enormous carved wooden panels. The coffered ceiling too had been fitted with a latticework of fine wood.

What had Mrs. Hancock said? *We never had a great deal of woods on Atlantis, most of the original forest had already been cut down, and importing timber for pyres was beyond the means of all but a few.* For the Bane, it was not marble that symbolized luxury, but wood, a costly rarity in his youth.

Titus forgot all about wood when he saw that not far from him, Fairfax lay crumpled in another containment cell.

That is not—

He pushed away the reminder from his conscious mind—instincts would take over. He rushed to the side of the containment cell that was a few feet closer to her. "Fairfax. Fairfax! Are you all right? Can you hear me?"

"And what is the matter with Fairfax, if I may ask?"

For a fraction of a second, Titus thought it was West, the Eton cricketer who had been abducted by the Bane, standing before him. But though the man bore a close resemblance to West, he was at least twice West's age.

The Bane's current body, then.

"It isn't like you to be speechless, Your Highness," said the Bane. "Be so kind as to answer my question."

Titus looked at the unconscious girl in the other containment cell. The main thrust of the lie would be the same, but he had a split-second decision to make. Did he play the cold-blooded opportunist or the distraught lover?

"She begged me to kill her so she would not fall into your hands. But I—" His voice shook at the sight of her, at the mercy of their enemy. "But I botched it."

"The arrogance of the young. To think you could thwart me and get away with it." The Bane shook his head, his expression almost sympathetic. "And where are your other friends, by the way?"

"They never left Lucidias—they all three together powered the last-mage-standing spell."

"They value their lives too cheaply."

"Better that than cleaving to life by any foul means."

"You, prince, are filled with the sanctimony of the young," replied the Bane.

"I hope that as the very ancient Lord High Commander lies asleep at night, he dreams of nothing but his own agonizing death— again and again and again."

Titus had wanted to hit a nerve. But the flicker of anger in the Bane's eyes hinted that he might have gone too far—and been too accurate. Titus could have kicked himself. The longer he kept the Bane talking to him, the longer the Bane's attention would stay away from Fairfax.

But now the Bane approached Fairfax's containment cell, which protected those on the outside against those on the inside, but not vice versa.

"*Revivisce forte,*" said the Bane.

She showed no sign of recovering consciousness.

"*Revivisce omnino.*"

The reviving spell should have been strong enough to counter the stunning spell Titus had used, but Fairfax remained motionless, not a twitch, not even a fluttering of the eyelashes.

"Highly inconsiderate of you, Your Highness," said the Bane. "For what I've planned for her, it would be much better with her awake and alert."

Titus felt as if he had been enclosed in a coffin lined with spikes inside. "I thought all you needed was for her heart to remain beating."

"True, but it makes for a far more powerful sacrifice when she is completely aware of the goings-on—up to the moment the contents of her cranium are extracted, that is. I have a very good spell for keeping the heart beating throughout it all, until that too is required in the last step."

At the horrors the Bane so casually described, Titus's throat closed. His still-bound hands clenched into fists, shaking.

"You love her, I see. Then you must be there to witness her final moments on this earth. It's the least you could do for her. The least I could do for such a pair of devoted young lovers."

"No!" He banged his shoulder against the wall of the containment cell. It was soft enough to absorb the impact of his weight but firm enough not to move an inch. "No! You will not touch her."

"And how will you stop me, without the aid of your magic book? You are in my domain now, Titus of Elberon. There are no surprises that you can wield against me."

"She will defeat you."

"I built these containment cells to be mighty enough for me. You can say many things about her, but you cannot say she is a greater elemental mage than I."

The Bane turned to Fairfax and pointed his wand. *"Fulmen doloris."*

Titus flinched. The spell was powerful enough to make the dead sit up and scream in pain.

She did not move or make a single sound. He could not believe it. Had he inadvertently rendered her permanently comatose?

"When you bungle an execution curse, you bungle it royally, young man," murmured the Bane.

He pivoted, his wand pointed at Titus, and such a conflagration of pain engulfed him, as if every square inch of his skin had been set on fire. He screamed.

"Hmm," said the Bane. "She really is insensate. In a few minutes, if she still doesn't come to, I'll put some actual flame to her person and see if that doesn't help."

Titus trembled. The pain that had overwhelmed him was gone, but its memory still burned.

"Now, since dear Fairfax refuses to cooperate, we shall have a chat, you and I, Your Highness."

There was something extraordinarily smug about the Bane's tone. Dread crawled over Titus with feet like those of a hundred millipedes.

"Let me ask you something. Why did Gaia Archimedes betray me?"

It took Titus a moment to recognize Mrs. Hancock's real name.

"Because you murdered her sister to prolong your own life."

"And how would she have known it?"

Titus hesitated. "She and your old oracle met and fell in love. And they exchanged enough information for that to come up."

The more truth he told, the greater the chance he would not be interrogated under truth serum.

"You mean Icarus Khalkedon? But he never remembered anything from his oracular sessions."

"That is what he wanted you to believe."

The Bane's eyes narrowed. After a moment he said, "I see. What else didn't I know about him?"

"That he was not in a true trance when he told you that I should be sent to a nonmage school and that Mrs. Hancock should be placed on site to keep an eye on me."

"Why you?"

"Because my mother was pregnant with me at the time, and you always saw the Domain as a potential threat."

"Was that the only instance in which Icarus lied to me during an oracular session?"

"It is the only one I know of. Mrs. Hancock said he planned to give several more correct answers and then kill himself."

"Such treachery. Which makes it even more heartwarming, I assure you, when it is one of his final answers that led me to this body." The Bane gestured at himself. "A fine specimen, is it not?

"I obtained this body almost eighteen years ago at the Sheikha Manāt Interrealm Hub in the United Bedouin Realms. It was exactly where Icarus said it would be, waiting for a connecting translocator."

Premonition sank its cold claws into Titus. Almost eighteen years ago. A young traveler. A disappearance no one could explain.

The Bane smiled. "I do not enjoy the process of taking over another body. It is necessary, but never pleasant. In Wintervale's case I had to allow myself to be surrounded by his memories for some time, so that I would be able to recognize the people around him and imitate him to a creditable extent. I did the bare minimum, which proved to be a mistake—it was just like that stupid, shallow boy to never think about his one fatal weakness. No, it was all cricket, his mother, Mrs. Dawlish's boys, and his old home in the Domain."

Titus wished his fist could connect with the Bane's nose and shove it straight to the back of his skull. "Wintervale was worth a hundred of you. A thousand."

The Bane shook his head. "You are a young, foolish boy, full of maudlin sentiments. You should have had some of your grandfather's pragmatism. He killed his own daughter to keep his throne. All you had to do was hand me the elemental mage and you could have reigned in peace for the remainder of your natural life."

"My grandfather was but an instrument you wielded. You were the one who killed my mother. I will set fire to the Citadel myself before I become your willing collaborator. And I will gladly be the last heir of the House of Elberon if it hastens the hour of your demise."

The Bane smiled again, but this time with a harder edge. "We digress. Now where was I? Yes, my failure to learn enough about Wintervale. After Wintervale died, when my consciousness traveled back, what should I find but that the body I'd been using since June, after Fairfax electrocuted its predecessor, had died during my absence, of an aneurysm of the brain, of all things.

"So it was on to the next body, this one. And with the dire example of Wintervale before him, I deemed it prudent to dig a little deeper into this one's mind. He seemed to be of a simple enough background. Before he was brought here, he'd been a student in the capital city of your great realm, a nice boy who enjoyed helping customers at his father's bookshop. He hiked in the Serpentine Hills and sailed off the coast—a cliché, almost, if one didn't account for his Sihar ancestry."

Titus fell back against the far wall of the containment cell—and slid to the floor.

"Does that sound familiar to you? It was so ordinary and colorless I was convinced there was no need to pay further attention. And then, about forty-eight hours ago, I thought to myself that perhaps I'd made a mistake in the execution of Princess Ariadne. Perhaps if I hadn't asked for her life, I would not have made such an implacable enemy of her son.

"Such violent emotions erupted in this one. Not that violent emotions aren't always running through the little peons. You cannot conceive of the tedium of always having to ignore their alternate tantrums and fits of despair. But in this instance the upheaval was cataclysmic. I had to find out the reason—it was hindering my mastery of the body.

"It was not easy. This one had actually gone through some effort to compartmentalize his memories. It was only hours ago that I finally broke through. And what a secret: a passionate love affair with none other than the late Princess Ariadne herself. Who'd have thought? Even I had mildly wondered about the identity of your father, Your Highness, and what had happened to him. To think I believed it had been some shenanigans of your grandfather's, when I'd had him here all along. It really is too bad that I didn't find out sooner. You would have traded Fairfax for your father, wouldn't you?"

Would he? Titus thought wildly.

"But it's too late now. You will have neither. Fairfax will give me another century of life. And you, it will give me great pleasure to watch you leave the shores of Atlantis a broken man. It won't just be Fairfax I will sacrifice for my health and longevity; I will use a good few parts of you too. Let's see, I shall require an eye, definitely an eye. Your wand arm, it goes without saying. Beyond that, it will depend on my mood. How would you like to be known as the Eunuch Prince?"

Titus could barely stop himself from wrapping his arms around his knees and rocking back and forth. Where were Kashkari and the real Fairfax? When would this nightmare end?

"In fact, before I apply fire to our dear Fairfax, I shall apply a blade to you. You won't miss a finger or two, will you?"

The Bane sauntered forward, a knife in his hand. Titus wanted to scream, but he could only whimper. Then, all of a sudden, he leaped to his feet and words rushed out of him like water from a collapsing dam.

"Can you hear me, Father? My mother named me after you. And she never gave up on finding you. I always wondered why she took part in the uprising against Atlantis. Now I know it was for you. That failed, but before she died, she asked me to promise her I would do my utmost to defeat the Bane, because it was the only way for me to ever see you."

The smile on the Bane's face became ever more smug, almost radiant. He seized Titus's still-bound hands. An ice-cold blade settled against Titus's thumb.

"She loved the vine that you gave her!" Titus shouted. "It climbs over a pergola on the upper balcony of the castle. I could always find her underneath it—it was her favorite spot!"

The knife lifted. "Son?" came a tentative whisper, without a shred of the Bane's arrogance.

Titus's heart almost burst out of his chest. "Father! Please help me! Please help all of us!"

The Bane laughed. He hooted and guffawed. "You believed that? Oh dear, oh dear. You actually believed that poor sod could overpower *me*?"

Tears ran down Titus's face. He was a child of six again, watching the flames go up around his mother, nothing but despair in his heart. "Please, Father. Do not let him do this."

The knife dug into his flesh.

"She loved you," he whispered. "She loved you until the day she died."

The knife moved away. He raised his head in incredulity. Had he succeeded at last, or was the Bane about to make another cruel play?

It was neither.

Across from him Fairfax whimpered. Slowly she pushed herself to a sitting position, one hand clutching at her head. Then she looked about at the unfamiliar surroundings.

Her gaze settled on the Bane.

She shuddered.

CHAPTER · 22

IOLANTHE AND KASHKARI EMERGED FROM the Crucible ready for assault. But the cave, its air still dusty, was silent—and dark.

They stood in place for several minutes, listening. Then Iolanthe set a sound circle. "I don't think anyone is here."

The ruse had worked as intended. The Bane believed he now had both the Master of the Domain and the elemental mage whom he had been desperately seeking for so long.

"But we still have the same problem," answered Kashkari, his voice hoarse but steady. "We still can't get up that cliff face."

Iolanthe grimaced. Did they fly around? They had no idea how far the escarpment stretched in either direction. Certainly beyond the range of their far-seeing spells.

Into their impotent silence came agitated clicks.

"What's that?" she asked.

"Sorry," said Kashkari. The noise stopped. "The last time we all left the Crucible together, Titus told me to take a small stone from the meadow, to keep the book 'open.'"

Kashkari had become their keeper of the last resort, as he had seemed destined to outlive them all. Since the Coastal Range, he had been the one to carry the Crucible on his person. Titus had taught him all the passwords and countersigns for the Crucible, and Iolanthe had given him the words to unseal the connection between their copy of the Crucible and the one they'd left behind in the Domain—in the unlikely event he left the Commander's Palace alive and needed to get out of Atlantis in a hurry.

"I was jangling the contents of my pocket," he went on, "and the stone was knocking against Durga Devi's prayer beads."

Kashkari, like the prince, almost never fidgeted. For him to be reduced to such nervous motions told her everything she needed to know about his frame of mind. She sighed.

The next moment she grabbed him by the front of his tunic. "I know how we can get our hands on a pair of wyverns—or at least I know where we can try."

Iolanthe murmured the words to undisguise the Crucible and felt about on the rubble-strewn floor of the cave until she had the book in hand. Next she had Kashkari "close" the book. Then she took him to visit the Oracle of Still Waters.

The oracle's pool captured the image of those who last looked into it. This was how Titus had circumvented the Irreproducible

Charm, captured her image, and given Sleeping Beauty her face. She hadn't known whether to give him a swift kick or to kiss him silly—she would worry about that later, if there was to be a later. Now she busied herself pitching her tent in the middle of the cave—once the tent had been sealed, light on the inside could not be seen from the outside.

With Kashkari standing guard at the mouth of the cave, she huddled in the tent, under a smidgen of mage light, and made changes to several stories in the Crucible. When she was satisfied with her modifications, she extinguished the light, packed away the tent, and entered the Crucible once again, Kashkari at her side.

Since the Crucible had just been "reopened," the meadow was quiet and peaceful, no treasure hunters trampling across the long grass yet. They flew toward Sleeping Beauty's castle.

"I'm carrying a two-way notebook that lets me communicate with Dalbert," she told Kashkari. "If something happens to me, you take it. The password is 'conservatory.'"

"Wouldn't be much use, would it?"

"You might think differently if you were to survive—let's not only prepare to die."

She didn't cling to any hope, but as long as she breathed, she would act.

They shot past the ring of impenetrable briar that surrounded Sleeping Beauty's castle and came to a stop. Below, by the gate of the castle, lay two wyverns, sleeping, their hind limbs in chains.

It was possible to bring out objects from the Crucible. In fact, it was necessary to keep the book "open" and instantly accessible. But until now, they had brought out only small, inanimate items: a jewel belonging to Helgira or a rock from the meadow before Sleeping Beauty's castle.

Now for something different.

"I've made it as easy as possible for us," said Iolanthe. "If we can't get the better of these wyverns, we don't deserve to ride them."

Kashkari exhaled. "Then what are we waiting for?"

"We meet again at last, Fairfax. Welcome to my not-so-humble abode," said the Bane, all graciousness and suave manners.

The woman who looked exactly like Fairfax regarded him with loathing.

"Are you all right?" Titus shouted. "Are you hurt?"

Briefly she closed her eyes. Of course she had been in pain—the Bane had tortured her in his effort to rouse her. But she had willed herself to remain perfectly silent and still to buy more time, giving up the pretense only to save Titus from certain mutilation.

"Hmm, you don't seem as delighted by our reunion," said the Bane. "I suppose I can't really blame you, considering what is about to happen."

Fairfax shuddered but did not speak.

"As much as I would love for you to say a few words of your own volition, I will hear from you soon enough when you begin to scream. Shall we, then?"

Titus stumbled—without notice, the containment domes had begun to move.

"Are you all right?" he called again to Fairfax.

She winced and leaned against the wall of the containment dome.

"This is not the end," he said desperately. "Not yet."

"Not for you," said the Bane. "You will live, with as many missing parts as it is possible to have and still remain alive."

Titus shook. Or perhaps he had not stopped shaking since he was first captured.

"Father, can you hear me? He already killed the woman you loved. Please do not let him harm the one I love. Please!"

"Oh, young love. How touching," said the Bane.

"We met because of one of Mother's visions. She had written that I would see a feat of tremendous elemental magic when I woke at two fourteen one afternoon. So I would have Dalbert wake me up at precisely that time whenever I was home in the castle. About seven months ago, on a perfectly clear, cloudless day, a bolt of lightning burst into being. It lasted and lasted until the shape and brilliance of it was imprinted on my retinas. I got on my peryton, vaulted to where the lightning had struck, and that was how I first saw her, half of her hair standing up."

The Bane, walking behind them, displayed nothing but a polite interest. So Titus kept on talking, telling his father everything about his entire time with Fairfax, the setbacks, the heartbreaks, the triumphs—everything except that it was not the real Fairfax in the containment dome gliding alongside his.

Corridors, ramps, stairs. He would have marveled at how perfectly the containment domes coasted along—or the countless intricate and expansive wood carvings that lined their path. But the only thing gripping his attention was the fact that they passed no one on their endless descent.

It was not surprising that the Bane should have a private route through his stronghold—both the Citadel and the castle were full of secret passages known only to the family and maybe a few of the senior-most staff. But this meant it would be nearly impossible for Kashkari and Fairfax to find them.

Titus's voice was wearing out. "I forgot to tell you, remember the copy of *The Complete Potion* that my mother defaced, the day she met you at the bookshop? What she wrote in the margins led Fairfax to bring down her first bolt of lightning. We are all connected in destiny, all of us."

They were no longer descending but in a straight passage, narrow enough that he and Fairfax were proceeding single file. A door opened to an enormous chamber.

An enormous chamber with a huge mosaic of the Atlantean maelstrom on the floor—exactly as Kashkari had described.

They had arrived at the crypt.

At the far end of the crypt, an elaborate sarcophagus sat on a raised dais. Before the dais were arrayed six plain, raised platforms in two columns. Five of the platforms were empty. On the last one lay West, the Eton student who had been abducted because he, like Titus's father, bore a striking resemblance to the Bane.

The containment cells stopped in the middle of the crypt.

"Only the worthy may proceed farther," said the Bane.

With a lightning-fast motion, he struck at Fairfax. Titus did not even have time to cry out before the Bane pulled back. Fairfax, her face contorted in pain, gripped her right arm. The Bane held a thick pick aloft and, an ever-delighted expression on his face, examined the blood that had been extracted.

"Very lovely blood," said the Bane, as he walked toward the sarcophagus. "I hope it will tell me that you will be an extremely effective sacrifice. But of course it's only formalities—we both know how powerful you are, my dear."

But of course the blood would reveal nothing of the sort. And as soon as that was done, the Bane would learn the truth.

"Are you sure you have body parts remaining that can be used for a sacrifice?" jeered Titus, even as his palms perspired.

"Trying to stall for time, prince? No, the time for talking is done."

Behind the sarcophagus, with only his head and his shoulders visible, the Bane busied himself with his infernal procedures.

"Do you ever dream of your children?" Titus made a last-ditch effort. "Do you ever see their bloody remains? What about your little granddaughter? Do you ever see her begging you to please not hurt her anymore?"

"That reminds me, it will give me great pleasure to remove your tongue, Your Highness," said the Bane, completely unruffled. "I will be doing the mage world a service, I bel . . ."

His voice trailed off. He raised his head and stared at Fairfax. She stared back at him. He returned his attention to his task, seeming to be repeating the procedure once more.

Again, he looked up.

Titus felt his blood turn into ice.

The Bane knew. He knew he had been duped, that the one who stood before him was not the one he had moved heaven and earth to find.

Slowly, he came toward them.

"Do not let him hurt my friend!" Titus cried. "Father, do not let him. Help us!"

The Bane stopped before Amara's containment dome. "Who are you?"

"I am but another one of your sworn enemies," said Amara, rising to her feet, her voice clear and proud. "There is no end to us. Every time one falls, another one will take her place. Your days are numbered, you vile old man. In fact, you will not live to see another s—"

The Bane lifted his hand. She slumped over.

"No!" Titus screamed. "No!"

The slight distortion in the air that had marked the outlines of her containment cell disappeared. The Bane lifted his hand again—and flung her twenty feet into a support column.

"No," Titus whispered.

The Bane was before Titus. "Where is she? Where is Iolanthe Seabourne?"

Titus heard himself laugh, a soft, half-crazed sound. "I do not know. You can pour any quantity of truth serum down my throat, and you will get the exact same answer. I do not know where she is."

The Bane's eyes burned into Titus's. "Then you will die too."

With the black tunics and half helmets Iolanthe had borrowed from the costumes being readied for Sleeping Beauty's fancy dress ball, she and Kashkari were scarcely distinguishable—at least in the dark—from any other pair of Atlantean wyvern riders. Half an hour into their flight, she saw, as he had dreamed, a faint pool of light in the distance.

She was scarcely breathing, and her heart felt as if all the blood had drained out hours ago. But she was long past any need for courage: desperation was a far better impetus.

A few minutes later, Kashkari said, "The light is coming from the top of a mountain. From *inside* the top of a mountain."

He was right—light was spilling out of the summit of a big,

conical peak. Iolanthe sucked in a breath. Now she at last understood the description of the Commander's Palace. "It's inside the caldera."

"Any chance you can awaken the volcano?"

As his uncle had.

"I wish that were the case. If there's magma anywhere near I'd have sensed it—nothing but solid rock underneath this one. Sorry."

Kashkari grimaced. "It wasn't as if the Bane would make anything easy for us."

Wyverns wheeled above the caldera, far fewer in number, however, than she'd been led to expect—even the Bane could not replace the hundreds of experienced wyvern riders he had massacred in the Sahara with a quick wave of his wand. But colossal cockatrices carried by oversize armored chariots were every bit as jaw-dropping and intimidating a sight as the description suggested.

Many guard towers stood upon the circle of peaks that surrounded the caldera—the brim of the erstwhile volcano itself. Soldiers patrolled various sections of the rim, and from time to time wyverns would land for a few minutes before taking to the air again.

"Let's put the wyverns down. Wyvern riders seem to do that regularly enough—we shouldn't attract too much attention."

They landed in the dark hollow of a ridge near but not at the top of the rim, on the outside of the caldera, and led the wyverns back into the Crucible. The meadow was again in an uproar, with

Skytower already at its edge. They left in a hurry, taking a brass key someone had dropped in the grass, to keep the Crucible "open."

Behind Iolanthe, Kashkari limped. She turned around. "You all right?"

"A little more time and I'll be good as new."

She braced her arm around his middle; he did not refuse her help. They stuck to the shadows as much as possible as they climbed to the brim of the dead volcano, looking around constantly.

The ascent was steep, but not particularly treacherous; no loose stones or little depressions perfect for spraining ankles. In fact, near the top, the land flattened noticeably. Even with Kashkari leaning on her, they made good time.

As the terrain underfoot began to tilt the other way, they crouched down next to a boulder—more to shield themselves from the nearest guard tower than anything else—and looked down upon the Bane's redoubt.

It was much, much bigger than she had anticipated. Even against this grand natural setting, the palatial fortress, on its own hill at the very center of the caldera, dominated by its sheer aggressiveness. She had imagined it would be foursquare like Black Bastion, but there was something maritime about the architecture of the Commander's Palace. Its walls seemed to meet at angles sharper than ninety degrees, its roofs looked like unfurled sails, and both its northern and southern extremities jutted out like a ship's prow.

Kashkari swore. "No wyverns land on or near the actual

palace—if we try to approach that way, we will be immediately marked as suspicious. Carpets will be a dead giveaway. We can't vault and we can't walk across the floor of the caldera past all those rings of defense. How the hell do we get in?"

Iolanthe took a deep breath. Her heart pounded and her hands shook, but it was as if the quantity of fear and anguish that had washed through her this night had somehow anesthetized her.

"We'll get in exactly as you foresaw in your dream," she replied with something that was almost equanimity. "How would you like to be the first mate of Skytower?"

Kashkari stared at her, probably thinking back to his prophetic dream. *I was in the air again, on a huge terrace or platform that floated forward.* "Skytower? I was standing on *Skytower*?"

"I don't know," Iolanthe answered. "But now you will."

When they had last gone into the Crucible to hide, some part of her mind had noticed the silhouette of Skytower. If she were to stand at the front of the command deck, she would not see the great rock formation below, in the shape of an upside-down peak, but would think herself on a floating platform.

And that was good enough for her.

Kashkari's jaw clenched. "Well, let's go take over Skytower."

Which was a far easier task than otherwise, given that now the Enchantress of Skytower and her second-in-command looked exactly like Iolanthe and Kashkari, respectively, after the modifications

Iolanthe had made to the illustration that accompanied the story, affixing their own likenesses, captured by the Oracle's pool, onto the characters' faces.

A short time later, they stood on Skytower's command deck, their crew of bloodthirsty marauders waiting for orders. But how did one take a tower the size of a mountain out of the Crucible?

By its steering helm, Kashkari recommended. The handling of the helm wasn't usually the second-in-command's task, but no one was going to deny him the use of it, especially not when the mistress of Skytower herself accompanied him, her hand on his arm.

"And they lived happily ever after," she said.

The night sky in the Crucible was replaced by the far brighter night sky above the Commander's Palace, which looked a good deal less impressive when viewed from the lofty vantage point of Skytower.

They had succeeded—they had taken out the entire Skytower.

The sudden appearance of this colossus stunned the Atlanteans. The wyvern riders gaped from their mounts; two armored chariots almost flew smack into Skytower; and cries of alarm and dismay echoed from below, from the guard towers and the rings of defenses.

Kashkari summoned his carpet. They had laid the Crucible carefully atop a battle carpet, so they could retrieve it immediately: anything brought out from the book would evanesce if it moved more than a short distance away.

Iolanthe caught both the carpet and the book.

"Where's the helmswoman?" asked Kashkari. "She can—"

He cried out and fell against the helm. Skytower rammed directly into the side of the caldera. The entire structure shuddered. The crew shouted. Iolanthe grabbed on to the railing.

Kashkari screamed. Skytower skidded starboard, its enormous base now scraping and scoring the inside slope of the caldera.

She pried him off the helm. "What's the matter? What's going on?"

He bent over, his fingers digging into her forearm. "Pain. Everywhere."

She gasped. "You are still connected to Titus via a blood oath, aren't you? You are feeling *his* pain. The Bane—the—"

If the Bane was torturing Titus, then he already knew Amara was not the elemental mage he wanted. What had happened to *her*?

She grabbed the helmswoman normally in charge of Skytower's navigation. "You see that building down there? Plow it flat. *Flat.* I want to see deep into its bowels."

Pain racked Titus. His internal organs were raked over burning coal, his sinews shredded apart.

"You interfering little snot," snarled the Bane. "You think you can keep me from what I want? I always get what I want."

Titus could not speak. He could not even scream. The pain ratcheted tighter and tighter. He was blind with agony.

He barely felt the shudder in the floor beneath him. The sound, like enormous millstones grinding together, only vaguely registered. But the next second his pain stopped. He collapsed to the floor of the containment cell, gasping.

The Bane stood listening. Titus could hear nothing—they were too far into the center of the hill on which the Commander's Palace stood. Which made the noise from a moment ago all the more remarkable. What had happened?

"Is Iolanthe Seabourne behind this?" demanded the Bane.

"I do not know." But he certainly did not think it was beyond her. What had she done? Caused an actual earthquake?

The entire palace lurched, again and again, as if its levels were being sheared off one by one. The jolts went straight to Titus's stomach. He clenched his teeth against repeated surges of nausea. Yet another hit. The ceiling of the crypt cracked. Stone and plaster rained down; dozens of wood carvings thudded to the floor.

The sounds changed, from those of brutal impact to something almost like a needle scratch, if the needle was the length of a street. Titus sucked in a breath. *Skytower.* Its great rock formation had a blunt end, but one of Skytower's secrets was that it could extrude a huge spike from that blunt end. And the helmswoman who piloted Skytower was said to be an artist with that spike, and could carve her name on a piece of stone no bigger than the seat of a chair.

It must be Fairfax. She had found a way, as she always did. He was on his feet, his face pressed against the wall of the containment cell, his fist pounding. *Come on, Fairfax. Come on!*

Something that resembled a wasp's stinger, if the wasp was the size of a phantom behemoth, tore through the ceiling near the southern wall of the crypt. He gasped. Beyond the shredded ceiling was the sky itself—Fairfax and Kashkari had managed to bulldoze the Commander's Palace.

In that jagged band of the harshly lit night sky, Atlantean forces were madly maneuvering. Titus tried to recall what he could of Sky-tower's crew. Did they have enough mage power to hold the wyvern battalion, the armored-chariot-carried colossal cockatrices, and all the other soldiers and war machines the Bane had at his disposal?

He glanced at the Bane, expecting to see the latter's face twisted with rage. Instead, the Bane was smiling. Titus's nascent hopes turned to ash. Why was the Bane delighted? What were his plans?

Wildly he looked about. Then he saw it, the round, transparent base of the other containment cell, gliding toward the opening in the ceiling. That very moment Kashkari and Fairfax streaked in on their carpets. Before Titus could shout in warning, they passed directly over the base of the cell.

Instantly the walls of the cell closed about them.

CHAPTER · 23

AS FAIRFAX'S AND KASHKARI'S CARPETS struck the invisible barrier, they cried out and fell in a heap.

"No! No!" Titus screamed.

It could not be. They had not demolished the Commander's Palace to be caught like rats in a trap.

The Bane laughed. "Why, thank you, my dear Fairfax, for taking the trouble to deliver yourself to me."

Titus fell back against the far wall of his own containment dome, his hands over his face. Not this. Not this bitter, senseless end. Not after everything they had gone through, all the sacrifices that had been made, and all the lives that had been irrevocably lost.

Inside the other containment cell, Fairfax was getting up. "You all right, Kashkari?"

Kashkari was slower to rise to his feet. "I'm fine," he said, wincing.

Fairfax's gaze landed on Titus. She raised her hand and rested it against the wall of her cell. "Your Highness."

Titus could only shake his head, trying not to break down and weep openly.

"Where is Durga Devi?" she asked.

From her spot, the pillar upon which the Bane had dashed Amara blocked the line of sight to where the latter lay.

"She is here."

"Is she . . ."

"I do not know."

Her containment cell glided across the floor toward the Bane. Kashkari gave a cry as they rounded the pillar and he saw Amara's crumpled form. Fairfax's throat moved at the sight of her own face on that too-still body.

The din of battle rose to a deafening pitch outside—the defenders of the Commander's Palace were throwing themselves upon the marauders of Skytower. But Titus scarcely heard anything, his attention fixed on Fairfax. There was a smear of dirt on her face and bits of rock dust in her hair, and he was reminded of the day they first met, seven months and forever ago.

The cell stopped six feet from the Bane. At last she looked upon the monster himself. She did not appear afraid, only weary beyond words.

"My dear, dear Fairfax," murmured the Bane.

"My lord High Commander," replied Fairfax, in her low, rich, slightly gravelly voice. "Or is it Palaemon Zephyrus? No, I forgot. Your real name is Pyrrhos Plouton, you nasty old man."

The Bane's good humor apparently could not be dampened by a few barbed words. "About to be an even nastier, even older man, thanks to you."

"You will not have me," she said flatly. "Nor will this cell hold me."

"This cell is built to be strong enough for me."

"I thought so," she said. "Step behind me, please, Kashkari."

A bolt of lightning left her hands and struck the wall of the containment cell, which lit up and crackled. The Bane's expression changed. He had built the cell to be strong enough for him—but he was not capable of lightning.

Suddenly Titus felt the Bane's wand at his temple.

"Stop or the boy dies," snarled the Bane.

"Keep going!" Titus shouted. "It does not matter if I die. Finish *him*!"

Fairfax hesitated.

"Do not think. Do as I say!" he shouted louder, even as his voice turned hoarse. "Break free now!"

A pain like ice gored him in the stomach. He fell down. Ice turned into fire, charring all his nerve endings.

"Be a good girl," came the Bane's honeyed voice, "and he won't suffer any more."

"No . . ." The possibility that she might listen to the Bane horrified Titus. "No . . ."

Her jaw worked. An agony like having his spine ripped out skewered through him. He convulsed, but he kept his eyes on her, willing her to hold firm. Her hands shook. Her whole person shook.

The Bane lifted his wand. Titus braced himself for worse. The Bane half dropped his hand, raised it again, and slid it to the side. Titus blinked, so confused and taken aback he only faintly noticed that he was no longer in pain.

The Bane waved his wand about like the conductor of an orchestra. A sneer twisted his lips, an expression of sheer disdain. Yet as Titus watched, that disdain turned into consternation. Then, outright anger.

The next second the walls of the containment cells disappeared. The Bane knelt down and lifted Titus. "Get off that base," he said to Fairfax and Kashkari, both flabbergasted. "I can't keep him away for long."

No, not the Bane. This was Titus's father, and Titus was looking into the kind, beautiful eyes that his mother had loved. "Father. Father!"

"You look just like your mother," said his father, hugging him tight. "You look just like Ariadne."

He kissed Titus on the forehead. "Someone stun me right now and put a spell shield around me. The Bane can't use me if I'm unconscious."

Fairfax and Kashkari raised their wands. But whereas Kashkari fulfilled Titus's father's request, Fairfax lifted a chunk of stone and sent it flying toward—

West, who was just sitting up on his platform. He promptly tipped over and fell onto the floor.

"Good thinking!" cried Kashkari.

With Titus's father unconscious, the Bane had turned to West. But now, with his last spare out of commission . . . Fairfax, Kashkari, and Titus looked at one another: faced with a clear path to the Bane's sarcophagus, they were at a loss over what to do.

A wall of flames roared their way.

The Bane's original body might not have fingers left to grip a wand, or even a tongue for speaking the words of an incantation, but his mind was perfectly functional. And the mind was all that was needed to power feats of elemental magic.

While Kashkari and Titus shouted for shields, Iolanthe raised her hands and pushed back against the fire. "Keep an eye on West and your father," she cried. "Keep them safe."

It had amazed her to hear Titus calling the Bane's current body "father." But it all made sense. Now if only they could defeat the Bane and get out of here.

She lifted one of the stone platforms and sent it crashing toward the sarcophagus, and then another—the best way to keep everyone safe was to keep the Bane busy defending his original body. She advanced. The fire he had summoned she kept sweeping toward him. "Do you enjoy being toasty, my lord High Commander?"

The third platform she smashed into the sarcophagus fractured the lid. With a wave of her hand, the split halves of the lid went flying.

"The ceiling!" Kashkari shouted.

Cracks zigzagged across the ceiling. Enormous slabs of stone fell. Iolanthe redirected the tonnage of debris toward a far wall of the crypt. The next moment, half of everything she'd just put away came zooming back, headed for Titus. With a yell she propelled the slabs off course.

Titus cried out. She screamed too, fearful he had been hurt, only to see that with all her efforts concentrated on keeping him safe, the Bane had managed to hurl a slab into Titus's father.

With a sinking heart she lifted up the slab. More fire erupted, a conflagration that engulfed the entire crypt. She hefted the fire upward, so that those who lay on the floor—Amara, West, and Titus's father—would be spared from the flames.

"We must keep advancing!" Titus called.

"The longer he stalls us, the more likely the mages of Skytower will be overwhelmed and he will be rescued," said Kashkari almost at the same time.

Iolanthe gritted her teeth and punched a lane through the fire. Titus and Kashkari marched on either side of her, applying shields. The pieces of decor had caught fire and were smoking mightily. The air shimmered with heat from the flames. The Bane's sarcophagus seemed to warp and wriggle.

More fire. More flying rocks. Despite the shields, she felt the skin on her cheeks blister, a scalding pain. Grunting with the effort, she again hoisted the flames a few inches higher, not wanting those on the floor to suffer.

Ten feet. Five feet. Three feet. They leaped onto the dais and stood over the now lidless sarcophagus. But all Iolanthe could see of the interior was a milky fog.

Kashkari prodded the tip of his wand against the fog. The wand was stopped by an invisible shield. Titus was already trying various incantations.

"Should I shatter the rest of the sarcophagus too?" Iolanthe asked.

"You can," said Kashkari. "But I doubt it'll help. I think the sarcophagus is just decoration—this inside shield is what truly protects him."

But how did they break through this shield, which the Bane must have spent decades, if not centuries, perfecting?

And they must do it soon. Outside the roar of wyverns was deafening. The stink of colossal cockatrices had already reached her nostrils. And the crew of Skytower were calling for her. "We have to get out of here, Skipper!" "Skipper, we can't hold them off for much longer!"

Had they come so far to be thwarted by a *shield*?

Titus and Kashkari whispered fiercely, trying spell after spell. She and the unseen Bane wrestled with each other via their command of the elements, locked in a stalemate. Sweat dripped down her face, an indescribable pain where it rolled past the blisters on her cheeks. Cries from the Atlanteans outside were becoming more aggressive, more triumphant. Soon armored chariots would crash through and it would be too late.

Out of the corner of her eye she caught sight of West crawling across the rubble-strewn floor of the crypt. Her heart very nearly leaped out of her rib cage: the Bane had retaken command of West's body. But when he raised his face and met her gaze, there was no malice in his eyes, only a great determination—it was just West, who had regained consciousness.

He inched along, dragging an injured leg behind him, making for Titus's father. When he reached the latter, he lifted one of the man's hands and pointed at the sarcophagus. *Of course.* The Bane's original body needed to be cared for, and who better to handle the task than his current body? It wasn't any spell or incantation that Titus and Kashkari could think of that would rescind the shield, but the touch of the current body.

"Stand back," she ordered Titus and Kashkari.

She aimed a bolt of lightning directly at the shield, then another, and yet another—not to damage the shield, but to keep the Bane worried and jumpy, focused only on Iolanthe's doings. And as she did that, she poked Titus in the side and indicated West with a tilt of her head.

Titus, after a similar initial moment of dread, understood. He leaped off the dais and brought his unconscious father the rest of the way to the sarcophagus. With Kashkari's help, they lifted him high enough to place his hand on the shield.

The milky fog cleared.

Iolanthe knew the Bane's original body had to be completely mutilated. Even so, she gagged. She didn't know how anyone could be so butchered and still be alive. The body had nothing below the waist. Both arms were gone. Ears, nose, lips, teeth—none remained. Only one eye stared out at her, with loathing, fear, and a covetousness that was a hundred times more vile than any disfigurement.

Titus and Kashkari, too, stared, staggered and repelled.

"Come on. Put it out of its misery!" shouted West.

She glanced toward Titus—he looked as paralyzed as she felt.

"What about you, Kashkari?" begged West.

A muscle near Kashkari's jaw leaped. He lifted his wand and pointed it at the Bane. As had happened with the ogre in the Crucible, the Bane's head disconnected from his body with an audible pop and a spurt of blood that sent all three of them scrambling backward.

They waited for a moment. For so long the Bane's every footstep had made the entire mage world quake. Iolanthe half expected the floor of the caldera to collapse in a cataclysmic convulsion and bury them under millions of tons of volcanic rock. But except for the spurt of blood, the Bane's death was as ordinary as anyone else's.

Kashkari dropped to his knees and retched. She hurried to him and dug out a remedy from her bag. Once he'd swallowed the remedy, she wrapped her arm around his shoulders and raised her waterskin to his lips.

Two feet from them Titus knelt next to his father, holding the latter's wrist in his hand with a grim expression. Then he closed his eyes for a moment, kissed his father on the forehead, and leaped off the dais.

Kashkari got up too. Most of the elemental fire had cleared, but many decorative pieces made of wood were still burning. Through the haze of smoke he tore across the rubble-strewn expanse of the crypt, his feet pounding on the mosaic of the great maelstrom of Atlantis. At his approach, Titus, who was already at Amara's side, looked up and shook his head.

Iolanthe covered her eyes. Kashkari's prophetic dream had come true, down to its every last detail.

A hand shook her by the shoulder. "We have to go. Now."

Titus. They embraced briefly, then busied themselves getting everyone onto carpets, Amara with Kashkari, Titus's father with him, and West with Iolanthe.

The ruins of the Commander's Palace burned. The scene above was greater chaos than any she had seen on the meadow of Sleeping Beauty's castle: wyverns shrieking, armored chariots careening, swords and maces from Skytower whirling about the fortress, a tornado of weaponry.

They darted up to the command deck, put their hands on the Crucible, with Iolanthe's other hand around Skytower's helm, and recited the password. As they arrived inside the Crucible, she realized the chaos on the meadow was no less, after all. But since they controlled Skytower, they were above most of the pandemonium, which made it easier to take off on their carpets in the direction of Black Bastion.

Her carpet had been suborned to Kashkari's, which allowed her to take a look at West's leg. Something had definitely been fractured, but she could give him no help beyond a full dose of pain-relieving remedy. "As soon as we get to safety, we'll have a doctor fetched for you."

But would there be safety at the other end? The monastery's copy of the Crucible most certainly had fallen into Atlantean hands. Was it in the Inquisitory, or worse, in Lucidias?

She pulled out the two-way notebook Dalbert had given her and wrote, *The Bane dead. The prince alive. In the Crucible, headed for the monastery's copy.*

The Bane dead. The prince alive.

It was all she wanted. Yet a black anxiety gnawed at the edge of her heart. Kashkari's prophetic dream had come true. What about Princess Ariadne's vision of her son's death?

She glanced at Titus. He happened to be looking in her direction. It was too dark to see his features clearly, yet she felt the same unease emanating from him.

Let him be safe. Let us outlive this night.

She found some burn potion, gave half to West, and applied the rest to her own blisters.

"That was quite impressive, by the way," said West. "Lightning bolts—now I've seen everything."

"How are you? Not too shaken up, I hope?"

"Completely shaken up. But we are safe now, right?"

If only she could answer that question with any confidence at all. "Hard to say. The Crucible itself is dangerous, even if—" She looked back and swore. "We are being chased!"

Kashkari echoed her imprecation. "They are towing spell accelerators."

"Are they?" Titus's question was sharp.

And his voice was unsteady.

"Did your mother mention spell accelerators in her vision?" Her voice too had risen an octave.

He said only, "Give me your wand."

Dum spiro, spero.

What happened to hope, when there was no more breath?

She handed him the wand and gripped his hand. "It'll be all right."

"I love you," he said. "And you will always be the scariest girl I have ever met."

A lump lodged in her throat. "Shut up and fight."

Several miles behind them, three cowl-like nets were being readied. Titus released his spells one after another; Kashkari did the same. After a minute or two of this rapid firing, Kashkari wrenched all the carpets up and to the right.

West yelped, his fingers gripping hard onto the carpet's edge.

"Kashkari has to keep the carpets steady when he and Titus aim, but then he has to swerve to avoid being hit by the spells cast by our pursuers," Iolanthe explained, panting with relief that they had not been hit. At least not this round.

West's response, after a pause, was, "The prince called you the scariest girl he's ever met. You are a *girl*?"

Eton College seemed to belong to the misty reserves of history, but it had been mere days ago that West, Kashkari, and Iolanthe met regularly for cricket practice. Of course West had every reason to continue to think of her as a boy.

She waved a hand. "That's not important right now."

They had covered approximately one-third of the distance to Black Bastion. *That* was important. Also important, that together

Titus and Kashkari had stunned several of their pursuers.

She wiped a hand across her brow. She was perspiring, and not just from nerves—the night, quite cool earlier, had turned unseasonably warm. The weather inside the Crucible always reflected that outside. Why would it have suddenly become hot on Atlantis?

Skytower had been directly on top of the Commander's Palace when they brought it back into the Crucible. Which meant the Crucible would have dropped right down into an inferno.

"Titus, can the Crucible catch fire?"

"Eventually, yes."

"We might be inside the remains of the Commander's Palace."

"Or we might have been deliberately set on fire," he said grimly, "to finish us off."

No matter what had happened, the result was the same. They were in for a broiling.

Sparks leaped on the grassland below. Smoke was already rising. The air rushing past her face was so hot she might as well have stuck her head into an oven. Titus and Kashkari, however, seemed to pay no attention to these developments, their focus solely on their spell-casting.

The grassland burst into flames. Distant woods too caught on fire, their burning branches crackling. Smoke obscured the sky, muffling the screeches of the wyverns in the distance.

What had Titus told her long ago about the vision of his death?

My mother saw a night scene. There was smoke and fire—a staggering amount of fire, according to her—and dragons.

All the conditions had been met.

"Yes. That's all of them!" shouted Kashkari.

She started. It took her a moment to understand that he was talking about their pursuers. While she'd been preoccupied with fire and doom, Titus and Kashkari had stunned every last wyvern rider in their wake.

And there, ahead, was the silhouette of Black Bastion through the billowing smoke, much closer than she had thought it would be. Hope shot through her, a starburst of happiness. The future that she had given up on was now back in her embrace, full of laughter and promises.

She turned to her beloved. For the first time since the Bane's fall, she wanted to celebrate. He was gazing at her too, with wonder in his eyes. They had done what they needed to do and they had survived. Now they would have all the time in the world to be young and frivolous. They would play; they would sit around; they would spend entire days not doing anything useful and not preparing for any great, awful task.

He smiled, he who so seldom had reasons to smile. She grinned from ear to ear. Oh, how lovely it was to be alive—and together.

He leaned toward her, his hand outstretched. The next moment he stiffened, his expression one of pain and surprise. Beyond him, in the firelight, Kashkari's face filled with horror. Spells that had been distance-cast took a while to reach their targets. And in his jubilation, Kashkari had forgotten to swerve one last time.

Titus fell.

CHAPTER · 24

"NO!" WEST SCREAMED. *"NO!"*

Iolanthe summoned a fierce updraft. *I will die by falling,* Titus had once told her. And so she had prepared. He was *not* going to die by falling, not while she was with him, not while she was the great elemental mage of their time.

"West, brace yourself." With a levitating spell she transferred a flailing West to the vacant spot left on Titus's carpet. "Kashkari, untether my carpet."

"Done!" said Kashkari.

She zoomed down to where Titus hovered in midair, kept aloft by her updraft, and pulled him onto her carpet. *"Revivisce omnino! Revivisce omnino!"*

He showed no reaction; his face still bore that expression of pained surprise. She gripped his wrist—no pulse. She put her ear on his chest—no heartbeat.

She could not believe it. She could not accept it. Surely he had been only stunned, not killed.

"Don't you dare die! Not now! Don't you dare, Titus!"

Kashkari, now floating beside her, tried spells of his own. Nothing, nothing at all.

Blood pounded in her ears. They must do something and they must do something fast. The Crucible kept no dead. Titus would be expelled from the Crucible if they couldn't think of something.

But what? What?

She gripped Kashkari's arm. "How do distance spells kill? How?"

"By instantly stopping the heart. But I can't think of any spells that would start the heart beating again."

Neither did she know of any such spells. Despair swallowed her. Violently she shook Titus by the shoulders—as if that would help. "Come on! Come on!"

"May I—may I offer a suggestion?" said West.

His carpet, still suborned to Kashkari's, had brought him down. She stared at him. What ideas could *he* possibly have that would be of any use?

West swallowed. "My father is a professor of biology at King's College, and he does experiments on the effect of electricity on muscle stimulation. You can command electricity. Can you try and see if that would get his heart muscles to contract?"

Iolanthe stared at him one more moment. What kind of arrant

nonsense was that? But beyond that fraction of a second, she did not hesitate.

She gathered a ball of lightning in her hands and aimed the sphere of electricity at Titus's chest. Once. Twice. Three times.

His tunic smoked. She waved away the smoke and put out the sparks. Kashkari already had his hand on Titus's wrist, his brows furrowed in concentration.

"There's a pulse!" he shouted. "Fortune shield me. There is a pulse!"

Now it was Kashkari whom Iolanthe stared at in disbelief. How was it possible? How was that at all possible?

"Don't just sit there," Kashkari ordered. "Put some air into him, damn it!"

Of course. Of course. She pried apart Titus's jaw and forced a current into his windpipe. He coughed and half sat up, a look of utter confusion on his face.

Tears filled her eyes. She kissed him madly, but very, very briefly. "Let's go. Let's go!"

The entire world inside the Crucible was burning. They flew through smoke and fire, with Fairfax holding the worst of both at bay.

When they arrived at Black Bastion, its occupants were running about in a frenzy, and they had little trouble gaining access to the portal. They also managed to leave Black Bastion in the monastery's copy of the Crucible without much ado.

There was the unpleasant question of where they would find themselves once they exited the Crucible, and Titus ought to prepare for that. But he simply could not pull himself out of his utter amazement at being alive.

Every other minute he would turn to Fairfax and ask, "Are you sure that I am still on this earth? Are you sure this is not the Beyond?"

She would simply smile and kiss him again. Though around the fifteenth time he asked, she said, "I rather think we'd all be cleaner in the Beyond."

It was true they were all in a state of appalling grime—the soot on her face had streaked from where her tears had run down. Worse, there was a gash on her arm and another one on her side, and she could not even tell him what had happened—or when.

He turned to West, probably also for the fifteenth time, and said, "If ever there is anything the House of Elberon can do for you, let me know."

West stammered for a bit, before he cleared his throat and said, "I'd still be stuck in that horrible place if all of you hadn't come. So I'd say we are even."

As Sleeping Beauty's castle—and the moment of truth—drew near, Titus fell silent, wondering if the worst was still to come. Fairfax placed her hand over his. "We'll get through it."

He raised her hand to his cheek, beyond grateful—no one who toppled the Bane could be said to have lived anything less than a remarkably full life.

"Look at that!" cried Kashkari.

A few miles ahead, a silver-blue flare shot high in the air. It expanded to take on the shape of a giant phoenix, shimmering against the night sky.

Titus was astonished. "It is the beacon of an ally—an ally of the House of Elberon."

He rushed to apply a far-seeing spell. Beneath the beacon, on the meadow before Sleeping Beauty's castle, stood a man, waving.

And that man was none other than one of Titus's greatest allies, Dalbert.

After Titus's speech on the balcony of the Citadel, mages had started launching incendiaries at the scores of armored chariots that hovered above Delamer and kept the city in a state of siege. The situation escalated rapidly. After some hesitation, Commander Rainstone, who had led the force that came to Titus and Iolanthe's aid in the Sahara Desert, decided not to wait anymore before taking down the armored chariots.

As it turned out, the raid on the facility under the Serpentine Hills that had so dismayed Titus had not destroyed the entire cache of war machines. In fact, the raid had been allowed to happen to fool Atlantis into thinking that the resistance had been brought to its knees.

With newer and better war machines that had been hidden elsewhere, mostly in the Labyrinthine Mountains, the Domain's forces downed the armored chariots and took over the Inquisitory. This last had happened only a few hours ago, and everyone had been waiting, in a state of finger-biting tension, to see what Atlantis's reaction would be.

The Bane's demise shifted the advantage decisively to those who had long opposed him, but the situation remained fluid and dangerous. Atlantis had a large standing military and contingents stationed all over the mage world. Who would control that structure in the power vacuum left behind by the Lord High Commander's death?

"We will need your help in making crucial decisions, sire," said Dalbert, after he summarized the events of the past few days.

All three copies of the Crucible that Atlantis had confiscated had been kept at the Inquisitory in Delamer—the Bane had not wanted anything that could possibly function as a portal for his enemies on Atlantis itself, but he had not wanted to destroy them in case they could be useful to him. Dalbert had made it a priority to retrieve the copies after the sacking of the Inquisitory and had brought them to a villa on the shoulder of the Serpentine Hills, where Titus's parents had often met during their clandestine courtship.

And so it was that Titus and his friends also found themselves in his parents' former love nest, a small, airy house with warm cream walls and decor in the colors of the sea. Dalbert had remedies, baths, and nourishment waiting for them, and while they refreshed themselves, he saw to West's leg.

Titus scrubbed himself clean. Then, in a soft, blue tunic that smelled of cloud pine and silver moss, he sat down in the dining room, next to a busily eating Fairfax.

"Hmm, already frowning," she said. "I see the joy of being alive doesn't last very long with you."

The one he loved knew him all too well. "Unfortunately, it is beginning to sink in that since I lived, I will be expected to actually govern. It almost makes me wish I were dealing with the Bane instead."

She rolled her eyes. "You idiot. Have you already forgotten what it was like to deal with the Bane? Run your damned realm and be grateful."

He laughed. "I deserved that, did I not? 'Shut up and govern.'"

"Yes, you deserved that." She shoved a chocolate croissant into her mouth and closed her eyes for a moment in undiluted bliss. "But here's another thought: you will do very well at it. In fact, someday you might be spoken of in the same breath as Titus the Great and Hesperia the Magnificent—not by me, mind you, just historians who don't know any better."

He laughed again, feeling light and blissful.

Outside, the horizon was at last turning a pale shade of fire. The longest night of his life had come to an end. A new day was beginning.

Kashkari had just joined them when Dalbert ushered in Commander Rainstone, who was on their side after all. Titus greeted her warmly and offered both her and Dalbert a seat at the table. Commander Rainstone analyzed the situation in greater detail. Then she said, "Under extraordinary circumstances, the High Council may approve of handing the reins of power to a sovereign who is still underage. These are certainly extraordinary circumstances, and I have no doubt that a unanimous approval will be forthcoming. Have you given some thought, Your Highness, to how best to proceed?"

Titus glanced at Fairfax—they had been talking about it before the other three arrived in the dining room. She nodded. He exhaled. "The Bane had long cut down anyone who might emerge as a threat to him. There is no one waiting to succeed him on Atlantis. It seems to me that the Domain must step in and play a large role in the near future, perhaps in the running of Atlantis itself.

"To do that, we will need, to some degree at least, the consent of the people of Atlantis. I propose that I take responsibility for what happened and provide a detailed narrative of the Bane's many secrets. It will come as a traumatic shock to most Atlanteans, but truth is the only remedy in a situation like this."

"I believe Mrs. Hancock has left behind an account of her

story—and the evidence she had gathered—in a safety-deposit box with the Bank of England," said Kashkari. "She was an Atlantean who had lost a sister to the Bane's practice of sacrificial magic—her words will carry significant weight."

"Lady Wintervale's words will also carry a great deal of weight," added Dalbert.

"Is she all right?" exclaimed Fairfax.

"She is well enough—she was held at the Inquisitory in Delamer. I have spoken to her, and she is more than willing to let the world know what the Bane did to her son."

"Here comes the more difficult part," said Titus. "The Bane had many loyalists who benefited greatly from their association with him. And there are Atlanteans who will feel resentful at their realm's loss of power and prestige. At the intersection of those two groups we may expect to find mages who will be determined to ignore the truth, no matter how well documented. And they will wish to seek vengeance for what they consider an assassination.

"Mrs. Hancock is no more—and she left behind no living family. Lady Wintervale has no one to worry about except herself. What about you, Kashkari, are you prepared to take credit for having killed the Bane?"

Kashkari was silent for a minute. "I know I have done it, and that's quite enough for me. I'm not willing to endanger my family to be known publicly as the one who accomplished the deed. Fortunately, my contribution in the matter can be obscured easily enough, but Fairfax . . ." He turned toward her. "Your role cannot be covered up."

"No, indeed," said Commander Rainstone. "The part of the great elemental mage will have to be told."

Fairfax frowned.

"Your Highness can extend the protection of the crown to Miss Seabourne," suggested Dalbert.

Fairfax blinked. "But that would require us to marry, wouldn't it? We are not even of age."

Becoming a princess consort, with all its commitments and obligations, was not what Titus wanted for her either. Not now, at least, not when she was at last on the cusp of achieving her dream of attending the Conservatory.

"If I may, I believe I have foreseen the solution," said Kashkari.

All eyes turned to him.

"Do you remember, Fairfax, when we were on Atlantis, and I thought I had dreamed of your funeral?"

Fairfax nodded.

"You told me then it took place before the great Angelic Cathedral of Delamer, where only state funerals are held." Kashkari looked around the table. "Since my sister-in-law passed away in Fairfax's form, why not hold a state funeral for her? The Bane's loyalists will not hunt for Fairfax if they believe her already dead."

"That's an ingenious idea," said Dalbert. "No one besides those in this room knows that Miss Seabourne returned from Atlantis, and we will happily hold that secret."

Iolanthe laid her hand on Kashkari's arm. "Are you sure?"

He smiled a little. "I will need to consult my brother, of course. But in the main, I believe Amara would have been tickled to have such a grand send-off."

Kashkari left to write to his brother. Dalbert departed on his many and often mysterious tasks. But Commander Rainstone remained at the table.

"If you don't mind me asking, Your Highness, Miss Seabourne, what happened to Master Horatio Haywood and Miss Aramia Tiberius?"

"Master Haywood died defending us with a last-mage-standing spell. Miss Tiberius is currently with Atlantean authorities, I believe—she betrayed us."

Commander Rainstone sucked in a breath. "Oh, that child."

"The apple doesn't fall far from the tree."

"So you know that she is indeed Lady Callista's flesh and blood, sire?"

This caught Titus's attention. "You know too?"

"After Horatio made the switch, I switched them back."

Fairfax gasped. "You were the one who switched us back?"

Commander Rainstone sighed. "You probably know that I read Her Highness's diary, Miss Seabourne, which I did under duress—Callista, my half sister, kept insisting that something terrible might happen to her child if I refused to find out what Her Highness might have foreseen. As it turned out, I read a vision of a man switching the places of two infants in a nursery, on a night during which there seemed to be a steady shower of fireworks outside the window.[5]

"As I left the hospital, after having been caught snooping by Her Highness herself, I saw the meteor storm overhead and realized that the streaks of falling stars were what Her Highness had foreseen. All at once I understood why Callista had been spending so much time with Horatio, because he knew an orphaned baby girl in that hospital, and because that girl was soon to go to a relative who had never seen her before.

"I made up my mind then that I would not let Callista do this. She would not steal someone else's child. I reversed the switch.

"I was afraid that Callista might treat her own child as a mere decoy. But that did not happen, as most of the time Callista kept her memories suppressed and didn't think of Aramia as someone else's child—though she was disappointed that Aramia was neither beautiful nor a born charmer.

"I spent time with my niece when I could. I wanted to be a different kind of influence in her life. And at first she proved to be a very rewarding child, bright, inquisitive, always attentive, and with beautiful manners. But later I saw that she was obsessed with winning her mother's love, the kind of obsession that didn't care what it crushed underfoot, or that this mother of hers was made of a monstrous indifference to just about everyone except herself.

"I pulled back my involvement with Aramia, but I must apologize here." Commander Rainstone bowed her head in Titus's direction. "Early on I had told her about Validus's sister wand. She gave the information to Atlantis, when the new Inquisitor wanted to know how he could find Your Highness, after your escape from their bell jar dome in the desert."

"Did you also tell her about the destination disruptor in my possession?" asked Titus. "The one that would have allowed me to use a translocator at Delamer East to get to Atlantis?"

"No. According to those at the Inquisitory, Aramia told them that it was Prince Gaius who had shown her the disruptor long ago." Commander Rainstone turned to Fairfax. "Miss Seabourne, please allow me to apologize to you also. I should never have spoken of Validus's daughter wand to anyone, blood relation or not. I hope you will forgive me for having put your life in danger."

"Quite to the contrary," said Fairfax. "I am *most* grateful to you for not letting me grow up under Lady Callista's influence."

They were silent for some time. Commander Rainstone rose and bowed to Titus. "With your permission, sire, I will return to my duties."

Titus nodded.

As she reached the door of the room, Fairfax stood up. "If you will excuse me, Commander. You and my guardian were friends—very good friends, I believe. Did you ever speak to him about what he had done?"

Commander Rainstone shook her head. "For a time I was as upset at Horatio as I was at Callista. But then, about a year after Aramia was born, I asked to meet with him. He said he was too busy just then. A year after that, he contacted me. But when we met, I realized that the only memory he had of Callista was the first time he saw her.

"Later that day I confronted Callista. But she didn't know what I was talking about either—her own memories were suppressed too. I left completely frustrated: I couldn't help him, nor could I find help for him. So I pulled away from Horatio, feeling that our friendship simply wasn't strong enough to withstand what he had done and who he had become."

Fairfax slid her fingers along the edge of the table. "And were the two of you ever . . . more than just friends?"

Titus remembered the picture Fairfax had shown him of Haywood and Commander Rainstone from many years ago —they had seemed completely taken with each other.

Commander Rainstone shook her head. "No, we were very, very good friends, but never more than friends. The one I loved was . . ."

She looked down at her hands before her gaze came to Titus. "The one I loved was Her Highness, sire, your mother."[6]

Iolanthe and Titus didn't even go to bed, but fell asleep on long sofas in the solarium. At some point she became aware that Titus was speaking to her.

"... approved of the transfer of power. I have to go. I love you."

She made some sounds. They were probably a series of *mm-mms*, but she felt he would know that she told him she loved him with a ferocity that would frighten most wyverns.

When she woke up again, it was afternoon and a steady shower fell outside. She walked out onto the covered balcony and sucked in a breath: the great bell tower of the Conservatory, less than half a mile away! And the red roofs of the colleges, soaring above the tree line. And if she squinted really hard, she could even convince herself she was looking at the flow of colorful umbrellas on University Avenue.

"I see you are up, Miss Seabourne," came Dalbert's voice.

She spun around. "Oh, Master Dalbert, I know you have no time to spare. But would you happen to have a lackey you can send out for a copy of last May's upper-academy entrance examination?"

Dalbert smiled. "Consider it done. In the meanwhile, I have a visitor waiting for you."

"Who is it?" Who else knew that she was here?

"Master Kashkari," answered Dalbert. "Master Vasudev Kashkari."

She exclaimed softly. "When did he arrive?"

"About half an hour ago."

Dalbert conducted her to the reception room, where Vasudev Kashkari was waiting. The family resemblance was obvious—the brothers had the same build, same dark, expressive eyes, and same elegant mouth. Yet the difference immediately struck her; there was a great gentleness to the elder brother. The younger brother, for all his impeccable manners, was driven. But Vasudev Kashkari was the kind to smile and laugh easily.

Or at least he must have been once.

They shook hands.

"Please have a seat," she said. "It's an honor to meet you."

"The honor is mine. You have accomplished what mages have been aspiring to for generations."

"Not without help. Not without the sacrifice of many." She already had tears in her eyes. "We could never have done it without Durga Devi."

"I went to see her just now," he said softly. "I was told that she looked like you, but still it was . . . it was something of a shock."

"I'm sorry you couldn't look upon her face one last time."

"I already did that before she left the desert. She told me exactly what she meant to do."

"So you knew she was a mutable?"

He smiled slightly. "I have never told anyone this story—her mutability was something we had to keep a secret—but I fell in love with her when she looked very different."

"Oh," said Iolanthe.

"You know that mutables can take anyone's form when they are children, but can only change form once when they are full grown?" She nodded.

"We met during a time when she probably should have stopped assuming the appearances of others. But she was reluctant to give up the freedom not to be stared at everywhere she went. So I first saw her as her cousin Shulini."[7]

Iolanthe had met Shulini, who was a pleasant-looking young woman, but hardly a beauty of Amara's stature. "What a story that must have been. I wish . . . I wish I'd had the chance to know her better."

"You saw how she conducted herself under the most extreme of conditions. In a way, you couldn't have known her any better than that. But yes, I wish you had met her under different circumstances, when she was simply a warm, wonderful person to be around."

Iolanthe's eyes once again welled with tears. "Did you . . . did you ever ask her not to do this? Not to go on a venture from which she would not return?"

He looked outside the window for a moment, at the rain that was still steadily falling. She noticed for the first time that he wore Amara's troth band around his wrist.

"I wanted to," he said softly. "I wanted very much to beg her not to leave. But she was more than the woman I loved; she was a fighter. And one does not hold back a fighter when the battle is on the line."

This man might not have personally ended the Bane's existence, but he was no less remarkable than his brother.

She reached out and took his hands in hers. "She was the bravest mage I have ever met. You and she both have my eternal gratitude."

Vasudev Kashkari gazed upon her a moment. "And you ours. Never forget that."

The story of the Bane's death was released that evening. Iolanthe read it in her copy of *The Delamer Observer*, fascinated even though she already knew everything. The article, which occupied nearly the entirety of the paper, ended with,

> *For their safety and the safety of their families, all who played important roles in these remarkable events have not been mentioned by name. To their extraordinary courage and sacrifice we owe our undying gratitude.*

For the next forty-eight hours, the entire city was wild with celebration. And then came the state funeral. Dalbert had secured Iolanthe and West an empty reception room at Titus the Great Memorial Museum, next to the cathedral. They arrived as the sun was setting, the windows of the cathedral ablaze in the dying light of the day. An enormous crush of mages, quiet, sober, and all dressed in white, thronged the length of Palace Avenue.

West's fractured leg had already healed. He could have gone back to England, but he'd wished to attend the funeral. While they waited for the procession to start, they chatted about his plans, hers, and all the marvelous things he had seen in the Domain. Then she said, "May I ask you a question?"

"Of course."

"You were quite interested in the prince, at the beginning of last—no, this Half. It used to make me a bit suspicious. I wondered whether you weren't an Atlantean spy—but you aren't. So why did you have so many questions about His Highness?"

A little color came into West's face. "I first saw him on the Fourth of June, when his family set up court underneath that huge white canopy. He was beautiful and angry. And, well . . ." West shrugged. "I thought of him all summer."

Iolanthe rested her fingers against her lips. "I never guessed in that direction."

"Promise me you won't tell him."

She was about to reassure him that Titus would hardly change his opinion of West because of something like this, when she realized that it was simply the request of a proud young man who preferred to keep his unrequited love to himself. "I promise."

As the first stars appeared in the sky, the hundreds of torches that had been placed along Palace Avenue burst into flames. The ethereal notes of the Seraphim Prayer rose, almost inaudible at first, then growing stronger, more impassioned. The funeral procession started from the Citadel, the biers that bore the departed not drawn by pegasus, or even phoenix, but carried on the shoulders of mages.

The crowd joined in the prayer, hundreds of thousands of voices raised together. "Do you leave as a ship sailing out of harbor? Do you return as rain to the earth? Will I guide you in the Beyond, if I hold aloft the brightest light here on earth?"

Five biers arrived at the plaza before the cathedral: Amara, Wintervale, Titus Constantinos, Mrs. Hancock, and Master Haywood—these last two represented by lifelike wooden statues. The Master of the Domain was one of the bearers of his father's bier, the Kashkari brothers for Amara, Lady Wintervale for her son, and Commander Rainstone for Mrs. Hancock. Iolanthe was touched to see Dalbert as a bearer for Master Haywood.

The departed were set on their pyres. The prayer rose to a crescendo, then faded into complete silence. The Master of the Domain, solemn and compelling, addressed the crowd. "Before you lie courage, perseverance, kindness, friendship, and love. Before you lie men and women who could have chosen otherwise, who could have inured themselves to the injustices of the world, rather than giving their lives to change it. Tonight we honor them. Tonight we also honor all who have gone before and paved the way, the ones we remember and the ones we have forgotten.

"But nothing is lost in Eternity. A moment of grace resonates forever, as does an act of valor. So honor the dead—and live in grace and valor."

One by one he lit the pyres. The flames leaped higher and higher, whipping, crackling. A child's voice, as clear and bright as the

Angels' clarion, rose with the opening notes of the Adamantine aria, "For what is the Void but the beginning of Light? What is Light but the end of Fear? And what am I, but Light given form? What am I, but the beginning of Eternity?"

With West's arm around her, Iolanthe wept.

Escorted by Dalbert, West returned to England the next morning. The Kashkari brothers took their leave of Iolanthe in the afternoon. They'd been moving about openly in Delamer, under the guise of rebels freshly arrived to discuss the situation with the Master of the Domain. But now it was time for them to head back.

She embraced both the brothers. "Look after yourselves."

"You too, Fairfax," said Kashkari. "And before we go, this is for you."

She accepted the handsome mahogany box. "For me?"

Kashkari nodded. For the first time in a very long time, there seemed to be a hint of mirth in his eyes.

She opened the box and burst out laughing. At the end of Summer Half, to thank Kashkari for the help he had given the prince and herself on the night of the Fourth of June, they had bought him a very fine monogrammed shaving set.

And now Kashkari had returned the favor and Iolanthe held in her hands a monogrammed shaving set with ivory handles and gold accents that would have made Archer Fairfax levitate with manly pride.

They were still laughing as they embraced each other again.

After the brothers were gone, Iolanthe looked at the shaving set for a long time, lifting each individual item and feeling its weight and shape, rubbing her fingers against the embossed initials on the top of the shaving brush.

And wished fiercely for the well-being and happiness of these remarkable young men.

When Titus returned to the villa that night, Fairfax was stretched out on a long sofa in the solarium, her eyes closed. As he approached her, he saw his mother's diary lying open on a side table, an entry plainly visible.

His chest tightened. What did he need to know now?

On top of the diary entry was a note from Fairfax. *Found this. Thought you would like to see it. For once, it's good news.*

26 April, YD 1021

The day his mother died.

For years I have prayed for a vision that I actually want to see. It happened today, a brief, intense minute. In that vision, I saw my son embraced by his father, both moved beyond words.

My face is wet with tears. I have no time to write down greater details, for Father has already arrived in the castle, and the appointed hour of my death is only minutes away.

At least now I can tell my son, not all will be lost.

Not all will be lost.

He read the entry a few more times, wiping away the tears at the corners of his eyes. After he closed the diary, he saw that he had read only half of Fairfax's note. The other half said, *I am in the Queen of Seasons' summer villa.*

The season inside the Crucible reflected that outside, except when the story itself overrode external weather conditions. At the Queen of Seasons' summer villa, it was always summer, always airy and lovely.

Lanterns hung from the trees. Fireflies twinkled among leafy branches. She sat on the stone balustrade overlooking the lake, gazing up at the stars. He climbed onto the balustrade and sat down next to her. She placed her arm around him and kissed him on his temple. "Happy?"

"Yes."

Her hand grazed his arm. "I'm about to make you happier yet."

His pulse accelerated. "I do not see how that is possible."

She placed something in his palm, something light and incredibly soft. A rose petal. "Look around."

He must have been blind—or only had eyes for her. Now he

noticed that there were rose petals everywhere, along the path, on the smoothly clipped lawn, to either side of them on the balustrade, and even floating on the lake below.

He laughed. "When you change your mind, you change it hard."

"Wait until you see the tonnage of petals inside. You'll be filled with awe."

He leaped off the balustrade and set her on the ground too. "Awe is my default position when it comes to you, lightning-wielder. Now let us see if I am man enough to stay put when faced with an avalanche of rose petals."

She laughed too. Hand in hand they walked into the villa, kissing as they closed the door.

EPILOGUE ✦

THE SCENT OF BUTTER AND vanilla enveloped Iolanthe the moment she entered Mrs. Hinderstone's sweets shop. The bright, trim establishment was one of Iolanthe's favorite places in Delamer. It served intriguing ices in summer, a very satisfying cup of hot chocolate in winter, and a quality selection of pastries every day of the year—and that was before one even came to the display cases of colorful confections made on the premises.

"Good morning, my dear," said Mrs. Hinderstone, beaming. She stood next to the till. Above the till, hanging from the ceiling, was a sign that read *Books on the dark arts may be found in the cellar, free of charge. And should you locate the cellar, kindly feed the phantom behemoth inside. Regards, E. Constantinos.*

Before Mrs. Hinderstone had taken over the premises, the place had been a bookshop run by none other than the Master of the Domain's paternal grandfather—though no one knew it then, not even the prince himself. Mrs. Hinderstone had kept some of the books, a rather large collection for her customers to browse through as they waited for their orders or drank their morning tea. And she had kept most of the bookshop's signs, including one that said *I would rather read than eat*. Iolanthe had immediately liked Mrs. Hinderstone for her self-deprecating sense of humor.

"Good morning," Iolanthe returned the greeting. "How are you?"

"I've been waiting for you to come in to tell you this. I've had so many potions and elixirs for my elbow over the years, but that draught of yours—it's a miracle! I can't thank you enough."

"All right!" Iolanthe smiled—she did very much enjoy being helpful. "Nothing feels as good as not hurting anywhere, does it?"

"Tell me about it. The usual for you today?"

"Yes, please."

"A chocolate croissant and a cup of café au lait for Miss Hilland," Mrs. Hinderstone said to her helpers behind the counter. She turned back to Iolanthe. "You are always up so early on Saturdays. Don't you go out and have fun Friday nights?"

"Oh, I do. Last night I went to an aerial polo game with my friends. The Conservatory's team won, so we celebrated by singing in the quadrangle, loudly and badly, until two in the morning."

Her throat was still slightly scratchy—it had been a riotous good time.

"But it's barely seven." The shop had just opened and was without its usual crowd, since it was so early.

"It's the only time of the week I have a chance at my favorite seat," said Iolanthe.

She had no idea why she always woke up the same time on Saturday as she did on school days. She never set her alarm on Friday nights, but every Saturday morning she opened her eyes as the sun rose.

One of Mrs. Hinderstone's helpers brought Iolanthe's coffee and croissant. Iolanthe opened her wallet.

"Absolutely not," said Mrs. Hinderstone. "That is on the house."

Iolanthe thanked Mrs. Hinderstone and took her tray to the small table by the window. The shop sat on the corner of Hyacinth Street and University Avenue, across from the Conservatory's famous statue garden. Mages came from all over the city for their early morning walk, and one never knew who one might see.

Ten minutes later, Mrs. Hinderstone herself came to refill Iolanthe's cup. "You know, miss, Iolanthe Seabourne used to come here as a child. If you don't mind my saying it, you look a bit like her."

"Why would I mind? Please, do compare me to the great heroine of the Last Great Rebellion."

They both chortled.

In fact, Mrs. Hinderstone was not the first to comment on Iolanthe Hilland's resemblance to Iolanthe Seabourne. Her second year at the conservatory, she had taken a class from a big, flame-haired professor named Hippolyta Eventide, and Professor Eventide had made a similar observation. But Iolanthe didn't mention it to Mrs. Hinderstone. That would be bragging.

Mrs. Hinderstone set down her coffeepot on the table. "And guess who came into my shop two days ago? His Highness!"

Iolanthe could not suppress a half squeal.

It was no secret that the Master of the Domain visited Mrs. Hinderstone's from time to time—one of the reasons that her place was so popular. But Iolanthe had never had the good fortune of running into him here.

"Yes, he did, and placed an order for a picnic basket to be delivered to the Citadel today."

She had no idea the prince picnicked. She thought he worked all the time—and maybe occasionally went for a long walk in the Labyrinthine Mountains.

"And you know what? After I took down his order, I kept thinking of you. He named everything on the menu that you like—summer salad, pâté sandwich, spinach quiche, and pinemelon ice."

"My goodness." That could easily have been a picnic basket she ordered for herself.

"You have met him, haven't you?"

"Once. At my graduation."

The prince had come to give out awards to the Conservatory's top graduates and hosted a reception for them afterward.

"Isn't he a very fine young man?"

"I for one am glad he is the Master of the Domain."

He had been very courteous to everyone present, even though Iolanthe could sense that he did not enjoy such occasions that required him to make small talk.

"We have not had one so worthy of that title in a while," Mrs. Hinderstone said decisively.

On Iolanthe's way out, Mrs. Hinderstone presented her with a large, beautiful box of chocolates, a thank-you gift. The chocolates attracted several friendly comments as she walked across the great lawn of the Conservatory.

On the far side of the great lawn, which was otherwise free of any arboreal species, stood a magnificent starflower tree, which the prince had planted in memory of his partner, the great elemental mage. On mild, sunny days, Iolanthe often spread open a blanket under the shade of the tree, to study or to share a scoop of pinemelon ice with her friends.

She reached home a few minutes before eight o'clock. Soon after she'd arrived in Delamer from the remote Midsouth March, she had been told of an opportunity to look after a professor's house while the latter did his research abroad. She'd applied for the position, never thinking it would come to her. But it had. And for living in this lovely house, all she had to do was to make sure that it stayed clean and well maintained.

Almost a bit too much luck for a very ordinary girl from the middle of nowhere.

She entered the rather modest-looking front door of the house, set Mrs. Hinderstone's present on an occasion table, and walked to the balcony at the back. The Conservatory of Magical Arts and Sciences sat on the hip of the Serpentine Hills. From the balcony, she had a spectacular view of the capital city, all the way to the dramatic coastline. She stood for almost ten minutes, gazing at the Right Hand of Titus, upon the ring finger of which sat the Citadel, the prince's official residence in the capital city.

With a sigh, she headed back inside to fetch the thick stack of laboratory reports sitting on her desk, waiting to be dealt with. As she walked out again, her gaze fell upon the portrait that had been taken at her graduation, of the Master of the Domain handing over her certificate and her medal of excellence.

She halted in her tracks.

The portrait had been moved from her nightstand to her desk, then to the top of the bookshelves, and at last to the back of a cabinet with all kinds of knickknacks inside. Still it distracted her. Still it made her stop whatever she was doing to stare. And remember.

And wish.

Stupid. It was so stupid it was humiliating. Girls all over the Domain were in love with the prince—at the annual coronation day parade they fainted by the score along Palace Avenue. Understandably enough—he was an attractive young man in a position of tremendous power, and the hero of the Last Great Rebellion, no less. But they were starry-eyed adolescents and Iolanthe was a woman of twenty-three in the last year of her postgraduate work. She taught advanced practicals to first- and second-year Conservatory students. And for heaven's sake, she was sensible and disciplined enough to grade their laboratory reports bright and early on a Saturday morning!

And yet it persisted, this somewhat unhealthy fixation on the prince. She didn't go to coronation day parades; she didn't buy memorabilia affixed with his likeness; and she never made a fool of herself in front of the Citadel waving a *Will you marry me?* sign—she didn't even go anywhere near the Citadel, if she could help it.

But his least doings mattered to her. She studied his schedule as published by the Citadel, followed media coverage of the ceremonial events he attended, and parsed the language of his statements and speeches for his true assessment of the state of the Domain.

It was complicated enough, the realm's transition to democracy from a millennium of autocratic rule followed by years of foreign occupation. On his twenty-first birthday, he had also made the unprecedented move to acknowledge his Sihar heritage.

The next month, as debate raged among her fellow students, with one of them declaring, "The Master of the Domain is the exception that proves the rule," she had stood up and asked, even as her palms perspired, "How many exceptions must there be, before you realize that the rule is only in your head? That you would never wish for yourself to be judged the way you judge the Sihar?"

That night she had sat down and written the prince a long,

impassioned letter. To her surprise, within days she had received a two-page reply in his own hand. When they had met at the graduation gala, he had immediately said, "You are the one who sent me the beautiful letter, are you not?"

They had conversed for all of three minutes. Afterward, she couldn't recall what they had said to each other. All she carried with her was a sensation of phenomenal intensity, the way he'd looked at her, the way he'd spoken to her, the way he'd taken her hand briefly before she'd had to yield her place in the reception line—as if she mattered more than the entirety of the Domain and it would cost him half his soul to let her go.

That was the first and last time she had seen him in person. Other people ran into him, but life seemed to have no plans to bring them together again. She could only watch from afar as he went about his grand destiny.

Truly it was madness, to look upon this distant icon and think that if only they could meet, they would be the closest of friends. He might be an exceptional man, but he was not a friendly one, and she was sure that in private he must be quite difficult in many ways. All the same, day in, day out, year in, year out, he remained the secret undercurrent of her life.

She realized that she had taken the instant portrait out of the cabinet and was tracing her finger along the edge of his charcoal-gray overrobe. This new generation of instant portraits captured the texture of fabrics, so that she felt the elaborately embroidered band that trimmed the hem, the silk threads smooth and evenly oriented beneath her finger.

Muttering an obscenity under her breath, she marched into the study and shoved the instant portrait onto the very top of the shelves inside a small closet.

Ninety minutes later, she had finished with all the reports. She made herself a cup of tea and took out some papers that she had to read for her own classes.

But she was restless. Instead of reading the papers, she left them on top of her desk and approached the window. It had started to rain, but she could still see the Citadel in the distance.

She shook her head. She must stop obsessing over him. What could she hope to happen even if she met him again? No more than another couple of minutes of his time. If he had wanted to know her better, he could have done it two years ago—he knew her name and her university; everything else he could have found out, if he had wanted to.

If he had *wanted* to.

That he hadn't contacted her subsequently was ample evidence that he had no such desires, that all the longing on her part was entirely unrequited: hard truths she must force herself to accept, however unhappily.

A rattle inside the small closet brought her out of her reverie. She glanced at the door of the closet, confounded and faintly alarmed.

Surely there could not be an intruder in this house: she had done the security spells—and she was quite good at those.

All the same, she pulled her wand from her pocket and silently called for a shield. The closet door opened and out stepped none other than the Master of the Domain himself, a grin on his face, looking gloriously young and gloriously happy.

Iolanthe was thunderstruck. Fortune shield her, had she begun to hallucinate? The prince, though always flawlessly courteous in public, was said to be aloof and solemn by nature, not given to mirth or merriment.

That she'd conjured a smiling version of him had to be proof that she was out of her mind. Right?

"Oh," he said, as he took in her shock and dismay. He cleared his throat and his expression became more serious. "I apologize. I am early again."

She was not hallucinating. It really was him, the Master of the Domain, standing not even ten paces away. And what did he mean that he was early again? Early *again*—when had he been early before?

"Sire," she said unsteadily. She should bow. Or curtsy. Or was curtsying too old-fashioned these days?

"No, do not bow," he said, as if he'd heard her thoughts. Then, after a moment, "How are your studies?"

"They are—fine. Going very well."

She couldn't stop gawking at him. His black hair was a little longer than it had been in the official portrait. He wore a simple fawn tunic over a pair of dark-gray trousers and wore it well—the tunic draped beautifully over his lean, spare frame.

"Did you have fun at the match last night?" he asked, smiling a little again.

How did he know she had gone to a sporting event? And why was he gazing upon her exactly as she would want him to, with tremendous admiration and something that approached downright covetousness?

"May I—may I offer you a seat, sire?" She somehow managed to keep her voice even. "And some tea? I also have some chocolate from Mrs. Hinderstone's shop."

"No, thank you. I just had breakfast."

She was beginning to feel terrifically awkward. How did one ask the Master of the Domain what in the world he was doing in her house? And how had he come through the storage closet, which was emphatically not a portal of any kind?

"Me too," she said, "at Mrs. Hinderstone's. She mentioned that you had been there in person two days ago."

"Yes, the picnic basket for us."

For us. Us! Should it feel so completely disorienting when dreams came true? She was asleep, wasn't she, this whole thing just one fantastical illusion?

He came toward her, until barely a sliver of air separated them. So close that she could make out the exact design on the decorative buttons on his tunic: a coat of arms unlike any she had ever seen before, with a dragon, a phoenix, a griffin, and a unicorn occupying the quadrants.

So close that she breathed in his scent of silver moss and cloud pine. So close that when she looked into his eyes, she saw every detail of the starburst pattern of his blue-gray irises.

"I have missed you," he murmured.

And kissed her.

In the mountains where she grew up, sometimes people rafted down steep, fast-flowing streams. His kiss felt exactly like that, full of danger and exhilaration, making her heart rattle and thump, ready to leap out of her rib cage.

He pulled back slightly and traced a thumb across her cheek, a caress like lightning. "You and you alone," he said softly.

Suddenly her head felt strange, a thousand brilliant dots of light hurtling about. Memories burst into her cranium as if from a geyser. She gripped his shoulder to steady herself.

He wrapped his arm about her. "Everything coming back now?"

A secret life unfurled before her. The diligent, mild-mannered candidate for Master of Magical Arts and Sciences was in fact the power beside the throne. Those long walks that he took in the wilderness of the Labyrinthine Mountains? That was time they spent together discussing, strategizing, and sometimes agonizing over difficult decisions. That historic speech he'd given when he'd announced his Sihar heritage and reforms he planned to undertake to make the Sihar full subjects, instead of merely guests of the crown? She had drafted a large portion of it—not to mention persuaded him to take the monumental step in the first place. And one entire summer, as well as a good chunk of an academic term her second year at the Conservatory, instead of being back in the mountains taking care of her elderly grandmother, as she and everyone else had believed, she had been at his side, in disguise as a male aide-de-camp, waging campaigns against remnants of the Bane's forces.

Of course, there had been the Last Great Rebellion, in which she had played an instrumental part. Grief shot through her as she remembered those who had been lost—Amara, Wintervale, Mrs. Hancock, Titus's father, and Master Haywood. She experienced a moment of searing disgust at the thought of Lady Callista and Aramia, who were now in Exile, along with Prince Alectus.[8]

And then, pure joy, as she looked upon the young man before her.

He was the one with whom she'd come through war and hell. The one with whom she'd changed the world. The one with whom her destiny would forever be entwined.

She smoothed a finger over his brow. "Titus."

"That is sire to you, young lady," he answered, teasing.

"Ha. Only when you address me as 'my hope, my prayer, my destiny.'"

He gave her a dirty look.

She laughed. "And how dare you take advantage of a poor, hero-worshipping girl?"

He gave her another dirty look. "I keep telling you to forget all about me in the meanwhile. But will you listen? And then when I misjudge the time, you look at me as if you have been on your knees a thousand years, praying for me."

She giggled. "I do get pretty pathetic, pining after you."

"No worse than me. You do not know how hard it is to have to wait a week every time before I can see you again. Sometimes I still think that anyone with eyes could have seen through our secret the day of your graduation gala, even though I tried my best to treat you exactly the same as everyone else."

Nobody had seen through it, but soon things would change.

She had always planned to assume a false identity to attend the Conservatory. But she had vacillated over whether to also assume a set of false memories, so that she would enjoy a purer, more unencumbered university experience, without being constantly distracted by what Titus had to deal with as the Master of the Domain.

In the end she had decided to give it a try, with many, many safeguards in place, and a blood oath she had demanded of Titus, that he absolutely must summon her to his side when the need arose.[9]

By and large, she'd had a marvelous time at the Conservatory.[10] But now that her time there was near an end, she had become impatient to be who she really was. As soon as she finished her master's degree, her true identity would be revealed—it still wasn't a perfectly safe world, but she was no longer deterred by the risks. After that, well, she looked forward to seeing how her life would unfold.

And today she would take the first step on that new path. "Ready for the Fourth of June? Ready for dear Cooper to fawn all over you?"

She hadn't seen Cooper, or anyone from Mrs. Dawlish's, since she left England on a hot air balloon.

Titus groaned. "As ready as I will ever be."

She kissed him, grinning. "Come. Let's go make him the happiest man alive."

Cooper squealed and lifted Fairfax bodily off the ground. "My God, I can't believe it. It really is you."

She laughed and lifted him in return. "Cooper, old bloke. I heard you've avoided becoming a solicitor after all."

The most unexpected twist in the entire saga was that Titus and Cooper had become semi-regular correspondents—regular on Cooper's part and semi on Titus's. Cooper never would have presumed to write to Titus, but his letters to Fairfax, sent to the fake address in the Wyoming Territory that Titus had set up, had come to Titus instead. And in those early years after the Bane's death, when Lady Wintervale had nearly been assassinated twice, Titus had deemed it too dangerous for Fairfax, who was supposed to be dead, to reply, even if it was to a nonmage.

So he had written back instead, putting his talent for lying into creating fiction. He found it relaxing to spin yarns of Fairfax, first as a Wyoming Territory rancher, then as a San Francisco hotel manager, and of late, a Buenos Aires businessman. He had also come to enjoy Cooper's long, rambling missives, full of news of their old friends' doings. Sutherland had not yet married a loathsome heiress. St. John rowed for Cambridge. Birmingham was now a proper Egyptologist, with eager sponsors for his excavations and avid audiences for his lectures.

"Thank goodness for that," said Cooper. "Being the private secretary to a very important man agrees with me. I am well on my way to becoming an insufferable fart."

He turned to Titus, blushed a little, and took off his hat, revealing a mop of luxuriant hair.

Titus shook his head. "Vanity, thy name is Thomas Cooper."

One time, remembering his long-ago dream of meeting Cooper on a Fourth of June, Titus had asked in a letter whether he had become heavy. Cooper replied that he had retained his girlish figure, but had unfortunately lost a great deal of hair. Titus, in a charitable moment, had sent him a case of anti-baldness elixir.

Fairfax slapped Cooper on the back. "My God, that is beautiful, Cooper. *Beautiful.*"

Cooper turned the color of a beet. The world's happiest beet. "I'm so glad to see the two of you. It's been far too long. And . . ." Some of the delight drained from his face. "And we aren't always guaranteed to meet with old friends again after many years, are we?"

In his latest letter, Titus had at last told Cooper that Wintervale and Mrs. Hancock had died long ago, in the same "palace intrigue" that had taken him away from Eton.

Fairfax wrapped an arm around Cooper's shoulders. "But today we are. All the old friends in the world."

They gathered up Sutherland, Rogers, St. John, and several other old boys from Mrs. Dawlish's and sat down to a plentiful picnic. Halfway through the picnic, Birmingham, their old house captain, arrived with, of all people, West, in tow. The young men turned aflutter at the sight of West, who had not only captained the Eton eleven, but had gone on to also captain the Oxford University cricket team. He was now embarking on a career as a physicist and shared a house in Oxford with Birmingham.

West held an animated conversation with Fairfax. Then he, Fairfax, and Titus together spoke for a while. When he left to join a conversation between Sutherland and Birmingham, Fairfax whispered in Titus's ear that West and Birmingham were "together."

He whispered back, "Do you think I am blind?"

She laughed, the sound of which was drowned out by an overjoyed squeal from Cooper. "Gentlemen, our friend from the subcontinent has arrived!"

Titus and Fairfax both exclaimed. They had, of course, met Kashkari numerous times in the intervening years—spent months together on campaigns, even. But this was special, to stand with him where it all began.

They ate, laughed, and reminisced. At some point in the afternoon, Titus, Fairfax, and Kashkari bade good-bye to the other friends and vaulted to London for a very long tea. They had much to talk about, as Kashkari was also planning to reveal the truth about his and Amara's involvement in the Last Great Rebellion.

The day was fading when Titus and Fairfax made their way to the house on Serpentine Hills where his parents used to meet. In the past six years, it had become a refuge for them too, a safe haven where they could shed their responsibilities and simply enjoy each other's company.

"You know how we always go to the Queen of Seasons' summer villa?" he asked, collapsing onto a long sofa in the solarium.

"Far be it from me to tire of the most beautiful place in the Crucible," she teased, sitting down next to him. "But go on."

He set their clasped hands on top of his copy of the Crucible. "Well, recently I went into the Queen of Seasons' *spring* villa and saw something unexpected."

The spring villa, on a high alpine meadow with riots of pink and mauve wildflowers, was every bit as beautiful as the summer villa. Titus pointed at a pair of travelers walking across the meadow, their faces glowing in the light of a brilliant sunset. "Look at them."

Fairfax sucked in a breath. "But they are your parents."

"Yes," he said softly. "She kept a record of his likeness after all, for me to find someday. And for me to see them happy and together."

They watched the young couple, their arms around each other, stroll past the villa and disappear beyond a bend in the path.

Then Fairfax took his hand. "I'm ready for whatever the future brings."

"Me too," he told her. "Me too."

1. (p. 74) **Redhull, Bernard**

YD 967–1014. Seer.

Known more for prolificacy than significance. Claimed to have never had a single vision about himself, but always about complete strangers. Sent out batches of letters every month to those who his visions concerned, when he could discover their identity. Best remembered as the one whose vision of a conversation between Lady Callista Tiberius and a friend spurred her to action, to duplicate all the measures enumerated in that foreseen exchange. *See* Lady Callista Tiberius, Horatio Haywood, Iolanthe Seabourne, Aramia Tiberius, Prince Titus VII.

—From *Biographical Dictionary of the Domain*

2. (P. 274) THE FOLLOWING is an excerpt from Hancock's written account:

Two months later I came across one more mention of Pyrrhos Plouton, in a letter by a remote acquaintance, exclaiming how he had not aged a single day in twenty-five years. It would appear that the first feat of sacrificial magic Plouton performed was so powerful it gave him not only unnatural longevity, but also seemingly unfading youth. This might be the reason he moved far away to become Palaemon Zephyrus: to avoid the kind of speculation brought on by his apparent agelessness.

Judging by all the sources I'd collected, both Pyrrhos Plouton and Palaemon Zephyrus—before the latter's encounter with the "giant serpent," at least—were fine physical specimens, suffering from no handicaps and missing not even a small toe. Which led me to conclude that Plouton must have powered his first sacrifice with a kidney. Organs are highly valued in sacrificial magic, but one could live a normal life with only one kidney and, perhaps equally important, give the impression of being whole and unmaimed.

—From *A Chronological Survey of the Last Great Rebellion*

3. (P. 299) THE TEXT of the note Seabourne left in Titus VII's laboratory before she departed Britain is as follows:

Your Highness,

I am going to kill you—eagerly and with great satisfaction. Perhaps I am speaking figuratively; perhaps not. You will find out. Likely too late.

But if it should be that both I and Fate somehow spare you, and you return here one day, victorious and in one piece, know that I meant what I said: I have no regrets about going to Atlantis, deadly prophecies notwithstanding.

And know that I have loved you all along, even while I plot your imminent demise. Maybe especially as I do so.

Now and always,

The one who walks beside you

—From *A Chronological Survey of the Last Great Rebellion*

4. (P. 325) THE PRACTICE of wearing troth bands goes back almost a millennium. Once a pair of lovers seals their pledge to each other and puts on the troth bands, the bands cannot be taken off unless one or both of the wearers pass away.

This irreversibility is likely the reason troth bands never became popular. Even the most sincerely devoted couples could drift apart over time. What, then, to do about this no longer meaningful symbol that cannot be removed unless one is willing to give up an arm too in the process?

—From *Encyclopedia of Cultural Customs*

5. (P. 387) THE TEXT of the entries Commander Rainstone read in Princess Ariadne's diary:

6 May, YD 1012

Why do I so seldom see good news? The lonely finding love and friendship. The just and brave rewarded for their courage and sacrifice. Or even a rapturously received new play—at least that would be something to look forward to.

No, instead I see death and misfortune. And when I am lucky, things that I cannot quite interpret one way or the other.

Now on to the vision. It is a hospital—or at least it looks like the maternity ward of a hospital, with a number of newborns in rows of bassinets. A man, in a nurse's white overrobe and white cap, his face covered by a protective mask, checks all the babies one by one.

He stops before two bassinets and looks at the babies inside for a long time. Then, with a glance to the window that looks out to the corridor, he quickly switches the babies.

So frustrating—the man is clearly committing a terrible misdeed. Yet because it has not taken place yet, I cannot do anything. Nor can I recognize the hospital, though I toured a number of hospitals last summer, especially in the provinces.

I will wait for the vision to come back and hope for more identifying information.

19 August, YD 1012

The vision came again. This time I could see that there are fireworks out the window, a steady shower of golden streaks.

Father's birthday or a feast day?

—From A Chronological Survey of the Last Great Rebellion

6. (p. 389) Commander Penelope Rainstone:

Sometimes the reports make it seem that my rupture with Princess Ariadne was permanent. That wasn't quite the case. Her Highness did dismiss me, since I read her diary without authorization and then refused to give a reason. But six months later I went to see her.

I made it clear that I could never confess why I'd snooped—Callista didn't want anyone to know that we were related, that her mother had indulged in an affair with a gardener during her marriage. But I asked Her Highness to please understand my dilemma, as a woman who also had secrets she couldn't tell the world.

She was silent for a long time, but then she nodded slowly.

I can't tell you how much that meant to me, her forgiveness. I offered to take a blood pledge, as a gesture of my gratitude and loyalty. She declined it, but said if I wished to, I could make that same pledge to her infant son.

I did. At the time I had no idea that years later the pledge, which bound me to His Highness, would enable me to break through the siege of the bell jar dome in the Sahara Desert.

The threads of Fortune weave mysteriously.

—From *The Last Great Rebellion: An Oral History*

7. (p. 392) Vasudev Kashkari:

I was twenty when I left home for the Sahara Desert. There was never any question that I wanted to be part of the resistance—even if my uncle hadn't been Akhilesh Parimu, I would still have wanted to contribute.

Not long after I arrived at my first rebel base, in the western Sahara, a courier came from another base. I watched her at lunch, speaking to and laughing with some of my friends. I wasn't in the habit of approaching girls, but there was something irresistible about her warmth and vivacity—and she had a lovely smile. At the next meal I mustered the courage and took the seat next to hers.

We got to talking. As it turned out, her mother was from the Ponives, my grandparents' native realm. So we talked more—and more. We were the last two to leave the canteen that evening. The next morning we met again for breakfast and talked until she had to leave.

When she was gone I walked around in a fog for the rest of the day. That night I wrote her, a few lines in my two-way notebook. She replied immediately and we kept on writing for hours. That became a pattern: every night we wrote to each other, about what happened that day and everything else under the sun. [Smiles] I had to get a new notebook every few weeks because we chatted so much.

I suggested many times that we should meet again. But she always found some excuse to demur. After four months, I had had enough and wrangled myself an assignment to improve the irrigation system at her base. But when I got there, no one on the premise knew who I was talking about. They all took turns with courier duties and nobody used the nom de guerre of Durga Devi. When I mentioned her connection to the Ponives, they pointed to this intimidatingly beautiful young woman as the only one with a mother from that realm.

My repeated questions in the notebook went unanswered. I didn't know what to do. I felt as if I'd been the biggest fool. I was also completely unsettled: I like solving problems, and problems that presented no rational solutions made me restless and irritable.

When I finished my assignment and was about to leave, a message came from her at last, begging me to stay at her base, even though she wasn't there and nobody knew anything about her. If I stayed, I would find answers, she said.

I agonized over my decision but in the end I stayed. I loved her and I needed to see her again. If staying at her base was going to lead me back to her, then that was what I'd do, despite my misgivings.

In the meanwhile, Amara was promoted to oversee supplies and logistics for the base, which meant we interacted at regular intervals. I found those occasions awkward: she was usually quite curt and never looked me in the eye.

And needless to say, my evening conversations with the one I loved had also become stilted and uncomfortable. I couldn't just pretend that everything was the same as before.

Three weeks in I told her that she had to see me face-to-face and tell me everything before another month was out. We argued back and forth and finally agreed to meet on a day six months in the future.

A week before our rendezvous, I saw her across the canteen,

chatting with a group of carpet weavers as if she hadn't a care in the world. I stared at her. She looked up at me and smiled—a friendly smile, but one without any hint of recognition.

Next thing I knew, Amara had her hand on my arm and was dragging me away from the canteen. We almost came to blows, she pulling on me and me trying to get back to the girl whose absence had consumed me for months.

"That's my cousin Shulini." Amara spoke directly into my ear. "You have never met her nor she you. I took her form when I went to your base."

I couldn't speak for my shock—mutables are so rare in real life that the possibility never crossed my mind. She explained that when she traveled away from the base she often took on Shulini's appearance because her own face made people stare. But she had to stop because she was becoming too old to 'mute at will, at least not without fear of ending up looking permanently like someone else.

I became angry. We'd known each other ten months by then. At any point she could have told me. Instead she chose to let me simmer in my own anxiety. She said she was afraid of losing me, since I never showed the slightest interest in her.

"How about this? You've lost me anyway," I said, and stormed out.

For a few days I showed Shulini around the base. She was a nice girl but there was no spark between us whatsoever, which made me even more incensed. Amara I ignored altogether.

But she didn't give up on me. She got us assigned to night patrol duty together. In the dark, when I couldn't see her face, but only hear her voice—that was why she'd spoken so little to me since I came to live at her base, because she still had the same voice. And I loved her voice, the sound of her laughter, the precision of her vowels, and especially the way she sometimes hummed a little to herself.

From there we started our reconciliation. It took me a while to fall in love with her face—I used to start every time I saw it, especially if we'd been sitting side by side for a while, talking without looking at each other. Later she would joke that she wanted to marry me because I was the only man who preferred her in the dark.

[Smiles again.]

And there you have it, our story.

Interviewer:

After you were reconciled, how long were you together?

V. Kashkari:

Three years eleven months.

Interviewer:

Too short a time.

V. Kashkari:

All good years are short, as are all full lives.

—From *The Last Great Rebellion: An Oral History*

8. (p. 412) **Prince Titus VII:**

The morning of the state funeral, I was informed that the Atlanteans had handed over Miss Aramia Tiberius. That afternoon, I had her brought in along with Alectus and Lady Callista.

In the short time since the Bane's downfall, Alectus had become an old man: he stooped and wore an expression of perpetual confusion. Lady Callista seemed to have lost much of the elegance for which she had been so admired—it was a twitchy woman who curtsied to me. Aramia simply looked terrified.

I addressed her first. "I see you are safe and sound, Miss Tiberius."

She had the sense to not say anything.

"Your Highness, why was I not allowed to attend my daughter's funeral?" Lady Callista interjected. "Why, indeed, was I not mentioned at all in the account you gave of how the Bane was brought down? My daughter was the great heroine of her generation, and you would have the populace believe that she was the child of those paupers from the Conservatory?"

I stared at her until she fidgeted and curtsied again. "I apologize for my outburst. Please forgive me, sire."

"Miss Seabourne was not your daughter," I told her.

"I might not have raised her, but I gave birth to her. My blood ran in hers and so did the blood of Baron Wintervale, the greatest hero of *my* generation."

"Baron Wintervale betrayed my mother."

"No, that is not possible."

"Ask his widow about it, if she will condescend to meet with you. As for your kinship with one of the bravest mages this realm has ever known . . ."

A blood assay had already been readied. I picked up the glass beaker. *"Sanguis densior aqua."*

The clear liquid in the beaker turned jellylike and slightly opaque. "I require a drop of blood from you and from Miss Tiberius."

They hesitated. Miss Tiberius pricked her finger first, squeezing out a drop of blood. The blood drop fell through the jellylike substance as a pebble in water, reaching the bottom of the beaker with an audible *plink*.

Lady Callista did the same.

I swirled the beaker. "If you are unrelated, your blood will not react."

The drops of blood, like two tiny marbles, tumbled along the bottom of the beaker. And then, as if they were magnets, they moved toward each other until they had joined into a single oval.

"Very close kinship, I would say."

"This—this can't be true. Perhaps through some coincidence we are distantly related."

Without a word, I performed another blood assay, this time using blood from myself and Alectus. Our two drops of blood also approached each other, but instead of merging together, formed something in the shape of a dumbbell.

"He is my great-uncle. And your kinship is far closer than ours."

"No," mumbled Lady Callista. "No."

She collapsed into a chair.

Miss Tiberius held completely still, staring at her mother, the woman for whose love she had committed treason.

I could have told her time and again not to bother to win Lady Callista's approval: Lady Callista disdained all who loved her—the only one to whom she had ever been devoted was Baron Wintervale, a man who only thought of himself, who took and took from those around him.

Earlier I had been of a mind to recommend a particularly harsh penalty for Miss Tiberius. But now I knew nothing I meted out could punish her as much as her mother's indifference—indeed, revulsion—at the thought of being related to her after all.

"Each of you can be charged with treason. I will, however, recommend to the High Council a less punitive course of action. Like all collaborators, you will have the chance to confess and seek pardon. Detail your dealings with Atlantis, and you will most likely receive a pardon. Conceal anything . . ."

I did not need to finish the sentence. "In the meanwhile, I will seek the High Council's assent in stripping Alectus of his princely appellation and privileges. All three of you are to pack up and leave the Citadel within twenty-four hours."

"But—but—what are we to do? Where will we go?" cried Alectus.

"I could but I am not seizing your personal assets. So you will have more than enough to find a place to live. I believe the same is true of Lady Callista."

"Can we not receive some leniency?" Alectus beseeched. "We are your family, after all."

"You are looking leniency in the face. Would you like to see my less lenient side?"

Alectus trembled. "No, sire. Thank you, sire."

"Good," I said. "I look forward to never seeing any of you again. Now leave."

As they shuffled toward the door I remembered something. "By the way, Lady Callista, the day before Miss Seabourne faced the Bane, she realized that she was not related to you, because her blood did not react to the blood circle you had set in the Sahara. I must say, I had seldom seen her more delighted."

—From *The Last Great Rebellion: An Oral History*

9. (P. 413) UNBEKNOWNST TO the general public, the heirs of the House of Elberon have always been proficient in the wielding of blood magic.

Most mages in the Domain are familiar with the story of the arrival of the Sihar, persecuted elsewhere and desperately seeking a safe haven. What is not taught in schoolbooks is that the Sihar, in gratitude, gifted Hesperia the Magnificent a copy of their most prized manual on blood magic, as well as the secret know-how to fabricate a folded space, a secret which later became lost among the Sihar but has been preserved by the House of Elberon.

—From *A Chronological Survey of the Last Great Rebellion*

10. (p. 413) **Iolanthe Seabourne:**

The night before the state funeral, the prince and I went to my guardian's apartment in Paris. Only four days had passed since the two of them sat down to tea only to be interrupted by the tracer's signal that my location had changed thousands of miles all of a sudden.

The tea service was still on the table in the *salle de séjour*. When I saw that . . . [Pause] Excuse me. When I saw that I cried.

We went to his bedroom and gathered up his things. He had very few possessions—it was only days before that we'd freed him from the fear circle at Claridge's. And everything was new, bought in anticipation of a long stay in Paris.

When we went into the spare bedroom, I'm afraid I cried again. I'd seen the spare bedroom when the prince and I had brought him to the apartment, but he'd rearranged the furniture and changed the wallpaper to make it look more like my room in our house at the Conservatory.

[Pause]

I sat on the bed while His Highness went through the rest of the apartment, until he called to me from the study. He had found a letter that had been hidden away. Master Haywood wrote that he was very much looking forward to my arrival in Paris, to spending time together in safety and anonymity. But if for some reason something should happen to him, he wanted me to have the incantations necessary to invalidate the Irreproducible Charm that he had put on me when I was a toddler.

For the day when I would live in easy, peaceful times and wish to capture moments of my life, like everyone else.

I'm not sure we've arrived at completely easy, peaceful times yet. But one of the decisions His Highness and I made before I assumed a false identity was to revoke the Irreproducible Charm so that I'd indeed live as normal a life as possible, which was what Master Haywood would have wanted.

Sometimes I look at the pictures on my walls of those terrific years I spent as a student at the Conservatory, and I wish—

Actually, I think he knows in the Beyond. He knows that everything he'd ever wanted for me has come true.

—From *The Last Great Rebellion: An Oral History*

♦ ACKNOWLEDGMENTS

Donna Bray, for whom I have run out of superlatives.

Kristin Nelson, ever my fairy godmother.

Colin Anderson and Erin Fitzsimmons, who outdo themselves with each cover in the series.

The entire team at Balzer + Bray and HarperCollins Children's, for an immensely enjoyable experience all around.

Dr. Margaret Toscano, for coming up with the Latin equivalent of "Open sesame."

Srinadh Madhavapeddi, for Vasudev's name.

The lovely and talented John Thomas, for coming up with one of the most important uses of Iolanthe's powers. The very kind Dr. Milan, for answering my questions concerning such a use.

My family, for making my peaceful, drama-free existence possible. I could expend any amount of ink and not say enough good things.

All the readers, authors, librarians, booksellers, and bloggers who have embraced and championed this series, I am beyond grateful.

And if you are reading this, thank you. Thank you for everything.